Martin Boylan was born in Belfast and educated at Queen's University. He started writing in Canada and had some short stories broadcast on CBC. Four of his stage plays have been produced – "Mick and Ed"(The Abbey Theatre), Thompsons (The Abbey Theatre), Georgina (The United Arts club) and The Making of Father Sullivan (Anglo-Irish Theatre, Tubingen, Germany). The latter play received the O Z Whitehead award for playwrighting. Martin has had over twenty radio plays produced by the BBC, RTE and Channel 4 radio – inclusive of comedy series. He also has a screenplay credit, "Thompsons", for RTE. He lives in Dublin with his wife, Catherine. "The Jealous God" is his first published novel. Councillor O Toole, an eight half-hour radio comedy series, was broadcast six times by Channel 4 radio – the novel and the radio comedy series are available on his website martinboylan.com

THE
JEALOUS
GOD

Martin Boylan

ISBN-13: 978-1533553140

ISBN-10: 1533553149

For Catherine

THE JEALOUS GOD

Chapter 1

The wedding party was almost over. From a constant, high-pitched chatter, there was now a buzz broken only by the odd unmistakable peal of a Belfast laugh. Marie raised the cold glass to her lips and sipped the wine. She rocked to and fro on the porch, her eyes squinting at the sun sinking into the Indian Ocean.

Rosaleen leaned over from behind and touched her arms. 'How are ya feelin', Mum?'

'Great, I never get sick of these sunsets. They're gorgeous.'

'John and I are going,' she said, pulling a footstool up beside the rocking chair and sitting on its edge. 'Do you know what they did? They tied one of those logs with all the fireworks to the bumper. And we can't get it off!'

'Ask Danny.'

'It's locked with a metal chain. And nobody has the key!'

Marie stood up, stiff and unsteady, 'One of them big logs? All the way to the airport! That's no joke.'

'It's okay, Mum. Sit down.'

'No, no, I'm seein' yas off.'

'Did you enjoy the wedding?'

'I did, love, I really did,' and she threw her arms around her daughter and burst into tears.

Danny, Michael, Agnes and John came out to the porch. Rosaleen pressed her face against Marie's neck just under her chin. She was smaller than her mother with a sturdy, firm body and thick blonde-streaked hair. Her pale brown make-up glistened, the eyeshadow was deep green. The top of her yellow cotton dress smudged her mother's lipstick as she rocked from side to side, saying, 'Didn't I tell you old blubber-lips would cry? Didn't I?'

Marie gave her a last great squeeze and let go. Rosaleen slid over towards John and slipped her fingers into his hand. Black hair slicked back, a boozy contented smile, he punched the other hand into creased, white linen trousers. Three-quarters Irish, he had the easy confidence of a second generation professional. She spoke without looking at her mother. 'You all know Mum – worried about losing her slave.'

'Slave? Sure you never washed a dirty cup in your life!'

'Mum! You'll be giving John a very bad impression.'

Marie folded her arms, 'I don't care. Anyway, sure it's too late now. He's signed up.'

They laughed.

Her son Danny, his hair prematurely grey and hanging over his left eye, always reminded Marie of Harry, her late husband – his prominent lips, always on the verge of a smile, the laugh that showed his upper gum, and especially the ambling gait of his walk. Agnes, her older daughter, had moist eyes but her face beamed happiness. She and Rosaleen were very close. Closer than the boys. As close as she and her own sister Rosaleen were once many, many years ago. Agnes was beginning to put on a bit of weight and, not yet thirty, she had the beginning of her mother's double chin. That was something she'd always hated about herself.

When she looked at Michael, the oldest, her eyes smiled. Wiry blonde hair, long freckled face, high cheek bones, arched eyebrows and the same green eyes that made him a sunparched edition of her father, Frank – he was the most Aussie looking of the family – she'd always doted on him. And when he became a priest …

Michael held her by the elbow. The arthritis in her knees sometimes made her rickety. 'I'm okay, son,' she said, brushing off his hand. 'It was just getting up.'

He put his hand back. She acquiesced. 'Ya'd think you were lowerin' me int' a coffin.'

'You'll live till you're ninety, Mum,' he said.

'Are you tryin' t' put a curse on me?'

They went through the living room of the summerhouse, still hot after the baking day, and strewn with towels and bathing costumes. It was a second home during the hot Western Australian summers and even the occasional hot autumn like now. In fact, there had been suggestions of a wedding on the beach. But Marie was having none of it. A reception in the summerhouse was fine, but Michael would marry them in a church. His church.

She had always encouraged his vocation, from the first inkling of interest all the way to his ordination. There was something about him that gave her great comfort, joy and pride. Watching him serve Mass. Remembering his birth, his scrapes. And out here there was more than just the ordinary pride any Irish mother would feel. The fact that her son was serving in the Church connected her with Ireland.

'How long is the flight to Bali?' she asked.

'Five hours.'

'I hate flyin'.'

It was on her lap in a plane that she carried Harry's ashes back to Belfast in a silver urn. She couldn't think of him without feeling sad. No, she never regretted coming out here for the advantages it gave her children, but neither of them really settled. Especially Harry. The first time he had a heart attack she went up to the hospital to see him. He opened his eyes and said: 'Don't be lettin' me die in this bloody country.' Well, he did. But she did bring back his ashes and bury them in Milltown cemetery. A grey winter's day with a few relations and a handful of old men who had played football with him. Trouble finding the family grave. Did she really want to put her family to that trouble when the time came? Yet, it was over thirty years ago that they had emigrated, and in a way they had never really left the Falls Road.

A small crowd had gathered at the front of the house. The car, a long beige Ford, was covered in technicolour stickers. Michael grabbed a spray-foam to add a 'Just', but ran out of space for the 'married'. Marie didn't like his nonclerical gear. Sandals, jeans and a cream see-through cotton shirt were just a bit too casual for a priest. Danny lit one of the fireworks on the log and it exploded, setting off a series of bangs. The children screamed. 'Don't be goin' too near them squibs,' said Marie.

Tony, Danny's eldest boy, tried to set off the fireworks on the second log with a smouldering taper. For a few seconds nothing happened, then a series of small explosions made the log jump and he leapt back onto the ground. Everyone laughed.

A postman crept up on Rosaleen who was laughing and talking to two girls from work. She signed his pad. There had been telegrams coming all day. He went back to his motorbike parked at the first of two spindly gum trees on the driveway between the house and the lane. Rosaleen tore open the envelope. 'Mum!' she cried, rushing up to Marie.

Her mother scratched her cheek and set her jaw. She knew Rosaleen was high. 'Who's it from?'

'Aunt Rosaleen.'

Marie felt a stab of emotion. The wedding invitation had gone unacknowledged. Not that she had expected her to come all the way from Georgia in America. But she had expected something.

'A telegram?'

'Not just a telegram, Mum! A money order! Guess? How much?'

'Youse young 'uns are money mad.'

'A thousand dollars! American!'

Marie took the crumpled money order into her hand. She caught her daughter's wide excited hazel eyes. The money was already spent on the new unit.

'I must write her a thank you note,' said Rosaleen. 'Really, I must. And after all the things we said about her.'

Marie read the telegram. 'Many congratulations to Rosaleen and John. Myself and Daniel are deeply sorry that we couldn't come. We are forwarding a money order for your wedding present and hope you will be very happy. Your loving Godmother, Aunt Rosaleen, Daniel, Ruth and Aaron.'

'Did you phone her, Mum?'

'No, but I wrote her a letter with the invitation.'

'She must think a lot of you.'

Marie shrugged.

'Like, she's my Godmother but she's never met me. And she never writes.'

'We're not great writers.'

'Maybe she'll visit us sometime.'

'Yeah, maybe. That would be nice,' she said, handing back the money order and the telegram. 'Ya know, you take after her in some ways. Except for the religion.'

Rosaleen laughed. She went the odd time to church.

'But you'll change. I was like you too when I was your age.'

'I'm gonna surprise you all, Mum. When I have the biggest and best house in Western Australia and about fifteen kids I'm gonna call it a day and go into a nunnery.'

'You're laughing now.'

Souped-up cars encircled the Ford, their horns screeching. Rosaleen leaned forward and kissed Marie on the cheek. 'We're off.'

Marie gripped her arms. 'Look after yerself, love. John'll be good t' you. He's a nice lad.'

Rosaleen turned and ran to the car. Michael, in his open-back van, led the posse. A teenager tied fireworks to the bumper on the Ford and lit them. Rosaleen dashed into the passenger seat and gave a last wave. The cars parted and the Ford sped through, sending up clouds of dust from the brown scrub, and then they jumbled behind it down the lane that led to the highway. A few seconds after they disappeared behind a buff-coloured ridge, more car horns added to the din.

Marie leaned against the peeling white post in front of the door. When the car horns became faint she pursed her lips, turned and went into the house, now strangely silent. The black-and-white wedding photograph of her own mother and father, with its old-fashioned round frame, was on the wall over the stone fireplace. She felt restless. She went up the stairs and closed the windows in all the bedrooms. She came back down and was just about to close the sliding door when a small shadow fell across the back porch.

'Where is everybody, nanny?' asked Gerry.

Agnes's nine-year-old son had a tough little face with a boxer's nose and closely cropped hair. His cheeks were streaked with marine-blue and orange sunblock and his scrawny frame was visible under the white, wet tee-shirt. He stood with a bamboo fishing rod in his right hand.

'They've gone to the airport with Rosaleen and John.'

His cheeks contracted. 'Without me?'

'They want us to mind the place.'

He was unconvinced.

'There's no point in standin' there with an oul puss on ya. They'll be back soon. Are ya not gonna help me keep the muzzies out?' she said, going over and closing two windows.

He put down his rod and closed a window, saying, 'I don't know why you're doing this.'

'I hate muzzies.'

'They're all inside. Can ya not hear them?'

'No,' she said, raising her hand to the insistent buzzing at her ear. 'Most of them stay outside until you put the lights on. Did you bring up the fish you caught?'

'No.'

'Why?'

He didn't answer.

'Go on down and get them an' I'll fry them for our tea – before the others come back. How many did ya catch?'

He smiled. 'Four.'

'Go on. Run.'

He dashed out the door, his bare feet flapping on the wooden boards, and ran across the sand towards the narrow wooden pier at the water's edge. His silhouette disappeared over a dune and then his bobbing head became just visible against the orange brilliant sky. She loved Gerry. She loved all the kids. And whenever she had her doubts about having made the right decision, all she needed to do was look at the kids. In Belfast, Gerry would have been a hard little nut in the wet back streets of the Falls Road, involved in God knows what. Here his world was a playground. A young country for young people. A lucky country. What opportunities! What houses! Yes, she nor Harry might never have felt at home, but the children …

He came into the kitchen, panting, and laid his trophies at her feet.

'They're a good size. What do you call that?' she asked, pointing at a plump fish with pink-tinged fins.

'That's a snapper,' he said proudly.

She lifted it, held it under the tap and slit it open with a small sharp knife. Blood spurted onto her hand, scarlet rivulets ran along the bottom of the sink. 'Do you not mind?'

'What?'

'Watchin' this.'

He shook his head.

'Do you know who hated the sight of blood. My sister Rosaleen. Ya cud never get her t' do anything like this.'

'Why?'

'Just her nature, I suppose. She sent a telegram today.'

'Did she?'

'And a money order for a thousand dollars.'

Gerry whistled. 'She must have plenty of money. She's in America, isn't she?'

'Yeah, but … I wouldn't say she's well off.'

She suddenly put down the knife, washed the blood off her hands and went to her handbag lying beside the settee. She took out a small brown notebook and flicked through the pages, stopped, lifted the cream-coloured phone and dialled a long number. She waited. Her legs were unsteady. She sat down. At the other end the phone was lifted and a man spoke in a deep Southern States voice: 'Hello?'

'Is that you, Daniel?'

'Yes.'

'Marie here, Rosaleen's sister … is Rosaleen there?'

'No, I'm sorry. She's gone to a meeting.'

'Oh. When will she be back?'

'Two – three hours. Is there anything wrong?'

'No, it's just, you know, it's my daughter's wedding day and we got – thanks very much for the present.'

'Your daughter got married?'

'Yes, my Rosaleen.'

'Maybe you could leave your number. Does she have it?'

'Yes – I don't know – maybe. Five-six-three-two-one is the local number.'

He repeated the number. 'I'll give it to her when she returns.'

'Thanks.'

'Did everything turn out all right?'

'Yes, oh yes. It was a lovely wedding.'

'Good. Good. I'll let her know you called.'

'Great.'

'Goodbye.'

'Goodbye Daniel.'

She put down the phone. The ice had travelled all the way from Georgia and touched her blood. Some people were like that. Daniel was one of them.

'Nanny! Do you want me to fry the fish?'

He was standing at the door with a fish-slice in his hand and a fillet dripping blood. His blue eyes had the brightness of a successful hunter.

'No, I'll do it. You burn them. Fresh fish only needs a minute on the pan.'

The phone rang. She snatched it up. Her face dropped when she heard the plaintive whine of Mrs Robertson. The church collection hadn't balanced again. She got rid of her in a couple of minutes and put down the phone. Gerry was standing in the doorway, a clean fish fillet hanging from his fingers.

'I can do them. I won't burn them,' he said.

'Okay. I'll cut, you fry.'

She went in and cut, cleaned and washed the fish. She spread flour on a plate and watched him fry them and they set up a table by the front window. She poured him a lemonade, herself a glass of white wine. They ate the delicious fish. The distant sky was orange-purple.

'They're taking ages, nanny,' he said.

'They've probably called in somewhere. Are you tired?'

'No.'

His eyes were beginning to close. He had been up most of the previous night.

'Go over and lie down on the settee there.'

'But I'm not tired.'

'Have a wee rest. Till they come back.'

He went over and stretched out on the soft, brightly coloured cushions, enclosed with a cane frame. His eyelids started to

9

drop. In a few minutes he was asleep. Marie took an enormous towel from a chair and covered his body. She sipped the wine. The deep purple was swallowing the orange, the shadows were indistinct. She glanced at the phone.

Sisters were much closer than brothers. She'd noticed that in her own. Whatever about Daniel, the telegram and money order meant something. Nothing should have ever come between them. Like when they were jiving in the living room all those years ago, you knew exactly what the other was supposed to do. The furniture against the wall and on the gramophone you put Bill Haley, Elvis, Cliff …

Chapter 2

Rosaleen was vaguely aware of the high-pitched chatter of the class. The smell of spilt milk, bread, the discomfort of her burgeoning breasts under the brown school uniform of St Monica's.

Cliff was gorgeous. At the record shop in Smithfield, on Saturday, she had stood for ages listening and hoping they would play 'Move It' one more time. Some said he imitated Elvis. That didn't matter. It was the music, the face, the way he moved –

A sudden echoing clatter of sturdy heels in the corridor, a swish of a navy-blue habit, the door banged. Sister Gertrude, cheeks weather-scorched, pink lips tight, stood in front of it and trained her small blue eyes on the class, now rigid with attention. She pointed a finger at Rosaleen and the girl beside her.

'Rosaleen Johnson! Joan McCormack – out!'

Eyes flicked across at the victims. One or two smiled at the randomness of the selection. They all watched the two girls troop forward and stand before the blackboard.

'The noise of this class could be heard at the bus stop down the road. Two teachers have put in formal complaints. Sister Veronica had to send the caretaker down to get me. You are all a complete and utter disgrace.'

The girls' eyes sought the grainy ink-stained desks, the floor, the windows overlooking the bog meadows below.

'And you,' she said, turning to Rosaleen and Joan, 'are the ringleaders.'

Joan, a thin and slightly gawky girl, and a full head shorter than Rosaleen, stood behind her friend's shoulder.

'I want you to write one thousand lines each: "I must not talk in class without the permission of the teacher." And hand them to me tomorrow morning at nine o'clock.'

Joan's eyes were like a rabbit's under the claw of a predator. Rosaleen's lower lip dropped and when the full implication dawned on her of what the punishment was for, she said: 'But I wasn't talking, Sister Gertrude.'

The nun's body stiffened, she clenched her strong hands into fists. 'I won't stand here and listen to lies. I saw you. Both of you. With my own eyes!'

Rosaleen returned her gaze. 'I wasn't talking,' she said flatly.

'Go outside the room. The pair of you. I won't have naked lies told to me in this class. I won't stand for it.'

The girls shuffled towards the door. 'And if I were you,' she threw after them, 'I would pray that Sister Veronica doesn't come along and see you.'

They slipped through the door and stood in the dark silent corridor. They could hear Sister Gertrude, in her rasping West of Ireland accent, hammering out a short discourse on the importance of discipline before launching into the life of St Brigid. Snatches of Miss Long's musings on Hannibal's crossing of the Alps came drifting along from a class further down the corridor. 'A thousand lines!!' gasped Joan.

Rosaleen's chin jutted, the skin on her face burned. 'She's a vindictive old cow.'

'But why us?'

Rosaleen knew the incident that sparked it. Pagans in Africa. Religious rituals with candlelight. Were they not similar to rituals in our church? Our church? She honed in and hissed: 'Obviously you have no faith.' That a question could produce such hatred startled and frightened Rosaleen. Why shouldn't she be curious? Why should there not be similarities? Why did she not try to answer the question? Why? Why?

'I think it was me she was after,' said Rosaleen. 'You were unlucky.'

'But you weren't talking either.'

'She doesn't care.'

'How are we going to do a thousand lines for tomorrow?'

Rosaleen folded her arms. 'I'm not,' she said.

The time dragged on. Joan's upper teeth gnawed at her lower lip and she stared balefully along the length of the corridor. 'If Sister Veronica comes – we're for it.'

Rosaleen relished that prospect. The principal had been fair in her dealings with her in the past. The shiny tiled floor and smooth mauve-painted walls echoed their tiniest movement. Rosaleen fidgeted, shook her limbs and rocked to and fro on her heels. Joan's pale face bespoke that she had accepted the fate of a powerless victim. A shrill bell rang, the class door opened and the face that emerged had not softened.

'You will report to me in the staffroom at nine o'clock sharp tomorrow morning. And I expect a thousand lines each – is that clear?'

'Yes, Sister Gertrude,' said Joan.

'Is that perfectly clear, Rosaleen Johnson?'

Rosaleen brushed past her to go into the classroom.

'Come back here!'

She stopped, turned and avoided looking at Sister Gertrude.

'I don't like your manner. You're an insolent girl. And I'm sure your parents don't approve of your behaviour. Marie never gave any problems in this school.'

There was a muted buzz in the classroom. Aware that something was happening in the corridor, the girls delayed coming out. Joan stood with her hands behind her back, Rosaleen's fists were clenched, her knuckles white.

'It's a question of attitude,' said Sister Gertrude. 'You have the wrong attitude. And if you keep it up you're going to have severe problems. Not only in this school – but in your life. Do you understand?'

The voice came from deep within Rosaleen, with a slight tremble on her lips. 'I wasn't talking.'

'Hah! And I suppose no one was talking. All these mute monkeys manufacturing a great wall of silence.'

'I don't know what mute monkeys were doing – I know what I was doing.'

'If you keep up this attitude – this arrogance – I don't see a future for you in this school.'

Rosaleen turned away.

'Think about it. Before you do anything silly,' she said, watching her hurry back into the classroom.

The girls had quickly formed themselves into groups and found a solution. The number of lines was divided by the number in the class and each girl would do an equal share of the lines. Rosaleen took her lunch from her schoolbag, grabbed a bottle of milk from one of the crates by the wall and went outside to the shed at the edge of the schoolyard.

The conspiracy gathered momentum in the afternoon. Lines were written on desks, on creaky benches, on knees. They were written during classes all afternoon and by the time the final bell rang pages were stacked at the front desks. Joan worried about the difference in handwriting, others assured her that Sister Gertrude wouldn't mind or care. Rosaleen didn't thank the class for their effort. Nor did she concern herself about gathering up the pages. She left that to a worried, frightened Joan.

After school she shrank from the celebrity status conferred on her by the girls. It was raining. Amidst a throng, she piled onto a red and white trolley bus. Sloping rods clicked into overhead lines and it whirred along the road to Ivy Drive.

Small terraced houses, lace curtains, green railings around a patch of a garden, and at number fourteen, three pruned Macready rose bushes tucked neatly in a line. From the bay window you could see its junction with the Falls Road where at night Lotharios hung about, strutted, and awaited the arrival of their perfumed belles.

Rosaleen was glad there was no one home. She put her wrinkled leather schoolbag down by the settee and went up to the back bedroom she shared with Marie. A double bed was shoved against the inside partition – she hated the way you could hear everything in her parents' room. Some day, when she was rich, she would get a big house with thick walls. Cliff Richard sulked in a black and white photograph above the bed, and beside him Bill Haley leaned down so that you could see his kiss-curl. Beyond the bright pink bedspread a square window overlooked small brick yards strung with washing. Opposite, atop a pigeon loft, a lone pigeon sat with its head down amongst its grey feathers.

She took off her uniform, shirt and tie, and hung them over a chair. Her underarms, just above the edges of her vest, were slightly sore from the thrust of her breasts – she felt them from the sides with the palms of her hands – they were too big and if they continued at the rate they were growing she would be a freak. Marie's were better. She had a figure. But they weren't a show.

She opened the old walnut wardrobe. In the mirror along the back of the door she caught her reflection and squirmed at the yellow pimple on the side of her nostril. She scratched it, hoping it would explode into smithereens. It just oozed and itched – she took up a tissue, dabbed it dry and then smeared on some sulphur acne ointment. A beam of sunlight cut through fine dust particles and fell on the hanging clothes. Her left hand fingered a heavy brown jumper, a grey pleated skirt. All her clothes seemed drab and heavy. To their right hung Marie's. A narrow black skirt, a flaming pink silk blouse, nearly a dozen jumpers and the whiff of perfume. Marie was off working in an office uptown. She could shop on her lunch break. She had money every week.

The outside door opened and slammed. 'Rosaleen!' shouted Marie.

Normally the sound of Marie's voice lifted her. Not today. She continued dressing slowly and went down the narrow staircase with the turn at the bottom into the small living room. Marie was motion. Still in her camel hair coat she was bent over, pushing the heavy settee against the wall. Her small heels slipped out of the shiny black stiletto shoes. Her slender legs reminded Rosaleen of the thickness of her own.

'Givus a hand,' said Marie.

Rosaleen pushed the other end of the settee. They set back the wooden chairs against the walls and partially shoved the dining table into the tiny kitchen. 'What's wrong with you?' asked Marie.

'Nothing.'

The story got told.

'I never made trouble,' said Marie, 'because I was afraid to say anything. But plenty of times I felt like it. Anyway, she's a cow. Remember – you only have another year to go. You can leave after your Senior. And don't let it interfere with your dancing career.'

Marie went over to the plastic bag lying by the door, pulled out a new single disc, lifted the top of the gramophone and put it on. The needle whirred around the outside.

'Who is it?' asked Rosaleen.

Marie rolled up her sleeves, pushed her left knee against the edge of her tight skirt, and, ready to jive in the girl's position, watched her sister's face. At the first chord of the guitars it beamed.

Rosaleen gripped Marie's left hand and twisted her around. She came back. They changed hands. Rosaleen pushed her out again and slowly she came back in to the rhythm of the guitars. She imagined Cliff's stance, the way he held his head to the side, the swivel of his legs.

They played and danced to 'Move It' six times. Then they played Buddy Holly's 'Rave On', 'Rock around the Clock' and 'You Ain't Nothin' But a Hound Dog'.

* * *

The evening meal was over and the girls were finishing the dishes in the kitchen. Frank Johnson sat at the table, chewed his lips and stabbed the bowl of his pipe with the pipe-cleaner. He had thick, wiry, prematurely grey hair and a lean hard body. Behind him his almost stain-free green overalls had been taken from the canvas bag, and both hung on two of the hooks strung out on the wall at the base of the stairs. Normally, on finishing his meal, he claimed the armchair by the Devon grate, turned on the small cream-coloured radio and smoked his pipe. Tonight his green eyes were downcast, his cheeks taut, and just above his neat white shirt and tie, his Adam's apple throbbed slightly. Across the table, now cleared of the plastic tablecloth, sat Eileen. He avoided looking at his wife.

Eileen glanced down at the front page of the Belfast Telegraph – bold black type proclaimed the red menace. She had wide-set brown eyes, the white with a tint of blue giving them depth, and the kind of open full-cheeked good looks that still turned men's heads. Her figure was curvaceous, ample, and she had long slender fingers. She flicked the paper to the side and joined her hands and said, 'I don't think she should do them.'

He didn't look up. 'Why?'

'Sister Gertrude's being vindictive.'

He gave his pipe bowl a few stabs. 'Maybe she doesn't mean her to do them all.'

'I believe Rosaleen.'

17

'Remember that row when I was paintin' the statues. Gertrude said they were too bright. They would've lost their brightness in a few months.'

'You shouldn't have done them again.'

'Ya can't win with them nuns.'

Eileen set her face firmly. 'A thousand lines by nine o'clock tomorrow morning? Rosaleen!'

Rosaleen came out, Marie stood at the entrance to the narrow kitchen with a cloth in her hand.

'What are you gonna do about these lines?'

Rosaleen shrugged. 'Nothing.'

'She's only pickin' on her, mammy,' said Marie. 'She doesn't like Rosaleen.'

'Maybe it's better not t' make a big thing out of it? Do some of them,' said Frank, 'maybe a couple of hundred?'

'For what? For sittin' there doin' nothin'! Mindin' m' own business.'

Frank threw his pipe to the side. 'Maybe she thought you were talking.'

'She's not blind,' said Rosaleen.

Marie leaned against the edge of the doorway. 'Everybody knows her,' she said. ' When Gertrude has it in for ya – ya get it.'

'I wonder should I go up and see Sister Veronica,' said Eileen.

Frank lifted his pipe and jabbed the bowl with a wire. 'That might make it worse,' he said. 'If Rosaleen makes some gesture …'

Eileen folded her arms. 'I could write a note to Gertrude,' she said. 'Say you could only do two hundred? – a hundred?'

They looked at Rosaleen's face. Her jaw was set firm. 'I don't see why I should do any,' she said, going around the table to the foot of the stairs. 'She's a liar. She's not fit to be in the position she's in. But she's not going to make a liar out of me.'

She went up the stairs.

Eileen and Frank looked over at Marie. Arms folded, red lips tight. 'I think Rosaleen's right,' she said.

'This isn't the first time she's been in trouble,' said Frank quietly.

'She's not a doormat,' said Marie. 'A lot of the teachers and nuns in that school expect ya t' say nothin'. Question nothin'.'

Frank folded his arms. 'You never got into trouble.'

'Well,' said Marie, after a pause, 'plenty of times I felt like sayin' somethin'. But I kept m' mouth shut. An' I'm sorry I did.'

Eileen sucked in her cheeks, Frank's eyes narrowed as he spoke. 'What harm did it do you? Ya got yer reference and yer certificate and a good job in an office down the town.'

'We were like sheep. Plenty of us felt like sayin' things. But we hadn't the guts. Rosaleen's different.'

'This just didn't start today,' said Eileen. 'We all know where it goes back to.'

Marie brought the cloth into the kitchen, hung it up above the sink and came back out. 'Why shouldn't she ask questions?'

Frank twisted around in the chair and plumped an elbow on the table. 'It's not just questions,' he said. 'There's ways of askin' them. And nuns and priests are funny. It can be dangerous t' try an' go into religion too deep.'

Marie shook her head. 'All she did was compare African tribal rituals to …'

Frank dug his elbow into the table. 'That's guaranteed t' get people's backs up!'

'How?' asked Marie, spreading her hands and going over to the Devon grate and leaning her backside against the warm shiny tiles.

'Because they're out convertin' the blacks t' Christianity – that's why. An' ya can't question religion too deep. Ya have to just accept.'

They were silent for a few moments.

'None of this solves the problem,' said Eileen. 'What's Rosaleen gonna do or say tomorrow?'

Marie shrugged. 'She won't do them. We all know that.'

* * *

Rosaleen left her schoolbag at the back of the chapel, slid into the last pew, kneeled down and joined her hands. She buttoned another peg on her navy duffle coat. St John's was still cold – bright, modern, with a simple white marble altar up at the front. There were only a few stragglers from the eight o'clock mass.

Her eyes were ringed. All night long the dramas had played back and forth. Aligned against her were Sister Gertrude, Sister Veronica, her mother and father, the whole class – on her side, only Marie. The opposition spoke: she was a well-known liar, a cheat, a chatterbox who was determined to be the centre of attention. Nothing they said was true. She knew what the truth was, and she would be judged on the truth.

She closed her eyes and said five Our Fathers and five Hail Marys. She imagined Our Lady. A beautiful, wise, serene and gentle face – the arms extended, comforting, understanding. Our Lady could see the truth. And behind her, Jesus – not meek, but strong, penetrating, the scourge of Pharisees, money-lenders and liars. She asked them personally, directly, for their help. In my hour of need let Sisters Veronica and Gertrude see the truth.

It was shortly after nine when she went into the classroom. The babble stopped suddenly. A flurry of sheets exchanged hands and Angela Murphy, a plump girl with a puckish smile, gathered them together at the front. Another girl stood lookout at the door. 'Joan's gone down with hers,' said Angela, proffering the sheets. 'There's slightly over a thousand.'

Rosaleen threw her schoolbag along the aisle to the approximate position of her desk. She turned and marched past a gaping Angela and the girl at the door. Behind her, the cries rang out. 'The lines! Rosaleen! You forgot the lines!'

Miss Kerr strode towards her with an armful of exercise books and flashed a tight smile. Rosaleen turned a corner and knocked the heavy brown door of the staffroom. Miss Giblin, a young teacher, opened it. Beyond her and the table where two lay teachers were sitting, stood Sister Gertrude with a large bundle of assorted sheets under her arm. 'Can I see Sister Gertrude?' asked Rosaleen.

Before Miss Giblin turned around Sister Gertrude had darted over. The skin on her face was crisp-clean and the almost bare eyelids came down slightly. She licked her upper lip and said, 'You have something for me?'

In an instant the young teacher caught the mood and retreated to the table. Another teacher brushed by as the two of them locked eyes. 'No,' said Rosaleen.

'You haven't done the lines?'

'No.'

'Have you a note from your parents?'

'No.'

Sister Gertrude paused and then said, 'You just decided not to do them?'

Rosaleen didn't answer.

'Come with me,' she said, heading past her and down the empty corridor towards the front of the school.

Rosaleen deliberately dragged behind and caught a glare when they turned a corner. She was nervous. But she had a sneaking confidence that Sister Veronica would see the justice of her case.

'Wait here,' said Sister Gertrude, as she marched straight into the principal's office.

The time passed slowly. She felt alone. She began to feel sorry for herself. Her eyes lit on a statue of Our Lady just down the corridor. Our Lady would help her. She would just go in and tell the truth and things would be all right. Eventually the door opened. 'Come in,' said Sister Gertrude.

There was something in her tone that made Rosaleen feel uneasy. In past dealings with Sister Veronica, she knew her to be fair. But another nun, the vice-principal, was involved now. And they had been talking for at least five minutes. Had they decided something already, without giving her a hearing? The expression on Sister Veronica's face was hard, serious. She sat behind a dazzling brown desk. The white band of her habit was plainly visible in the reflection. To her left, at the side of the desk, stood Sister Gertrude with her fingers lightly touching a pile of sheets.

'Sister Gertrude tells me that she gave you some lines.' She paused. 'You refused to do them?'

'Yes.'

'Why?'

'I wasn't talking. I didn't deserve to get them,' she said, glancing over at Sister Gertrude who seemed to have momentarily removed herself from the proceedings.

'Sister Gertrude says you were talking.'

'I wasn't.'

Sister Veronica looked down into the reflection on the desk. 'You and Joan McCormack were given lines. Joan handed hers in this morning.'

'She didn't.'

'What do you mean?'

'They aren't her lines.'

'Are you accusing Joan McCormack of something?' interjected Sister Gertrude. 'Are you?'

'She didn't write a thousand lines last night.'

'There they are!' she said, prodding the sheets of paper with her finger. 'While you, one of the biggest chatterboxes in the class, have done nothing.'

'I did nothing because I was guilty of nothing.'

Sister Gertrude flapped her hands. 'It's wilful and deliberate disobedience,' she said. 'An affront to the authority of the school.'

'I will not be punished for something I didn't do.'

'Why did you do none of the lines?' asked Sister Veronica.

'Because I wasn't talking! I was sitting there doing nothing!'

Sister Gertrude, so as not to breathe the same air as the accused, held back her body and spoke precisely. 'Not only are you determined to disregard the authority of the school but you are prepared to accuse Joan McCormack – a girl who has seen fit to do her lines – of a crime.'

'I didn't accuse her of a crime.'

'Then what do you mean she didn't do her lines,' she said, her fingers drumming the paper sheets on the desk. 'She handed these to me ten minutes ago!'

'I said they weren't her lines. And they're not. Nobody could do a thousand lines in one evening.'

'You're accusing her of wilful deception?'

'I'm accusing her of nothing. The girls in the class did them. They knew we weren't talking. They knew we weren't to blame. I refused to take their lines because I'd done nothing wrong.'

'The issue,' said Sister Veronica coldly, 'is your disobedience to the vice-principal of this school.'

Tears streamed down Rosaleen's cheeks. 'If you don't believe me, Sister Veronica, look at the lines. They're all different. Do you think the class would have done them if we had done anything wrong? We weren't talking and we were punished for the whole class!'

She rubbed her wet cheeks with her fingers. Sister Gertrude stared straight ahead, oblivious to her sobbing presence. And the ice had spread to Sister Veronica. Her lips contracted; the eyes, which Rosaleen had seen laughing sometimes, had shut out the light; the black eyebrows, flecked with grey, rose. She gently joined her hands and sat still, like a predator. 'I'm surprised at your behaviour, Rosaleen Johnson. Your family has always had good relations with this school and it saddens me to see you treat the vice-principal of this school in such a disrespectful –'

'But I wasn't – !'

'Please be quiet. I've heard both sides of this. Indeed, I can only reflect that in the whole six years of attendance at this school your sister never once had to be brought in to see me over an important disciplinary matter like this.'

Rosaleen sobbed and her shoulders shook.

'You'll have to stop this,' said Sister Veronica, 'you're behaving like one of the first years.'

Sister Gertrude shot a sideways, contemptuous glance. Rosaleen saw this and it stopped her sobbing.

'You're too old for this kind of behaviour,' she continued. 'But we have to have discipline in the school and you know the punishment for breaches of this kind. However, Sister Gertrude, being the person she is, has asked me to show leniency in this case. If you promise to do the lines by tomorrow morning she's prepared to overlook your omission today.'

Rosaleen glanced over at Sister Gertrude. Her beatific eyes were directed towards the Sacred Heart of Jesus picture on the wall opposite. Sister Veronica's face was stone. She knew in an instant what had gone on in the five minutes before she had entered the office.

'I won't do them,' she said.

Sister Veronica pulled her fingers free and laid the palms of her hands on the desk. 'Then you leave me no choice,' she said. 'You're suspended from the school for two weeks. I will be writing a letter to your parents today to explain our position. You can take your schoolbag and go straight home after you leave this office. Do you understand?'

Rosaleen fought back the tears, turned, went to the door and put her hand on the handle. She hesitated, half expecting to be called back. No one could be so brutal. Unjust. She turned the handle and slipped into the corridor. In the office she had felt brave, now she was afraid. She would have to go back to the class for her schoolbag and they would see the state she was in. What would it matter? She was right. Let them all rot in hell.

The statue of Our Lady was on her left. Where was she? Did she hear her prayers? Had she no influence over those two battle-axes? Where was truth? Justice? Were they only words?

When she marched into the class she quenched the babble momentarily. 'What happened?' 'What did ya get?' She answered no one. She dragged the schoolbag along the floor and put it on at the door. 'What did you do?' asked Joan. Anne, Mairead, Siobhan – the girls with whom she sat around the transistor in the milk shed – followed her out into the corridor. She couldn't speak. She hurried along, turned three corners and went out onto the Falls Road.

A cold blustery wind ruffled the bushes behind the drab green railings in the City cemetery opposite. She wouldn't get a bus. She would walk home. Head down, she plunged ahead. At a street corner a car screeched to a stop. She didn't notice the glare, the chopped words. A fudge of dusty gardens, red trolley buses, Ford Prefects, grey stone walls. By the time she had reached the stately Broadway Cinema she had made up her mind: She wasn't going back to St Monica's.

Chapter 3

Today, like every work day for the past month, when she walked through Pattersons factory gates, Rosaleen wondered if she had made the right decision. Most said she was lucky to get a job. But the weeks of arguments and rows after she left St Monica's had unsettled her. Not that she would admit it to her parents. To them she was a pig-headed stubborn girl, who would cut off her nose to spite her face.

The factory was a large, six storey, red-brick block, with drab rusty protective wire around the ground floor windows. She went up the dusty staircase to the first floor. Already the sewing machines were humming with twenty-odd girls leaning over white handkerchiefs. A couple looked up as she made her way to the end of the first line, where five girls were already sewing.

Unfriendly looks, she thought. Pattersons was, predominantly, Protestant, even though it was within easy walking distance of the Falls Road. Some had warned her. But a job was a job and the money, three pounds ten shillings a week, was reasonable. She could plan, for the first time in her life, what she would buy.

She was glad she was in before the supervisor, Mrs Gregg, whose first question – where do you live? Her dour face went instantly deadly.

Rosaleen thought she might only last a few hours, but she was determined not to pack it in, or give them an excuse to fire her. And her hard work – folding, piling and boxing the handkerchiefs, had by now won a grudging respect. Mrs Gregg was still a face better avoided until later in the morning.

Drawing together several bundles of handkerchiefs to pack her first box, she noticed the light go on in the office to her right and could make out Hilary's blonde hair behind the opaque glass. She liked Hilary. She was sure her friendliness and warmth had made some of the others feel guilty. And a few had come over and made an effort. Hilary made the breaks worthwhile.

Mrs Gregg appeared to her left and hovered over the girls at the machines, casting the occasional glance her way. A morning greeting, at this stage, would have astounded her. But there had been a subtle change since Hilary had broken the ice. Not actively friendly, but less hostile. Rosaleen concentrated until her arms and hands were moving in a quick rhythm – then her mind was free.

A wave of resentment started in the pit of her stomach, moved to her skin and pulled it tight. Her anger grew hot: at the school, the nuns, her parents, the Church. She was Joan of Arc, tied to the bonfire, and they were a gloating, baying mob around her. Yet they were the ones deserving of punishment. In the high court of the Lord, where truth and justice were all, she was innocent.

'We're doing the luxury ones after the break,' said Mrs Gregg. 'You'll have to be careful. They're easy to wrinkle.'

Rosaleen nodded.

'You haven't done luxury before?'

'I don't think so. What are they like?'

'Yellow, red embroidery.'

'No.'

'Come down to me after the break. I'll show you,' she said, turning and drifting down the aisle to her left.

Mrs Gregg was a bulky woman. She had a round face and red cheeks and features that could have been described as homely except for the set of her chin and wide-awake eyes that said: go on, defy me if you dare! She cruised around the aisles like the captain of an old galley-ship.

Rosaleen drifted back into her dream world. She banished the nuns and her parents. She smiled at Cliff. He was mad about her. He loved big girls with muscular shoulders, enormous breasts and legs like tree trunks. He wanted to strut for her, woo her. He wanted to make her his real live, living doll.

The hooter honked that it was time for a break.

On cue, Hilary came to the door of the office and waved to her. As Rosaleen walked towards it, she was aware of the furtive glances from the other girls as they drifted towards the makeshift canteen at the end of the room. Working in the hum of the machines, she didn't feel too isolated. Now that they were silent and the girls were chatting in groups, she felt excluded. But she had a friend.

Hilary's office was a cheerful cube in the factory cavern. Her back was turned. She was bent down, filing away letters into a cabinet. On the desk, beside the typewriter, sat a large bottle of lemonade, two clean glasses and two Mars bars. Rosaleen sat on the neat, red velvet stool beside the desk. There was an autographed picture of Cliff Richard on the wall behind the typewriter, and family photographs beside funny cartoon cuttings. The office was personal, neat and colourful. And the letters, packages and money that crossed the desk seemed to offer a lot more interesting work than packing hankies.

'Let me pay,' said Rosaleen, drawing some copper coins from her small brown purse and sliding them onto the table.

'Hush! Don't be bothering me,' said Hilary, still peering into the files.

'I have to pay.'

Hilary stood up. She wore a white blouse and a black skirt that wasn't quite tight and came to just below her knees. She threw her large frame into the swivel chair. Rosaleen liked her brazenness, the lively hazel eyes that half closed as she jabbed her hand over the Mars bars and lemonade bottle. 'Pattersons pay,' said Hilary.

'But …'

'You're okay. Yon director fella. Ya know the one that's always comin' in t'luk at the girls' legs. Well, the price of sin has gone up. It's now two Mars bars and a large bottle of lemonade.'

'You're terrible.'

'You don't know the half of it.'

'But I'm definitely getting something tomorrow.'

'Don't be botherin' yer head. There's loads of bars in the big office upstairs. They get boxes of them for nothin'.'

'Are you sure?'

Hilary lifted the coins and put them back into her hand. 'Save them for the collection.'

'What collection?'

'The church collection. You see, it's only right we should be taking money from the devil and giving it to the Lord.'

Hilary poured the lemonade. They tore paper off the bars and bit off chunks. 'I shouldn't be doing this,' she said, jabbing her waist with her elbow. 'But I can't resist them.'

'What kind of work are you doing?' asked Rosaleen.

'Letters. Invoices. Stamps. Petty cash … but sometimes,' she looked out the door and lowered her voice, 'I do things for the group. If it's slack, you know?'

Rosaleen stopped chewing. 'What group?'

'Our group.'

'What do you do?'

'Organise gigs,' she said, sinking her teeth into the bar.

'… music?'

'Everything. Community stuff. Table tennis. Bible classes. Religious discussions. Music. Top twenty stuff. It's great crack.'

For the last couple of months, Rosaleen had been reading and thinking a lot about religion. Her experience with the nuns, her unanswered prayers, the endless rows with her parents who seemed to have taken the nuns' side, had jaundiced her. Not towards religion in general – she felt she needed to believe, and Christianity, for her, expressed profound truths – but she couldn't accept the nuns' naked abuse of power. When they acted as they did they were ignoring the teaching of Jesus.

'I read the Bible,' said Rosaleen.

'Why don't you come?'

Hilary had clear, flawless skin, except for one pimple at the tip of her chin. She was devouring her Mars bar. She was fun. She had confidence. She wasn't aggressive. 'It's no big deal,' she said, popping the last of her bar into her mouth. 'There's lots of people from different denominations. Catholics too. The Reverend Prichard likes a big mix. Dolly all sorts.'

Rosaleen had seen photographs of him in the Belfast Telegraph. Tall, broad-shouldered, strong-chinned – he had been leading a protest against something somewhere. The accompanying article was, she thought, unflattering. But what she remembered most from the photograph was his expression – injured, resolute. 'Are they old?' she asked.

'No, there's loads our age. We break up into groups. Argue. Discuss. Agree. Disagree. Fight. Make up. Just like any family.'

'When?'

'Next Wednesday. Eight o'clock.'

* * *

It was a dark, wet wintry Belfast evening. From the northeast, the wind blew over Napoleon's nose and funnelled into the Lagan valley. Rosaleen met Hilary at the City Hall and they took the bus over the bridge to the church on Ravenmount.

She was nervous. Not about Hilary, who was chatting away beside her, but the Reverend Prichard had already established a satanic reputation on the Falls Road. That Hilary herself could be so nice and friendly, and talk about Prichard with such warmth, was reassuring. But in the back of her mind she still had a fear. Evil did stalk the world. It took many forms. And lately she had begun to question a lot of things she had formerly taken for granted.

The church itself was a surprise. Modern, red-brick, with a total lack of the ornate imagery she was used to. Inside, it was homely and simple with an elevated wooden pulpit at the front, and a much lower roof than most Catholic churches. More, she imagined, like a community hall; there actually was a hall, similar and smaller, and built on the ground beside the church.

They went through the church to the hall. Inside, about twenty young people were scattered in groups. Some played table tennis, a few threw darts, and a cluster of toe-tapping girls and a boy had gathered around a gramophone playing the Everly Brothers' 'Bird Dog'. Hardly anyone turned around to look at her. They hung up their coats and Hilary introduced her to three girls and a boy her own age at the gramophone table. She was embarrassed and could feel herself blushing. Hilary sensed this and lifted a single black disc from the pile of records on the table. 'What do you think of this?' she asked, showing her the label.

Rosaleen didn't recognise the name and shook her head. Hilary then drew out Bill Haley's 'See You Later Alligator.' She nodded.

The time flew. More young people drifted in until there was around forty. Rosaleen had expected their accents to be posh. Only some were. But their dress, compared to her grey pleated skirt and loose brown cardigan, seemed a lot more fashionable.

She tagged along as Hilary's shadow for about an hour and observed. They seemed different from most boys and girls her own age that she knew. Catholic boys and girls tended to hang around in single sex groups and there was little contact except at the céilidh or hop. Here there seemed to be an easy-going social mix.

At the break Rosaleen and Hilary sat down at a round table beside Eileen, a girl of about eighteen with striking brown eyes. Rosaleen envied them their snug tight belts and the wide skirts, like the professional rock-and-roll girls wore. They were joined by Mark. His curly ginger hair and open, freckled face were wet with sweat. His hands were large and well scrubbed, the skin slightly calloused. He wore a neat white shirt, a bright yellow tie in a Windsor knot and navy drainpipe trousers. A matronly lady, Mrs Turnbull, distributed a plate of biscuits and four small bottles of lemonade.

'Who's gonna be leader?' asked Mark, flicking the straw in between his lips. 'Hilary? You're the bossiest.'

They laughed.

'I'm sick of being boss. You take a turn.'

He shifted uncomfortably in his chair. 'What about your friend?'

'This is Rosaleen's first night.'

'Eileen, how about you?'

'No, no, no,' said the girl, shaking both her head and the lemonade bottle.

Mrs Turnbull put down four Bibles on the table and a brown envelope.

'We can't decide on a leader. What'll we do?' asked Mark.

'Vote,' she said, moving on to the next table.

'It's three to one,' said Hilary.

'All right,' he said, lifting the brown envelope and passing a Bible to each girl. 'I know when I'm beat.'

He opened the envelope and read. His clear blue eyes hardened, he put his left hand on the Bible and said: 'Why was Jesus killed?'

There was a pause. Rosaleen became aware of the sudden drop in the level of talking around the hall. Eileen cast her eyes down, Hilary and Mark closed theirs, Rosaleen, not quite knowing what was expected of her, half closed hers. She noticed a sharp change in their expressions. From smiles to serious intent. She knew that a light or frivolous remark would be frowned upon. It was like the high seriousness of church, when religion was at its most intense – and she liked it.

There was virtual silence around the room now. After a few moments, someone spoke at another table – Rosaleen didn't catch what he said – but the tone was different to what had gone before. When Mark spoke he startled her, as if she had been woken from a trance.

'Because they hated him.'

'Who?' asked Hilary.

'The people in power. The big bugs. They were afraid of Jesus. They thought he might be God.'

Eileen raised her head. 'Why would they try to kill God?'

'Because … because they didn't believe in God. At least not our God. The Christian God.'

'What kind of God did they believe in?' asked Hilary.

'A Jewish God,' said Mark, 'a slimey kind of God.'

'Not all the Jews were slimey,' said Hilary. 'Remember, Jesus was a Jew.'

His eyes grew spiky and he pointed his finger. 'The ones that crucified Our Lord were worse than slimey. They were …'

'They obviously didn't believe he was God,' said Eileen. 'Like who would try to kill God?'

'Satan,' said Mark.

'Did they think he was Satan?' asked Hilary.

Mark looked at her as if she had two heads. 'Our Lord and Saviour Jesus Christ?'

She spread her hands. 'It's possible.'

'No, no, no,' said Mark, shaking his head and leafing through the back of the Bible to the Gospel section. 'There is nothing Jesus said that could be open to anything of that nature.

Everything he says is against Satan.'

'But Satan does come in many forms,' said Eileen, a quiet voice from the edge of the table.

Rosaleen sat fascinated, lightly fingering her red Bible. She hadn't experienced discussions like this before. Young people, slightly older than herself, discussing and even questioning sacred religious texts. She shared their interest and excitement. It gave religion its important place.

'What do you think, Rosaleen?' asked Hilary.

The skin on her face burned, the brown jumper seemed too warm and the sweaty fingers of her right hand fanned the back pages of the Bible. 'Doesn't … don't the Gospels say?' She was ashamed of her lack of detailed knowledge. 'Didn't the high priests ask Pilate?'

She was delighted that the three of them nodded. Pleased, she continued. 'We understand it that the high priests handed over Christ to Pilate. They wanted him killed.'

'But why?' asked Hilary.

'Because he was a threat,' said Rosaleen.

Hilary came again. 'To who?'

'Rosaleen's right. He was a threat to them,' said Mark. 'That's why they wanted him killed. They wanted him out of the way.'

Eileen spoke. 'They weren't gangsters.'

'How do you know?' asked Mark.

'They were always trying to trip Jesus up,' said Hilary. 'That's clear from all the Gospels.'

Eileen plonked both her elbows on the table and cupped her chin between her hands. 'Who?'

'The Sadducees,' insisted Hilary. 'They controlled the temple.'

'I told ya,' said Mark, nodding his head. 'He got the big bugs' noses up.'

Hilary opened her Bible. 'Let's see what Luke says about it …?'

They compared what each of the Gospels said. They argued with and questioned each other. Rosaleen found herself joining in more and more and she could see they were very interested in hearing an outsider's viewpoint. She was in the middle of explaining her understanding of a Gospel statement, when the main door of the hall opened and the Reverend Prichard came in. She paused, the pitch of the conversation dropped and all eyes turned towards the door. She fudged the point she was trying to make and let Eileen speak.

Dr Lesley Prichard gave Mrs Turnbull a friendly tap on the shoulder, took off his navy Crombie overcoat and vigorously rubbed his hands together. He was big, over six feet, broad-shouldered, with jet black hair combed back on his head and slightly to the side. A small wave fell into a curl on his forehead. 'Don't pay any attention to me,' he said, with a flick of his hands. 'What you're discussing is important. Just think of me as the abominable no-man. I don't exist except when I'm looking for some of Mrs Turnbull's scones.'

Laughter rose. His hand reached out and his arm went around the lady's shoulders. 'They haven't ate all of them, have they? They're a hungry lukin' lot all right. Sorry about the interruption.' He punched the air. 'Go back.'

They obeyed. Rosaleen stole glances at the Reverend, who was now eating scones, sipping tea and regaling Mrs Turnbull with side-splitting stories. His voice, a resonant, manly bass, seemed to rise from the centre of his frame right up to the rafters. Without trying to, he dominated the hall. A change had happened. The centre of gravity had shifted. His newspaper photographs didn't do him justice. Clear, smooth skin, a slightly large chin and nose – she could swear his grey eyes were looking over his teacup and straight at her, and they made her a bit afraid.

'Rosaleen?' she heard Hilary say for a second time.

'Yeah?'

'John's Gospel.'

'Oh, yeah.' Her index finger went to the page of the Bible and ran down the text. Were the words jumbled? Why was she confused? She blushed. 'Could somebody else –?'

Mark took over. He read respectfully. Rosaleen listened but the words went over her head. She couldn't concentrate. Dr Prichard had begun moving among the tables. A joke, a hand on the shoulder, a pat on the back, hands jokingly around a young man's neck to throttle him, then, drawing back to make a serious point for a minute or two. Mrs Turnbull went to and fro, feeding him scones and information. He nodded and looked in Rosaleen's direction. No sooner had she dived into the Bible than he was upon her. 'Welcome to our humble abode, Rosaleen, have they been looking after you?'

'Yes.'

'Nice that you should come and visit us on such a miserable evening. The devil does his best – but it's not good enough. Is it, Hilary?'

'No, Dr Prichard.'

'Well, Rosaleen, you're sitting beside some of our star players in the Bible studies. Manchester United approached us about transferring Mark here – and when the Red Devils want you – you must be good.'

The four of them laughed.

'And Hilary here,' he continued, 'is one of our star performers.'

'I am not!' she protested.

'Now, Hilary, we all know about the unshakeable hold modesty has over you. But there are limits. Bill Haley was on the phone the other day – asking me to let you front his rock-and-roll group the next time he's in Belfast.' He turned to Rosaleen. 'She was at his concert, you know? And – she talked to him direct.'

'I only got him to sign a photograph,' said Hilary, her eyelids lowered bashfully. 'I'm not a real fan – it was for my sister. And the tickets were free.'

'You shouldn't deny it. There's worse sinners in this world than teenage girls with bad hearing and eyesight.'

Smiles all round. He lifted the typed sheet, read and put it down. He sucked in his lips slightly and his chin edged forward. 'Any thoughts? Conclusions?'

There was a pause.

'We think Jesus was killed because he was a threat,' said Mark.

'You don't mind if I have a biscuit,' said Dr Prichard, leaning over and picking one up. 'What do you think, Eileen?'

'They didn't know Jesus – they thought he was a criminal.'

'I think they did it because they were afraid of him,' said Hilary.

Dr Prichard leaned his hands on the table, then he reached out and pulled over a chair. He sat down and crossed his legs. 'Rosaleen?'

She coughed and shifted on her chair. 'I don't … like, I'm new – this is –'

'Just tell us what you think,' he said softly.

'I think … what he did in the temple. The money changers. The animal traders. When he drove them out –'

Dr Prichard joined his hands together and nodded. 'Yes,' he said, 'I think you're all on the right track. The temple, you see, represented the established Jewish religion. Power, money, image – a deep concern with the outer trappings of religion. Not the spirit – Jesus hated that. When he rode into Jerusalem on a donkey and the great crowds went with him to the temple, he was throwing down the gauntlet to the Jewish aristocracy. They controlled all the sacrifices – a monopoly – they were materialists. And when they saw the thousands that supported Jesus they were afraid and felt they had to do something. That's why they wanted to kill him. But the crucifixion – that was more. Even then it was considered barbarous. So they just didn't want to kill him – they wanted to humiliate him and deter his followers. But Our Lord and Saviour wasn't afraid of their supposed humiliation – he knew exactly what they were doing – and he understood the consequences. He foresaw everything.

'Each generation – you, I, have to read The Book and look into our hearts to redefine the spiritual purity that Jesus first preached. There are so many obstacles.'

He stood up. 'I will deal with this at the meeting on Friday night. Will you come?'

Hilary, Eileen and Mark nodded. The question seemed to be addressed to the group in general but Rosaleen felt it was especially addressed to her. And they seemed to be waiting.

'… I don't know. Friday is – awkward.'

'Some other time,' said Dr Prichard. 'We try to put on a good show, don't we, Hilary?'

She smiled.

'Maybe not up to the standard of Bill Haley and his Comets, but –'

'Better,' said Mark.

'You'll be scaring Rosaleen off, Mark,' he said. 'No, we'll leave it as an open invitation.'

'Maybe some other Friday,' said Rosaleen.

'Anytime. We're a family. We meet regularly. And you're always welcome. Always,' he said, smiling and moving on to the next table.

Soon the group began to break up. A handful of young people went out the door. Hilary closed her Bible and turned to Rosaleen. 'Will we play a couple of records before we go?'

Rosaleen left Hilary at the City Hall. She caught a trolley bus, sat on the blue worn shiny seat and looked through the misty window. The Falls Road was deserted. She had enjoyed the night. The skin on her face felt as if it was glowing. What was it? The music was good, the table tennis okay – the discussions? When had anyone ever listened to her the way they had tonight? They weren't faking it. They were actually interested in what she had to say. Her views were important. This wasn't something carved in stone. It was living. And her views were part of that living thing. Is that what they meant by a living church?

When she got home, Frank was dozing by the fire; Eileen, her glasses slipping down on her nose, was knitting a cardigan. 'Where's Marie?' asked Rosaleen.

'Bed.'

'This early?'

'Late night last night.'

She'd forgotten. Marie had been out with Harry the night before. Or was it Eddie? And she thought she had smelt something that was both sweet and nauseous off her breath. She wasn't drinking, was she? She felt like telling someone about the night she'd had. Not her parents. That would be impossible. She went into the kitchen, drank a small glass of water and came back out.

'Where were you tonight?' asked Eileen.

'Playing table tennis.'

'– table tennis?'

'Yer always on at me about exercise. I got some.'

'Where?'

'A hall down the road,' she said, going up the creaky stairs.

The bedroom was cold. She threw off her clothes, wriggled into pyjamas, slipped into the warmth of the bed and curved into Marie's body. Her sister stirred, then oozed back into sleep. She would have liked to talk. Tell her everything. Hilary was wonderful. The way she threw herself into things. Mark was nice too. And the Reverend Lesley Prichard? She saw his grey eyes, the American-style smile, the humour. He wasn't the droning priest from St Paul's nor the cold, guarded bitchy nuns. He wouldn't be afraid of standing in a thunderstorm and getting wet. How the newspapers had lied about him. But wasn't that typical? Hadn't the nuns lied to her too? A lot of people in authority weren't interested in the truth. That was obvious.

And what had her night been about if not investigating the truth? Through the gospels. That was religion. Real religion.

Marie stirred and raised her head from the pillow. 'Where were you?' she asked sleepily.

'Guess?'

'– guess what?'

Marie's head flopped back and down, she muttered something, then was quiet.

Chapter 4

Rosaleen turned off the Donegal Road and went up Broadway towards the Falls Road. The day was damp and close. She felt sweaty and itchy, the fluff from the factory got into everywhere, but she was looking forward to hearing the Reverend Prichard speak at the church meeting tonight. The last few weeks had been eventful.

Hilary had organised low key meetings at lunch-time where they discussed religion. Everyone's opinion was valued. The Bible was often referred to and interpreted for its relevance. Rosaleen liked going. She loved the open, challenging atmosphere. Nothing was swept under the carpet, everything was faced in the open.

Often across the table she found another girl coming out with criticisms she felt were true about the Catholic Church. And nothing was more eventful than the discussion about the papacy. Rosaleen had only vague ideas about its history, which she put forward, matter of factly. Hilary, in the same friendly manner she did everything, questioned some of her facts and suggested she consult some books on the subject.

One evening Rosaleen went to the Belfast Central Library and asked for a few reference books. She piled them on the solid wooden table under the large dome and started reading. Nothing had prepared her for the shock. She thought the first book might be black propaganda but the others largely confirmed it. The Borgia Pope, Alexander VI, was just one of a whole catalogue of monsters. Each book, even the ones with sympathetic Catholic authors, couldn't hide the evil perpetrated by the Popes. All in the name of power and money, and as far removed as it was possible to get from the original teachings of Jesus. Even the lauded St Peter's Basilica at the centre of the Vatican – built on a grandiose scale with money squeezed from the poor by selling them fraudulent indulgences – seemed a replica of the temple Jesus had cleansed in Jerusalem. No one, she came to believe, could interpret the Papacy as anything other than anti-Christ.

When she had recovered from the shock, she began to think. The history of the Papacy was depressing. Did the nuns at school know about it? They must. But they covered it up. Just like they had done with her at school. In the interests of power and authority, they had covered up the truth.

She turned off the Falls Road into Ivy Drive. Marie would be home. She smiled. Her sister always brought sunshine into the house. She was perfume, glamour, a job in an office uptown. And she had stood behind her in the row with the nuns. But she hadn't discussed the religious meetings with her. Why?

As she approached the house, the beat of Bill Haley's 'Rock Around the Clock' came from behind the white lace curtain in the bay window. A writhing figure was just visible. The front door was open. She turned the round brass handle of the living room door and went in.

All the furniture had been pushed against the walls – even the china cabinet had been moved. Marie, red tight jumper, flared black skirt, lipstick, make-up, mascara, hair tied back with a white band, slim legs on cloud-tipping stilettos, dashed forward without a word and removed Rosaleen's brown duffle coat and flung it over the arm of the settee. She pushed her left hand into her Rosaleen's right and spun around.

Rosaleen caught sight of herself in the mirror above the Devon grate: greasy, mousy hair tied back with clips, pasty complexion, an old fluff-flecked brown cardigan and a drab, grey, pleated skirt. Her sister's sinewy movements were confident and sexy. 'Why am I always the tank?' she asked.

Marie was too lost in the music to reply. When the record ended she hopped over, put on 'Move It' and became the tank for its duration. They swapped roles again, twice, and used up their stock of five records in about fifteen minutes. Rosaleen – catching a sight of her now beetroot face to cap her other deficiencies – gave up first and flopped down on the settee.

Her sister, still full of vim, slunk over to her handbag on top of the china cabinet and picked out a silver cigarette case. Holding it in the hand of her outstretched arm, she sprang it open – fluttered her eyelashes and beamed a smile at the invisible man. 'Thank you,' she said.

Rosaleen watched. Two slim fingers dipped into the case, then abruptly withdrew. Marie's head tilted back, her eyes half-closed and her lips curled. 'I only smoke filter-tip,' she said haughtily.

A second dip brought forth a filter-tipped cigarette. 'My pleasure,' she said, inserting it into a black cigarette holder.

From her handbag she produced a mother-of-pearl lighter that she flung at her sister. Rosaleen caught it and lit the small gas flame. Marie practised a long, slow elegant puff on the unlit cigarette as she sashayed across the room. She bowed her head, lowered her eyelashes, let the tip of the cigarette touch the flame and sucked in. Then she straightened up and shimmied over to the mirror – a lip-curling, sideways-glancing, sultry look – suddenly she burst out coughing.

'This never happens to Lauren Bacall,' she said, patting her chest. 'Fancy one?'

'Ma will be in soon.'

'Yer workin', aren't ya?'

'Still –'

'It's not her money,' she said, taking a cigarette and poking it between her sister's breasts. 'Yer a big girl now.'

Rosaleen brushed her hand away. 'Stop that!'

Marie swanned in front of the mirror pulling her jumper from the back in a vain attempt to emphasise her almost flat chest. 'You're nearly a C, Rosaleen. How do ya do it?'

'Marie!'

'Have you got them Charles Atlas chest expanders stashed away somewhere?' She pulled again. 'Have ya? No, I think they only work for men.'

'Do you ever think about anything else?'

Marie turned and looked her in the eye. 'What else is there? Go on – tell me –'

Rosaleen tutted and delved into the Woman's Own magazine on the settee beside her.

'If you made half an effort with yerself ya'd be a walkin' bombshell. Luk at me!' she said, holding in her breath and jutting her chest forward. 'This belt is pushin' m' stomach right up int' m' chest – an' they still wudn't knock the eyes outa yer head.'

'Marie!'

'Do ya know the best geg? Eddie? Predictable as that clock when he leaves me home. Standin' at the entry down there.' She jabbed her waist. 'His hands twiddlin' down here. A thirty-second snog. Up another wee bit. Thirty seconds later – another two inches. Ya wudn't need a stop watch or measuring tape with Eddie. He's gettin' all hot now, eyes glazed, nearly closed, his tongue floppin' aroun' like a hooked fish. Finally his eyes actually close. I can just see the picture playin' in front of his dirty wee mind. There he is – tremblin', gaspin', shakin' at the thought of his nicotine stained fingers claspin' half-a-dozen Kleenex.'

Rosaleen squealed a laugh and threw down the magazine. 'Marie! You shouldn't talk like that.'

'Why?'

'It's not nice.'

'Hah! Eddie's a twiddler. Now, Harry – Harry's more of a fumbler,' she said, gripping bits of jumper and flesh around her waist. 'Like as if he's lukin' for half a poun' of nice plump sausages.'

'Are you still goin' out with both of them?' She paused. 'There'll be trouble.'

'What do you think of Eddie?'

Rosaleen wrinkled her nose. 'He's all right.'

'Do you fancy him?'

'No, I don't. Whatever gave you that idea?'

'Nothin'.'

'Me fancy him?'

'Do ya like his Tony Curtis?'

'– it's all right.'

'He does luk a bit like Tony Curtis.'

Rosaleen thought for a moment. 'Know what I saw him doin' last Saturday?' she said, folding her arms. 'Before he called t' the door for ya? He juked into the entry – tuk out this plastic brush and mirror – combed each side about ten times. Then he twiddled the curly bit in the middle.'

'I told ya he was a twiddler.'

'When he caught me lukin' he nearly dropped the mirror.'

'He makes a big effort. That Italian suit he wears cost nearly twenty poun'.'

'I said t' m'self – where does she get them?'

Marie pulled the cigarette out from the holder and threw it into the fire and sat down beside Rosaleen. 'Eddie's in big demand,' she said. 'Don't be coddin' yerself. The girls in our office think he's a big hunk.'

'– a big hunk of what?'

'I think you and him cud –'

'– what?'

'Wud ya fancy goin' t' St Theresa's tonight with him?'

Rosaleen turned her head slowly towards Marie. Her mouth opened but no words came.

'All ya have t' do is doll yerself up a bit. I'll lend you one of m' jumpers. It'll stretch.'

Rosaleen looked away.

'Well, you could wear your own clothes if you like but you'll only be lettin' yerself down in front of everybody. Luk at ya now –'

'I work in a factory – I dress like everybody else. What way do ya want me to dress?'

'You should be makin' more of yerself – like even m' Ma says it. And as for style she's outa the ark.'

'You work in an office.'

'Still – there's no harm in puttin' yer best leg forward. An' St Theresa's isn't a bad wee hop.'

'I'm not interested.'

'In St Theresa's or Eddie?'

'Both.'

'Why don't you go to the pictures then? There's a good one on at the Gaumont.'

'I can pay m' own way int' the pictures.'

Marie leaned back on the settee, folded her arms and crossed her legs. 'Well,' she said, 'I've fixed you up tonight.'

Rosaleen concentrated her gaze straight onto her sister's eyes. 'Fixed me up with what? A date?'

'No, a banana.'

'You have a nerve. Tryin' t' dump one of your cast-offs onto me.'

'Eddie isn't a cast-off.'

'Hah!'

'He's just sort of … in limbo. You know, never allowed to enter heaven or sit at the right hand of Marie Johnson.'

'Anyway, I've made arrangements tonight.'

'You can't, Rosaleen. I'm serious about this. You can't.'

Rosaleen stood up. 'Can I not?' she said, heading towards the stairs.

Marie pulled her by the arm. 'I'm serious. Really. There'll be murder if ya don't.'

'I've made no arrangements with anybody.'

'But I have.' She paused. 'Both of them are comin' here tonight. Eight o'clock.'

'How –? What– ?'

'Ya see, Eddie rang me on Monday and asked me t' go t' St Theresa's tonight. An' he's not a bad fella. He has his good points. Like, he only uses about half as much Brylcreem on his hair as Harry – an' ya know the way it gets over yer face, neck an' shoulders. Well, Harry got two tickets for the Ritz tonight, so …'

Rosaleen gazed into the fire for a few moments. 'There'll be ructions,' she said.

'It's about time you got started –'

'Is it?'

'You and Eddie – I'm tellin' ya, I'm not jokin' – you and him could –'

'– what?'

'You never know. Anyway, Harry's more my type. Ya see, there's two kinds of men. Leg men and breast men. Harry's a leg man –'

'What's wrong with my legs?'

'Nothin'. Honest. I just – I just – well, my – Harry told me my legs cud be in films.'

'Did he?'

'Lauren Bacall.'

'The legs?'

'Maybe he's exaggeratin'. Slightly. Now Eddie's definitely a breast man. There isn't a shred of doubt about that. And I don't think I cud bear t' disappoint a man that much.'

Rosaleen bit her lower lip. 'And you think I–?'

'Well ya wudn't have t' live with the insecurity of him finding out.'

Her eyes heaped contempt on Marie. 'With his twiddlin'?'

'They all chance their arm. Sure ya'd think there was somethin' wrong with them if they didn't.'

'I wouldn't.'

'You don't go out with men.'

'I wouldn't be bothered.'

Marie let out a sigh and stared at the fire for a few moments. 'What'll I tell him?' she asked.

'I've already arranged to go out tonight.'

'Where?'

'A meeting.'

'Rosaleen, you're making a gigantic mistake. Eddie McGoldrick's been askin' about ya. Plenty of times. He has a great job. He's never missed a day at Hughes Bakery in his life. Do ya know what yer doin'? Do ya know what yer passin' up? You and him cud be the match of the century.'

'Yeah, me and King of the Twiddlers.'

'Ah Rosaleen, don't pay any attention to that. I was exaggeratin'. He's harmless. Do you think I wud let you go out with somebody who'd … who'd do anything?'

'Ya can talk all ya want. I've made arrangements with the girls at work.'

'Where are ya goin'?'

'Ravenmount.'

Two wrinkles folded neatly across Marie's forehead. 'Doctor Prichard?'

'Yeah.'

'That's a Protestant church, isn't it?'

'Yeah.'

The wrinkles deepened. 'You shouldn't be goin'.'

'Why not? It's only a church. People discussin' religion.'

'Don't ya get plenty of that in yer own.'

'I'm interested. The girls at work are interested in our religion. I want t' see what theirs is like.'

'Don't be tellin' m' Da.'

'Why not?'

'You know what he's like.'

'Religion's your own affair.'

'Not in this house.'

'Well mine is. You know, Marie, you should read some of the history of the Catholic Church. A lot of the popes were awful monsters.'

'Don't be talkin' like that, Rosaleen.'

'Why not? Why shouldn't you speak your mind? Why should the truth be hidden?'

'I don't know. I don't know what the truth is. I do know that the nuns treated you badly. And this house hasn't got over it yet. But you know m' Ma and Da. Ya can speak yer mind on anything ya like in this house – except politics, religion and sex.'

'And do you think that's right?'

'I don't like rows.'

Rosaleen's eyes grew bright. 'They have different ideas, you know, Marie,' she said. 'They believe in the Bible. Pure and simple. They don't believe in Our Lady and all the saints we pray to. They like ordinary Catholics – but they reject the pope.'

'What's all that got t' do with you?'

'It's important! Did you ever think why you believe and do the things you do? Like, do you believe what Jesus meant you to believe?'

'I don't know. What difference would it make?'

'What you believe? Your religion? Your immortal soul?'

'Rosaleen, I go to Mass – the odd time to confession. I say the odd prayer. But that's it. I don't understand it. And I don't try to understand it.'

'You don't care what happens to your immortal soul?'

'Of course I do. Why do you think I'm passin' Eddie ont' ya? Agh, go on, be a dote – listen, Rosaleen – wudn't it be better if you went out with Eddie tonight an' saved his soul instead of goin' t' this oul meetin?'

Rosaleen folded her arms and looked away. 'I'm not interested in savin' Eddie McGoldrick's soul,' she said.

'What sort of a Christian are ya?'

'Good, I hope. And I want to stay good. That doesn't mean goin' out with King of the Twiddlers.'

'I have a brainwave,' said Marie, pointing her finger in the air. 'You go to your meetin tonight.'

'I'm definitely goin'.'

'An' I'll fix ya up with Eddie for Friday night.'

'Marie!'

'Luk, I'll have t' do something. I can't devastate the poor fella altogether.'

'Can't you go out with him yourself on Friday night? Isn't that what you've been doin' for the past two months? Two timin'?'

'Yes, Rosaleen. But I've seen the light. I want to be like you. Good. I want to save my immortal soul.'

'You're not funny.'

'I've promised to go to a party with Harry on Friday.'

'Saturday?'

'There's a party for Agnes who's goin' t' Canada. I cudn't miss that.'

'Sunday?'

'Eddie's workin' on Sunday night.'

Rosaleen cast her eyes down. She hadn't ever been on an official date. Last year two boys had walked her and Ann Fagan home from a céilidh. But they were schoolboys, around her own age. Eddie looked fairly grown up.

'It's you he asked out,' Rosaleen said.

'He fancies you.'

'Hah!'

'Really.'

'How do ya know?'

'I can tell,' said Marie, her eyelids dropping in a knowing kind of way.

'Yeah, right.'

'I'm serious. You didn't see the way he looked at you that night you walked by us.'

'He was too busy admirin' the brass buckles in his shoes t' even look up.'

'No, you're wrong,' said Marie, scrutinising her face. 'He's dead keen.'

'– Friday night?'

'You won't regret it, Rosaleen. Honest.'

The brass doorhandle turned and Eileen breezed in carrying a plastic bag. There was an extra bounce in her step, excitement in her eyes – the girls knew she had been on a successful shopping expedition. When she took off her beige overcoat, her new dress emitted a blaze of colour – autumnal reds with muted yellows, in a swirling design where two large fans merged just between the breasts – figure-hugging from the waist up, slightly low cut with a wide skirt. 'What do you think?' she asked, twirling around and letting the hem rise until she had to pat it down with her hands.

Marie purred. 'It's gorgeous, Mammy. Really gorgeous,' she said, feeling the soft material.

Eileen did another less flamboyant twirl in front of Rosaleen, whose upper lip slipped down behind the lower. 'Well?'

'It's nice,' she said, without conviction.

A wave of doubt flitted across Eileen's eyes, her chin dropped and her lips parted. 'I can take it back. You don't think it's too … young.'

Marie shook her head. 'Get away.'

'Is it warm?' asked Rosaleen.

'I'm prayin' for a heatwave,' said Eileen, pulling the shoulders slightly with her fingers so that the top lay evenly and turning from side to side to examine it in the mirror above the Devon grate. 'You can't get a really good winter dress unless you pay an absolute fortune. This was in the sale. Guess the price?'

Rosaleen shrugged.

'At least thirty poun',' said Marie.

'Thirty-five – reduced to twenty-one. I cudn't resist it.' She moved forward and backward, examining herself from different angles. 'Frank'll kill me.'

Marie folded her arms and nodded. 'You were dead right, Mammy.'

'And –' said Eileen, dipping into the plastic bag at the foot of the settee and pulling out a small box. She prised out a bottle of perfume, opened it and dabbed some onto her neck. She waved the bottle under her daughter's nose.

Marie purred. 'Can I wear a bit of this tonight?'

'You only need a dab,' said Eileen, handing her the bottle.

Marie put on a couple of dabs and handed the bottle to Rosaleen who held it under her nose and sniffed. 'It's nice,' she said.

Eileen tucked her hands into her waist. 'Nice? Nice? Is that the limit to your vocabulary?'

'What do you want me to say?' said Rosaleen, handing back the bottle. 'I said it's nice.'

'Well you could say that its "sensuous odours wafted you away to exotic shores on distant sun-kissed islands" – that's what the box says.'

'Rubbish!'

Marie took the bottle and sniffed again and purred. 'Do you think it'll have that effect on my date tonight?'

'I wouldn't bet on it. Who's the lucky man? Eddie?'

Marie glanced at Rosaleen, whose face went scarlet.

'Harry?'

Marie nodded.

'Tweedledum, tweedledee,' said Eileen.

'Hah! Well you didn't exactly marry the King of Siam, did you?'

'Times have changed,' said Eileen, taking the perfume bottle off Marie. She went over and put it on the top shelf of the china cabinet. 'I left school at fourteen. In the hungry thirties. A tradesman was a good catch then.'

'So you married m' Da for his money. Well, you could have fooled us.'

'You have an education, Marie. Your Senior. We were threw out t' work in the mills when we were fourteen. The world's your oyster when you get an education. You can walk into any office in this town and slap your certificate on the desk.'

'Well, actually, Mother,' said Marie, stretching to the tips of her stilettos. 'We of the educated classes do not slap certificates, like dead fish, on the desks of prospective employers. Proles from the back street slap fish and other unseemly articles on desks. But not certificates of education.'

'A certificate gets you taken by the hand. Do ya think Rosaleen wud have ended up in a factory on the Donegal Road if she'd stayed on and got her Senior?'

Rosaleen glared at her mother. 'I hated that school.'

'There was nothing wrong with it.'

'The nuns were awful.'

'Marie got through it.'

'Sister Gertrude was a dragon.'

'She was always a lady to me. And Marie. Are the people you're workin' with a crowd of angels?'

'No … but they're nice.'

'Well they weren't always nice.'

'How?'

'It's only in the last couple of years they've employed any Catholics in that place. And only on the factory floor. Do you think you would've got a job in the office? Certificate or no certificate?'

'It's a lot better than school.'

'School's only for a couple of years. And if it's used right you can set yourself up for life. If I hada had half your chances –'

'I'm happy where I am,' said Rosaleen, going over to the foot of the stairs. She turned abruptly. 'And if you must know I think that dress is miles too young for you. I certainly wouldn't walk down the street beside you wearing it.' She turned and went up the stairs.

Eileen's lips tightened. She went over to the mirror and examined herself.

'Don't be payin' any attention to her, Mammy,' said Marie, directing admiring glances at the dress. 'She's only tryin' t' get yer back up.'

Eileen went forwards and backwards in front of the mirror and turned sideways each way. 'I could bring it back,' she said. 'Is it too young?'

'No. Definitely not. It makes you look younger, but that's the idea, isn't it?'

'Rosaleen can be very cuttin'.'

'She doesn't mean it.'

'You were never anything like her. All right, the nuns were … but she's so stubborn. No, there's no holdin' her. Never even did her exams. And all that education for what? A packin' job in a hankie factory.'

'She's plenty of time.'

'No, she hasn't,' said Eileen, turning her back to the mirror. 'That's the sad thing about life. Ya think ya have time for so much. But time surprises everybody. Especially girls.' She glanced back at the mirror. Yellow flames from the coal fire cast a pale light around the room. A dreamy look came into her eyes. 'I used t' see m'self sauntering along Bondi beach. We got the papers out, signed them, did the interviews. But when it came to the bit.' She paused. 'Frank wudn't leave. He cudn't leave here … all that sunshine. I'd have a permanent tan, like Liz Taylor. Don't you be making the same mistake.'

'Harry's not keen now. But you never know –'

'It's the childer. That's what I'd be thinking about.'

'Well I don't want t' scare him off. Just yet.'

'Why don't you ... help Rosaleen?'

'I do.'

'She won't listen t' me. But if you ... she could be makin' an awful lot more of herself.'

'I am helping her.'

'Good.'

'I have just lined her up with ... Eddie.'

Eileen screwed up her face. 'Eddie? Your Eddie?'

'Some girls lay down their life for their sisters. I'm doing more than that – I'm laying down my man.'

'He's too old.'

'Eighteen? She's nearly sixteen.'

'She's only fifteen. And a young fifteen at that. When I said help her – I meant about her dress an' things like that. Not throwin' her t' the wolves.'

'Eddie isn't a wolf.'

Eileen lifted the brass handle of the poker at the side of the Devon grate and stabbed a lump of coal. Flames slithered up the chimney. 'D' ya see the get-up of him?'

'Eddie is only a sheep in wolf's clothing. Honest. Ya see, the drainpipes, the buckled shoes, the Italian suit – that's only a front. He wudn't harm a fly. In fact, Harry's more of a wolf.'

'Harry?' she put back the poker and stood up.

'In relative terms. But they're both pretty harmless.'

'You're the expert?'

'Well I have been conducting my research out in the field. And times may have changed from the thirties, but there are still a lot of pretty harmless men aroun' –'

'No man is entirely harmless,' said Eileen.

'M' Da?'

'Oh yeah! It's a battle. And don't forget it. Why do ya think we've only two in our family?'

Marie made a goldfish mouth and her eyes like small saucers. 'God's will,' she said.

'I saw the writin' on the wall. Families aroun' here with hardly a crust. Nine an' ten childer. There's a house in Ballymurphy with twenty-six childer in the family. In the mornin' it's like the pictures comin' out. No. There's no man entirely harmless. Even Frank. An' he's not the worst. No. I had t' stand up t' Frank and the church.'

'Who was the worst?'

'Well, Frank eventually got the message. Anyway, he'd no choice.'

Marie sprang open the cigarette case in front of Eileen who shook her head, saying, 'No, I'll wait till after.'

She took one herself and lit it with the lighter. 'What about confession?' she asked.

'I found a harmless enough wee priest down in St Paul's. But I had t' educate him. It wasn't the other way aroun'. Actually, it was a bit of a geg – ya cud tell by lukin' aroun' the chapel an' what priest they were goin' to how many childer they had. Father McCarthy was three or less.'

Marie's red lips sucked hard on the filter-tip, drawing the smoke deep into her lungs. 'I won't have more than two, even if it means leavin' the Catholic Church,' she said.

'Don't be lettin' yer father hear that kind of talk. You need your faith. I'd never give mine up. And you'll find the same.'

Rosaleen's footsteps rattled the stairs. They exchanged meaningful glances and sat down, Marie on the settee, Eileen in the armchair by the fire. Rosaleen had brushed her hair and changed into a white blouse and another grey pleated skirt, but this one was crisply ironed. 'Is the tea ready?' she asked.

'Would your ladyship let me get inside the door?'

'I'll get it myself.'

'No,' said Eileen, getting up. 'I can see from the way that you've changed your clothes – that you must be going somewhere real important. And I wouldn't like you to be usin' up all your energy on somethin' as trivial as your tea.'

'What is it then?'

Eileen looked across at Marie. 'What's for her tea?' she asked.

'You made it. I only lit the gas.'

'Spanish onions, Irish carrots, Scotch potatoes and prime sirloin.'

'Stew,' said Rosaleen listlessly.

'How'd ya guess?' asked Eileen.

'You never bought prime sirloin steak in your life.'

'Are you callin' our butcher a liar? He's a very sensitive wee man.'

'It isn't the butcher who's a liar. I'm leavin' in ten minutes.'

'Marie! Go to it! Get this girl her grub or heads will fall.'

Marie smiled, got up and went through the narrow doorway into the kitchen. Rosaleen, deliberately ignoring her mother, pulled the table out from the wall and slumped into a chair.

Eileen joined her hands. 'Is your majesty going somewhere this evening?' She asked. Then, after a pause, 'Somewhere important?' And, still trying to catch her eyes, 'It must be very important.'

'It's important to me.'

'And me. And Frank. And Marie. Such a momentous occasion.'

'Who said it was momentous?'

Eileen smiled indulgently. 'Is he takin' ya t' the pictures?'

Rosaleen turned her head away.

'Well make sure he has you back by half-eleven.'

'I'll be home before eleven.'

Marie came out with two plates of stew and spoons, which she put down on the table before them, saying, 'That'll put hair on your chest.'

Rosaleen scowled.

'Sorry,' said Marie, trying to stifle a giggle. 'Bosom.'

Marie and Eileen burst out laughing. Rosaleen wearily lifted a piece of potato with her spoon and into her mouth.

'Now don't be laughin' at her, Marie,' said Eileen, wagging her finger. 'This is her first date and she's promised to be back by eleven.'

'Who said anything about a date? You do make a lot of presumptions around here.'

'Oh – if it's not a date, what is it then?'

'That's my business.'

'You're not sixteen. We're entitled to know where you're going.'

'Are ya?'

'Yes, we are,' she said firmly.

The door opened and Frank came in and closed it. He swiftly hung up his jacket behind the door, put his canvas bag in a small cupboard under the stairs and took out a pair of soft green slippers. In a well-practised motion his feet went into slippers at the same time as his hand reached into the side pocket of his jacket for his pipe, matches and leather pouch of tobacco. Turning to put these on the mantelpiece, he stopped suddenly. 'Am I in the right house? Will I go out and come in again?'

Eileen turned around before him, displaying the dress. He nodded his head approvingly. 'How many weeks' wages is that gonna set me back?'

'I got it for half-nothin' in the sales.'

'The last time ya said that we had t' go t' the bank,' he said, putting his stuff on the mantelpiece and turning his back to the fire. He looked beyond Eileen, to his daughters. 'Why are yas all dolled up? Is there a party on tonight?'

'They're goin' out,' said Eileen.

His eyes examined Rosaleen from head to foot. 'You've changed,' he said.

She shrugged.

'I'm just tryin' t' take it all in. I'm not used t' all this glamour.'

'I'll dress whatever way I like.'

'Don't get me wrong. I'm all in favour of change and colour. When Father Wilson asks me to paint a few statues with all the nice reds, blues and golds instead of the oul black railings, I'm as happy as Larry. But you haven't had that oul cardigan ya wear off yer back for about two years.'

'I only bought it last Christmas.'

'Well it seems like two years. When you buy an article of clothin' it's as if somebody stuck it on yer back with superglue – never to be taken off.'

'The girls at work like that cardigan.'

'Why wudn't they? You'll never be a threat t' any female with that death-shroud aroun' yer shoulders.'

'Luk, I'll dress the way I want. It's my wages that's buyin' the clothes. An' I'm entitled t' buy an' wear what I like.'

Marie went out quickly and brought in two more plates of stew and spoons. They sat eating in silence for a few moments.

'Sure you never go anywhere,' said Frank. 'Except the factory.'

Eileen picked out a dark bit of carrot and placed it on the rim of the plate. 'Well, she's goin' out tonight,' she said.

Frank let go his spoon and spread his fingers. 'Hallelujah! Marie, go on out there an' see if there's a blazin' comet in the sky.'

'There's no rush,' said Eileen, 'she's plenty of time.'

Marie caught Rosaleen's injured look and said, 'You'd ruin good clothes in the factory.'

Frank gave a wry smile. 'Are we gonna get a glimpse of the apparition that's responsible for this – how do you say it – "haute couture"?'

'It doesn't have to be a boy,' said Eileen.

Her husband popped a lump of potato into his mouth and shook his head. 'If he's anything like that pair chasin' Marie,' he said.

Marie flicked her empty spoon at him. 'You know nothin' about style.'

'Style?' said Frank, leaning back from the table. 'I've nothin' against style. Luk at the suit I wear t' Mass of a Sunday. I've had bookies ask me where I bought it – a fella even tuk me for a doctor one night. I'm all in favour of style. I saw one of your – I dunno what you'd call them – on the road the other night. Spindly legs in them ridiculous drainpipes, the big bulges at the knees, two-inch thick sponge soles an' where most ordinary people have shoelaces – big brass buckles. He was walkin' over t' the bus-stop like a constipated cowboy, his buckles janglin' like a donkey's bridle.'

Marie threw her spoon into the plate. 'Daddy!'

'Don't be gettin' me wrong, Marie – I've nothin' against them. That dour oul road out there cud do with a few pantomime characters t' liven it up.'

'Harry is no pantomime character,' said Marie, flicking the rim of her plate with the tips of her polished fingernails. 'Harry is a clerk in J.P. Wards.'

Frank pulled back his chair, got down on his knees, blessed himself and joined his hands.

'Lord,' he said, 'forgive me for insultin' one of yer right hand men at J.P. Wards. I really didn't mean any offence an' I take back everything I said about his –' he stifled a guffaw '– Edwardian sky-blue business suit, his classy buckled shoes, and his –' he tried to catch Marie's eyes '– what do you call the hair?'

She looked away.

'Tony Curtis duck's arse.' He twiddled the grey hair at the front of his head. 'Do you think I've enough curls t' wear the style?' he asked, getting back up to sit at the table.

'You've heard of the green-eyed yellow monster,' said Marie.

Frank raised the spoon to his lips, saying, 'I didn't know his eyes were green.'

'I think he cuts a dash,' said Eileen.

'He'll dash nowhere in them trousers. These teddy-boy suits are ridiculous. Where's the style in somethin' that wud make a cat laugh?' He moved his head, trying to catch Rosaleen's downcast eyes. 'Are we in for a bit of entertainment tonight?'

She slapped her spoon into the half-full plate and flashed a look at Frank. 'If you ask me, people think too much about clothes and other stupid things in their lives. There's much more important things than that. And it shows you just how much the level of conversation – in a supposedly religious household – has sunk, when all we can talk about is clothes. When was the last time anyone in this house talked about Jesus Christ? About what he means in our lives? And I'm not just talking about going to Mass on a Sunday. I'm talking about real religion – the experience of religion. And the truth of religion as revealed in the Gospels. When did anyone ever talk to me about that? No. Never. Not once. The girls I work with know more about religion than the two of you put together. Excuse me,' she said, jerking back the chair, standing up and stepping over to the foot of the stairs. Without turning around she grabbed her duffle coat off the hook, twisted the doorknob and almost caught her foot as she slammed the door behind her.

They listened to the fading beat of her heels hammering the concrete.

'What was that about?' asked Frank.

'You can overdo the teasin',' said Eileen. 'She's only fifteen.'

'Is she goin' out with a fella?'

'I don't know.'

'Marie?'

'She might be seein' some girls.'

'From work?'

'– I think so.'

The pale skin on Frank's face tightened and his eyes narrowed. 'We should never have let her go and work there,' he said.

'Is she better on the dole?' said Eileen. 'Hangin' aroun' the house.'

'Nobody else aroun' here works in Pattersons.'

'There's another Catholic there,' said Marie, gathering the plates together.

'Who?' asked Frank.

'– I think there is.'

'Father Wilson asked me last week. He said nothin'. But I cud tell –'

Marie stacked the plates, putting the spoons on top. 'What?'

'– that a young girl of her age could be exposed to –'

'Other girls? Father Wilson's behind the times. All that stuff's disappearin'.'

'He's nobody's fool.'

'You wouldn't get any of the young priests carryin' on like that.'

'He's been good to us. Thanks to him I've had ten years steady work. I've painted in every chapel in the town.'

'You're a good painter, Frank,' said Eileen. 'And you're reliable.'

'The town's full of good, reliable painters.'

'The statues are special work.'

'I didn't develop the skills overnight. It's easy for youngsters like Marie and Rosaleen t' think things have always been quiet here. I had a good paintin' job in the shipyard years ago and I was warned off – you remember, Eileen? We'd started goin' out together.'

'True –'

'Warned off?'

'Somebody let off a bomb. You could go in, I suppose, but –'

'The times are changin', Daddy.'

'– it can get nasty. All of a sudden.'

'Our office is mixed. And nobody cares what religion anybody is.'

'That's the way it should be,' he said.

'Then isn't Rosaleen doin' the right thing?'

'No. An office uptown is one thing. A job in a factory like Pattersons is another.'

'What's the difference?'

Eileen joined her hands and knitted her fingers together. 'Rosaleen's just going through a phase,' she said. 'She's takin' religion a bit deep.'

'Father Wilson has looked after my interests and the interests of this family for the last ten years. He knows his religion, and he knows this city. Now he didn't say anything to me. But it was a warning.'

'About what?' asked Marie.

Frank paused for a few moments, his eyes cast down, his fingers nervously touching the surface of the table. 'Doctor Prichard has a clique there,' he said.

'I never heard Rosaleen mention Doctor Prichard,' said Eileen.

'He has groups. People who've been trained.'

'In what?'

'If they get a Catholic t' turn –'

'Come on now, Frank,' she said, shaking her head.

'No, I'm serious. If they get one t' convert. To become a Protestant. They parade her in front of these huge congregations.'

'Our Rosaleen?' protested Eileen.

'I've heard Father Wilson preachin' about it. It's goin' on all the time. They're lookin' for converts.'

'Not our Rosaleen?' Eileen repeated.

'It cud be anybody. You, me – Marie, Father Wilson, The Pope. The way they work. It's a form of brainwashin'. Just like the communists in Russia or China.'

'She's goin' out with Eddie on Friday night,' said Marie.

'What's that got t' do with it?' asked Frank.

'– I just thought I'd mention it.'

'Spindly legs?'

'Bulls-eye.'

'Where's he work?'

'Hughes Bakery.'

'That's mixed, isn't it?'

'No, it's mostly Catholic,' said Eileen.

'Where's he live?'

Marie chewed her lips. 'Down the road,' she said.

'Which end?'

'He's definitely a Catholic!'

Frank sucked in his cheeks, his eyes were now sullen. 'Don't you be cheeky,' he said. 'The pair of you have been given a lot of freedom. Maybe too much freedom.'

'For God's sake, Da. She's only goin' out with a few friends from work.'

'I'm glad t' see her gettin' out of the house,' said Eileen.

'The first time, as far as I know,' added Marie.

Eileen stood up from her chair and lifted the plates and spoons. 'It's her age,' she said. 'Who's any sense when they're fifteen? You're makin' a big fuss about nothin'.'

'We'll see,' said Frank, folding his arms. 'We'll soon see about that.'

Chapter 5

Rosaleen climbed the stairs of the trolley bus and sat on the back seat. There were only two other passengers. She felt angry, harassed and nervous. Even Marie had joined in tonight. She looked through the rain-splattered window. In the dark, the narrow streets had closed in on the Falls Road and as the bus clicked and hummed its way to the city centre, she was glad to be leaving it behind, yet nervous at crossing the bridge to a sermon in a Protestant church at the other side of the city.

Hilary's smile at the City Hall reassured her. What could be wrong with going to a religious sermon in another Christian church? Yet the nerves no sooner fled than they were back. Excitement too. Hilary was talking about Sammy, a teenager who kept passing the office door when they were having lunch, but Rosaleen smiled and only half-listened. The face she saw was the Reverend Prichard's. His grey eyes. His strength. His humour. His confidence. His certitude. Did he ever experience the fears she felt?

They got on a bus. It sped through the city centre and over the bridge. Hilary nodded to a lot of passengers as they got on and passed by. Clean-shaven, well-dressed men and smartly turned out women. Girls their own age and younger too. The bus slowed down, traffic began to clog the road. On either side, people marched along the pavement. There was a palpable buzz, an excitement in anticipation of some event. Ahead three buses had stopped behind each other and passengers streamed from them towards the Ravenmount church.

'Is there always this many?' asked Rosaleen.

'Packed to the gills. We might as well get off,' she said, standing up.

Most of the passengers stood up and waited for an opening in the aisle. They filed off and converged with other streams from the buses, the cars and the narrow streets off the main road. The crowd didn't walk across the lawns, it marched along the paths and up the steps into the red-brick church. As it slowed in the doorway, a bright lamp shone upon a mass of covered heads.

Rosaleen hurried after her friend, down to a pew directly in front of the pulpit.

'You sit there and keep my place,' said Hilary, going up to a table opposite the centre aisle.

Three girls were waiting. When she spoke they immediately followed her example and started loading Bibles, leaflets and brown wooden plates with green baizes into their arms. They split and hurried up the aisles, distributing as they went and returning for more.

The crowd packed around Rosaleen. A man apologised after nudging her from behind. She explained to a well-dressed lady that the place beside her was taken. Four doors, two on each side of the church, were open; two temporary scaffolds had been put up and a steady trek of young men were cramming the three tiers with fold-up chairs. Men climbed up, tested the planks for steadiness, then sat down. One waved to a woman in a pew near the back.

Rosaleen could feel the lady beside her encroaching an inch or two. She feared there would be no room for her friend. These people were strangers. Their expectant conversation rumbled all around her. A woman squeezing past apologised and gave her a broad confidential smile, a kind of recognition that they were sisters. Rosaleen felt like an impostor. She didn't feel she belonged anywhere. But she wanted to be there – among all those expectant people waiting to hear Dr Prichard speak. He had, after all, spoken to her personally. And look at the crowd that had come here tonight. No ordinary man could command this attention – she felt privileged and special. That he had talked to her as an equal was a great honour.

To her right a chair fell off the scaffold. All eyes turned. A young man produced a hammer and its sharp ping rang out against the dull buzz of the discussion. Hilary, ever competent, was organising extra seating at the base of the scaffold – but even her face was red and tense with the strain. The crowd pushed against the pews at the back of the church – men funnelled through the centre aisle to the steps of the altar. The air was hot, clammy.

Hilary made her way back to the centre aisle and climbed the steps to the pulpit. Her voice croaked into the microphone for a few words before she began. 'Could the people at the back and side doors move out a little, please.' She paused. The crowd were quiet. 'Could they? We have speakers at each of the doors. Everyone will be able to hear. Just move back two or three feet and allow a space for people to move in and out. Thank you.'

The church, quiet for Hilary's words, now erupted into loud talk. With men perched high on the scaffolds and people crammed at the front and back – it had the whiff of danger like an ancient amphitheatre.

Rosaleen was proud of Hilary. So young, so capable. When her friend returned she tried to make herself smaller so that she could fit in – it was a struggle. The talk grew louder. A surge of people from the back caused a ripple down the aisles. Hilary stood up – her head swivelling around, her fingers flicking the gold shiny edges of the red Bible – and stared towards the back. Rosaleen had never seen her like this before. Her own body grew tense.

Suddenly the talk stopped. Hilary came slowly back down into her seat. From the far right, Rosaleen caught a figure moving rapidly towards the centre. Dr Prichard, wearing a black suit, white dog-collar, and carrying a Bible in his left hand came down to the front, gave a slight bow and smiled.

He walked down a few yards, turned between a gap in the pews and ascended the steps to the pulpit. He put down the Bible. His head turned in a wide arc from left to right and he gazed with serious intent upon the people. There was no coughing. Just an absolute stillness. Then the lights around the church dimmed and a spotlight shone upon the pulpit. His black hair glistened and he seemed to grow in size, casting a shadow on the people behind him who were turning their heads to see. He stood well back from the microphone, his limbs, body and manner relaxed.

'I hate microphones,' he said. 'They're a technological abomination. But tonight there are good people outside the doors of this church. And if their faith lets them brave the rain to attend this meeting, then I will brave any number of technological abominations.' He gave the microphone a hard flick with his finger – a resonant, discordant ping echoed around the church. Everyone laughed. 'But that doesn't mean to say I have to love them.' They laughed again. 'I see in front of me a lot of faces. Good people gathered here on this rainy night, to give thanks to Our Lord Jesus Christ.' Rosaleen felt that for a few moments he was looking directly at her. She shivered. 'And I welcome, each and every one of you, to the assembly under this –' He peered up at the ceiling towards the back right hand side of the church. 'Did James Brady get that roof fixed? Is there a James Brady in the church?'

A dapper man with an impish face and a tight little smile, seated halfway down, put up his right hand – in the other he carried a cap. 'Would you stand up, Jimmy, and let the people get a good look at you?'

Jimmy got up. 'There he is,' continued Dr Prichard, 'the Lord's special agent for leaky roofs. No, not James Bond, James Brady.'

He cocked an ear over the microphone. Jimmy's words, in a granite Belfast accent, were mostly swallowed up. 'Special tiles?' he announced into the microphone. And then, directly to the congregation. 'Well, it seems that the Lord's special agent needs "special" tiles to fix the roof. Now, I didn't bring this up to embarrass you, Jimmy – but I was distracted by that woman in the red hat – third row from the back. You see, her head was movin' this way, and then that way – and I thought maybe I had only shaved one side of my face or something.'

Everyone laughed. He paused, bent slightly, and spoke softly. 'But no – a voice – a wee voice inside my head said: she's trying to avoid that leak.'

Jimmy spoke again and his words were swallowed up. 'I notice you didn't sit there yerself,' said Dr Prichard. 'And you have the oul cap handy. Get a couple of chairs from the old presbytery and put them in the aisles. Okay?'

Jimmy rapidly made his way to the side aisle. 'The Lord's special agent has a lot of talents and I don't need to remind regulars of the sterling service that Jimmy has given this church over the last couple of years.' He leaned back on his heels and rested his hands on the plain wooden surface that circled around him. Rosaleen could just see the edge of the closed Bible – no notes were visible. His eyes searched the church, hungry for contact. She saw him looking directly at her again.

'I would like to extend a special welcome to new sinners,' he said. 'And just in case there's any new sinners out there tonight feeling that maybe they're not "good" enough to be assembled in this congregation, all I can say to them is – when it comes to sin –' he spoke with an American accent out of the side of his mouth '– you ain't seen nothin' yet.'

The laughter rose and he waited for it to die down. 'Was there ever as many Olympic champions assembled under one roof?' And after a pause. 'No, I don't mean swimmers, Jimmy – I don't think the lifeboats will be necessary.' Again the laughter rose. 'Not yet anyway.'

Rosaleen was beginning to relax. Hilary was becoming the girl she knew in the office at lunch-hour. Here, in the church, there was laughter, fun, and a hint of drama or excitement to come.

Dr Prichard, with an expression that suggested he was speaking aloud to try and explain something to himself, continued in a conversational tone. 'A few days ago I was walkin' in the park when I was approached by a poor man. He asked me for the price of a cup of tea – my instinct was to reach into my pocket and give him a shillin'. That is what my instinct said. When you see suffering the Christian way is to alleviate it as soon as possible. But ... I also smelt alcohol. There was a bottle lying by a park bench. I knew, as God is my judge, that if I reached into my pocket and gave that man a shillin' – it would make me feel good, make me feel more Christian, but it would not alleviate the suffering of that poor soul one iota. The shillin' would have been spent on another bottle of wine and he would have slipped further and further away from God.'

He leaned towards the microphone, his voice dropped to almost a whisper but it still seemed to carry to the back of the church. 'I talked to that man. I offered to bring him home with me to eat, have a bath and a good night's sleep. He accepted. The next morning my wife gave him breakfast and a decent set of clothes. I gave him a pound and the names and addresses of good people where he could find lodging. He left.' He paused again, sucked in his cheeks, and added softly: 'Tonight I see that same man among the congregation.'

There was a short silence, then a few claps, followed by more and more until it built up into a crescendo and echoed around the church. Rosaleen joined in. She had been taken unawares. She had been following the story attentively until she heard the word 'wife'. She had assumed that he, like the Catholic priests, was unmarried. Wife? She couldn't imagine a wife standing beside him. Maybe he had just invented her as part of the story.

He was standing well back from the microphone now, his head bent over, his black hair glistening, waiting for their silence. Their prolonged clapping had let him know where they stood. He raised his head and surveyed the congregation in a wide arc. Then, as he stepped forward, the movement of his body and limbs stiffened. His chin slipped forward slightly, his expression darkened and his eyes were full of concentrated energy. When he began to speak in his deep resonant voice, Rosaleen shivered.

'Thou shalt have no other Gods before me. Thou shalt not make graven images, or any likeness of anything that is in the heaven above, or that is in the earth beneath, or that is in the water under the earth: thou shalt not bow down thyself to them, nor serve them: for I the Lord thy God am a Jealous God, visiting the iniquity of the fathers upon the children unto the third and fourth generation of them that hate me; and showing mercy unto thousands of them that love me and keep my commandments.' He paused for a few seconds, and added, 'Exodus. Chapter Twenty.'

The colour of his face, a healthy light pink, began to grow pale. He stood well back from the microphone, the stiffness left his body, his movements backed the words. 'Walk into any Roman Catholic church in this city. Or any other city. What do you see? Legions of graven images. Sanctuary lamps and candelabras stuck before sickly prints of the virgin and other saints. It's like Madame Taussauds in London.'

Grim smiles spread around the church. Rosaleen was taken aback by the suddenness and ferocity of the attack. But she wasn't repelled. Here was a good man. A brilliant preacher. A seeker of truth.

'Did Jesus Christ, the Jesus we know through The Book,' he said, patting the Bible beside him, 'ever intend that his place of worship, his church, be turned into a gaudy palace?

'No, he did not. Jesus was a simple man. He was the son of God but he also was a simple, humble man. He was the son of a carpenter. Was there anything in his demeanour that bespoke the gaudy Roman palaces of the Catholic Church? Did he want his place of worship turned into a Hollywood picture palace?'

When he paused this time, there were a few coughs, and heads were consciously shaken from side to side. Rosaleen was beginning to feel herself part of the congregation, part of the shared emotion and energy that was focusing directly on Dr Prichard. In the past few months she had hated the nuns and the way they represented the Catholic Church. Was he defending Jesus? Seeking Jesus? Throwing light on the abominable practices and history of the Church she had been born into. Was he a true cleansing spirit?

'Ladies and gentlemen,' he said, 'I have a confession to make. I have been in one of these … palaces. I have observed their … priests. In my capacity as a minister of God I felt it my duty to observe. I bore witness to the machinations that took place upon their altar.

'Could you? Or I? – sense the presence of Our Lord and Saviour Jesus Christ in such a palace?'

He paused and looked around the church, then down at the people directly in front of him – Rosaleen felt his eyes connecting directly with hers. 'I didn't. No – what did I feel? I felt anger. I felt an anger that burned within me that Jesus Christ, that paragon of goodness and light, should be blasphemed by this travesty of a religion. And you, my fellow Christians, would have felt that same shame, that same anger, at this travesty of your Christian faith.'

Rosaleen's lips parted, her mouth went dry. Had she not felt the same over the past few months? What had he found out?

'Today we have Hollywood to churn out streams of moving pictures. They titillate the senses, fill people's heads with corrupt images of material success. And the people fall for it. We see this. We can recognise it for the triumph of Satan's will – posturing in his glamorous materialistic rags. And when our eyes and senses have feasted on this piffle we can turn to –' his hand moved over and his fingers tapped the Bible – 'The Book. There we will find no glamour. No urge to indulge the senses. Simple acts. Simple words. The words of Our Lord.'

Rosaleen immediately sensed what he was doing. The world was corrupt. But the devil was clever in the way he covered up corruption so that most people were fooled. Dr Prichard was chipping away at the rotten facade.

'We can see and recognise these modern Satanists. These Hollywood moguls must have their daily fix: a ready supply of poison to the veins so that they can endlessly churn carnality into dollars. They know how to divert the people. How to seduce, tempt and lure them away from the path of righteousness. We can see and smell the evidence of these modern Satanists at every street corner. But who? Who were the people that did that very same work for the Church of Rome? Who were they?'

Rosaleen felt herself being carried along – it was a quest, a search for evil.

'Artists! Sculptors! Architects! The pomp of human arrogance. The egotistical artists who prostituted their talent to the power of the Vatican. The popes gave them money and they in their turn fed fat the appetite of the multitudes. With their images, with their titillation, they bloated the senses of the poor, unsuspecting people. Yes, they succumbed to the temptation of power and money and built an edifice – not a church – all the Romanist buildings that you see around you are little Vaticans. They built an edifice to political power and money; an altar at the shrine of corrupt popes who had usurped the message of Jesus for their own nefarious ends.'

This hit Rosaleen with such force that her brain went into a swirl. At first she couldn't see the connection. Beautiful pictures, statues ... then she remembered the renaissance pope Julius II who sold indulgences to build St Peter's and to finance his wars. Who forced Michaelangelo to paint the Sistine Chapel? Beauty without, corruption within.

'Ordinary Catholics know nothing of this,' he said, matter of factly. 'The real history of the popes – the most damnable collection of villains that ever disgraced the human race – is buried deep in the vaults of the Vatican. And their modern disciples, the priests, befuddle the ordinary people with gobbledegook Latin texts. They perform tricks on the altar – the old smokescreen and incense trick – or S and I, as it is known by the three-card trick merchants at the racecourses.'

A rumble of laughter greeted this. Rosaleen felt uneasy. It wasn't right. Nor was she prepared for the next move.

'And – wait for it,' he reached into his jacket pocket, took out his wallet and with a trace of contempt picked out a white communion host. 'They claim that they can transform this wafer ... and a jug of wine –' He cocked his ear with the left hand, his right held the host aloft and he looked down at a man bent over in laughter '– no, Peter, a jug of wine – not whiskey. Or punch. There'd be too much spirit.' The man's face was screwed up and he was shaking.

Dr Prichard waited a few moments, then he scowled and thrust his right hand up into the air. 'This wafer! And a jug of wine into the body and blood of Our Lord and Saviour Jesus Christ? Is there anything in "The Book" that gives a mere priest, a so-called minister of religion, the right to perform miracles?'

Rosaleen cast her eyes down. She felt there was something wrong. But she wanted to believe him. Yes, she very much wanted to believe him. Maybe he was … right. She looked up. His grey eyes burned with righteous anger, he placed the communion host on his wallet and his hands closed into fists.

'No, there is nothing. Presumptive pride. The sin of Lucifer. And how comfortable that fallen angel must feel at the seat of pomp and power – the Vatican.'

Suddenly, within a few seconds, in silence, his body began to relax. His fists uncoiled and his hands came gently together. The colour returned to his face as the anger drained away. He bowed his head, his eyes were now slightly misty. Rosaleen thought they were looking directly into hers, and when he spoke the words confirmed it: 'We have in our congregation tonight some ordinary Catholics,' he said softly. 'My quarrel is not with them. I know that most ordinary Catholics are good living people. My quarrel is with the Catholic Church and its preposterous claims, its lies and falsehoods, and its corruption of the word of Our Lord. I wish to extend to all our Catholic brethren, assembled here tonight, the hand of friendship and peace.'

Dr Prichard turned over his hands and gently raised them. 'I think,' he said, 'we should all stand up and sing a hymn in praise of the Lord.'

Rosaleen, without deflecting her gaze from his face, rose with all the assembly. The organ music began for 'The Lord is my Shepherd' and around the church the people launched into song. She didn't consider herself a singer but she sang. She felt part of something big and the experience was totally unlike anything she had gone through before. Rich, intense, dramatic – and above all, reflecting in many ways her own feelings over the last few months: recognising evil, challenging and striving to overcome it. There was no despair along this path – there was too much to do, too much to overcome. But still something nagged at her. The host? The laughter?

More hymns followed. Some rousing, some peaceful and serene. Then the collection plate, filled along each pew and emptied at the end. Her sixpence was tiny among the large coins and notes. And finally a promise of dramatic revelations in the coming weeks. When Rosaleen stood up with the people to go, there was no doubt that she had been at an event.

Hilary led the way up to the table at the front – already the girls were loading it with Bibles, booklets and envelopes. She directed two girls towards the back of the church, stacked a pile of envelopes and turned to Rosaleen who was hovering at her shoulder. 'Would you bring these into Dr Prichard?' she asked.

Rosaleen hesitated. 'You mean –?'

'The room just over there,' she said, pointing at the corner.

'Well –'

'It's a top job,' said Hilary with a smile. 'The mules collect the Bibles, special secretaries bring in the envelopes.'

'Okay,' she said, letting her friend stack them into her hands. 'Just over there?'

'That's right.'

A lady came up and asked Hilary a question. Rosaleen turned and went over to the short corridor, dimly lit, which led to a grained, wooden door at the end. She went up and knocked. There was no reply. Just as she turned, a large figure loomed from behind a red velvet curtain and put a hand on her shoulder. She jumped.

'Rosaleen, isn't it?' said Dr Prichard.

'Yes,' she replied, shaking.

'I always spook people when I come out of there. Somebody called me Dracula last week.'

'Hilary told me to …'

'Come on in,' he said, opening the door and going into the room. There was a small plain desk with a few framed photographs. He took the envelopes from her and piled them on the desk. 'You get some right headbangers writing to me, you know.

This fella last week was inviting me to visit his church – I only learnt at the end of the letter that it was on another planet.'

Rosaleen smiled.

'Transport problems,' he said, reaching out and feeling the metal kettle on the shelf to the side.

'I'll just go ...'

'Sit down there. You won't go without a cup of tea,' he said, flicking the switch on the kettle. 'And Hilary has all that organised to a "T". You know it's the women that keep this church going – you could kill all the men off and nobody would notice. But everything, and I mean everything, would fall apart if it wasn't for the women.'

He warmed the brown, glazed teapot, measured out three spoonfuls of tea from a tin, filled it up and spread his large hands around it. 'Ah, it's hot,' he purred. 'There's nothin' like a hot cup of tea after a meetin – that's M'Creadie's tea. Blended by a wee man from Portadown. The best.'

He took off his jacket, hung it on a hook behind the door and swirled the teapot. Rosaleen couldn't help but compare this domestic man with the one she'd just seen in the pulpit. Her eyes drifted to the photographs. An old minister with an elderly lady – both country looking and old-fashioned. Then a family photograph of himself with a young, slight woman who had a baby in her arms, beside a boy of about three. Dr Prichard was staring directly at the camera; the woman's eyes looked up towards the side of his face. There was something frail about her, thought Rosaleen, the eyes too big for the face, the cheeks hollow. The children were gorgeous.

'You wouldn't think it,' he said, pouring the tea, 'but I'd say I lose about two pints of fluid out there.'

'Two pints?'

'Most of it in sweat. At least that's what I say. My enemies say I use up about ten pints of fluid – most of it from spittin' at the congregation.'

'No.'

'They say I should issue towels to the people in the first five rows. Take off your coat.'

'I'm all right, thanks.'

'Make yourself comfortable.'

She sat down on a chair to the side of the desk, opposite him. Dr Prichard lifted a plate of biscuits off the shelf and held it towards her. 'Have a few,' he said.

She picked a couple from the plate.

'This is the reward side of the night, after all the pain I inflicted on you in the other place.'

'No.'

'I do get very warm in there,' he said, loosening his white collar with his fingers and taking it off. 'I be very nervous.'

'You wouldn't think –'

'Everytime I climb up into that pulpit. You don't know what rubbish is going to come out.'

'Well, I enjoyed it.'

He bit off a piece of biscuit and swallowed some tea. 'Did you?'

'Yes.'

'Thank you.'

'Very much.'

'– you came with Hilary?'

Rosaleen nodded.

'Your first time?'

'Yes.'

'I always dread preaching to people. Especially the first time. It's such a … responsibility. And even though you know The Book back to front, and you have full confidence in the divine words of Our Lord, you're always aware of how vulgar your own voice sounds delivering such marvellous words; and the hopeless inadequacy of your own words.'

'I thought you spoke very well … though I didn't agree with all –'

He smiled. 'I wouldn't expect you to – Hilary has told me about some of the arguments you have. What specifically –?'

'Well,' said Rosaleen, looking down at his feet, 'I didn't like the way … you know … the host.'

'Did it shock you?'

'– no, but – well –'

'Hilary told me what a tough nut you were,' he said, waving a biscuit in the air. 'I want to challenge your deepest beliefs.'

'Why?'

'Because they're wrong.'

'I don't necessarily agree with the Catholic Church. You see, I like to try to understand what Jesus meant, but they –'

Dr Prichard lifted the red Bible from the shelf and held it in his hand. 'The word of Our Lord is very precise,' he said. 'Certain people have seen fit to make it complicated.'

'I understood what you said tonight.'

'Do you think if I had succeeded in communicating the word and spirit of Our Lord tonight there would be any doubt in your mind – your doubts, and the doubts of many, many members of my congregation – are a reflection of my inadequacies.'

'No –'

'I'm a sinner. You're a sinner. We're all sinners. Mercilessly flawed sinners groping in the dark with one infallible guide,' he said, tapping the Bible, 'The Book.'

'I read the Bible a lot.'

'I know. And from what Hilary has told me and from the little time I've spent in your company, you have read the book with all the discernment of a fine young mind.'

'– it's difficult.'

'Belief. True religious belief does not come easy. And I don't mean the shallow kind of belief many believers have. A prop. A hook to throw a rope around at the edge of the abyss. No. That's not real, true belief – that's fear. The kind of belief I mean is only arrived at after a long struggle. You pray to God.

You travel a path strewn with rocks, boulders of doubt. But sometimes. And only sometimes – you see a chink. Only a chink of light. And the light is of such a powerful intensity that it illuminates the world and you know in your heart and soul that it can only come from God. And you never, never arrive at the source of this light – nor do the rocks and boulders of doubt diminish – but you know in your heart that this path will lead to salvation.'

'Are you ever confused?' she asked.

'Every hour, every minute, every second of the day … about the world. Life. But not about the goodness of God. Or his beloved son, Jesus Christ.'

'You didn't speak tonight like you had any doubt. You believed, you really believed what you were saying.'

'Yes, I did. But next Wednesday might be different. You'll have to come next Wednesday and see me fall flat on my face.'

'I can't.'

'Why not?'

'Well – it might be difficult.'

'I know.'

'It's not that I wouldn't want to come. Like, Hilary's very nice and your sermons are … wonderful. You know, you'll not believe this, but sometimes I fall asleep at Mass.'

He laughed and leaned back in his chair. 'No!'

'Yes. Honest, I do.'

'Is that not an excommunication offence?'

Rosaleen smiled.

'I suppose if they did that there'd be no Catholics left on the Falls Road,' he said. 'But I do think when you preach the word of Our Lord that you have a duty to keep the congregation awake. And if a bright girl like yourself is falling asleep, then it must be the sermon.'

'It's the same Bible.'

'Or the priest.'

'The one in St Paul's … he drones on and on, Dr Prichard.'

'The ability to induce sleep is not confined to priests. There are pastors in our church that put me to sleep. In seconds. But that's a human frailty that has nothing to do with religion.'

'I really enjoyed your sermon.'

'Come again.'

'– no.'

Dr Prichard munched a biscuit and swallowed some tea. 'Hilary has told me about some of the discussions you've had at work,' he said, and then, wagging his finger, 'No doubt when you should have been working! That's neither here nor there. But it is right that you should question Hilary's beliefs. Your own beliefs. My beliefs. You see, it's only by questioning that you can strip away the extraneous matter. The tinsel that dazzles the eye and diverts the soul. If a religion can't stand up to continuous scrutiny – if it contradicts The Book – then there is something seriously wrong with that religion.' He paused, joined his hands together and meshed his fingers. 'I'm glad that you came along here tonight.'

'So am I.'

'Do your parents know?'

'Well, my sister –'

'It took a lot of courage for you to come to this church tonight. I know that.'

'My family don't –'

'– what?'

'– think much about religion.'

'Some Catholics think I am anti-Christ.'

'I don't.'

'But they, I'm glad to say, are Catholics who have never had personal dealings with me. I have friends who are Catholics. And they know what I think of their church – I make no bones about that. But they are good, nice, intelligent people. Like yourself.'

'I'm not, really.'

'And is one sermon enough?' He paused. 'Is it? Or will you come again?'

'I'd like to. I really would.'

Dr Prichard leaned over and took her right hand gently between his hands. 'Rosaleen, it's good enough that you came. Once. Even once,' he said.

'It's just that I don't think it would –'

'I understand. Totally and utterly. I have a much greater understanding of your kind of difficulties than you give me credit for. And I admire, really admire your courage.'

Rosaleen wondered for a moment if it really was her he was talking to. His hands were large and strong, the skin soft and dry. 'I'm not courageous,' she said.

'You are.'

There was a knock at the door.

'Come in,' he said, standing up and taking her by the hand.

Hilary, her face flushed, came in carrying a pile of leaflets that she put on the desk.

'Would you look at the state of me,' he said, brushing the crumbs off his trousers. 'Stuffin' m'self while the women do all the work.'

'Sure it's nothin',' Hilary said with a smile.

'And thanks for bringing along Rosaleen. We had a great chat, didn't we?'

Rosaleen smiled and blushed as he led her to the door.

'You're a great team,' he said. 'And how are yas gettin' home?'

'The bus,' said Hilary.

'No, you won't. It's a rainy oul night and it's late for two young girls like you. Special agent James Brady is not only in charge of a leaky roof – he also looks after a leaky car.'

'The bus is fine,' protested Rosaleen.

Dr Prichard took both her hands. 'Look,' he said. 'Tonight you came here to visit our family. The members of our church are all family. You did us an honour. And the least we can do is see that you have a lift home.'

The two girls, hurrying to keep up with his giant strides, followed him into the corridor and through the church, now almost empty. They waited while he had a huddled conversation with James Brady, who was waiting in a back pew. James nodded and quickly disappeared through a side door. Dr Prichard gently put his arms around their shoulders and walked them to the church steps.

Rain poured through the pale light that died a short distance into the empty grounds. The main road ahead was deserted. Dr Prichard, peering into the darkness, pulled them back a little to avoid the rain. A black Morris Oxford swung around sharply and stopped in front of the steps. James got out and opened the back door nearest the steps.

'Run! Quick!' urged Dr Prichard, flying down the steps and ushering them into the back seat. 'See you soon!'

James slammed the door and ran around and got in. The girls waved to Dr Prichard who stopped at the top of the steps and waved back. Rosaleen had only been in a car twice before. The engine hummed sweetly, the inside smelt of polished leather. As it sped towards the city centre Hilary chatted about Mrs Gregg from Pattersons. Rosaleen half listened. Soon they were upon the City Hall. 'I'll get out here and get the bus,' she said.

James wheeled around into Royal Avenue. 'Dr Prichard told me t' see you to the door.'

'I'm all right,' protested Rosaleen.

He swung into Castle Street, towards the Falls Road. 'That was his instructions,' he said.

Hilary was now talking about Alison, one of the girls who had been collecting in the church. Knots grew in Rosaleen's stomach. Small groups of men hung around pub entrances. Soon they were within a few hundred yards of Ivy Drive. 'Let me out here,' she said. 'I'm home.'

He pulled into the kerb, stopped and went around and opened the back door. A group of youths at a street corner over the road stared across. She thanked him, said goodbye to Hilary, and got out. The youths watched the car do a U-turn and speed back towards the centre.

Rosaleen was relieved. She walked steadily along the pavement. She didn't feel tired. The night had been exciting. And she felt like talking.

Marie stepped out of a chemist's doorway.

'What's wrong?' asked Rosaleen.

'Nothin',' said Marie, hugging her camel hair coat, tied with a belt at the waist.

'Where's Harry?'

'He caught the bus.'

They walked on for a few moments and turned into Ivy Drive. The concrete surface glistened in the wet, the street was empty. 'What are you gonna say?' asked Marie.

'About what?'

'Where you were.'

Rosaleen said nothing.

'I told them you were seeing a couple of friends from work.'

'The truth's always the best medicine, isn't it?'

'I don't know about that. M' Da nearly had a fit. If he knew …'

'Maybe we all should go.'

'Where?'

'Ravenmount.'

Marie stopped in her tracks. 'Wait a minute! Rosaleen!' she called after her sister who hurried through the door of the house and into the living room.

Rosaleen had already hung up her coat when Marie arrived. Eileen, who had changed into a cardigan and skirt, was busy putting wool into a coloured bag. Frank's fingers crackled the edges of the newspaper, his eyes bored into its centre.

'Who'd like a cup of tea?' asked Marie brightly.

'Count me out,' said Rosaleen, disappearing into the kitchen.

'Mammy? Daddy?'

Neither replied. Rosaleen reappeared in the doorway with a small glass of water in her hand. Frank's face was taut. Eileen patted down her hair and got up. 'I think I'll join ya,' she said, giving Marie an edgy glance.

'Where were you?' asked Frank abruptly.

Rosaleen finished her water slowly, lowered the glass from her lips and spoke: 'Out,' she said, turning around and going back into the kitchen.

'What's it like outside?' Eileen asked Marie.

'A bit of rain. Cold enough.'

Frank watched the doorway. 'Out where?' he snapped.

Rosaleen reappeared. 'With friends.'

'From work?'

'Yes.'

'Where'd ya go?'

Rosaleen paused, Marie ran her tongue along the lower edge of her lip, Eileen gave a nervous smile. 'A meeting,' she said.

'What kind of meeting?' he asked, his fingers digging into the newspaper.

'A union meeting.'

Frank slackened his grip on the newspaper, some of the hardness went out of his eyes. 'A union meeting?'

'Is that a crime?'

'Well, you better watch your tongue.'

Rosaleen shrugged and went over and up the stairs. Frank's eyes followed her and then returned to the newspaper. Marie went into the kitchen, filled the teapot and lit the gas.

'How was the pictures?' asked Eileen, coming in and standing at her shoulder.

'Not bad. Funny. Doris Day.'

'Union meeting?' she whispered.

Marie didn't look at her mother. She watched the blue gas flames lick up around the brown enamel teapot and replied quietly, 'Yeah.'

Eileen pursed her lips and caught her daughter's eyes. 'Union meeting?' she repeated.

'Yeah,' said Marie, less convincingly than before.

Eileen turned and went into the living room. When Marie poured the three cups of tea, she didn't join her parents. She took her cup into the tiny bathroom off the kitchen and removed her make-up. Underneath, her skin was pale and soft with only the minor blemish of a small pimple at the tip of her chin. When she finished she threw most of her tea into the sink, went through to the living room, said goodnight and went up to the bedroom.

She switched on the small bedside lamp and began to remove her clothes. Rosaleen lay with her hands cupping the back of her head, eyes closed.

'How was it?' asked Marie.

'What?'

'The meeting. What was it, anyway? It wasn't a union meeting, was it?'

'Well,' said Rosaleen, smiling.

'Great gas?'

'Yeah, it was.' Marie stopped undressing and looked at her sister's face, her eyes now wide open. 'He was great. I never heard anybody like him. Very funny … and great power.'

'Dr Prichard?'

'You should come. You really should, Marie. You have to hear him live. Don't bother about the rubbish you read in the newspaper.'

'Are you tryin' t' put m' Da int' an early grave? That's all he needs – two religious nuts in the house.'

'You're believing all the lies you read about him. He's not like that at all. I was talking to him.'

'Where?'

'His office. Presbytery. He's a very homely, family man.'

Marie hung up her skirt and jumper. 'Yeah,' she said, throwing a shiny blue nightdress over her head. 'So was Hitler.'

'Don't talk like that now, Marie.'

'Move over, will ya? My feet are freezin',' she said, slipping under the duvet. Her arms and legs curled into the warm body of Rosaleen who was still gazing up at the ceiling. 'So he's married, is he?'

'Yeah.'

'What are ya gonna wear on Friday?'

'Friday?'

'Eddie. The big date.'

'Agh –'

'He's dead keen. What are ya gonna wear?'

'Do I have to go?'

Marie reached over with her hand and switched off the lamp. 'He'll commit suicide if you don't,' she said.

'What have I t' wear?'

'That is the question. Now that is the real question. What are you gonna wear for this big date on Friday night?'

Chapter 6

The neon signs winked brightly. Good suits, technicolour girls. Pubs filled, tills rang. Catcalls, wolf-whistles, bus queues, perfume, aftershave, Lotharios, Cinderellas, dances, pictures. The Friday night surge onto the road crackled and glowed with anticipation.

Eddie McGoldrick rolled his shoulders as he walked towards the corner at Ivy Drive. His cheeks were sucked into a slight hollow, eyelids heavy, corners of his lips curled; his jacket had a finger-tip length of thin, blue and navy stripes, and there was a razor crease on his drainpipe trousers. His black leather shoes with brass buckles and one-inch thick sponge soles lightly stroked the pavement under the bright streetlights.

At the corner he glanced apprehensively at his rolled gold Timex watch. He peered down Ivy Drive. He looked at his watch again and stepped into the doorway. His hair, Tony Curtis style, was well oiled and combed back at the sides, with the front loosely shaken into curls dangling on his forehead. From his trouser pocket he took out a flat plastic brush that fitted neatly into the palm of his hand, and from his top jacket pocket he picked a small oblong mirror and held it longways in front of his face – there followed two quick brushstrokes on each side and vigorous plucking in the middle to create more dangling curls on his forehead.

Dissatisfied, he plucked a bit more and examined his fingers for dislodged hairs, flicking them away. Then he used the brush more gently, overlapping the curls in the middle of his forehead. He turned the mirror sideways and beamed an enormous smile, giving his teeth a vigorous rub with his index finger. He put back the brush and mirror, took out a cigarette and lit it.

A Morris Minor revved towards him, beginning to groan up the hill. His eyes followed it up to where he stood, and then off into the centre of the city. He glanced at his watch. He paced to and fro, moving his head, peering down the dimly lit street. He glanced at his watch again. He tapped it with his index finger.

Marie pulled back the front bedroom window curtain a few inches and looked out. 'He's there!' she shouted. 'Wearin' the new suit. Yer honoured.'

'Don't be gawkin',' said Rosaleen, from their bedroom at the back. Standing in front of the large wardrobe mirror, she was absorbed by her appearance – freshly washed hair tied back with a white band, a light sheen of powder and lipstick, green eyeshadow, a tight red jumper, four-inch stilettos, and a black skirt held up with a plastic belt. She pulled the belt until it hurt, then let go.

Marie came in. 'You'll ruin the effect,' she said, putting her hand down on the belt and pulling it in again.

'I have t' breathe.'

'Ya don't breathe with yer stomach. Push yer chest out.'

Rosaleen rolled her eyes.

'It's all about posture,' continued Marie. 'You slouch. If ya stood up straight your stomach would stay in and your chest would come out. Your shoulders are hunched over yer breasts. Look at Marilyn Monroe – she doesn't hunch her shoulders.'

'I'm not Marilyn Monroe.'

'She's not as tall as you are, ya know? She doesn't slouch and she doesn't hunch her shoulders – that's why everybody thinks she's mammoth.'

'Marie!' Rosaleen examined herself sideways in the mirror. The change was, well, startling. And from the side her figure was, well, full. 'I don't even wanna go out with this fella,' she said.

'You only think that,' said Marie, dabbing a little light powder on a spot at the side of Rosaleen's chin. 'It's nerves. Ya'll get on like a house on fire. Eddie's great with the oul chat.'

'Will you go up and tell him I'm sick?'

'Try these earrings,' she said, taking a small gold pair from the dresser and clipping them on. 'You're lucky with your ears – I've no lobes. Nice, aren't they?'

'I am sick.'

'You look gorgeous, really. You're a knock-out. Just dander up, say hello, go over to the bus stop an' down t' the pictures. That's the great thing about the pictures on a first date – you don't have t' talk much.'

Rosaleen flopped back onto the double bed, her eyes closed.

'Stop the messin', Rosaleen, will ya? Now ya can't be leavin' the fella waitin' out there all night.'

'You go.'

'I can't. Get up,' she said, pulling her by the arms.

Rosaleen allowed herself to be pulled upright. She brushed a few pieces of fluff off her skirt, saying, 'All this is your fault.'

'You'll be thanking me in years to come.'

'For what?'

'He's a good lukin' fella – have a peek?'

'Did you say peek? Or puke?'

'Serious now –'

'I've seen him.'

'Come on,' said Marie, going out the door and down the stairs.

She went over and stood with her back to the fire, hands against the tiles. Eileen, sitting on the armchair reading the newspaper, looked over her glasses. 'Well?' she asked, smiling.

Tottering steps rattled the top of the stairs, a few clomps around the middle – and then she emerged at the bottom with her left hand against the wall. 'Where's the jacket?' she asked, her eyes directed at the floor.

Marie darted over and took the white jacket off the coat hanger behind the door. She held it for Rosaleen to fit her arms through.

Eileen watched, her lips parted, in silence. Catching Marie's manic head movement and its obvious signal, she spoke hurriedly. 'You look ... great, Rosaleen.'

'Doesn't she, Mammy!' exclaimed Marie. 'A knock-out – wouldn't you say?'

'... great,' gasped Eileen.

Rosaleen, not looking at her mother, went to the table. 'Where's my handbag?' she asked.

'Here,' said Marie, lifting it from the side of the sofa.

She tottered forward, put the strap of the bag around her shoulder and twisted the handle on the door. 'See yas,' she said, using her left hand for balance as she launched herself into the hall.

Marie followed and peeped around the edge of the front door. Rosaleen's tall figure was veering across the street. She staggered slightly on mounting the pavement, clutched the railing for a few strides, stopped and steadied herself, then continued towards the corner. Marie came back in.

'Yer lucky yer Da wasn't here,' said Eileen.

'What's wrong with her?'

'She looks over twenty.'

'Agh, Mammy, don't you be gettin' like him. She's only makin' the most of her assets.'

At first Eddie thought the figure was too tall, then that it was more like a grown woman's than a girl's, but as she came closer and he recognised her, his mouth opened. The lie of the soft white jacket and the strap of her handbag merely emphasised her burgeoning breasts – his eyes, drawn towards them like a magnet, cast themselves down at her stilettoed feet. His mouth was dry. He managed to look up and say: 'Hi.'

In an instant her face, figure, perfume and hair energised every sexual molecule in his limp body and made him want to remember all the snappy lines from a million films – but none could be dredged up from the short-fused circuit above his neck that was now more turnip than brain. 'Ya came –' he mumbled.

She was looking straight at him, and the more she looked the more he "Oh, God, I better say something smart and clever" felt. 'Well –? Hmmm –?' he stammered.

Were those strangulated noises coming from his mouth? Why doesn't she say something?

'Not a bad night,' he said.

There was a long pause before she spoke. 'Where do you want to go?'

'I'm easy,' he said, bubbling air through his lips. 'Pictures?'

'What's on?'

'Jailhouse Rock is on at the Gaumont.'

Rosaleen's nose twitched. 'Elvis?'

'It's supposed to be good.'

'Is there anything else on?'

A wave of relief came over Eddie. They were talking. He still couldn't bring himself to look directly at her chest but he could think of something, even if it was stupid. 'There's a Cliff Richard film at the Hippodrome,' he said, without enthusiasm.

Rosaleen's eyes sparkled. 'Oh?'

'But a mate of mine said it was lousy.'

'Did he?'

'Worse than lousy.'

'I like Cliff Richard.'

A quiver of revulsion went through Eddie. Two nights ago he had heaped abuse on this excuse of a singer. Now this vision before him was uttering heresy. But she mustn't be beyond saving. She mustn't.

'– well –'

'His singing.'

'Well, in this film I heard he doesn't do much singin'. He tries to act and play the bongo drums and things like that.'

'Elvis is too –'

'– what?'

'Disgusting.'

He looked into her face. Glamorous, wide-eyed. His mouth opened – he couldn't let her see the horror he felt – how could this beautiful vision be uttering such heresies. 'Elvis – disgusting?' he asked.

'Yeah.'

But there were limits to what you could take in the line of heresy. Even from – some things were so black-and-white. He would have to risk putting her straight. His hands spread out, his shoulders went up, the words came: 'Elvis puts his whole … he puts himself … he makes … he's real excitin'. Like, compared to Elvis, Cliff Richard is a nancy boy.'

'What's a nancy boy?'

Eddie looked away from her, dug his hands into his trouser pockets, licked his lips and got out. 'A nancy boy is ah … he's a – like, he does what his Ma tells him.'

'Are you a nancy boy?'

Eddie's head swivelled around and his eyes gave her a quick dart. He threw his cigarette end on the ground and rubbed it out with the sole of his shoe. 'My Ma does what I tell her,' he said.

Rosaleen looked at him as if to say, 'Pull the other one.'

'I've been workin' near four years,' he added.

'Have ya?'

'I'll be outa m' time in six months. A fully qualified baker. How long have you been workin'?'

'Seven months.'

His eyes said: 'Who are you tryin' to fool?'

'I have,' she insisted.

'Ya've only been workin' three months. Four – max.'

'Have I? And how do you know?'

'Marie told me.'

'So yas were talkin' about me?'

'Naa.'

'Yas mustn't have had much t' talk about.'

'Plenty.'

'And she told you three months?'

'I can add things t'gether. Ya don't have t' be Einstein.'

'I've been workin' nearly seven months.'

'Well, we'll not fall out over it, okay? I'm just makin' the point that I have a bit of … experience.'

'At bakin'?'

'In Hughes, I'm assistant to the Master Baker.'

'Is that important?' she asked, her eyelids coming halfway down her eyes.

He scrutinised her face, trying to work out if or how much she was trying to tease, then he looked down and put his foot on the already extinguished cigarette and squashed it again. 'There's only one Master Baker,' he said.

'Ohhh,' she purred, her eyes now wide.

'Anyway, we're gettin' away from the point. Are … are we to go and see the King of Rock an' Roll in a great action film about convicts and criminals – or are we gonna see an English nancy boy tryin' t' play the bongo drums?'

'Why did you come here tonight?'

Eddie swivelled around just as the lapels of her jacket subsided – it seemed as if her large breasts were moving up towards him. His eyes became riveted, his face hot, his legs slightly unsteady – he suddenly looked off at a bus coming down the road. 'Come? Here? Tonight? Me?'

'You were supposed to be going out with Marie.'

'Well,' he said, pulling the neck of his shirt with his fingers.

'Am I the consolation prize?'

He tried to look into her face but his eyes were drawn down towards her chest. 'Naa,' he said, turning away.

'Well –?'

'It was my idea.'

'Was it?'

'Yeah.'

'When?'

His eyes fell on the cigarette end. He kicked it towards the grating on the road. 'I thought you were more my type.'

'Did you?'

'Yeah.'

'And how did … you … you know?'

'Well, ya just know,' he said, eyeing the cigarette end that had just stopped short of the pavement's edge. 'Ya know all right.'

'How?'

'Ya just know when a bird's your type.'

'But how?'

His eyes went up to her face, then down towards her chest and quickly off to his right. 'Any fella – knows,' he said.

'Just by looking?'

'Well – there's a wee bit more to it than that. Like – ahm –' His eyes returned to her chest, then he glanced away and loosened his collar, '– personality plays a big part in it.'

'So you asked me out for my personality?'

'Well … yeah, and other things. Like – ah – how – style, how ya luk. Like I wudn't ask out any bird I'd be ashamed t' walk down the street with.'

'Ohhh,' she purred, and then sharply, 'why?'

'– well, ya wudn't want yer mates slaggin' ya.'

'About what?'

'– being seen out with a –'

'Is there many?'

'What?'

'Girls you'd be ashamed t' walk down the street with?'

'Enough.'

'So I'm privileged?'

'Look, there's a lot of birds an' they have … no style.' This time he was able to hold his gaze directly on her face. 'They mustn't watch the pictures. Or go anywhere. Or luk at anybody who really knows how t' dress. They've no class.'

Rosaleen's lower lip dropped and she blushed. 'You mean ?'

'You're okay,' he said, flicking his right hand. 'Tonight you have the gear on. An' ya luk … ya luk great. But I have seen ya sometimes when you weren't doin' full justice to … you know? Ya luked like a kid. But tonight – ya've really got the gear on tonight. That's why I wanted t' take ya t' this Elvis film. Ya cud pick up a lot of tips.'

'Tips?'

'Both of us. I might see somethin' even. Ya have t' keep up. I was wearin' this real hick suit up t' a few months ago an' I went t' this picture an' saw Frankie Avalon – I knew the minute I saw it. That's me. It was the style, the cut, the way he moved – the tailor in Burtons didn't know what I was talkin' about. He musta been near thirty. But I got a camera and went down t' the pictures. Ya know, took snaps of the posters outside – but I still had to explain everything to him,' he said, running his fingers along the underside of the collar. 'And he still didn't get it exactly right.'

'– do I look like a good thing?' asked Rosaleen.

Eddie drew back, his face blushed and he turned away. 'Naa. Who told ya that?'

'Nobody. I heard one of the fellas at work talkin' about a girl one day.'

'Ahh,' he said, with understanding.

'He didn't – it didn't seem to mean … what it's supposed to mean.'

'You're not a good thing,' he said dismissively.

'And is that good?'

'Course. A guy wudn't like t' be seen out with a good thing. More than once.'

'Why?'

'You ask a lot of questions.'

'I want to know.'

'Well … it's very complicated. There's different reasons a guy mightn't like t' be seen out with a bird. She might be a good thing? Or a screg? Or a bat? Ya know what I mean?'

'Do you think I'm any of them?'

Eddie suddenly dried up. He looked into her face. Her eyes were lovely. 'No … you're a peach,' he said. 'That's why I asked you out.'

'Did you? Really?'

'You're the kind of bird I admire. From a distance, usually. Cause you're shy, you know? An' ya don't go t' dances. So it's hard just t' walk up an' … but your sister goes t' dances. An' ya say t' yerself – well, somethin' might happen.'

'A miracle?'

'I fancied ya. But I didn't plan anything.'

'Neither did I.'

'But I'm glad. True Bill. There's nobody else in this town I'd prefer t' take t' see Elvis Presley tonight.'

'Is it Elvis Presley or me you want to see?'

'You.'

'Or Marie?'

He stepped closer and tried to put his right hand around her waist – she brushed it off.

'Marie's history,' he said. 'She got me … close to you.'

'You mean you used her?'

'I noticed ya – I had, really. If there was any other way I'd have – but ya don't go anywhere. What wud ya have said if I had just walked up t' ya on the street?'

'I would've said you were straight.'

'And walked on –'

'Not devious.'

'I'm not devious. I'm one of the straightest guys you cud meet. Honest. True Bill.'

'Eddie, do you ever think about –?'

'– what?'

'Religion.'

Eddie looked up beyond the streetlights to the dark sky, then he swung around with an expression as if he hadn't heard her properly. 'Religion? – Mass? Yeah, I go to Mass. Just the same as you.'

'I mean … do ya think about it?'

'– at Mass?'

'About religion in general?'

'– at Mass I think about films, futball matches, and women –'

'Why?'

'Is this twenty questions?'

'I'm interested.'

'Religion's boring.'

'It doesn't have to be boring. It can be exciting. Better than any film. All it needs is the right people to understand and teach all the wonderful things that are in the Bible.'

'What wonderful things?'

'Everything. Everything about our lives.'

'What have I got in common with a bunch of Arab shepherds from the Middle East?'

'A lot more than you'd think.'

'How –? … I'm not interested. Anyway, I don't understand it. So how can you get interested in something you don't understand.'

'But it can be made simple.'

'Can it?'

'The Bible is simple.'

Eddie knitted his brow and stared into the ground, then he looked up. 'Ya didn't bring it with ya, did ya?' he asked. 'In your handbag?'

'No.'

'Thank Christ.'

'I don't want that kind of talk, Eddie. It's blasphemy.'

He turned around, hunched his shoulders, and turned back again. 'Okay,' he said.

'Are we going to see Cliff Richard?'

'It's a poxy film.'

'I'd like to see it.'

Eddie bit his lower lip, his eyebrows came down slightly, then he looked over at her and smiled. 'All right,' he said, leading the way. He searched for a gap in the traffic and went across to the middle of the road where he waited. She came, stiff-bodied, one foot in front of the other. He eyed the legs aloft the stilettos. 'We'll go to see the nancy boy. But I'm tellin' ya – yer gonna hate it.'

Leaning into her shoulder, he ambled towards the bus stop. 'Plenty of guys in our place saw it,' he said. 'They hated it – and even the girls didn't like it. But if that's what you want – are you sure you won't think about it? What have you got against Elvis anyway? Wait a minute! Do ya know? There's a scene in the Elvis film where he sings with a bunch of convicts in a church. I was readin' somewhere that Elvis is really interested in religion …'

Chapter 7

The red and white trolley bus turned onto the bridge and groaned. A burst of sunshine warmed Rosaleen's face. She closed her eyes. The air was hot. In the daytime everything was different. To her left a ship drifted away from the dockside wall and headed towards the lough.

This was her first visit to Dr Prichard's house. She was unsettled, nervous. Hilary was supposed to have come too. Instead, her sister, Jennifer, had brought a note to the City Hall: she had the flu. Rosaleen considered going back home. But the invitation, delivered after Wednesday's meeting, was one that made her feel privileged and obliged. Besides, she was curious.

A cloud covered the sun. In the darkened window she saw her image – a round, white hat that she wore to chapel, crisp-clean face, bright trench raincoat, cream-coloured blouse with a ruffled top, grey pleated skirt, one-inch heels – she smiled. Different, very different from the outfit she'd worn the previous evening on her date with Eddie. She smiled again, broader.

She'd told her parents she would be at St Paul's chapel. And then at Joan's. But they weren't lies. They were fibs. Necessary fibs to keep the rollercoaster from going off the rails. And what had her life been for the last few months, if not a rollercoaster.

Sometimes she felt the danger – like now, with no one to talk to – and she shivered. For she knew perfectly well what her parents, or all the Falls Road, would think of her visit.

And it wasn't as if she didn't care, for she did. She would have liked to be able to explain to them. But that was impossible. They wouldn't understand. Maybe sometime in the future. But not now.

She counted the traffic lights and bus stops, got off and turned down a leafy avenue. Solid, red-brick, detached homes, tarmacadam driveways, stately cars. She stopped in front of Dr Prichard's house, modest by the avenue's standards. A mauve Morris Minor sat in the short driveway. She expected this, and was pleased. With his following, he could have had any car or house he wanted.

She went up to the brown, paint-grained front door, lifted the brass knocker – then hesitated. Against the background of the light breeze combing the trees, she heard the sound of a child's voice from behind the house. She knocked three times.

Hurried steps, the door sprang open. A friendly make-up free face, full rosy cheeks, an altogether more robust figure than in the photograph. Mrs Prichard had wide-open, alert hazel eyes, and, Rosaleen noticed gratefully, sturdy countrywoman's legs. Only the hair, mid-neck in length with a parting down the middle, was the same. Hands tucked into the waist of her blue-patterned apron, she smiled.

'Is Dr Prichard in?'

'Come in, Rosaleen,' she said, holding the door well back. 'Hilary rang this morning and we were worried you wouldn't come.'

'I got the note,' said Rosaleen, stepping in and waiting.

'Great,' she said, putting out her hands to receive her hat and coat. 'Can I hang them up?'

Rosaleen handed over the hat and slipped out of her coat. Mrs Prichard hung them on an old-fashioned hatstand behind the door, saying, 'They're out the garden. The meal's nearly ready. Do you want to join them for a few minutes?'

'Sure.'

She led the way through the bright hall and into the smallish, gleaming kitchen. A smell of roast beef, potatoes, the damp feel of steam. Through the pane-glass windows of the back door, Rosaleen saw Dr Prichard about twenty yards down the lawn. A small boy, seated on a swing, gripped the chains with both hands as the minister – his face red, his shirt sleeves rolled up, his tie flapping about his shoulder – stood behind him and pushed. To his right, a young man dressed in a navy-blue suit held a young baby girl in his arms. She wore a white dress, a soft pink hat and her face was joyful. Mrs Prichard opened the door.

'Come on and give us a hand,' shouted Dr Prichard. 'I'm wrecked. He has me wrecked.'

Rosaleen walked slowly down the concrete path. She was conscious of the young man's gaze. Her cheeks glowed. He was big, his body a little too angular for a suit, and his stance – feet planted wide apart on the grass – was definitely country. The skin on his face was flawless and gave off a golden gleam. He had short blond hair, blue eyes, half-smiling lips, a prominent chin set firm and his arms were wrapped awkwardly around the baby.

Dr Prichard looked over as she approached. 'Are you any good with babies?' he asked.

'Me?'

'No, it's your shadow I'm talking to.'

'– all right.'

'Well, take Ruth off that dope over there,' he said, nodding at the young man. 'You push here, Daniel, and give me a break.'

The young man smiled and shrugged. Rosaleen went over and gingerly held out her arms. He offered the baby up like it was a precious gift. It started crying. Rosaleen winced.

'Have you met Rosaleen?'

'Can't say I've had the pleasure,' he said in a lazy American accent.

He held his large hand loosely towards her. She gripped the baby with her left arm and slipped her right hand into his. He shook it firmly. His hand was strong, the skin hard. She rocked the baby to and fro. The crying grew louder, the eyes closed, the gums showed and saliva dribbled onto her dress. Mrs Prichard threw open the back door and came up. 'It's her feed time,' she said.

'No,' said Dr Prichard, 'I think she got a good look at Daniel's face – he was hidin' it from her.'

She took the baby off Rosaleen and rocked it. The crying settled into a whimper. 'Ours is nearly ready,' she said, going back in.

Daniel was positioning himself behind the swing, looking for a place to put his spread-out hands. The boy on the swing looked shyly up at Rosaleen. 'Do you know the lovely girl, Sam?' Dr Prichard asked of him.

Sam shook his head.

'That's Rosaleen. Rosaleen's a new member. One of our family.'

The boy nodded. Rosaleen wasn't aware that she had applied for membership. But she didn't mind. She noticed that he had his father's eyes and mouth, though his build was much slighter.

'Are you gonna be nice to her, Sam?'

His head nodded.

Dr Prichard turned to Rosaleen. 'You're elected,' he said.

She laughed and went to stand beside him, a few yards from the swing. They watched Daniel. A firm push into the middle of Sam's back almost tipped him over.

'You'll puncture his lungs,' said Dr Prichard. 'Lower down. Push the seat.'

Daniel beamed an American smile. The swing went up and back, wobbling slightly. 'He doesn't know his own strength,' said Dr Prichard, aside to Rosaleen. 'A pity about Hilary. I was just tellin' her on Wednesday. You don't wear enough clothes, you young 'uns. This is a damp climate.'

Rosaleen immediately considered what she was wearing and wondered how she could make herself look warmer.

'You turn all the men's heads,' he continued, lightly touching her shoulder. 'But what's the use of that if you get pneumonia.'

She wrapped her arms across her upper body.

'You're a pretty picture today,' he said.

She smiled and looked at the grass.

'How am I doin'?' asked Daniel.

'You're not as big an eejit as ya luk. Is he?' he said, turning to Rosaleen.

'Thanks, Dr Prichard,' said Daniel. 'That's the nicest thing you've said to me since I arrived.'

'Well, if you were as big an eejit as ya luked, ya'd be back home in America by now.'

'I suppose that's some kind of Irish compliment, is it?'

'Ya can take it whatever way ya like,' he said, and then, turning to Rosaleen, 'He's been atin' us outa house an' home since he arrived.'

'Why are you making those unrighteous remarks about me?'

'The truth is never unrighteous,' said Dr Prichard, winking.

'In my next ministry I think I'll go to Australia.'

'They mightn't let you in – they're very particular.'

'I have a brother there. And their steaks are bigger.'

'Do ya hear that, Rosaleen? Not content with atin' us outa house an' home – he insults us.'

'Well,' said Daniel, puffing now from the effort. 'Your portions are pretty small. Especially when you consider the work you're expected to do for it.'

Dr Prichard turned to Rosaleen, 'He calls that work. That's the type of person they send me.'

The swing was riding up high, the hinges creaked. 'That's high enough, Daniel,' said Mrs Prichard from the back door. 'Time to eat.'

Sam screwed up his nose. 'One more time, Daddy,' he said.
'The general has spoken, son. You can come out later.'

They went into the kitchen. Mrs Prichard was cutting beef
and laying the slices on plates along a narrow cream worktop.
Her husband led the way into the dining room. The walls
were stark white and bare except for two family photographs,
the same two Rosaleen had seen on his desk, and a large photograph of the young Queen Elizabeth's coronation directly
opposite the garden window. Beyond the linen-covered table,
formally set with silver and white napkins, two leather arm-
chairs were placed in front of a fireplace where a few large
lumps of coal were burning. The mantelpiece had a brown
wooden frame around two vertical lines of shiny navy tiles
that rose up along the sides of a black iron grate. The carpet
was deep blue, like the tiles. What struck Rosaleen was the
absence of knick-knacks, even any children's toys. The dark
polished surfaces and the cold feel of the room didn't seem to
reflect Dr Prichard's nature at all. She supposed his wife had
picked the decor and furniture. The front room she passed on
the way in was completely empty of furniture – did they only
live in one or two rooms?

Dr Prichard placed Sam on a cushion-stacked chair and
sat down at the head of the table. To Rosaleen's surprise, his
wife placed the first plate of meat in front of her. Mrs Prichard
became a blur, her lips tight, her eyes full of concentration as
she rapidly packed the table with dishes of vegetables and
potatoes. Rosaleen noticed that while the silver and the linen
napkins appeared to be brand new, the dishes and plates, in
faded blue and pink patterns, showed a few years' use.

Daniel, standing behind the chair opposite Rosaleen, was
talking softly to Dr Prichard about wheat – bushels, acres,
yields. A final blur of blue and Mrs Prichard set down a dish
of buttered carrots and a jug of water on the table before sitting
down beside Sam. She swept a few brittle strands of brown

hair from her face. 'Help yourself, Rosaleen,' she said, sticking a tablespoon into the carrots. 'Don't be shy.'

'Will you say grace, Daniel?' asked Dr Prichard.

He sat down opposite Rosaleen, put his hands flat on the table and looked at its centre. 'We thank you, Lord, for what we are about to receive.'

A flurry of hands followed a short pause, the food spread around the plates. Mrs Prichard cut up potatoes and small bits of meat for Sam. She then tied a bib around his neck.

'Were we boring you with all that farm talk, Rosaleen?' Dr Prichard asked.

'No.'

'Rosaleen's a city girl.'

'Oh I've been to the country,' she said brightly. 'A couple of times. On holiday.'

'There's a lot of city slickers in our community. But we're not short of country bumpkins either.'

'That's very reassuring,' said Daniel, sticking his fork into a large potato.

Mrs Prichard passed the dish of carrots to Rosaleen. 'Sure we're all country people, Lesley. You're from the country, I'm from the country. Most of the people in Belfast have relations in the country. Where are your parents from Rosaleen?'

About to say The Falls, she paused and stopped cutting her meat. 'They're from … they're from the city,' she said, diverting her eyes onto the plate. She could feel her face blushing and hated it.

'There may be a bread shortage this year,' said Dr Prichard, looking sideways at Rosaleen. 'Storms. Hurricanes have hit the breadbasket of America. Daniel was telling me they had a hurricane in his part of the country.'

'And a tornado,' added Daniel. 'I visited the house of one of the parishioners. All the furniture had been sucked from the bottom floor, right up through the stairs into the landing and the bedrooms. Like a giant vacuum cleaner. Do you have storms here?'

'Nothing like that,' said Dr Prichard.

'Have you been to America, Rosaleen?' asked Daniel.

'No,' she said, giving him a shy look. 'But I would like to see it.'

'You're young,' said Mrs Prichard, pouring Rosaleen a glass of water. 'You've plenty of time for travel. Don't be getting married young. Take my advice. Don't be making the mistake I made.'

'I wasn't in any hurry to get married,' said Dr Prichard. 'That I can remember.'

His wife put down the jug and let out a hearty laugh. Her uneven yellow teeth showed and wrinkles spread from the corners of her eyes and mouth. 'You remember what suits you to remember,' she said.

'I wasn't,' he insisted.

'I should have used a tape recorder.'

He began to smile.

'That was my mistake,' she continued. 'Then every time it comes up you just press the button.'

Rosaleen watched Daniel eating. Though his hands were big, his movements were short and precise. His face was much more boyish than Dr Prichard's. But the expression had the same good-humoured sureness. 'What's your part of America like?' she asked.

He stopped eating and thought for a few moments. 'It's different from here. Flat. Very flat. In the Spring the corn is green and it stretches for miles and miles, like the sea. And in the summer the colours change into a kind of light gold. The sky changes all the time too and under it you get this vast space spreading out all over the plains where there isn't even a single house and if you stop and listen the only sound is the wind. Mostly a soft, light sound. Sometimes not even that. And all around, you have this silence. But that's only above the ground. Because, if you lie close to the earth you can hear all these insects – that's a world of its own too. One year we had a swarm of locusts – they ate everything – even bits of the houses. That's one of the things you get to understand quickly – God doesn't let you take anything for granted.'

'I was on holiday on a farm two years ago,' said Rosaleen.

'What kind of farm was it?' Daniel asked.

She spoke for some minutes, without inhibition. Mrs Prichard piled more food onto her plate. At home all the plates were filled in the kitchen from pots and pans, and brought straight out. Here they served from the dishes on the table. A step upmarket. She liked that. She liked the atmosphere too. The easy good humour. The love. And the sense of mission – that was something that really attracted her. What was life without a sense of mission?

After the meal Mrs Prichard put Sam down for a nap and made tea. Chairs were placed around the fire and they exchanged stories. Some humorous, some serious. Rosaleen noticed that when she mentioned anything to do with the Catholic Church, their level of interest heightened. Especially Dr Prichard. His face grew taut, the eyelids came down and he leaned forward. Gradually he drew her out on the reasons she left school.

'What kind of trouble?' he asked.

'Nothing. It was nothing, really. Well –'

'Did the nuns make you leave?'

'No. I decided myself –'

'To leave?'

'– yes.'

There was a short pause.

'Did they put pressure on you?' he asked.

'– well –'

'It's all right if you don't want to talk about it.'

'Yes. Actually they did.'

'It doesn't surprise me. We hear stories. Many from converts. Stories that would shock you. They're not for young people's ears.'

'I didn't do anything,' said Rosaleen. 'That was the point. And they ... they wanted me to tell lies.'

'The nuns?'

'Yes.'

'And you wouldn't?'

'No.'

Dr Prichard's features began to soften. All their eyes were riveted on Rosaleen's face. Where some months before she had only received the scorn of people in authority, she was now the object of admiration and respect. 'I just wouldn't accept their version of the truth, because it was wrong,' she added.

'That takes courage,' said Dr Prichard.

'Not really. I didn't think. I just –'

'– did what you thought was right.'

'– yes.'

Dr Prichard nodded and joined his hands together. 'The forces of darkness come in many forms,' he said. 'They're not always easy to recognise. But they must be opposed.'

'I just thought –' said Rosaleen.

'– that you were being asked to do something wrong?' suggested Dr Prichard.

'– yes.'

He looked at his wife and Daniel. Their faces had become serious, concerned. They returned his gaze and awaited guidance. 'What you say, Rosaleen, fits in with other cases – here – Scotland, and America. Isn't that right, Daniel?'

The American squinted at the fire for a few moments before nodding. 'We've had cases. Horrible cases,' he said. 'The same pattern. Blind obedience. And tight control, all the way through to the Vatican.'

'It was only one school,' said Rosaleen. 'And two nuns.'

Mrs Prichard pressed her lips together and gave Rosaleen a sympathetic nod. 'You're a young girl, Rosaleen. Very young. That was no way to treat a young Christian girl.'

'I'm glad I left,' she said. They watched her face, waiting to hear more. 'The time since I left has been the best time of my life. I've done so many things. Made new friends. Bought my own clothes. Go out to see people. Go places I would never have had the nerve to go to. Last year I would never have gone to your church.'

'So we have the nuns to thank,' said Dr Prichard.

Daniel smiled and closed his eyes like a conspirator. 'I wonder,' he said, 'should we try to recruit these nuns.'

'Why? Sure aren't they doin' a great job where they are. With nuns like that we just have to sit here and all the women of the Falls Road will be fallin' into our laps.'

They all laughed: Daniel, his head falling back, shoulders shaking, Mrs Prichard burying her face in her hands; Rosaleen smiling from ear to ear. When the laughter had died, Mrs Prichard sucked in her cheeks and said: 'What about your family, Rosaleen?'

She shifted in the hard leather seat. 'My parents didn't want me to leave school.'

'That's understandable,' she said, nodding her head slowly.

'But I couldn't stay. I just couldn't. I remember that day I walked out. I made up my mind. Nothing would change it.'

Dr Prichard looked over at his wife and rubbed his lips softly together. 'I don't think you could look on leaving school in those circumstances as just an ordinary leaving of school,' he said. And then, turning to Rosaleen, 'You felt they forced you to leave?'

'Yes.'

'It's similar to the case in Glasgow,' he added.

'Yes,' said Daniel, 'but they went even further there. They expelled the boy.'

'Did they?' asked Mrs Prichard, aghast.

He nodded and said, 'His parents used their influence to prevent excommunication. You see, once that whole thing starts, it's nearly impossible to stop.'

The word 'excommunication' hit Rosaleen like a slap. All right, she wasn't going along with all the Catholic Church's rules, but there wasn't anything that drastic. 'There's nothing like that in my case –'

'Oh, I didn't mean,' he stammered, '– I meant –'

'Don't be too sure about it,' said Dr Prichard. 'If old Beelzebub from the Vatican gets wind of it, anything's possible. It's not so long ago they suspended Catholics in the South for attending Protestant churches.'

'They wouldn't!' exclaimed Rosaleen, her cheeks growing slightly pale.

'Nothing they do would surprise me. But in your case I think the chances are extremely unlikely. Even an old fool like the present pope wouldn't be as stupid as that.'

Mrs Prichard gave her a soft, kindly look. 'I think you should obey your parents, Rosaleen,' she said.

'I do. In most things. Except when I think they're really wrong. In important things.'

Dr Prichard leaned towards her. 'What age are you?' he asked.

'I'll be sixteen on the sixteenth of May.'

'I'd say your parents are good people,' Dr Prichard said. 'And very fond of you.'

'Oh they are. The best in the world. And most of the time we get on really … it's in the last – my sister was the only one to – since then –'

'And you must think of them.'

'I do …'

He stood up and laid his hand gently on her shoulder. 'It's about time we moved. Right, Daniel? Are you ready?'

The American rose and stretched his limbs. 'What unspeakable chores have you in store for me today?'

'Since today's the Sabbath the chores are slightly less unspeakable than they were yesterday. I want to show you plans and a model for the new church in Monaghan. And give you some material for your lectures – you might be able to use it.' He turned to Rosaleen. 'Daniel will be pastor in a new church in America. Can I give you a lift into town?'

'Yes please,' she said.

'We'll stop off a few minutes on the way to get my papers. But we won't be long.'

Dr Prichard, Daniel and Rosaleen drove to the church on Ravenmount Road and went into the office. The desk had been cleared and a small wooden model of a church placed on the top of it. Dr Prichard, with childish glee, lifted the roof – under it there were tiny figures of men and women in the pews. 'The great thing about this one, or so the architect tells me,' he said, 'is that the dead zone will be eliminated. We may not have to use microphones at all.'

Rosaleen smiled, knowing well that with his voice, a church hardly existed where he needed a microphone. Daniel nodded a lot when Dr Prichard was talking, asked questions, and when they huddled over the lecture notes he positively purred. Before they left he stacked a box full of them and then carried it to the car.

She asked to be let out at the City Hall. That was fine. She had enjoyed the day, even without Hilary. In fact, the day had probably been more enjoyable because she wasn't there. The attention was nice. And Daniel had added a bit of … well, she looked forward to seeing him again.

Chapter 8

The pubs spilled their crowds onto the city centre streets. Young men cut a path to the Kingsway, the Orchid, the Orpheus and the Plaza. Band music wafted over the busy streets. In the doorways of the dancehalls, the pungent scent of Saturday-night girls mingled with the beery breaths of Lotharios. Queues formed at bus stops all the way along Royal Avenue and into Castle Street. Trains of buses edged along the sides of the kerbs, their conductors guarding their platforms until they headed the queues.

Rosaleen could feel Eddie pull on her arm as they turned into Castle Street. She was almost used to the high heels but she still couldn't walk as fast as him, even though he had altered his walk from a John Wayne-ish full steam ahead to an ambling right-to-left, left-to-right gait. His elbow was jutted out so that she could slip her hand through his arm. This was something she wasn't particularly comfortable with, but the habit seemed so ingrained she didn't want to make an issue of it.

He was wearing the other half of his wardrobe – a bright, grey pin-striped Italian suit and black sponge-soled shoes with silver buckles. He wore each outfit on alternate Saturdays with the occasional flash of a new tie. Eddie was going with Rosaleen.

In the half-step behind him, Rosaleen wasn't too sure what she was doing. Tonight, in her make-up, nylons, tight skirt and jumper, she was one thing. And she kind of enjoyed that, in so far as it went, despite the difficulties. But with Eddie you could only go so far. There were obvious limits. And lately she sometimes had the sense that her life was changing direction – as if a part of her was moving away from Eddie, her parents, her religion, her home … but not Marie. They were still great. They talked about everything. Well, nearly everything. Tonight Marie had helped her get ready. And even though she didn't understand and probably disapproved of the changes, she did not judge or condemn. But with each passing week, the centre of her life was more … Hilary, the meetings at work, her active helping in the church at Ravenmount, Dr Prichard, Daniel … Daniel had extended his training visit … these were becoming the familiar, the important.

Her hand lay lightly on the smooth cloth of Eddie's sleeve. He was busy analysing the movie – a few laughs, not a lot of action. They might have been better going to the John Wayne film instead. Maybe next Saturday? He asked, his eyes searching for the nod. She looked away.

The queue dissolved quickly. They rode near the front at the top of the bus. She refused Eddie's offer of a stick of Wrigley's Spearmint chewing gum, with a smile. Predictable as a clock, like Marie said. Sweeten his breath for their tryst at the entry corner.

In the beginning she enjoyed it – the taste, the smell, her power to attract, arouse. And she liked his good looks, clear skin and hard slim body. But tonight she wasn't looking forward to it. Nor had she for the last couple of times. He hadn't changed. She had.

They got off and walked down the short distance to the entry beside the first house. She felt a tug on her arm, then his hand slipped into hers and gave a light pull. She slowed down and stopped. He looked into her face, puzzled. Rosaleen recognised this as the first phase of the battle: how far up the entry should they go. Too far was complete darkness, risk and gritty battle. Not far enough meant the neighbours gawking at every kiss. The right distance allowed some light from the lamps but sufficient darkness to prevent outright identification. Rosaleen selected the right distance and prepared for war.

This began, in the usual harmless fashion, with Eddie closing his eyes, putting his arms and hands around her back, and approaching her lips with his. She liked his kissing: gentle, the Wrigley Spearmint breath, a touch of aftershave and a slightly rough chin. His tongue, with its impertinent prising between the teeth, was less likeable. But the real problem was the hands.

Eyes closed, she could feel his left hand beginning to creep down to her waist. Her right elbow jutted out. His hand hesitated, her elbow stopped, his hand moved onto her waist, her elbow was poised. His fingers began to creep under her jumper, her elbow pushed his arm back slightly. His fingers persisted, her elbow became relaxed. His fingers crept up under her jumper, her elbow clamped them. They pushed for a few moments, in vain, and retreated to the back.

They kissed for a few moments, his tongue slipping momentarily between her teeth. His left hand, still under her jumper, came sliding towards the front – she clamped his arm tightly with her elbow. He tried to move it – he couldn't.

They continued necking, then he tried to move his hand again. She clamped it tighter. His left hand retreated quickly to her back, she relaxed her elbow. Still necking, he put his right hand under her jumper – her left elbow became poised. His right hand moved forwards and backwards under her jumper around the waist, up towards her back. Her elbow relaxed and then, just as his hand was about to slide around to the front, she clamped it and drew back.

'What are ya doin'?' she asked.

His eyes were slightly glazed, the mouth open, the breath rapid. 'Nothin',' he said.

'Hmmm?'

'Nothin' much.'

She withdrew his hand and straightened her jumper, saying, 'It's always the same, isn't it?'

Eddie winced and shook his head. 'Ah, com' on –'

'Com' on what?'

He closed his eyes and moved his lips towards hers. 'Com' on, let's –'

Her hands pressed against his chest. 'What?'

'You know.'

'You tell me, Eddie. Tell me what I know.'

'You know,' he said, trying unsuccessfully to put his hands around her waist. 'You know what I mean.'

Rosaleen held his hands firmly. 'I think, Eddie –' she said.

Puzzlement creased his face, his eyelids came down. 'Yeah?'

'– that you should find –'

'– what?'

'Another girl.'

The puzzlement became disbelief, the eyes owlish. 'Why?' he gasped.

'Because –'

He let go her hands, twisted to the right and turned back sharply. 'Tonight? That?' he asked, nodding his head at her waist.

'We're wasting each other's time.'

'No.'

'You want something.'

His eyes burned with incomprehension. 'Me? Want something? What makes you think that?'

'It's always the same.'

'What?'

'This,' she said emphatically, folding her arms.

'I don't know what you're talking about. Honest.'

'How long have we been goin' out together?'

He shrugged.

'Three months.'

'– yeah.'

'And it still hasn't –'

'What?'

'Penetrated –'

Eddie spread his hands and looked directly into her face. 'What was I doin' wrong? Eh?'

'Look, Eddie, I'm not –'

'What?'

'– what you're looking for.'

His face collapsed, the light went out of his eyes. 'Naa,' he said, taking out a cigarette and lighting it.

'It's plain, isn't it?'

'Naa.'

'You should go out and find someone –'

'Why?'

'You're happy with.'

'I'm happy with you.'

'Me?' she gasped.

'Yeah.'

Rosaleen fixed her eyes on the silver buckles of his shoes – they caught the lamplight and sparkled. 'How?' she asked, not lifting her eyes.

'You're my type.'

'I'm not, Eddie.'

'We like the same music. We like to dance. And we like the same pictures – mostly.'

'That's not everything.'

'Where's the beef?'

'Sometimes I wonder –'

'What?'

Her eyes shot him a glance. 'If we talk the same language,' she said.

Eddie stepped back, took a deep drag from his cigarette, shook his head from side-to-side and then turned around to face her. 'Language?'

'We seem so –'

'What?'

'There's a big –'

'Have you been readin' magazines?'

'Hmmm?'

'Women's magazines.'

'What if I have?'

'One of m' mates at work is havin' trouble with his bird.'

'And –?'

'Well he didn't have any trouble before –'

'– she started readin' women's magazines?'

'I'm not sayin' he's a hundred per cent right.'

'Magazines have nothing to do with what I'm –'

'Yeah?'

'Trying to say.'

'Okay.'

'I just think that we … that you are barking up the wrong tree.'

'Me?'

'Yeah.'

'– I don't get ya.'

Rosaleen took a deep breath, looked out towards the street and exhaled it slowly.

'What did I do wrong?'

'It's me. We're different. You're different from me. We feel different about … basic things.'

'– I don't get ya.'

'Just think. For one minute. One second. Maybe a few seconds. About what you do.'

'– at the bakery?'

'No, here. In this entry. For the past three months.'

Eddie's lips clasped the tip of the cigarette, his cheeks hollowed and he stared up at the stars for a few moments. Then as the smoke raced from his nostrils he looked into her face. 'I don't think much about it,' he said.

'I know you don't think much about it.'

'I just –'

'– yeah?'

'Sorta –'

'Sorta what?'

'Do somethin',' he said, shrugging his shoulders and spreading his hands. 'What do ya expect me t' do? Stand here like a tube with m' hands in m' pockets?'

'Eddie!'

'I kiss you goodnight. Is that such a big crime? A hangin' offence?'

'There's nothing wrong with a goodnight kiss.'

'Well?'

'You just don't want a girl like me –'

'But I do,' he said, throwing down his cigarette and squashing it with the sole of his shoe. 'That's where you're wrong.'

'I'm not.'

His hands slid onto her waist. 'I could go out with plenty of birds. Good things!'

'Well, why don't ya?'

'Because I'm not –'

'Interested?'

'No, I am – but –'

'But what?'

'I don't feel – it wud only be – there's birds I know and you wud only have to – one of the guys at work has to get married.'

Rosaleen's eyes grew wide, her lips parted. 'Who to?'

'A bird.'

'A good thing?'

'An' he's got two years t' go in his apprenticeship.'

'Where are they gettin' married?'

'Search me. But I know one thing –'

'What?'

'The Master baker doesn't like it – he's been put on baps full-time since the news broke.'

'Is that bad?'

'Nobody likes being put on the baps. Ya have t' start two hours early an' yer always knackered.'

'I feel sorry for her.'

'What about him? His job's on the line and he cud be on baps for life. Never able t' go anywhere. Absolutely knackered.'

'Everybody'll know.'

'Course,' he said, putting his arms around her waist. 'I don't mind. I want you t' stay the way you are.'

'Then why do you –?'

'I'm just goin' through the motions. Honest. I'd be just as happy wearin' boxin' gloves.'

Rosaleen leaned back against the rough wall and folded her arms. Her upper teeth bit into her lower lip. 'Anyway –' she said emphatically, looking above Eddie towards the row of lighted windows at the backs of the houses.

His eyes tried for contact, in vain. 'We're okay, eh? Didn't I take ya t' the Cliff Richard picture? Didn't I even buy ya his record?'

'You don't –'

'– what?'

Her eyes finally made contact. ' – care about religion,' she said.

Eddie turned away, his face lit palely from the street lamp, and winced.

'See, even when I mention it.'

'Luk, Rosaleen, I'll take ya t' any amount of poxy Cliff Richard pictures. I'll get ya every one of his sick imitation Elvis records. But I won't – I won't go to those bloody meetings.'

'Why?'

'Well – for starters – they're Protestant.'

'Are you afraid?'

'Me? Afraid?'

'You won't even discuss anything about it.'

'What?'

'The Bible.'

'You shouldn't be goin' t' them meetings.'

'Why?'

'They have a bad effect on ya.'

'Have they?'

'Yeah.'

'And you can say that! Without even havin' the courage t' attend one of them.'

'I don't need t' go t' see the effect.'

'What effect?'

'On you. The way you look. Think. I can tell when you've been t' one. They're different sort of people. They look different. They think different. They are different.'

'You don't understand, Eddie.'

'Don't I?'

'When you look into religion. Really look into it. You begin to feel and see things clearly. And when you see and understand, you want to share ... you want other people to be able to see too.'

'There's nothin' wrong with my eyesight,' said Eddie, holding up his hand between them. 'That's my hand. Clear as daylight. Straight in front of my nose.'

'But that's only one form of reality. There's another, deeper reality. And religion helps us to see it.'

'What religion?'

She hesitated. '– the Bible.'

'They're not right.'

'What's wrong with them?'

Eddie rubbed his forehead with his hand and closed his eyes. 'Everybody ... has their religion,' he said. 'Don't they? Why don't they just keep it? Why do they have t' go t' meetings an' discuss it?'

'– they don't have to.'

'Exactly.'

A breeze blew down the entry and swept Rosaleen's hair onto her face. The lamplight caught Eddie's eyes – determined, baffled – staring towards the street. She swept the hair back on her head and asked: 'Will you come?'

'No.'

Her hand went down along the wall until it touched the strap of her handbag. 'Goodnight,' she said, picking it up and moving towards the street.

Eddie followed a few steps behind. 'I'll see you next Wednesday,' he said.

'No.'

'What's wrong?'

'Not this Wednesday.'

'We see each other every Wednesday.'

'I can't,' she said, hurrying across the street.

He stayed at her shoulder up to the railing of the house. 'When will I see ya? When?' he asked, his hands spread out in a desperate gesture.

She went straight into the hall and stopped. Her hand touched the brass round handle of the inner door. The crackled sound of Radio Luxembourg playing Buddy Holly's Maybe Baby came from the living room. She glanced over at Eddie. His arms spread across the short path, his hands gripping the railings. A few weeks ago she would have smiled and arranged something. 'We'll see,' she said, twisting the handle and going in.

When the door slammed behind her, she felt a twinge of guilt, maybe even regret. She restrained an impulse to go back out. And begin what again …? She put her handbag on the settee and waited a few moments. Then she went over, opened the door and peered out. He was gone.

'What are ya doin'?' Marie shouted from the kitchen.

'Nothin',' she said, closing the door.

'Cuppa?'

'Okay.'

Rosaleen sat down at the table. There was something different about the room. She ran her finger along the top of the skirting board just above the table. Not a speck of dust. There was no sign of the newspaper even. Marie brought in two brown mugs of tea, put them on the table, switched off the radio and sat down.

'Who did the house?' asked Rosaleen.

'M' Ma.'

'Tonight?'

'Yeah.'

'Why?'

Marie shrugged. Rosaleen suspected she was holding something back. The way her eyes had avoided contact for an instant. 'Well,' she said, wrapping her long fingers around the mug, 'where did Eddie take you?'

'The Ritz.'

'Any good?'

'Pillow Talk. Doris Day and Rock Hudson. It was funny.'

'Rock's a hunk.'

'Not bad.'

'And did King of the Twiddlers like it?'

Rosaleen smiled and shook her head, the hair fell in front of her face. 'I got a bit of peace,' she said.

Marie sucked in her cheeks, her eyes became eggs. 'Could this be the start of something big? Getting a bit of peace from King of the Twiddlers is not an everyday event.'

'But only while the picture was on.'

'All hands on deck at the interval,' said Marie, playing a piano with her fingers. 'All that pent-up twiddlin' energy.'

'We had an ice-cream at the interval.'

'He never bought me an ice-cream – he must be serious about you.'

'And saved all his energy for a finale in the entry. Does Harry go on like that?'

'They all graduate from the same school.'

'Pathetic, isn't it?'

'Ah, sure, God love them. Can you imagine how neurotic they'd get without something t'twiddle with? It's really a social service we provide. Feels on heels.'

Rosaleen giggled, choked on her tea and dried the dribbles on her chin with a tissue. She looked across at her sister. Their eyes met. Invisible laugh lines. She loved her, really loved her.

'Can you keep a secret?' asked Marie.

Rosaleen's fingers gripped the mug, her lips parted, she didn't have to answer. Her sister dashed over to her black handbag and took out a small crimson velvet box. She flipped up the lid to show a one-stone engagement ring.

'Are you engaged?'

'A reward for services rendered. Beyond the call of duty. Twiddlin' booty.'

'Are you serious?'

'He's mad about me.'

'Are you –?'

'He dragged me into the shop this afternoon. What could I do?'

'It's a gorgeous ring.'

'Do you really like it?'

'It's lovely. Really lovely – and it's not too big. I hate the big engagement rings with the big diamonds.'

'So does Harry –'

Rosaleen took the ring from the box and slid it onto her finger. 'It fits,' she said.

'Another few years of twiddlin' endurance and a sparkler like that cud be yours for the askin',' Marie said.

'I cudn't. Honest.'

'Eddie's not a bad wee lad.'

'No, but –'

'Don't strike him off your list – yet,' she said, putting the ring back in its box. 'And not a word to m' Ma an' Da.'

Rosaleen grinned and returned a conspiratorial nod. 'Where are they?' she asked.

Marie lifted the box and went over and took her time about putting it back into the handbag. When she turned around her eyes were downcast.

'What's wrong?'

'I think they know about you,' she said softly. And then, emphatically, 'Not from me. I never said anything. I played dumb.'

'Who?'

'Father Wilson sent for them – he – he must know something. Somebody must have given him your name.'

Rosaleen's fingers clenched the mug. 'It's none of his business,' she said. 'Why can't they all just leave me alone?'

'– they're worried.'

'About what?'

Marie shrugged.

'A person's beliefs are private. And they're entitled to stay that way.'

Marie sipped her tea and waited a few moments before speaking. 'Do you not think ... that maybe you're taking it a bit far?'

'No!'

'Just an opinion,' said Marie, folding her arms and pushing back against the chair.

'I think I have the right to decide for myself.'

'Sure –'

'I'm not stupid. I have intelligence. God-given intelligence. And I won't be treated like some kind of idiot.'

'Rosaleen, I'm on your side. I want what's best for you.'

'– I know that.'

'It's just – I don't – I don't see things the way you do.'

'But you would, Marie, if you read the Bible. Read it. Or come with me to one of the meetings. Just to hear Dr Prichard. He makes it so clear and simple – it's as plain as the nose on your face. The trouble with religion is that a lot of people try to deny the Bible its basic simplicity. They try to confuse people.'

Marie diverted her eyes away from Rosaleen, saying, 'I'm not so sure.'

'About what?'

'It's effect ... on you.'

'Marie, these past few months have been the happiest of my life.'

'Have they?' she asked sharply.

The edge in her sister's voice made her hesitate. 'I've never been so ... spiritually contented,' she said. 'And I won't let anyone. Anyone take that away from me.'

Familiar footsteps approached from the outside. Rosaleen sprang up from the chair and clattered up the stairs. Her feet were silent when the door handle was given a violent twist. Marie's shoulders sagged and she winced when she saw Frank lead Eileen into the living room.

'Is she home?' he snapped, and then his eyes fell on the two mugs.

Eileen, without taking off her coat, straightened the cushions on the settee and armchair.

'She isn't asleep, is she?' he asked.

'Just gone up.'

'Give that table a wipe, will you?' asked Eileen.

Marie lifted the two mugs and glanced down at the clean polished surface. 'What's wrong with it?'

'Just give it a wipe,' insisted Eileen.

Marie went into the kitchen. Frank, his hands dug into his tweed overcoat, paced between the settee and the armchair. Eileen fidgeted with and plumped a few cushions and when her daughter returned with a cloth, she added, 'There's some polish in the cupboard.'

'Polish?'

'Father Wilson's comin',' said Frank.

'At this time of the night?'

'It's about a very serious matter.'

Marie stood still, the cloth bunched in her right hand, and observed her parents with detachment. 'Rosaleen,' she said, throwing the cloth carelessly onto the table.

Eileen darted forward and gave the table great scrubbing wipes. 'Are ya not gonna do it?' she snapped. 'Have Father Wilson think he's comin' int' a pigsty.'

'I'm not joinin'.'

'You'll do what you're told,' said Frank, stepping over to stand at Eileen's shoulder. 'Yas have had too much freedom. The pair of ya.'

'It's wrong,' said Marie.

'What?'

'What you're doing!'

'This house has been too lax,' he said, wagging his finger. 'For a long time now. There were things goin' on under our noses and we ignored them. And nobody knew just how far things had gone.'

Marie glanced over at her mother. 'I'm surprised at you,' she said.

'It's not like I thought, Marie.'

'Really?'

'I thought anything she was involved in was harmless too.'

Frank sat down, got up, stuck his hands into his pockets, sat down, and got up again and said aloud: 'From the day –' then he lowered his voice, but his agitation only seemed to increase '– from the day she started work in that factory I never felt right about it. I felt it in my bones. And I can't say I wasn't warned.'

'What are ya afraid of?' asked Marie.

'If you can't see the danger,' he said, his head jutting forward. 'An innocent wee girl being lured into one of them dens and subjected to the most intense form of brainwashin' known t' Western man.'

'What? Socialising with a few girls from work?'

'It's not as innocent as it sounds,' said Eileen, taking the cloth back into the kitchen.

'They're only the outriders for Prichard. They're the scouts bringin' them in so that Mister Svengali can get t' work.'

Marie folded her arms and bit her lower lip. 'She seems happy,' she said.

'Happy!' Frank barked.

Marie stood back. His eyes roasted the air between them. 'Do you know anything about your sister?'

Eileen appeared at the doorway. Her stone expression showed where her support lay.

'We're very close,' said Marie.

This seemed to goad Frank. He flashed a bitter smile at his wife before looking his daughter directly in the eye. 'Did you know that she's under their instructions? No, I don't expect ya did. Do ya think they want t' warn her family before she's trapped in their clutches? Does the name Mary Conway mean anything t' ya?'

'No.'

'You tell her, Eileen.'

Frank stepped back and leaned his hand against the door. Eileen came in, sat at the table and looked straight across at the embers of the fire. '... seventeen years of age,' she said. 'A convent girl from Newry. She was gonna start teacher training college. And now –'

'After they've been workin' on her,' added Frank.

' – she turned,' said Eileen.

Frank pushed himself away from the door and fixed his eyes on Marie. 'They're paradin' her around halls in Scotland,' he said. 'With a renegade priest. It's a cabaret. Makin' a mockery of the Mass. Lost, lost to her family and her religion.'

'I wudn't have believed it,' said Eileen.

Marie shook her head from side to side. 'No, not Rosaleen,' she said, 'I cudn't believe that about her.'

Frank dug his hands deep into his pockets, saying, 'I just hope we're not too late.'

'– I don't believe it,' continued Marie.

'Neither did I,' said Eileen. 'Until tonight.'

Marie switched her gaze back and forth between the two of them. 'What did Father Wilson tell you?' she asked.

Eileen left it to Frank. '... he's been investigatin'.'

'Rosaleen?'

'The whole set-up. The system. The psychology. The way they work on immature minds. He was able to describe to a "T" what's been happening.'

'All right, she's been a bit serious about religion. But I honestly haven't noticed that big a change.'

'That's part of the technique.'

' – according to Father Wilson –' Marie interjected.

'No, Marie,' said Eileen with a shake of the head, 'he understands it. He really understands it.'

Frank nodded and used his right hand to emphasise the points as he spoke. 'I think we should let the man speak for himself. We can only understand it up to a point. Religion's like that. This is a case for the specialist who really knows about religion. We can only see the tip of the iceberg.'

'She's only fifteen,' said Marie.

'That's the way they work,' explained Frank, 'get them young –'

'I think it's only a phase.'

'How do you know?' asked Eileen. 'How do any of us know?'

'Every teenager goes through phases.'

Frank wagged his finger in front of his daughter's nose. 'What other teenager on this road do you know that's goin' through it? Name one! There's none of them. Not one. They're out dancin', enjoyin' themselves, or goin' t' their Mass on a Sunday. Not trottin' over t' listen t' Svengali two or three nights a week.'

'It's not two or three nights a week.'

'Do you think she's tellin' us the truth when she goes out?'

'Why not?'

Frank sucked in his lips and squeezed them tight before speaking. '– she was supposed to be out dancin' last Wednesday.'

'Yeah.'

'She was over at Prichard's.'

'How do you know?'

'We know!' said Frank, shaking his fist.

'You were spyin' on her?'

'We were spyin' on nobody. She's fifteen years of age. And directly under our charge.'

'Well, I don't think you're going the right way about it. All right, maybe she is under … his influence. He influences a lot of people. But do you think this is going to make her any less under his influence?'

Frank half-closed his eyes and gave a quick nod of the head. 'Father Wilson is an experienced priest,' he said.

'He's a good priest,' said Eileen. 'You can't deny that, Marie. And he's been good to us.'

'Rosaleen's stubborn. Once she gets a thing into her head. Everybody gangin' up on her?'

'Who?' asked Frank.

'What do you call this?'

'She was seen goin' int' one of Prichard's meetings. She even got up and spoke.'

'– what did she say?'

'You've heard the rubbish she comes out with.'

'Maybe if we just took it easy. Let it run its course.'

'It's too late for that.'

'I'm worried,' said Eileen, knitting her fingers together on her lap. 'None of us know how far this has gone.'

Frank gripped his temples with his fingers and gave them a vigorous rub. 'Father Wilson isn't the type of man to do anything unless it was extremely serious. Direct intervention is the last resort,' he said, going over to the foot of the stairs. 'Rosaleen! Come down here!'

Eileen's eyes shot him a warning. 'Now, Frank,' she said, 'don't be rushin' at it like a bull.'

'We'll sort this out tonight.'

Her high-heels clattered and stomped on the stairs. Marie thought this unusual – she normally slipped out of them at the earliest opportunity. But when her sister emerged at the bottom she understood the reason: standing straight up in her heels, with her arms folded, she was taller than her parents. Frank was standing well back with his arms crossed over. He stared straight at her for a few seconds, speechless, and then looked down towards the settee.

'What is it?' she asked.

'There's a few things we want aired,' he said.

'Is there?'

His eyes were still cast down towards the settee, as if he couldn't bring himself to look at his daughter in her burgeoning Saturday night finery. 'Yes, there is,' he said. 'Me and Eileen got a bit of a shock tonight. We thought we'd raised our family, our daughters, to be honest with us. That if they were worried about somethin' they wud come to us. That they wud at least consider our feelings and give us our due respect when it came to important matters in their lives. That they wud tell us the truth and not deliberately deceive us.' His eyes rose up and gazed directly into Rosaleen's face. 'But it seems that one of our daughters has betrayed the trust we put in her.'

'I don't know what you're talking about,' she said, giving Marie a glance.

'Where were you last Wednesday night?'

'With girlfriends.'

'What girlfriends?'

'The girls from work.'

'At Prichard's church?'

Arms folded tighter, head tilted back, chin slightly forward. '– yes, what of it?' she asked, the tip of her tongue licking her lipsticked upper lip.

Frank's head jutted slightly as he took half a step forward and said: 'I'll have no cheek here tonight.'

'We're concerned, Rosaleen,' said Eileen.

'About what?'

'Well, we heard –'

Frank couldn't stop himself, the words shot out '– that you were givin' a congregation of Protestants a lurid picture of what it was like t' be educated by nuns in a Catholic convent.'

Rosaleen looked over at Marie, who had moved around behind her father with her back to the Devon grate. Marie shook her head slowly, but she knew the information hadn't come from her. 'It wasn't a congregation,' she said.

'What was it, then?' he asked.

'People.'

'Forty? Fifty? Five hundred? Five thousand?'

'What does the number matter?'

'I told you about the cheek.'

She shrugged and spoke after a pause. '– twenty, thirty.'

'And you slagged your religion in front of them?'

'I told the truth.'

Frank's body seemed to be twisting into hard knots under his overcoat. 'Just because you can't get along with the nuns,' he said, 'just because you're a misfit and have t' leave a good education t' work in a Protestant factory – this gives you the right to slag a whole religion.'

'I didn't slag a whole religion.'

'What did you do?'

'I told the truth.'

Eileen, her eyes glassy, stared across the room at nothing in particular. 'They were using you, Rosaleen,' she said.

'No.'

Frank shook his head in disbelief as he spoke. 'And who orchestrated this – this show? No prizes for guessing the name of the holy Master Director.'

'There was no show. It was just a religious meeting where people were asked to volunteer to talk about their religion.'

'And you volunteered?'

'Yes.'

'Can't you see what they were doing?' said Eileen, spreading her hands wide. 'Why do you think you were invited?'

'Because I'm interested in religion. Because I'm not only interested in the narrow views of the Catholic Church.'

Marie closed her eyes and pressed two fingers against them as Frank leaped in to reply. 'What can you know about such things? The church is thousands of years old. There's scholars who have been studyin' holy books for years and years, and still they don't pretend to understand them. And you, not sixteen years of age, think you know enough t' get up on a pulpit t' preach against your faith.'

'I wasn't up on a pulpit,' said Rosaleen, her arms unfolding in a quick, thrusting movement. 'And I wasn't preachin' against my faith.'

'We have evidence.'

'What evidence?'

'A witness.'

'Who?' Her hands went into her waist, her elbows jutted. 'What did he say I did?'

Frank's body seemed to wilt under his overcoat. '– I never felt so ashamed,' he said.

'We were very hurt, Rosaleen,' said Eileen.

'What did he say?'

'He said you made a mockery of your religion.'

'I did not!'

'That you were under an evil spell.'

'That's ridiculous,' said Rosaleen, stamping her foot and nearly toppling over. Her hand gripped the edge of the wall at the foot of the stairs. 'I'm not going to stand here and listen to this.'

Frank moved forward, ready to thrust himself between Rosaleen and the stairs. 'You will,' he told her. 'You will stand here and listen to us. And you will stand here and listen to Father Wilson.'

'Father Wilson?' she asked in disbelief. Her eyes sought Marie behind her father.

'I'm against it, Rosaleen,' she said.

Frank shot Marie a hostile glance and moved his arm between Rosaleen and the stairs. 'Maybe you can tell him all the things you think are wrong with your religion,' he said. 'Maybe you can set the poor fool right?'

'Maybe I can,' she replied, brushing his arm away with her hand.

Frank twitched. His foot went across the first step. Rosaleen swivelled around and was just about to step over his leg when there was a soft knock on the front door. They froze.

'Now, I'm warning you,' said Frank, 'I want you to show the proper respect.'

Eileen got up as she spoke. 'Rosaleen, we all want to help. If there's something wrong. If you're worried about something, we can all talk about it and discuss it like a family.'

Caught between her mother and Frank, whose full body was now blocking the stairs, Rosaleen went over and stood on the other side of the Devon grate from Marie. Another soft knock came from outside, this time closer. 'Why him!' snapped Rosaleen. 'Why did you send for him?'

'Because …' Eileen faltered.

'Because we need him,' said Frank. He twisted the door handle, opened the door a few inches, nodded and then slipped through pulling it gently behind him.

'Is she there, Frank?' asked a priest wearing a black suit and dog collar.

'– yes.'

Father Wilson, a stocky man in his mid-forties, had a bald high forehead and a creased face. His eyes appeared glassy as he screwed them up behind horn-rimmed spectacles, rubbed his hands together and stared off down the street. He obviously wasn't relishing the task ahead and Frank sensed this, as he stepped out of the hall to join him.

'I think it might be better if I see her alone,' said the priest in a low voice.

'Now?'

'The sooner the better.'

'Fine. We can go down the street to Eileen's cousin.'

'I won't be long. I just think there are some things that should be got across to her. As soon as possible.'

'Of course, Father.'

Frank turned and led Father Wilson into the living room. The priest smiled and nodded to Eileen and the girls. Marie's face was solemn. Rosaleen bit her lower lip and stared at the floor.

'Have a seat, Father,' said Eileen. 'Would you like a cup of tea?'

'No, no, thanks – it's too late.'

Frank dug his hands deeply into his pockets, saying, 'He just wants a few words with Rosaleen. Alone.'

'Is it any trouble?' asked Father Wilson.

'No, no, no,' said Frank apologetically. 'We can go down to Ann's.'

Eileen and Frank moved to the door and turned to face Marie, who was trying to catch her sister's eyes. 'Will I stay?' she asked Rosaleen.

'No.'

'You're sure?'

Rosaleen replied with a curt nod. Marie joined her parents and they went out, closing the door behind them.

After a few moments, Father Wilson spoke. 'Your parents are worried,' he said, taking off his glasses and giving the lenses a rub with his handkerchief.

Rosaleen thought his grey unfocused eyes looked sinister.

'We're all worried. Do you know that?'

'No.'

'Well, we are,' he said, putting his glasses back on. 'You see, we realise the danger. We know how they work.'

'Who?'

'Prichard. And his cohorts. We've studied their techniques.'

'What techniques?'

'The methods. The methods they used to ensnare.'

'Father Wilson, I'm not a rabbit.'

His eyes gave off a momentary flash of anger. His mouth opened slightly, then closed as he rubbed his hands softly together and continued. 'You're an intelligent girl. But intelligence isn't everything. There are higher things in life than intelligence – there's the means by which we can glimpse the mystery at the heart of life through our faith. And faith lies beyond intelligence, beyond reason.'

'I know what faith is.'

'Do you? Do you really understand the true meaning of the faith you've been brought up in?'

'No.'

'Of course you don't. You can't. You're too young. Your mind's too immature. You're confused.'

'I'm not confused about everything.'

'But you are confused about important things.'

'No.'

'I'm afraid I have to contradict you, Rosaleen. Reports

reached me. Accurate reports by a first-hand eyewitness of you misrepresenting your faith to a crowd of –'

'I misrepresented nothing.'

Again his eyes flashed anger and his lips trembled slightly as he spoke. 'I beg to contradict – '

'I told the truth about my experience with the nuns in the convent. And every word of it was the truth.'

He flattened his lips and pulled a face. 'Really?' he challenged.

'Every word, every syllable, every comma and every full stop.'

'You must have a remarkable memory.'

'There are some things I never forget.'

'Everyone who goes to school has unfortunate experiences. Do you think you can damn a whole religion for one or two minor misdemeanours by a couple of neurotic nuns?'

'I did not damn any religion.'

'I have on report in my files, verbatim, every word that came out of your mouth at that meeting.'

'Well, if the words in your files say that I damned my religion – then all I can say is that the words were taken down by a damned liar.'

The colour bleached from his face. His hands, hanging limp at his sides, trembled. 'That's enough of that oul talk,' he said, his Belfast accent now becoming thick. 'Your father warned me about your cheek.'

'Did he?'

'And it won't wash with me. Here are the facts: you attended a meeting in a Protestant church organised by enemies of the Catholic religion and you have been most wilfully used by evil people to attack and undermine the tenets of your most holy faith.'

'I never –'

'Enough!' he cried, raising the palm of his right hand. 'Just remember, Rosaleen – you are a mere girl of fifteen years. Your parents are your sole guardians under the law of this land and you have distressed them deeply.'

'If I did, it was not deliberate.'

'Whether it was deliberate or not, you have done them a most wilful wrong. How would you feel if your own daughter walked off and joined a sect that attacked your own religion as if it was an anti-Christ?'

'I have joined no sect.'

'Do you realise the distress? The utter distress you have caused them?'

'No, I don't.'

'Well, you have. If you had been with them earlier in the evening when I told them the facts – I have never seen such desolation. It was worse, much worse than if I had told them … you were pregnant.'

'I did not want to hurt my Mammy and Daddy.'

'I have witnessed their devastation. You can take my word for it.'

'All right.'

'All right what?'

'I'll take your word for it.'

Father Wilson tilted his head and gave her a quizzical look. His eyes and face softened slightly as he spoke. 'Are we finally getting somewhere? Are we?'

'I'm sorry that I hurt my parents.'

'Good. Repentance is the first step. We're not too late. We can repair the damage.'

'What damage?' she asked, narrowing her eyes slightly.

'The damage to your parents, the Church and above all – to your immortal soul. Can I not get it through to you just how serious this is? You have come within a hair's breadth of excommunication. Do you know what that means? Do you know the significance of that? Banishment. Complete and utter banishment from the sacraments, the body of the church and probably your family. Do you want that?'

'No.'

'Well, they are the possible consequences of your actions.'

'What actions?'

'Surely you're not trying to deny what you have said and done?'

'No, I don't deny it. You have what I said on paper. I can't deny it.'

'Good. That is the first step. To admit your guilt. Now I want you to promise me that you will never again go into that particular occasion of sin.'

Her lips parted slightly, her eyes were puzzled. 'What –?'

'Prichard's church. His meetings.'

'– I can't promise that,' she said with a slow shake of the head.

Behind the glasses, his eyes blinked. 'You can't what?' he asked.

'– I enjoy them. I go with the girls from work. They're part of my social life.'

His hand clasped his forehead. 'Part of your social life?' he stammered. 'His anti-Catholic ravings are part of your social life?'

'It's not true he raves against Catholics,' she said.

'I know what goes on at his meetings,' said Father Wilson, his temper fighting the words. 'His newspapers publish the same muck. How anyone could go there and listen –?'

'He loves the Bible. He loves its truth. He loves the words of Our Lord. He fears what the Catholic Church is doing to the word of Our Lord. He wants Christ to speak directly to the people through the Bible; not through the Catholic Church.'

Something snapped in Father Wilson. His face collapsed, his lips crumpled and he stared into her face. 'I can see, Rosaleen,' he said, 'that damage has been done.'

'What damage?'

'I must ask you to promise me that you will not go to that church again. That you must not see Dr Prichard. That you must not go to these meetings.'

'I can't.'

'You mean you won't give me your voluntary promise?'

'No, I can't.'

'Then you leave us no option. You will be forbidden to attend.'

'No!'

'I know the stage you're at. They'll work on you until you won't want to have anything to do with your family or church. And you'll be lost, lost forever. Never to see your father, mother, sister again. Is that what you want?'

Rosaleen shook her head. 'No, you don't understand,' she said.

'That's exactly how it will be.'

'I will always be close to my family, especially Marie.'

'I know how they work – it's like a drug. You're at the beginning now and don't realise what's happening to you –'

'I will always love my family.'

'When they have you… when they know you're theirs…when the drug has taken its full effect – they will give you a new family.'

'No –'

'And you will be lost.'

'No, no, no.' she said, 'that can't happen.'

'It will,' said Father Wilson, a soft sadness coming into his voice. 'Believe me, Rosaleen. You may think I'm an old inflexible parish priest, but I have seen these things happen – I know the power and the effect it can have on young minds.'

Rosaleen stared beyond Father Wilson. To the jagged glass prisms and reflecting light patterns of the hall door. She didn't feel anger at him now. He was wrong. Her world had always been in this room, this house, her mother, father and sister. What he was suggesting was unthinkable. 'We will always be close. My Mammy, my Daddy and Marie,' she said.

'Not if it happens –'

'What?'

'Why do you think I'm being so hard on you? I want to save you. I want to save you – for your Mammy and Daddy and your sister.'

Rosaleen looked around the room. The family pictures on the wall, the gramophone, the settee. Father Wilson was an important man. He was pleading with her. This was her world, the world she had known most of her life. Her other world was across the bridge. Sometimes it seemed that that was where she wanted to be – but only sometimes. And she loved that too. 'Why can't I keep my new friends?' she asked.

'They're trying to take you away from your family and church.'

'No.'

'They are! Believe me, Rosaleen, that is what they're trying to do.'

'I can't have both?'

'No. It's not possible. That's why I'm here. Tonight.'

'Then –'

'We want what's best for you.'

He watched Rosaleen's face, his eyes apprehensive and expectant. She rubbed the wet palms of her hands tightly together. In the silence, her troubled eyes flicked around the room as if she was hardly aware of his presence. 'I can't just ignore them,' she said finally.

For the first time the tension began to ease in Father Wilson's face – his expression less crushed, the colour returning. 'No,' he said.

'I must say goodbye.'

'To who?'

'My new friends.'

'I think we can be fairly flexible about that, Rosaleen,' he said, taking off his glasses and giving them a wipe. 'Just remember – all this is for your own good. It's how we – the church, your family – express our love. We don't want to lose you.'

'I understand.'

'I'm glad we had this talk,' he said, rubbing his hands together. 'I'll tell Frank and your mother that we had our talk – ' and then, more hesitantly, ' – and that we reached a satisfactory agreement. Will I tell them that?'

'Yes.'

He smiled, gave a quick nod of the head and went out the door. Rosaleen didn't move. She had been put under pressure. Had agreed something. And she would try to do what she had agreed. She had to do something to keep the whole thing from exploding. She hadn't planned what had happened these past few months. Nor did she want an disaster. In a few moments, her parents and sister would be back and they would all try to be nice to each other. But she wasn't happy. Her world, everything she had known since she was a baby, was too important to her now to even think of blowing it up. And that was what she had stopped. That, at least, was something to be thankful for.

Chapter 9

The almost full summer warmth of the sun made the top of the bus like a hothouse and Rosaleen sweated under her trench coat. Her face was pale, her eyes sad. The crossing of the bridge had been a familiar route these past few months. When the solid red-brick outline of Ravenmount church came into view, she stood up, clutching a large brown envelope, and made her way down the stairs.

The airy grounds with the neat, trimmed lawns and bushes were a welcome contrast to the grey, dusty Falls. The doors of the church were open. Inside, a few men in overalls were working on the scaffolding – the same scaffolding where people had crammed on that first night to hear Dr Prichard speak.

'Rosaleen!' the familiar voice boomed out from the body of the church.

Some yards beyond the workmen, his head bobbed up from a pew. Dr Prichard in his dog collar, black vest, and shirt sleeves rolled up, was bent over double. A shockwave of black hair dangled over one eye. 'The return of the prodigal daughter,' he said, hardly looking up.

She smiled and went up the centre aisle very slowly. His eyes were concentrated on a brown leather box. Turning a silver knob very slowly, he said, 'This is a new contraption for measuring sound. You see, you can arrange things to eliminate microphones altogether.'

'I don't think you need any amplifying,' she said.

He half-closed his eyes as he peered down at a white dial. 'I don't know whether that's a compliment or insult.'

'It's a compliment.'

'Thank you, kind lady. And can I return the compliment and say how lovely you're looking on this glorious spring day?'

She knew she didn't look lovely. But she held her tongue.

'Where have you been?' he asked pseudo-sharply with an upward glance.

'Nowhere.'

'That's the kind of answer that covers a multitude of places. And sins.'

'I wasn't –'

'I'm only joking,' he said, standing up and putting his arm around her shoulders. 'We missed you. A lot of people were asking for you.'

'I haven't … I haven't been …' she faltered.

'Were you ill?'

She hesitated.

'Hilary said you haven't been to work,' he said quietly. 'Were you not feeling well?'

The tears welled up in her eyes, her lips compressed, her head dropped. The echoing metal clatter from the workmen suddenly stopped. She thought she was the object of their attention, that they were laughing at her.

'Com' on, love,' he said, giving her shoulder a soft squeeze. 'Let's go into the sanctuary. Away from all this babble.'

They walked over to the corner, down the short corridor and into his office. The model church had been moved and placed on the floor along the back wall. The desk was covered in sheets of paper with longhand writing. 'You've caught me in the middle of my scribblin',' he said, gathering the sheets together and stacking them into a pile at the corner of the desk. 'You'll have a cup of tea? McCreadie's? No tea-bags. The real thing.'

She nodded and sat down on the chair in front of the desk. He switched on the kettle, arranged the cups and saucers on the tray and tore open a packet of biscuits. 'Chocolate bickies?' he asked temptingly, with a smile.

She smiled back. He squeezed them out onto a large plate and said, 'Have as many as you like. There's a full box in the pantry. One of our members is in a strategic position in a biscuit factory.'

She smiled again.

'Take them,' he urged.

She lifted a biscuit and started eating it. The kettle boiled quickly. He warmed the pot, put in three spoonfuls of tea, left it on the tray to draw, and popped a dark chocolate biscuit into his mouth. 'Sinful, aren't they?' he said, his cheeks going hollow with the sucking and chewing.

'This is for Daniel,' she said, placing the large brown envelope on the desk.

'He was asking for you.'

'The photocopies.'

'He missed you. We all missed you. Your contribution to our debates.'

'I … I can't come any more,' said Rosaleen.

Dr Prichard stopped chewing. Then, after a pause, he finished the biscuit quickly, joined his hands together and leaned over the desk. 'Why?' he asked.

'It's just … I can't … I promised my Mammy and Daddy.'

'They forbade you?'

'– yes.'

He shook his head slowly and closed his eyes. 'We meet so much misunderstanding,' he said. 'It doesn't surprise me. Not their fault or yours –'

'It's not my decision,' she said, and noticing that the chocolate was spreading over her hands, she put the biscuit back on the plate.

'No. Of course not.'

'I love coming.'

'Do you?' he asked, smiling and looking directly at her.

'– yes. I do.'

'And you're a good girl.'

'I don't know about that,' she said, casting her eyes downwards.

'You are. And you're very brave. It takes a lot of courage for a Catholic girl to come here.'

'I love it.'

'It's a pity.'

'I'll really miss your sermons.'

'Just scribbles,' he said, waving his hand at the pile of sheets on his desk. 'You hope that all those pages will yield up something worthy of fifteen minutes attention.'

'Your sermons are brilliant.'

'No.' He coughed and a light blush came to his cheeks. 'Sometimes they're adequate. Mostly –'

'These last few months have been the happiest of my life.'

'Really?'

'I mean it.'

'Well we feel … we feel privileged to have …' his voice trailed off. He stood up awkwardly and poured two cups of tea. When he had milked and sugared them, he slumped down in his chair and said, 'Well, let's look on the positive side – you've had a few months coming here. It gave you a chance to examine our horns. In detail.'

'Father Wilson came –'

Immediately the colour left his face and his features were cast in stone. He jerked in the chair, his eyes bored into the shiny surface of the desk, his fingers joined together and coiled around each other. 'I see,' he said, 'the heavy artillery.'

'He came around to the house. And we talked. You see – there was someone. At one of the meetings.'

'A spy.'

'He knew everything. But that didn't matter. To me. I never told any lies.'

'I know that, Rosaleen.'

'I didn't mean anybody any harm. I didn't feel I was doing wrong. I wasn't trying to split up or attack anything.'

Standing up abruptly, the chair shot back. 'Rosaleen,' he said seriously, 'in the few months you've been coming here we know you as a girl of the highest principle. What did Father Wilson say?'

'He … he …'

'I can guess.'

'He told me that I might –'

'– go on –'

'That I might lose my family.'

Dr Prichard moved around the side of the desk and towards the door. A hammer banging a metal pole could be heard from inside the church. His hands, down by his side, were clenched. 'Is that how you feel about us?' he asked, without turning around. 'That we're trying to lure you away?'

'No –'

He turned, came back, pressed his hands against the surface of the desk and looked directly into her eyes. She shrank back a little. His grey eyes had the same look she'd seen on a few occasions in the pulpit. 'What kind of man would put that sort of thing into a young girl's head? Lies … falsehoods … fear … hate …'

'I honestly feel –'

'What?'

'– that he is genuinely concerned.'

Dr Prichard gave a sudden laugh and stared into the desk. 'I would like to believe that,' he said. 'Unfortunately, past experiences teach me differently. He's in the grip of the terrible power of the Roman Catholic Church.'

Rosaleen caught his eyes as they glanced up, and she shivered. There was something in the way he spoke that went beyond language and meaning – a profound all-embracing certitude in his vision. And she herself? Did she not have all those same self-professed doubts about that organisation. 'It's not simple,' she said.

'No, you're wrong, Rosaleen. The truth is simple. The devil complicates the truth. For his own ends.'

She opened her mouth to speak but nothing came out.

'He's using you. And your family. I've seen it before.'

'I don't see –'

'I'll tell you what I see, Rosaleen. I see us losing you. All of us – me, Daniel, Ann, Hilary – we all hold you in the highest esteem. You're a remarkable girl.'

'Me?'

'Yes, you.'

'No –'

'We don't want to lose you. We don't want to give up what we've experienced these past few months. We want it to continue. But, if your parents –'

'They –'

'You must … we will miss you,' he said, taking both her hands and pulling her up.

There was a knock at the door and it opened. Daniel, dressed in denims and a bright blue shirt with his sleeves rolled up, opened the door wide. With his golden skin and brown leather shoes, he reminded her of a cowboy.

'Hey, where've you been?' he asked, beaming a broad sunshine smile. It went immediately when he saw her face.

'Here's your photocopies,' said Dr Prichard, briskly lifting the envelope and handing it over. 'She's been slaving away on your rotten photocopies.'

'You haven't?'

'I meant to bring them,' she said, flapping her hands and finally putting them into the pockets of her trench coat.

'There was no hurry. Really –' he said softly.

'I had them done ages ago. It was just –'

There was an awkward pause, finally broken by Dr Prichard. 'She's had some difficulties, Daniel. And we've had a talk.' He put his arm around her shoulders and they moved towards the doorway. 'Will you give her a lift?' he asked, placing the car keys into Daniel's hand.

'The bus is fine,' protested Rosaleen.

'No!' exclaimed Dr Prichard, holding up the palm of his hand. 'We look after family members.'

'What about the new chairs?' asked Daniel.

'Don't bother about them now. Take Rosaleen off and see a few sights. Your time's short enough, Daniel. You might as well see a bit of the place.'

'Thanks.'

Daniel led the way through the corridor and up the centre aisle of the church, followed by Rosaleen and Dr Prichard, still with his arm around her shoulders. The workmen were taking a break and the church was almost silent.

'We may not be seeing Rosaleen again,' said Dr Prichard.

Daniel shot her a piercing glance. She looked down, her face crimson. 'You're not coming?' he asked.

'It's not her fault. But! Who knows what the good Lord has in store for us? Maybe it was all that work you were giving her, Daniel.'

'No!' exclaimed Rosaleen.

Daniel gave an inscrutable grin. His metal heels crunched the hard tiles and his long lazy strides kept him well ahead up to the church steps.

'Tell your parents I was asking for them. And they're welcome to visit us anytime they like. Cream buns and tea guaranteed,' said Dr Prichard with a smile.

She hurried down the steps. Daniel waited for her to pass, shrugged and went after her. 'No need to hurry back, Daniel,' they heard Dr Prichard call out behind them.

Rosaleen kept her head down until she came to the mauve Morris Minor. When she looked up, Dr Prichard was waving from the top of the steps. She waved back. Daniel opened the passenger door and she slid in. The carpets were spotless, all the surfaces gleamed. A strong smell of polish. No ornaments.

Daniel, his large frame squeezing into the driving seat, hunched his shoulders over the wheel. His lips puckered and he said, 'Are you in a hurry?'

She shook her head.

'There's a nice river walk not too far from here. Would you like that?'

'Okay.'

He started the car. The engine purred. He stomped on the pedals, got their feel, and moved out onto the road. The traffic was light, the bridge empty, and even the gasworks tanks looked clean under the bright sunlight as they swung west. No conversation passed between them until they reached Shaw's bridge, beyond the city limits. 'Will this do?' he asked.

She nodded and got out. Her shoes were the sensible low heels she'd worn to work. Conscious that they made her legs look heavy, she buttoned the lower part of her coat and waited. Compared to her, he seemed lightly dressed. 'Are you not cold?' she asked.

'No, I've been workin' all mornin'.'

'Still, if the sun goes in.'

'Don't worry.'

They went through the wooden gate and along the towpath. The river was high and brown from the previous day's rain. To their right, green banks rose up to a large stately house. Across the river, dense thickets of trees ran along the bank. 'This really is the country,' she said.

'Yeah, it's pretty.'

They went around a series of bends where bud-laden branches drooped over the towpath, then came to open fields.

Horses came near and snorted behind thin bushes. An abandoned mill and waterwheel across the river, this side a putting green. And birdsong everywhere. They continued to a split in the river and crossed a narrow wooden bridge to the island in the middle. Following the sound of fast water, they reached a small waterfall.

'Are there places like this where you come from?' she asked.

'Sure,' he said, nodding slowly. 'Different. But some are even prettier.'

'That's hard to imagine.'

'Yeah, it is.'

They sat down on a dead tree trunk and watched the brown water boil at the foot of the falls.

'Is it true?' he asked.

'What?'

'What Dr Prichard said.'

She gazed at the river. Its force bent and flattened the reeds and bushes. She hadn't been this close to it before. Passing over the bridge it had merely meandered below. Now it had real force.

'What would you do if your parents told you not to go to a particular church?' she asked.

He shrugged.

'What would you do?'

'It hasn't happened.'

'But what would you do?'

'Well – I guess it would depend –'

'On what?'

'– how I felt about that particular church. If I thought it was a living church. True to the word of Our Lord and Saviour, Jesus Christ.'

'Suppose you felt all that.'

'Yeah.'

'And they still said you couldn't go.'

'Well, they couldn't, could they?'

'Why not?'

'I'm twenty.'

She smiled. 'So I have to wait till I'm twenty.'

'– no.'

'How long?'

'I don't know. Anyway, they shouldn't.'

'What?'

'Stop you going.'

She said nothing for a short time. 'Well, I promised.'

'They don't know how … how good … if they came they would see what a true man of God he really is. You know that, Rosaleen.'

'I'll miss you.'

Daniel got up, walked a few strides away and turned. 'I know … it's difficult,' he said. 'They're your parents. And I understand … but we can … I … I would like to keep in touch … with you. Would … will you?'

'Yeah,' she said brightly, 'I would like that.'

'You won't be fifteen for … that long. Who knows what will happen? But we can promise to keep in touch, can't we? They can't stop you from doing that. That's not against the Catholic religion … as far as I know …'

'I don't care.'

'I'll write to you.'

'Will you?'

'Promise. Word of honour.'

'I'd like that.'

He paused and said, 'Want to go further up the river?'

They went over the narrow bridge, continued further up the river for a quarter of an hour, and then turned back. Daniel walked alongside her, his arms gently swinging. When he spoke, he turned his head and looked at her face – it reminded her that Eddie's eyes were always drifting down to her chest.

She would have liked Daniel to hold her hand, but it wasn't important. She felt that he wanted to touch her – and she liked that, even though he didn't. There was something about Eddie's predictable, mechanical compulsion to grab her that was not nice, and boring. Restraint could be nice. And sexy.

Back at the car he jangled the keys in his hand. 'Suppose we went to a movie?' he asked.

'– well?'

'If I go back early he'll give me all kinds of chores.'

She smiled.

'I'd prefer to go to a movie with you.'

'Which one?'

They had fish and chips in a café opposite the Ritz. Outside, workers were hurrying home. She sipped tea. The smell of vinegar. Steam clouding the windows. The way he hunched over the table – anxious, she felt sure, that this might be the last time he'd see her. The sound of the Everly Brothers singing All I Have To Do Is Dream on the juke box in the corner. It was all so lovely and sad, she thought.

In the almost empty cinema, they sat near the middle. A romantic technicolour film, Doris Day, a handsome leading man, sleigh rides by moonlight. She took off her trench coat. Underneath, she wore the cream blouse with the ruffled neck and the pleated grey skirt. Her arm lay beside his. Occasionally their shoulders touched. Caught up in the humour, love and froth, she identified with Doris Day. She was so beautiful, fresh-faced, American – like Daniel. Compared to America, Ireland was grey and dreary.

Darkness and a light fog had come down on the city when they came out. A man walked by, his coat collar turned up, a cloth cap flat on his head, a bronchial cough: he became absorbed in the mist. As she crossed the road, the yellow lights looming out of the fog, she had the sinking feeling that the colour was draining out of her life. The America of Doris Day had technicolour, her world had various shades of grey, with the exception of what she was being forced to give up.

'Is America really like that?' she asked, getting into the car.

'Some of it. Though we never have snow in the winter. Up north it's like that.'

'And the rest of it? The houses?'

'The houses pretty much … Logran, where I live, has houses like that.'

He switched on the inside light and examined the control board. She looked across at his face. So smooth and open. The eyes clear and blue. Like an American prairie sky, she imagined.

'Maybe you could come out sometime. In the future.'

'Yeah.'

'For a holiday. You might like it.' He paused. 'Which way is home?' he asked, starting the engine.

She directed him up the Grosvenor Road, a shortcut to the Falls. Off, to the right and left, the houses squatted in the fog and belched out smoke. Today was a dream. Another world. But she had made a promise to her parents. And she would stick to it. For the moment.

'Stop here,' she said, a short distance from the top of her street.

The car slowed down, drew into the kerb and stopped. The engine kept running. 'Will I walk you to your house?' he asked.

'No. I'll get out here. How long will it be before you go back home?'

'A few weeks.'

'Will you write?'

'Sure.'

'Promise?'

'Word of honour.'

'You have my address?'

'In my notebook.'

'What is it?'

'Fourteen Ivy Drive.'

'Tell me about everything. Hilary, Dr Prichard – everything.'

'Sure. And will you write back?'

'Course!'

She got out quickly and ran down the street. Behind her she heard the car rev and move off. When she came close to her house, she stopped running and walked slowly. The lights shone dimly out of the windows. She had spent a lot of time there lately. It was her prison. She opened the door and went in.

Her father looked over from reading the paper at the fireside. Eileen, her glasses down on her nose, sat at the table, holding a pencil over a soft paper dress pattern. Without a word, Rosaleen went straight through to the kitchen and filled a glass with water.

Frank looked across at Eileen. She let the pencil fall from her fingers, pursed her lips and gave him a hard stare. His fingers crackled the edges of the paper; his eyes bored into the middle of the sheet.

A few seconds later Rosaleen came out and went up the stairs.

Eileen lifted the pencil and looked up at Frank. He crackled the paper louder, saying, 'How long is this gonna go on for?'

Eileen didn't reply. She traced a line over the surface of the paper.

'Do you know where she was?'

'There's been enough rows, Frank. I think it's better that we just let it lie.'

'She's ignoring us. As if we weren't here.'

'What do you suggest?'

Frank stuck the newspaper into his lap. 'We should at least know where she's goin',' he said.

'Do you want to go up and ask her?'

He lifted the paper and plunged it down between the chair and the wall. 'If we let her get away with this – there'll be worse trouble.'

'What do you suggest doing?'

'I don't know,' said Frank, scratching the back of his ear. 'I would've thought women would know how to talk to each other.'

'So it's my fault.'

'I didn't say that.'

'You can't make people talk. Not if they don't want to.'

'Where does she get money?'

'Marie.'

'She talks to Marie, doesn't she?'

'Yeah.'

He took his pipe off the mantelpiece, packed it with tobacco and lit it. 'What are we supposed t' do then?' he asked with a shrug.

'Nothin'.'

'Just wait?'

'Unless you can think of somethin' better.'

His eyes went down to the flickering yellow flames of the fire. Gas hissed up the chimney. 'We don't know what she's doing, do we? And that's not right, is it?'

'No, it's not,' said Eileen, slowly drawing a long line on the paper in front of her. 'And you still haven't told me what you're going to do about it.'

Chapter 10

The weather hadn't changed in two weeks. It was still bright and warm, with the early summer flowers bursting out of their buds. Rosaleen sat on the top deck of the bus, where she could see everything. The grounds of St Dominic's school, the Children's Hospital. Her brand new cotton dress – pale yellow, speckled with small violet flowers – felt fresh and cool against her skin. Marie had bought it for her, barely two hours ago.

You need something to cheer you up, she said. And she did, having spent the morning in the dole queue in Corporation Street. The jobs on offer were boring and badly paid. But that wasn't really what was getting her down. Marie was good to her, very good. She knew instinctively how she felt. It was nearly two weeks since Daniel had promised to write.

Each morning she listened for the familiar patter of the postman, the single flip and flop of the letterbox lid. A stupid bill or advertisement – it was the same this morning. A letter dropped. Down she came in her bare feet – nothing on the Devon grate, a rumble in the kitchen. A peek around the edge to make sure it hadn't been left anywhere else.

She now supposed he must have promised to write because it was too awkward to say anything else. Carrying her grey, pleated skirt and white blouse in the plastic bag, she struggled down the stairs of the bus. Her stilettos caught on the last step. She wobbled onto the pavement, straightened up and sauntered towards the top of Ivy Drive. Image was important, she decided, and she wasn't in a hurry.

As she turned the corner, she saw Eddie dressed in his blue Italian suit at the entry. Instinct propelled her towards the shop doorway. Too late, he'd seen her. Instantly, she was sorry that he might have seen her make the move. Wearing his good suit, one hand dug into his pocket, the other raising a cigarette to his lips – he cut a forlorn figure. She walked towards him and managed to smile.

He flung his cigarette end on the ground and squashed it with the sole of his shoe. 'Where've ya been?' he asked, his eyes fixed on the ground.

'Nowhere.'

He continued to squeeze the last spark out of the cigarette end.

'How come yer never in?'

'I'm busy.'

His eyes came up. 'Doin' what?'

'– lots of things.'

'Like –?'

'I don't have t' tell you what I'm doin'. Ya don't own me.'

He looked down, circled around the cigarette end, and said, 'I thought we were doin' a line.'

'Well –'

His eyes flashed up, in anger. 'Are ya seein' somebody?'

She gripped the plastic bag tight, the blood warmed her face. 'I don't think –'

'If ya are – come right out an' say it. Straight t' m' face. Don't be sneakin' behind m' back.'

She felt the blood was shooting to the top of her head. 'I'm not sneakin' behind anybody's back.'

'Who is it? Have ya met somebody at one of them meetins? Is that why yer never in when I call?'

His eyes were hard beads. She felt his aggression.

'No,' she replied.

'I don't believe ya.'

'Eddie, the last night we were out, I tried to –'

'What?'

'Tell you.'

'Ya never mentioned anybody. I remember. I remember everything. Every detail. Do ya think I'd be here – who is it? It's some guy, isn't it? Some eejit that holds yer hand at these loony meetins.'

'They're not –'

'That's where you met him.'

'Well, if that's what you –'

'That's it. Isn't it? That's the reason. Why didn't you tell me?'

'You never –'

'Give me a chance. No. Ya just ignore me.'

'I asked you to go to the meetings plenty of times.'

'But ya knew I'd refuse, didn't ya? Ya didn't let on there was somebody else.'

'I never –'

'Do ya think I'd have let ya go on yer own if I knew there was somebody else? You lied to me.'

'I didn't.'

'You told me you went with a bunch of women.'

'Yeah!'

'Where did ya pick him up? What kinda meetins are they? Do yas play musical Bibles?'

'Eddie!'

'You never really wanted me to go.'

'I did. I thought you would benefit. Spiritually.'

Eddie's head jutted out from the collar of his suit, he screwed up his face in a wrinkled mass of incredulity. 'Spiritually?' he spat out, before turning away in disgust.

'That's all.'

'So yer dead worried about my immortal soul?'

'Well –'

'An' ya cudn't give a shit about the rest of me.'

'That's not true.'

'Isn't it? Do ya know how many times I've been up t' yer door the past weeks? Standin' here like a tube. An' never once did ya even come out.'

She looked at him in silence.

'You cudn't give a shit whether I lived or died,' he said.

'Look, Eddie, I haven't been deliberately avoiding you. I've been very busy. And I've had a lot on my mind.'

'Like what?'

'Personal things.'

'I know what ya have on yer mind. Some Bible-thumpin' nancy boy!'

'I'm goin' in,' she said sharply, swinging away from him.

He caught her arm. 'No, wait, Rosaleen. Please – I didn't mean it.'

'I don't like that kind of talk.'

'Luk, tell me this – true-bill. No messin'. Is there someone?'

She let his eyes catch hers, then she looked away. His mouth hung open, his eyes roved over her face. 'There is someone, isn't there?' he asked.

'No,' she said, shaking her head. 'There's no one.'

'You're sure?'

She nodded.

'Okay. Okay then. I'll go.'

'Where?'

'The meetins. You get me a Bible an' I'll go. And don't make it a big one – I want one that'll fit inside m' pocket. I don't want people laughin' at me.'

'It's not that simple.'

'What do ya mean it's not that simple? Aren't ya always sayin' how simple the Bible is? How any eejit cud understand it? Well, here I am – one ready, willing and able buck eejit – exactly what yer meetins are cryin' out for?'

'No –'

'Do ya think I'm too stupid t' understand?'

'No –'

'Well, what –?'

'You don't really want to go.'

'I do, honest.'

'You want to go for the wrong reasons.'

'I don't, honest – what reasons?'

'Eddie, I know what you think.'

'Well, Jesus, Rosaleen, you know more than I do.'

'Anyway, I may not be going –'

'Where?'

'To the meetings.'

'– does that mean ya'll have more time then? Ya'll be able to go out?'

'No.'

Eddie spread his hands wide and they jigged up and down to the beat of the words '– what? Tell me – what? – what? Is it –? Is it engaged you want? Do you want – will I get you a ring or somethin'?'

'No, Eddie, it's not –'

'What the hell do ya want me t' do? I'm hangin' aroun' here day an' night. I'll buy a dozen Bibles, I'll go t' any bloody meetins, I'll get ya an engagement ring – all I want ya t' do is tell me what you want.'

His hands flopped down along the sides of his jacket. She found it hard to speak and stole a quick glance at him. His misery reflected her own. One letter could have changed everything for her, just as going along with him could have erased his pain. But that would be dishonest. 'I don't want you to do anything, Eddie,' she said. 'It's not you. It's me.'

'Jesus –'

'I need time. To think. To be by myself.'

'Would you fancy a holiday in Portrush? I've saved a few bob an' I know a woman with a guesthouse. Everything straight. Nothin' out of order.'

'I would – if I could go by myself.'

'Yourself? Why do ya never think of us doin' things? Together.'

'You're older, Eddie. You're mature.'

For the first time the tension in his face began to ease. 'I suppose I am,' he said. 'I'll be a qualified baker next year.'

'You're ready for things that I'm ... not ready for.'

'You think so?'

'I'll have to mature. I'll have to grow up,' she said with a smile.

Eddie squeezed his lips together and rolled his head from side to side. 'If I were you,' he said, 'I wudn't take too long about it.'

'I'm not sixteen.'

His eyes flashed directly at the burgeoning bosom of her summer dress. 'You look more,' he said. 'A lot more.'

She blushed and hated herself for it. 'Well –'

'Will you see me next week?' he asked.

'Next week?'

'Yeah.'

She pressed her lips together. '– alright.'

His eyes drifted towards the pavement. 'What night?'

'Can we leave it loose?'

'Loose?' His eyes flashed up, accusing.

'Okay, what day?'

'Saturday, seven o'clock?'

'– alright.'

'Pictures?'

'Yeah.'

He broke into a smile and fumbled in his pocket for a cigarette. 'Good. That's good,' he said.

'I'll see ya,' she said, moving across the street.

He lit a cigarette and watched her. The shiny brown hair, the bright new dress, the lightly-tanned skin – even in the shade of the houses, she sparkled. When she reached the front door she turned and gave him a gentle wave.

She was sorry she had made the date. It would only prolong things. Stepping into the hall, she saw that the inside door was about two inches open. She silently pushed it wide and went in. Dragging, scraping noises came from upstairs, near the back of the house, their bedroom. She froze. Just as she was about to retreat, she noticed her father's tweed jacket behind the door, his green canvas bag hanging on the brass hook at the bottom of the stairs. A glance at the clock showed three o'clock – hours before he normally came home. She hurried up the stairs.

The light was on in their bedroom. The bed had been pulled out from the wall and two cardboard boxes tipped over. Dusty dolls and ornaments had been dumped on a chair. Dresses, tops, skirts were strewn over the dresser. At the back, just under the window, her father, bent down on his knees with his shirt sleeves rolled up, held open exercise books in his hands. He gave her a scalding glance and returned to the books.

Her mouth fell open. 'What's wrong?'

'Where were you?' he asked abruptly.

'Downtown.'

'Doin' what?'

'Corporation Street.'

'Anywhere after that?'

'The shops.'

'Who with?'

'Marie.'

'Marie?' he asked with a trace of sarcasm. 'We'll see when she comes in,' he said, standing up and throwing the exercise books on the floor.

'They're mine!' she shouted on her way over, picking up the soft-backed books.

163

He brushed past her.

'What are you doing in our room?'

He ignored her and looked over the stuff lying on the bed, the dresser, the chair, the floor.

'You have no right to be here,' she snapped. 'What are you looking for?'

He continued to ignore her. In an instant, she recognised and felt her dependent subservient state in a house where her privacy could be ignored at will. She stamped towards him. Her face was white. 'Do you hear me?'

His eyes locked onto hers. 'You tell me who you were seeing, and I'll tell you what I'm looking for,' he said.

He swung around, went through the doorway and stomped down the stairs. She looked around the room. She felt like smashing something. Why had he carried out this desecration of her room? Hadn't she stopped going to the meetings, left her job, gone down to the Corporation Street dole queue! She dashed down the stairs, almost toppling against the wall at the bottom.

He had gone into the kitchen. She went to the door. He poured water from the tap into the metal teapot.

'What were you doing up there?' she asked.

He stared at the teapot, turned off the water, put the lid on, moved it onto a ring and lit the gas with a match. The blue flames licked around the black bottom.

'What do you mean, who was I seeing?'

He said nothing.

'What you did up there. That's wrong. You know that. You're treating me and Marie with no respect.'

His cheeks went in, his stained upper teeth gnawed at his lower lip. 'Marie doesn't come into it,' he said.

'What were you after?'

She blocked the doorway. His eyes flicked at her as he spoke. 'You promised you wouldn't go near him again.'

'Who?'

'Prichard.'

'– I only – I had some photocopies. I left them back. That's all. Where's the harm in that?'

'Photocopies?'

'Yeah! I'd promised to get them done before –'

'Just photocopies?'

'Yeah.'

'And why would you need to go walking along the Lagan just to give back a few photocopies?'

He lifted the teapot, flung it into the sink, turned off the gas and stepped over to the doorway. She backed into the living room.

'Who've you been seein'? Who've you been cavortin' with? I want the truth. Is it Prichard?'

'No.'

'One of his kind?'

'I'm not answering –'

'– that doesn't surprise me. Not one bit. You've a lot to hide. If it's up in that room or anywhere else in this house I'll ferret it out. I'll expose your lies.'

'I'm not a liar.'

His eyes ran up and down the yellow dress. 'Is that what you wear when you go to see him? How many fifteen-year-old girls do you see out on that road dressed like that? No. That's not a schoolgirl's dress, is it? Does he ask you to dress like that? So that you look like a twenty-year-old tart?'

'Marie bought me this dress.'

'Does Marie know what ya've been up to? Takin' from her, takin' from everybody so that ya can flaunt yerself to – who is he? One of Prichard's cohorts?'

'Who are you talking about?'

'Do I have t' tell ya his name? I wondered why ya were coming down every mornin' for the post. How many more did ya get?'

'Did you take my letter and open it?'

'That man should be locked up behind bars. Interferin' with children!'

'Did you?' she asked, going towards him.

'I'll use any means I deem fit to protect my children against the likes of that.'

'Where is it?'

He looked away, then back.

'The letter. It's from Daniel, isn't it?'

'So.... you remember his name! What were you doing going off into the wilds of the country with one of Prichard's cohorts? What were yas up to? What were yas doin'?'

'You opened my letter?'

'It's my property. You're a minor. It's evidence. Evidence of his involvement with a minor. That letter will sink him and the rest of his mob.'

'Give me it.'

'Do you think I'm an eejit? Do ya? I'm keepin' it. And any others that you have hidden in your room.'

'Where is it?'

'When I think of it? The age of ya! Out cavortin' with one of his —'

She stepped over to the door and flicked back the lapel of his jacket. The pale blue tip of an envelope stuck up from the inside pocket. She plucked it out and read her name in neat, black fountain-pen writing just as her father dashed forward. He gripped her wrists, saliva spluttered from his mouth. 'This is how you repay us. Cavortin' aroun' the countryside with Prichard and his lieutenants. Throwin' yerself at them like some shameless trollop!'

He pushed her hard. She fell back against the settee cushions, bouncing to the side, grasping the letter. She rolled along the settee and stood up, just in front of the Devon grate. Yellow flames, from the loosely packed slack in the grate, slithered up the chimney. His arm and hand stretched forward like a poker. 'Give me it,' he said.

With both hands, she hid it behind her back. He lunged forward, his arms encircling, his hands wrenching hers apart. She let out a cry. The letter fell to the floor.

He snatched it up. 'Is this the dirt? The filth you want? Is it?' He spat on it and tore and twisted the envelope and pages, thrusting them towards the fire.

She dove down, grabbing the pieces as they fell, knocking against his body so that he twisted around. His right hand suddenly squeezed into a fist and clattered her ear. The force swung her body around, the inner arm of the armchair became a fulcrum, and her head smashed against the corner of the Devon grate. She gave out a sharp cry, then a dull groan seemed to come from her throat.

Frank froze. His daughter's legs slid over the armchair and lay contorted around each other, against the lower edge of the Devon grate. Between the groans, she sobbed. 'Rosaleen! Rosaleen!' he cried, pulling her legs and dress away from the flames of the fire.

The sobbing increased. He stood over her, his eyes wide in horror. He knelt down and leaned forward. Her hands crept up and felt the side of her face. Blood trickled from between the fingers. He pulled the chair back. 'Rosaleen!' he said, tugging at the dress to cover her legs.

She kicked out her foot, just missing his knee. 'Go away!'

He went into the kitchen. She struggled to her feet, holding both hands over the side of her face. He came back with a towel and held it towards her. She pushed it away, turning towards the mirror. There was a gash above the partially closed eye, and bruised swollen skin from the temple to the chin. 'Look what you've done,' she said.

He couldn't speak. A crooked vein in the middle of his forehead throbbed. His hands pawed the air, afraid to touch her. 'Rosaleen, I didn't mean –'

She stared down at the blood on her hands, then at his face. 'How could you do this to me?'

His fingers pressed gently into her shoulders. She swung away, catching him with her elbow against the ribs. He fell back against the Devon grate, the flames visible between his legs, his arms spread out. He was drained of venom and anger.

She knelt down and greedily grabbed the bits of pale blue paper into her hands and stood up.

His gaze was piteous. He seemed paralysed.

'You'll never get the chance to hit me again,' she said, turning and running out onto the street.

Her heels clattered. A woman wheeling a pram along the pavement pulled it back. Through the tears, the Falls Road was a jumble of colours. Behind her a thick, hateful voice was calling her name. A trolley bus pulled to a stop across the road. She ran, jumped on, climbed the stairs and sat on the first empty seat.

A small boy caught sight of her face. Staring, he tugged at his mother's sleeve. Rosaleen looked down at the bits of paper bunched in her left hand. Her right hand went up to touch her throbbing temple. Sticky blood was caked on the inside of her fingers. Behind, the jingle of coins, a cheerful conductor. She had no bag, no money. She had left the house with absolutely nothing.

She sprang up and pushed past the conductor. His snubbed cheerfulness. Glances at, then away. Off the bus. She had gone only two stops. Grey granite walls of St Dominic's, another school, another prison. Her head, face, eye ached. A holy show. Towards town. Few cars, no walkers except her mad self, in stilettos. What did she need? She needed a friend.

Chapter 11

The town was busy. Where the sun shone on the west side of the City Hall was busy too. People stretched on the grass and lounged on the seats. Rosaleen picked a quiet bench in the shadows of the east side, and sat down. Her head and face still ached and the field of vision in her right eye was narrowed to a slit. She was tired. And her toes felt squashed and sore. But her biggest worry was her appearance – the blood and the bruising.

She laid out the pale blue pieces of paper on the bench. There were smudges on the official church notepaper, but she could still read the writing:

Dear Rosaleen,

I'm sorry I haven't written sooner but the pace has been hectic here this last week. Anyway, I'm not a great writer and the few times I did sit down I got up again pretty quick. But here goes, good or bad. The first thing is – we all miss you – especially me. The good doctor teases me but I can tell he misses you too. Hilary, David and Ann were also asking after you. I don't know why they ask me – maybe they see me as your official protector. Though what my parents would make of that I wouldn't like to tell you – they weren't gone on me coming to Ireland. And the idea of me protecting anyone would be like just so much moonshine to them – my size doesn't matter – they still think I'm a kid.

When the time comes to go – a few weeks ahead – I will take with me some truly wonderful memories. Some from the church here in Ravenmount where I really did find my vocation – if I could preach the scripture with one hundredth of the divine spirit that Dr Prichard can put into his sermons – then that would be a true miracle. And he has also given me a lot of practical help. I used to just read from The Book – the Lord has given him the marvellous talent to arrange and express words (unlike this fool here). His power comes from the way he touches the essence of Jesus Christ through language – no one can use language better than the Irish – and he is a genius among geniuses.

The other thing we share, Rosaleen, is the feeling of family. This is hard to talk about, never mind write – it's more a warm glow when we're all together – usually in his house or the church. You know what I'm talking about, don't you, Rosaleen?

But probably the nicest memory I'll bring back to America with me was that day we went walking along the Lagan. There are just some days when everything seems right with the world and that was one of them. It was an awful pity we didn't have more – maybe, in the future, when things are better with your folks, we can. I will definitely be coming back for more!

There are many things I like about you. Your beauty, your charm, your spirituality, your courage – how's that for starters? Do you think I might be getting the hang of this writing game? Serious though, it may not be possible to meet up before I go home – but please write – give me something to take back with me. Have you got a new job? Hilary says there's still a place in Pattersons. How's your sister, Marie? Do you think your parents will ever let you come back to Ravenmount church? How do you yourself now feel? There's so much I want to know. Write soon.

Yours sincerely,
Daniel Upshaw.

A rush of warm feeling and sadness ran through her as she read. She read it again – some of the sentences three or four times. What a nice man, she thought, to have written something that would make her feel so good. Then suddenly, anger struck. The gnawing pain was evidence of the horrible scene. How, in the name of God, did that gentle letter produce such violence?

She saw on the ground next to her a small, crumpled, brown paper bag, slid the pieces of the letter together and put them inside. All around her, women and girls were adding a splash of colour to the grey of Belfast...young children in buggies... teenagers coming from school. School? That now seemed like a million miles away. Her path lay in another direction. But where exactly? Where would she go?

She started a process she'd been using lately to make decisions. You ruled out all the things you wouldn't do, all the places you wouldn't go to: home, her relations – they would only contact her parents, or worse, Father Wilson. She would only embarrass Marie if she turned up at her office – and she might try to persuade her to go home. Hilary would help – but there were too many people at Pattersons. Her old friends at school wouldn't understand. That left Ravenmount.

She got up, crossed the busy street and started walking towards the bridge. She kept the discoloured side of her face to the wall and was surprised how few people seemed to notice it. But all along the pavement, with each laboured step, her resolve diminished. Did she really want Daniel and Dr Prichard to see her like this? No, a thousand times no. A few days or a week in a dark cave. A cheap hostel, a room – anywhere would do. But she hadn't even the money to take a bus.

No more did she notice the fleeting technicolour of the city. Violent waves of feeling. Her feet ached, especially her toes, the sweat wetted every inch of her skin. All she wanted was a cool resting place. On the bridge, the late afternoon traffic was gathering pace. She considered hopping on a bus, then decided against it. How stupid she was to leave herself without any money whatsoever.

Heavy limbs dragged worn heels along the gravel path at the side of Ravenmount church. She climbed the steps and pushed against the main door. It was locked. She slumped down on the warm top step, closed her eyes and covered her face with her hands. It wasn't quite dark, but it did blot out the world.

A few minutes passed.

'Can I help you?'

The voice was friendly. She looked up. It was Jimmy, the caretaker, carrying a rake.

'I was looking for Dr Prichard or Daniel,' she said, keeping the right side of her face covered.

'They're in the office. Go through the side door. Do you know the way?'

'Yes, thanks,' she said, standing up.

He turned and headed towards freshly cut grass. She sighed. Her dress was no longer sparkling, cool and fresh. It was sticky, and all the walking seemed to have made it slip further down her chest – the type of slippage that gave the men in the gallery at St Paul's downward squints. Utterly unsuitable for Ravenmount church, where they had only seen her in grey pleats and a cream or white blouse. They had never seen a stilettoed, cleavage-flaunting Rosaleen with a battered face. She winced, pulled up the shoulders, tugged her dress at the back and went around to the side entrance.

Inside the church was cool and dark. The scaffolding along the sides had been removed, and tiered benches with cushions put in their place. All the walls were plain red brick, interspersed with wooden framed windows and beams. Not an image in sight. Yet, as Rosaleen clumped her way down the aisle, she felt a presence – a real feeling that she was in a spiritual place. The noise she was making seemed out of place.

She took off her shoes, felt the soothing coolness of the plain stone floor and went silently to the office door.

As she approached she slowed down. Behind the door there was an eruption of talk, then a sudden burst of Daniel's unmistakable laughter, followed by an oratorical stream from Dr Prichard – he was onto a humour lode, and when he struck that he mined it for all it was worth. The laughter increased. Rosaleen raised her hand to knock, then hesitated. She didn't really want to intrude, spoil their fun.

The door swept inwards, the side of Daniel's head came plunging out, she jumped back, turning sideways. A white smile beamed directly at her, then it collapsed. She kept her head down.

'Rosaleen,' he said softly.

'Who is it?' asked Dr Prichard from behind the door.

As it slowly swung open, she came into view. The smile left Dr Prichard's face. He shoved the book he was carrying into the nearest shelf and came to the door. His eyes flicked between Daniel and Rosaleen, his face was white. 'Come in,' he said.

She didn't move. Daniel's hands jerkily rubbed the sides of his dark trousers, he went from one foot to the other, his hard blue eyes staring.

'Come inside, Rosaleen,' said Dr Prichard. 'Come on in.'

She bit her lower lip, tears welled up in her eyes. Dr Prichard put his arm around her shoulders.

'Will you have something? Can we get you anything?' he asked.

She shook her head.

'You look warm. Get her a glass of water from the kitchen, Daniel.'

He shot through the door. Silently Dr Prichard pulled around a comfortable armchair, plumped two cushions on its seat and placed it behind her. Slowly she sank into it, her hands squeezing the paper bag on her lap.

'Don't say anything until you're ready. If you want to say anything at all. Okay?'

She nodded slowly.

'Have you been to hospital?'

She shook her head.

'You'll have to go.'

'Why?'

'Your eye. It's nearly closed. It'll have to be checked. Treated.'

Bustling footsteps came from the corridor. Daniel came in carrying a large tankard, the water spilling over the edge.

'Give me that,' said Dr Prichard, taking it from him and reaching for a small glass on the shelf. 'There's enough water in this for a horse.' He poured out a measure. 'Rosaleen is a young lady. In case you haven't noticed.'

Daniel stood back. In his black trousers and round collared shirt he looked more ministerial. His lips had become thin, the skin on his face taut and his eyes gazed on Rosaleen with an undisguised anger and concern.

She sipped the water. Daniel's gaze didn't waver. Dr Prichard plucked at his lower lip with his fingers and looked at the floor. After a couple of minutes, he said, 'Do you want to tell us what happened?'

Her eyes flitted between their faces. 'My Daddy did it,' she said.

Dr Prichard's fingers froze, a shudder spread through Daniel's limbs and he flapped his arms around each other.

'Why?' asked Dr Prichard.

'He saw a letter. From Daniel.'

Daniel's mouth fell open, he gulped in air. He turned around and a noise came from him that sounded like something between a growl and a groan.

'Sit down, Daniel,' said Dr Prichard calmly.

He sat on a seat behind him and closed his eyes.

The doctor chewed his lips and said nothing for a few moments, then he asked, 'Was there anything improper in the letter?'

She gazed at the floor and shook her head.

'No!' exclaimed Daniel. 'There was nothing. Absolutely nothing that could be construed by anyone who wasn't – I never – you have – have you the letter, Rosaleen? Let him see the letter.'

She began to open the crumpled brown paper bag.

'No,' said Dr Prichard, waving his hand. 'I know. I know Daniel. Anyway, no letter could justify that. I'm very sorry, Rosaleen, that we have brought this upon you.'

'It wasn't you. Or Daniel. It was me he was getting at.'

'For coming here?' asked Dr Prichard.

'He told me to stop coming. I haven't been. It was me. Me he was getting at. The letter was an excuse.'

'How could anyone,' said Daniel, spreading his hands. 'I asked about you. I wanted to know how you were getting on. Where's the …'

Dr Prichard leaned forward and took her hand. 'What do you want to do? Now?' he asked.

'I don't know.'

'We have to take you to the hospital. Is that all right?'

She nodded.

'Then … it's up to you. Do you want to go home?'

She shook her head.

'Anyone you know? Relations?'

'No.'

'Hilary?'

Her face brightened. Daniel came up and stood beside her. Dr Prichard took her hand between both of his, saying, 'We have to be careful, Rosaleen. You're very young. I, we – our whole church has enemies in this city. We want, we really want what's best for you.'

'I trust you,' she said, looking straight into his eyes.

Standing up, he dropped a bunch of keys into Daniel's hand. 'Bring her straight to the casualty department of Parkway Hospital. Ask for Dr Stevenson. I'm going to make a few phone calls. The first thing is to get all the medical attention you need. After that …'

Daniel lifted his white collar from the shelf.

'No,' said Dr Prichard, raising his hand, 'I don't think it would be wise to draw attention to yourself. Wear an ordinary shirt.'

She followed Daniel into the corridor and through to the back of the church. He disappeared into a room and came out wearing a checked shirt. 'How are you feeling?' he asked, his hands trembling slightly at his sides.

'Okay.'

'Is it sore?'

'A bit.'

They went out to the car park behind the church. The roads were beginning to clog with traffic. They slotted in and drove to the east side of the city. Leafy avenues, large polished cars, open spaces. Daniel didn't speak. She sensed his tension.

When they drove into the grounds of the hospital, she said, 'It's not your fault, Daniel. I asked you to write. You did nothing wrong.'

He gave her a weak little smile. But the hurt was in his eyes.

At the hospital reception desk they were expected. Dr Stevenson, around thirty, with bright eager brown eyes that rarely seemed to blink, ushered them into a private room off the main waiting hall. He asked Rosaleen a number of questions on her physical well-being. When it came to one on how the injury happened, she said, ' A fall against the fireplace.' He hesitated, then left the form blank. Afterwards he shone a bright light into the injured eye and examined it.

They went to the X-ray room. Dr Stevenson brought in a nurse and they took two X-rays – head on and sideways. Then she was brought into a room where a camera had been set up on a tripod. The shuffling from room to room was beginning to annoy her.

'What's this?' she asked sharply.

'A camera,' said Dr Stevenson, a little startled.

'Why?'

'Dr Prichard –'

The door opened and Hilary came in. She immediately burst into tears. Dr Stevenson retreated, Daniel shuffled his feet and wrung his hands. Rosaleen hugged Hilary. In the mirror beyond her friend's blond hair, she saw her own face. The entire right side was black and blue. Hilary squeezed her tight.

Dr Stevenson waited for a minute, then he said, 'Dr Prichard asked me to take a couple of photographs. For the records.'

'Okay.'

She broke free from Hilary and sat down on the chair in front of the camera. She was conscious of all their eyes: Daniel's and Hilary's, hardly able to look at her without having to turn away, and Dr Stevenson's steady gaze into the top of the camera.

'Will I smile?' she asked with a grimace.

'No, I don't think that would be appropriate,' said the doctor. 'Just look straight ahead?'

'Yes.'

His thumb pressed the button, a blinding flash followed the click.

* * *

As soon as Eileen saw the house, the only one on the street with the lights off, she knew something was wrong. She hesitated at the iron railing – looked around her – and crept up to the open front door. She considered calling for a neighbour but then, gingerly, reached her hand across and turned the handle of the inside door.

'Rosaleen? Frank?' she called.

A figure wearing an overcoat moved in the gloomy far corner of the living room. She jumped back. Then she recognised the grey hair and square-shaped forehead of her husband, slumped down into the armchair.

'Frank? What's wrong?' she asked, feeling for the switch with her hand and flicking it on.

His right hand covered his eyes. He removed it slowly, blinking at the light. Eileen looked at the dead fire, the empty kitchen, then Frank.

'Where's Rosaleen? Did she not make the tea? Who let the fire go out?'

'She's gone,' said Frank, his hands gripping the wooden arms of the armchair.

'Where?'

Frank said nothing.

'Gone where?' asked Eileen, lips pursed and flinging her handbag onto the settee. 'Did you have a row?'

'I'm sick of the disobedience in this house. I'm sick and tired of it.'

'What disobedience?'

'Everything.'

'What did she do?'

'She's been gettin' away with murder. No other family on the road has this trouble.'

'What was it about?'

'She's still involved.'

'With who?'

'Prichard.'

Eileen winced and put her left hand on the mantelpiece of the Devon grate. 'Involved? You mean she's still going?'

'I mean involved.'

'She's gone? Over there?'

'I don't know!' he exclaimed, throwing up his eyes.

'Was she in when you came home?'

'No.'

'Then how –?'

'I don't care where she's gone. I'm finished. Absolutely finished. I'm washing my hands of her.'

Eileen took a deep breath and sat down on the settee. 'Who started the row?' she asked.

'What is this? An inquisition? Whose side are you on?'

'I'm trying to find out what happened.'

'I told you what happened. She was disobedient.'

'Cheeky?'

'Don't you be interrogatin' me, Eileen. It's Rosaleen that's causing the trouble.'

'Will you tell me what happened?'

'I don't know where she is. Nor do I care.'

Eileen sucked in her lips and stood up. 'Fine. That's just fine. You're setting a good example on how to behave,' she said, going towards the kitchen. Her eye caught dark marks on the wallpaper beside the Devon grate. She stopped dead. 'What's that?'

'What?'

'There. On the wall,' she said, going over to stand beside him and looking over his head. He bent away from her. 'What is it? That stain wasn't there this morning. The wallpaper's ruined. Is it tea? Coffee?'

He got up and walked towards the door and stopped. She leaned over and scraped off one of the spots with her nail. 'What sort of a row did you have? Is it blood?' At another spot, a thin dark line smeared across the wallpaper. 'Is it blood?' she repeated.

'I didn't mean …'

'Did you hit her?'

'…it was only a slap.'

'A slap?'

'She attacked me … I didn't mean … she fell over the chair, hit her head …'

'Where is she?' Eileen asked icily.

'I don't know. I honestly don't.'

High heels clattered on the pavement outside. Marie came bustling through the doorway, her arms hugging a black bag close to her camel hair coat. Frank retreated towards the Devon grate. 'Do you like it?' Marie asked of her mother.

'What?'

'The dress? Where's Rosaleen?'

There was a short silence.

'Did she not come home? She got a new dress in the Co-op at dinner time. Did you not see it?'

'No.'

Marie looked at her father, his eyes cast down, the dead fire, her mother's pinched face and the quiet kitchen. 'What's wrong?' she asked with a sigh.

'There was a row,' said Eileen.

'About what?'

'You better ask your father.'

'I'm tryin' t' bring some sort of order t' this house. Some sort of ordinary, normal behaviour.'

'What did you do?' asked Marie, her eyes now hard.

Eileen rubbed the spots on the wall with a tissue. 'Did you notice anything this morning, Marie?'

'A letter for Rosaleen. I put it on the mantelpiece.'

'It was from him,' said Frank, raising his eyes and directing his gaze at each of them in turn.

Eileen swallowed hard. 'From who? Dr Prichard?'

'One of his cohorts. She's carrying on behind our backs. Cavortin' out in the country with him. Tryin' t' turn her head with rubbishy letters.'

'Did you open her letter?' asked Marie.

'Yes! I did.'

'Daddy, you've no right –'

'Haven't I?'

'– to open anybody else's letter in this house.'

'We know whose side you're on. It's me and Eileen that's responsible for her behaviour. And I'll search that room up there until I find any other evidence.'

'You won't search my room,' said Marie.

'Oh, are you afraid of us seein' what you're up to? What are you hidin' up there?'

'It's none of your business.'

'Well, I'm makin' it my business,' he spat out. 'You two can plot all you like. You can give her all the money and buy her all the dresses you want – but I'm followin' this through to the bitter end.'

'Is that what the row was about?' asked Eileen. 'A letter?'

'She's still in cahoots with them. I'm tellin' ya!'

Marie's eyes bored into him. He leaned back against the wall and his head went down into his overcoat as if he was getting smaller. Eileen examined the tissues in her hand. 'Is that Rosaleen's blood?' she asked.

'She might have cut herself when she fell,' said Frank.

'Did you hit her?' snapped Marie. 'Did you?'

'I'm sick of the lack of respect in this house.'

'Where is she? Where's my sister?'

'I'm sick of all the women in this house gangin' up on me. I can't even come home and have m' tea in peace.'

Marie's white fingers gripped her bag as she spoke. 'Oh, you're very brave, aren't ya? Are ya proud of yerself? Hittin' a fifteen-year-old girl?'

'Do you know where she is?' asked Eileen plaintively.

'No.'

'Is she hurt bad –?'

'– her eye might –'

'Did she go to the hospital?'

'I don't know! She just ran off –'

They stood in silence for a short while, lost in their own thoughts. A car revving up the street broke the spell.

'Frank, do you think it might have been bad enough for her to have to go to the hospital?' asked Eileen.

He dug his hands into his pockets and nodded slowly.

'Come on, Marie, we'll go down to the Royal.'

They went out onto the street, not bothering to close the door. The sound of their heels began to fade. Frank rubbed his eyes and temples with his fingers. The light was really annoying him. He stepped over, switched it off, closed the door and went over and sat down on the armchair.

Chapter 12

Rosaleen, wearing the same yellow dress, now crisply clean, sat in the passenger seat of a navy blue Ford Escort, driven by Daniel. The mid-morning traffic was light. Her hands were sticky. She glanced over at Daniel – tweed jacket, cavalry twill slacks, light blue shirt – gripping the driving wheel. He tensed his arms and said, 'I don't think it's a good idea.'

'I need to get my things.'

'You can buy new –'

'No.'

He was silent. She felt like making a stand. Events were moving fast. Too fast.

The first two nights in Hilary's room had been like a convalescent holiday after a nasty shock. Records, long discussions, analysis, dreams, what she would do. Then cars started coming to the house. Frequent phone calls, hushed conversations. In one, Hilary's father had mentioned Stormont and Rosaleen's name. Things were happening. A swirl of events, with grave consequences, where no one, including Hilary, seemed to know exactly what was happening.

On the third day she was invited to another house. Large gardens, a spacious bedroom from where she could see out across the city to the Black mountain. She was now even further away from Ivy Drive.

But she didn't like it – this feeling of being on the run. Except when she looked in the mirror at her now blue and yellow face, and re-ran the scene of her and her father. He needed to be punished.

'I didn't want to move out of Hilary's,' she said to Daniel, who was staring at the road ahead.

He sucked in his lips before replying. 'Do you not like Henry's?'

'Nothing to do with Henry. I just don't see –'

'Dr Prichard thinks it's necessary.'

'Why?'

'There's people. They'll make things difficult.'

'Who?'

'Lots of people. You'll find out pretty soon. Unless you want to go home again. Do you?' he asked.

'No.'

'Well, they know about Hilary. Where she lives.' He turned his head, looking at her sideways. 'I think you would really like America. I'd like you to see it. Maybe if you just think about Henry's as one of the staging posts on the way to America.'

For her, America now seemed like the other side of the moon. The day was dull and calm. A few shoppers meandered up the dusty Falls. Girls went to middle-aged women very quickly on the Falls Road. America was one long, exciting, technicoloured dream.

Ivy Drive came into view. She sensed Daniel's nerves, saw the blood rising in his face. Her stomach began to tighten.

'Suppose your parents are there at the house?' he said.

'They'll be out at work.'

She wasn't sure. But she wasn't telling him that. When you had decided to do something, assume the best. Daniel slid down the gears and the car came to a stop at the head of Ivy Drive.

'Will I drive down the street?'

'No, wait here,' she said, turning the door handle. 'I might be a while. I want to pack a case.'

She got out. Her stilettos clattered on the concrete pavement. The street was deserted except for a startled grey cat that watched her all the way to the wood-stained front door. It was shut. She looked across the street at all the windows. Lace curtains, half-rolled blinds, potted plants. Behind them there could be a million eyes. She lifted the end of her dress and swung a leg over the railing. Crouching down she tilted up a red brick and slid out a key. Back at the door, one last nervous glance at the prying windows, then through to the living room.

Silence. No change. Except the faded stains on the wallpaper to the right of the Devon grate. Upstairs, the unmade bed, Marie's pink French night-dress on the chair. She pulled out the large case from under the bed. Opening it, she tossed out a handbag and two old pairs of Marie's shoes. From the wardrobe she plucked dresses, blouses, skirts. Bunches of underwear, socks, two pairs of nylons from the dressing table drawers. Flat-heeled shoes, even old ones she'd worn to school, were flung into the case. Make-up powder, eye-liner, sulphur acne ointment, tampons – all into a plastic bag and stuffed down. Four Woman's Own magazines, all the pictures of Cliff Richard, carefully folded after peeling the sellotape off the wall. Joey, the furry rabbit she slept with, was packed into the side.

The dark green photograph album stopped her buzzing. Weddings, babies, one large one of her and Marie at Helen's bay, aged ten and twelve. She remembered the day, the heatwave, the sunburn, the pain. It was Marie who brought her to the hospital. She flipped out the photograph, then others – only of herself and Marie.

The case was more than full. The catches wouldn't stretch across. She sat on the lid and managed to click one in. Bumping her way down the narrow stairs to the bottom, she threw the case into the middle of the room. It rolled over on its side. She went through the kitchen and into the tiny bathroom. Creams, toothpaste, a toothbrush, aspirins – all in a plastic bag. She came back out, knelt down and opened the case.

An approaching shadow. The door sprang open. Marie, her camel hair coat flapping, stood over her. Their eyes locked together for a few seconds.

'Did he do that?' she asked.

Rosaleen nodded.

Marie's unmade-up face was white, her fingers clasped the material of her coat. 'He deserves everything he gets,' she said.

'I fell back over the –'

'Where've you been?'

'With friends.'

'Who? Prichard?'

'No.'

'Why'd you just disappear? We were frantic.'

She lowered her eyes. 'I'm sorry.'

'What's this for?' asked Marie, pointing her foot at the case.

There was a pause, then Rosaleen said, 'I'm going away.'

'Away? Are you mad?'

'I can't stay.'

'Why not? Nobody'll touch you, Rosaleen. I promise you that. Nobody will lay one finger on you. Over my dead body.'

'It think it's best.'

'Why?'

'I've definitely made up my mind. I may go to America.'

'America? Are you out of your head? You've never been beyond Bangor, never mind out of the country.'

'Not immediately.'

'Rosaleen, you're going nowhere. There's been ructions all over this road. Paddy Bolger's gonna bring it up in Stormont. The police are involved. It's gonna be in the Irish News, the Tele, the radio … the whole country is gonna know about you. You won't be able to go anywhere.' She lifted the lid of the case and plunged in her hands. 'You're taking everything

– shoes, clothes, Joey, even photographs – where do you think you're going?'

'I don't know, Marie. I only know that I'm not staying. And I trust the people I'm going to.'

'Prichard's gonna be in big trouble.'

'It's not him. It's me. I'm going of my own free will.'

'No! You're not. I know you, Rosaleen. You're my kid sister – I've looked after you, I've fought beside ya an' against ya. I've slept in the same room as ya all my life.' Her eyes sought Rosaleen – she glanced away. 'You've changed – do you know that? They've changed you. You're not my Rosaleen. They're taking you away from me. From all of us!'

'No – nobody's taking anybody away. They encourage families to stay together.'

'And what do you call this?'

'I need to go. Now. For a while.'

'No.'

'It's just a temporary thing.'

'Rosaleen – if you go, this won't be a temporary thing. You've been building up to this for months. You've become secret. You've told lies.'

'Only because –'

'You told me you were going t' dances an' you were goin' t' them meetins.'

'To stop rows.'

'To stop rows? With who? With me?'

'I thought you might –'

'Rosaleen, have I ever told on you? Have I? I've always fought yer corner. I told them t' lay off an' let ya –'

'I know, I know, I'm sorry, Marie.'

'You've hurt me.'

'I didn't mean … everybody was so … against me.'

'I've never been against ya.'

'Not you. Not you, Marie.'

'And now you're –'

'I would've told you but … they –'

'They who?'

'They said there'd be trouble.'

'Yes, they're right. Kidnapping a minor is a serious offence.'

'I've not been kidnapped. I'm going of my own free will.' She closed the case and stood up. 'I better go.'

Marie stepped back towards the door.

'You won't! I won't let you,' she said. 'I won't let you go through that door. I'll keep you here till they come home. We'll all stop you. You're only fifteen and we have a legal right t' keep ya here.'

'You won't stop me, Marie,' said Rosaleen, slipping her hand through the handle of the case.

'Do ya think I'm gonna let ya go off t' God knows where? With strangers tryin' t' take ya away from us?'

Rosaleen lifted the case and stepped forward, staggering slightly from its weight.

'There's somebody waiting for me,' she said.

'Who?'

'A friend.'

'One of Prichard's crowd?'

'He's a good friend. He helped me. He took me to the hospital.'

'Rosaleen, I would've done that. If I had been here m' Da wouldn't have touched ya. I'd have taken a knife t' him – an' he knows it.'

'I don't want that, Marie – I don't want anything like that. I've caused enough trouble. Now my friend is out there.'

'Where?'

'In a car. He's waiting.'

Marie folded her arms tight. Her eyes were hard, her face pinched.

'He's going to take me to a safe place.'

'You're safe here. With me!'

'No. If I stay, what happened before will happen again.'

'No.'

'I know it will. I won't, I can't do what they want. It's my life. I want to do what I know is right.'

'You can do that here. With me.'

'He won't let me.'

'We'll stop him – together.'

'You've got your own life.'

'I don't care. Honest. I don't care how many rows there are. It'll be me and you.'

'Please.'

'What do you think it's gonna be like if you go away?'

'Things'll die down. Later, when everything's settled, we'll make arrangements.'

'What kind of arrangements?'

'I don't know. Look, Marie – I'll have to go – he's waiting,' she said, moving forward slightly with the case.

'You're not leaving this house!'

Rosaleen put down the case.

'I'm going to meet someone. He's a friend. A good friend. I'm going away for a short while. When things are okay – I'll be back.'

Marie didn't budge. She looked at the case, Rosaleen's tense, white hand around the handle, her face.

'If you try to stop me – I'll never forgive you.'

Marie felt as if the blood was draining from her body. She slowly unfolded her arms and turned sideways towards the sofa. Rosaleen stepped forward and opened the door. She lifted the case, lurched out through the hall and zigzagged along the pavement. Ahead, the Escort began to nose out from the corner. A backward peek saw her sister slumped against the doorway. She lowered her head and plodded on.

Running, rattling heels behind her. She turned. Her sister's tear-stained face, her enveloping arms hugged her tight. She let go the case and hugged her back. After a few moments they broke.

The Escort, backing down alongside the kerb, came to a halt. Daniel got out and came around to the pavement. His arms hung loosely by his side, his face was red.

'This is Daniel,' said Rosaleen.

He stepped forward and offered his hand to Marie. She ignored it, snapping, 'Where are you taking her?'

He looked sheepishly away, lifted the case and went around to the boot of the car. Marie's eyes followed him.

'I'm okay,' said Rosaleen.

Marie pulled the coat around her slim body that now appeared skinny; her eyes were puffed, her hair uncombed. 'Have you not got a tongue in your head? I said, where are you taking her?'

In one quick, easy movement, he shoved the case into the boot.

'Rosaleen?' he offered.

'I'm asking you. You're the one that's taking her away.'

'It's up to your sister,' he said gently. 'I'm doing what she wants.'

'I'll be in touch,' said Rosaleen, putting her arm around her hunched, narrow shoulders.

Marie slid away, leaning back against the railings and spreading out her arms. She gripped the bars and watched them get into the car. It crawled up the street, puffing blue smoke out the exhaust and turned right onto the Falls Road. Eyes down, she walked back to the house. A white lace curtain in the window of the house opposite moved and a grey head appeared. She didn't notice. She went in and closed the front door behind her.

All the way along the Falls Road and down into the town centre, Rosaleen and Daniel were silent. Finally, just past the City Hall and within sight of the bridge, he said, 'I'd like to meet your sister sometime. In the future. When things are more normal. I think I would like her a lot.'

Rosaleen saw her sister's face. In the boot of the car was almost everything she owned. She hadn't wanted to run into Marie. She was the one person she could never imagine leaving. Yet that was what she had just done.

The river looked grey and black under the bridge, as if it absorbed all the light. She was afraid. Was rejecting all the negative alternatives really the best way? Was she doing the right thing? She couldn't sleep in that house, she knew that. She couldn't look in the mirror without feeling hatred. That wasn't right. Yet she was afraid of what she may have set in motion. She had the distinct feeling that people were moving into fixed positions, and no one, including herself, was prepared to compromise.

The car swung left just over the bridge, away from Ravenmount Church and Dr Prichard's house, and towards Henry's. Action, secrecy and self-preservation were the order of the day. It wasn't what anyone wanted, but it was the only way. And still she saw her sister's face.

'Rosaleen,' said Daniel, 'I think you should think of this as the beginning of a big adventure that will hopefully take you to America. You'd like that, wouldn't you?'

She gave him a weak smile and lowered her eyes.

Chapter 13

Early the next day, Rosaleen spent an hour in the bathroom at Henry's. She finished off by applying light powder to her face, particularly the discoloured skin around her eye. Then Hilary called. She brought a box of Cadbury's chocolates, a present from the girls at Pattersons. Rosaleen wondered if they thought she was a hospital patient. Just as Hilary was getting into her stride with the office gossip, a phone call summoned her away. Alone, she tried reading the Bible. But she couldn't work up the required concentration. A magazine diverted her attention for a while. Still the time dragged.

She had lunch, a quiet affair with Henry's wife, Margaret, being overly polite and trying too hard to please. Rosaleen didn't like the constant fussing, as if she was a delicate porcelain vase. After the meal, Daniel arrived and Margaret disappeared.

'We have to go,' he said.

'Where?'

'Away from Belfast. Up the coast.'

'Why?'

'I think we should trust his judgement,' he said, with a trace of impatience.

She returned his look, with interest.

'I'm sorry,' he added.

She walked past him to the door and went up the deep-carpeted stairs. Following behind her, he waited until they reached the top before he spoke again.

'I'm sorry,' he repeated. 'There's been a lot of people hasslin' me. I couldn't even use the Ford – I had to get a car from a man in Portadown. And he was late.'

The way he said 'Port-a-down' told her just how foreign he was.

'Don't mind me,' she said, 'I'm only the passenger. The car's much more important.'

'No, Rosaleen, I've just –'

'Why did nobody ask me?'

'About what?'

'What I wanted.'

'I – we – thought –'

'Dr Prichard hasn't even contacted me.'

'He's being watched. There's newspaper men outside the church at this very moment.'

'I just thought I could have been consulted.'

'It's for you that we're doing it. Really, Rosaleen. That's the truth.'

'All right,' she said, after a pause, 'I'll go.'

She opened the gleaming white door and went into the sunlit bedroom. Gathering up her things from the chairs and the dresser, she threw them back into her case. Daniel stood on the landing, and leaned his head into the doorway.

'If you'd like to bring your case out,' he said, 'I'll carry it down the stairs for you.'

She turned and looked at him.

'Out?'

He blushed and wiped his hands down the sides of his cavalry twill trousers. 'The Reverend told me on no account to go into your bedroom.'

She blinked at him.

'… it's a procedural thing,' he muttered.

'Suppose I break my back lifting it,' she said, eyeing the case, 'then where would you be?' She snapped the case shut and dragged it over to the door. 'Lucky for you and your procedures that I have a strong back, isn't it?'

Lifting the case, he smiled weakly and lumbered down the stairs behind her. At the bottom she plucked her trench coat off the hook, put it on, patted her freshly washed hair and looked off into the distance.

'I'm not the General in this operation,' he offered. 'When I came over here I didn't expect to end up in the middle of a civil war.'

'Did you tell Dr Prichard you don't want to do this?'

'I didn't say I didn't want to do it. I just –'

'Don't like the hassle.'

'Well –'

'Why don't you ring him? He'll get someone else.'

'Look, Rosaleen, I'm not complaining.'

'I better say goodbye to Margaret –'

'She's gone – I told her.'

'So – are we all set, or are we not?'

'Yes, we are,' he said, opening the front door and tilting sideways to balance the heavy case.

She followed him down the stone steps onto the gravel driveway to the dark green Morris Oxford. He put the case in the boot and went around and opened the passenger door. She got in. He banged the door shut and went around to the driver's side and squeezed in. She could see by the set of his jaw that he was annoyed. He started the car and drove out onto the road.

'I'm sorry,' he said, after some minutes of silence. 'I'm sorry for being selfish. I should be making allowances for what you've been through. And I feel privileged – I really do – to be helping you.'

'Okay,' she said, after a pause.

'Is there anything you really want? Anything?'

She thought for a few moments, then she said, 'I think I should be making a decision. A clean break. I want to join Ravenmount church.'

Daniel turned his head to catch her face and smiled.

She smiled back. 'How do I go about it?'

'I don't think there's any formal process,' he said, sliding his hands freely around the rim of the wheel. 'We're a family. You're part of that family now. But I heard them talking back there – when you're sixteen, it's more straightforward.'

'Thursday fortnight,' she said, folding her hands into her lap.

They rolled through the drowsy mid-afternoon traffic of the city and went up the Antrim Road, towards Napoleon's Nose. She pointed out the steps of Bellevue Zoo – the Johnson family had visited it the previous year. Soon they were on the high, flat plateau of South Antrim, and shortly afterwards heading down towards the hook that formed Larne harbour.

When they reached the coast, a brisk breeze was blowing in from the sea and a fine spray lashed the winding road. The inside of the car was snug and warm. This was her first time along the Antrim coast. Yellow gorse on the steep slopes. Green multi-hued patchwork fields under rainwashed caps. Rathlin Island, low and stark on the horizon. A grandeur of headlands, lush glens and pretty villages. She liked this journey. She liked the company. Her tension eased.

Near Waterfoot, on the far side of a squalling shower, Daniel turned off the main road into a leafy lane. A short distance on, they came to a large stone house. There were hens pecking around the untidy, spacious garden. A sheepdog circled the car and stood off. Behind the house, white sheep and lambs peppered the hillside.

A woman with spiralling grey hair and sturdy church-going shoes came hurrying towards the car. Mrs Moore wore black woollen stockings – they disappeared under a thick, shin-length tweed skirt. The flapping wings of a grey cardigan covered her rolling, plump shoulders and a heavy navy cotton blouse was carelessly tucked in at the waist. Her bright blue eyes radiated energy, kindliness and zeal, and when her ruddy face came close to the car window, you could see thread-veins on her cheeks and nostrils. She tried to wrest the case away from Daniel – and when he successfully resisted, skipped like a goat up the stone steps to the porch.

Rosaleen smiled and replied politely to her questions. She had met a stream of women these past few days, all energetic and excited to be part of the great conspiracy. Rosaleen didn't particularly take to them, but Mrs Moore's open, friendly manner and strong country accent made a difference. 'Would you like some fresh baked scones and soda bread? Sure you would. Come on in,' she said.

The living room was large, with high ceilings and comfortable old furniture. A patchwork, quilt-covered settee had been pulled towards a blazing turf fire. The table was set with brown bread, scones, a small pot of blackcurrant jam and a bowl of farmhouse butter. The air was dry with the heat of fresh baking, and its smell was everywhere.

Mrs Moore firmly gripped Rosaleen's shoulder as she led her to the end of the settee closest to the fire. 'You're safe here,' she said with a wink. 'They won't get ya in this place.'

Rosaleen smiled and sat down.

'Nobody but Daniel will know yer here. And after that – it's up to you. Isn't that what you want?'

'Rosaleen would like to become a full member of our church,' said Daniel.

Mrs Moore clasped her hands together and closed her eyes.

'Of course,' he added, 'that can't be official for a couple of weeks.'

'God doesn't pay any attention to that oul nonsense,' said Mrs Moore. 'It's what goes on in the heart that counts – pieces of paper don't matter.'

Daniel nodded.

'I'll get the tea,' she said, disappearing through the door to the kitchen.

'A lovely woman,' he said.

'How long do you think –?'

'Do you not like it here?'

'No, it's fine – I just –'

Daniel looked at the floor, covered in a thick beige and green rug. 'The truth is – I don't know. I have to go back to Belfast now. Then it'll depend –'

'On what?'

'The situation.'

'So you don't know?'

'No. But I'll be back tomorrow. For certain.'

A dog barked loudly outside. They both looked at each other. Rosaleen got up to go to the window. 'That mightn't be such a good idea,' he said.

She stood still. An outside door opened in the room to the right. There was some garbled talk, then the door closed. Rosaleen sat down again.

'He's an oul pest,' said Mrs Moore, bustling into the room with a large blue porcelain teapot. 'Higgins from down the road. Handy enough with his hands but never around when you want him. He'll leave a couple of bags of turf. Have ya not started – what's keepin' ya? Eat up!'

Mrs Moore was good on local gossip. She gave cutting character descriptions of three of her neighbours and several other locals. Rosaleen noticed that she always prefaced her characterisation with a friend or foe nuance. Who could be relied upon and who couldn't. Here, in the Glens of Antrim, Rosaleen learned for the first time that there was a strong population of Catholics. To her credit, Mrs Moore spoke highly of them, if not their church. She reserved her special wrath for Protestants – certain alien brands of Presbyterianism. But Rosaleen couldn't detect any real malice in her, and was sorry to hear that she was a widow with no children.

Daniel left a couple of hours later. She watched his car drive off into a strong wind that was swirling dark clouds over the glen. Off towards the road, distant lights sparkled in the darkness.

Walking back into the living room she felt lonely. She would have loved to go up to bed and snuggle up to Marie, or have a chat with Hilary.

'Come in here and get something to read,' said Mrs Moore, leading her into a study off the living room. 'Take as many as you like – I don't bother much with books – my husband was a great reader, God have mercy on him.' Dusty bookshelves rose from floor to the ceiling. There were even leather-bound volumes with an antique look. Rosaleen wondered where to start looking. 'I have to go ready your bedroom – it's a while since it's been used.'

When she'd gone, Rosaleen plucked a thinnish volume off the shelves: '*Kidnapped* by Robert Louis Stevenson' was printed in gold letters on the cover. She opened it at the first page and read:

I will begin the story of my adventure with a certain morning early in the month of June, the year of grace 1751, when I took the key for the last time out of the door of my father's house.

Rosaleen's skin went goose-bumpy. Had she done the same?

One book was enough. She drifted back into the living room and went over to the large window nearest the door. The heat died quickly, away from the fire. Drawing back the curtain, she looked out. She could see nothing but reflecting light. She went over to a white-washed alcove directly opposite the settee. On the floor was an old Singer sewing machine, and beside it a yellow tablecloth was draped over a box-shaped object. She peeped under the cloth – it was a large wooden radio. On the dresser in the living room directly opposite, there was an empty space. Had Mrs Moore deliberately moved the radio?

She went over and sat down by the fire and re-opened the book. But she was still wondering about the radio. Would anything she heard on the News make her change her mind? No, of course it wouldn't. She started reading.

Before she had finished the first page, she was gripped by the story – so much so, that some time later she hardly noticed Mrs Moore's figure gesturing at the door, to follow her into the kitchen for their tea.

The enticing smell of boiled bacon and cabbage was matched by the taste. There was more gossip and reassurances that she was safe and doing the right thing. Afterwards, when Rosaleen said that she was tired and would like to go to bed, Mrs Moore led her up to the bedroom at the front of the house. Despite her efforts with an oil heater, and a turf fire in the small grate, the room was still cold.

Ten minutes later, the old lady brought up two hot water bottles. She caught Rosaleen sorting Hilary's box of chocolates into the nutty and dark ones, and the rest. Two soft centres were all Mrs Moore would accept.

Alone again, Rosaleen changed into pyjamas and got into bed. Her feet pushed one hot water bottle down towards the bottom, her hands fondled the other across her stomach. She reached over to switch on the bedside light, jumped out of bed, ferreted out from the case a heavy white jumper, put it on and leapt back in. Perching the box of chocolates against a plumped up pillow, she sucked each chocolate slow and good and read. Outside there was a gale, somewhere beyond the sea the Isle of Mull, where David Balfour was washed ashore. In here she was warm and cosy. She could forget about everything, absolutely everything else until the morning.

When she awoke – for an instant she couldn't remember where she was. The air was like ice. Her eyes fell on the chocolate box – there were only four left. She lifted her small, rolled gold Timex watch from the table. It was stopped. She had forgotten to wind it. The book was lying on the floor with the corner of a page turned down. She lay still. The wind had dropped.

Downstairs, towards the living room, there was the murmur of a voice, followed by music. Had Mrs Moore brought out the radio? She got up, shivered in her cotton pyjamas, ran out onto the landing and into the old spacious bathroom. It was even colder than the bedroom. A day for the navy woolly leggings she had wisely brought.

In ten minutes, wearing her grey pleated skirt, heavy white jumper and low-heeled shoes, she went down the stairs. But before she reached the bottom, the music stopped. Bustling movement and a bumping noise came from the living room. She went in. Mrs Moore stood awkwardly behind the settee, her face even redder than the day before.

'Did you have a good sleep?' she asked, her right hand making a vain attempt to pat down her wiry hair.

'Great.'

'I'll get your breakfast. Sit down by the fire there till it's ready.'

Rosaleen went slowly over towards the settee and, just before sitting down, she said, 'Did you hear the News?'

'What?'

'The News? On the radio?'

'There's never anything on the radio,' she said, turning and going off into the kitchen.

Rosaleen looked over at the alcove, where the tablecloth covering the radio was slightly more crumpled than it had been the night before. She walked over and touched it with her hand. It was warm. She went over and picked up the red Bible lying on the dark dappled marble mantelpiece. She tried reading some verses in Samuel about David, but her attention wandered. She was still with David Balfour and Alan Breck Stewart in the Scottish Highlands. She put the Bible back on the mantelpiece, slipped upstairs to the bedroom to retrieve the novel, and came back down.

Submerging herself in the story she felt a great kinship with the characters – their flight from everything they knew and loved. But in her case, she reassured herself, it was only a temporary thing. To teach certain people a lesson. Not a final cleavage. No, it could never be that, she said, as her eyes drifted towards the faded page.

After a large Ulster fry, Mrs Moore cleared and washed the dishes, resolutely refusing Rosaleen's offer of assistance. 'Sure it's your holidays, love,' she said.

But the suggestion of a walk along the beach or up a lane was met by a look of alarm. Daniel's imminent arrival was put forward as a deterrent. And, since Mrs Moore had to do messages, Rosaleen must stay in and guard the fort.

This meant several hours alone, reading the novel, stoking the fire with turf and stuffing herself with scones and jam.

Eventually, when her eyes got tired reading, she dragged the radio out of the alcove and switched it on. Music and a talk show were the only programmes she could find. She put it back and began to walk around the house, exploring the rooms. In one bedroom she saw a wedding photograph of Mrs Moore and her husband. She was much, much younger. Then she heard a car arrive in the gravel driveway. It was Daniel in the green Oxford.

From the porch she thought his beige polo neck and black anorak made him look like a fisherman. As he closed the car door she thought his face was tense and drawn, but when he came up, he beamed her a broad, white American smile and said, 'How's it going?'

'Okay.'

She would have loved him to put his arms around her or at least kiss her on the cheek but he just stood there rubbing his hands together as if he was about to say his prayers.

'Will we go in?' he asked, opening the door.

'I'm sick of being stuck inside.'

He hesitated for a moment, then looked worried. 'Let's talk –'

She walked in and over to the settee, threw herself down and folded her arms.

'Where's Mrs Moore?' he asked.

'Out.'

'Have you heard the News?'

'That's the radio over there,' she said, pointing her finger at the alcove. 'Hidden under that cover.'

He walked to the edge of the alcove.

'I wouldn't go in there if I were you – I think it's out of bounds.'

He smiled, came back over and sat down on the chair opposite her.

'I need fresh air,' she said.

'There's been developments.'

'If I don't get some fresh air, I may start acting funny.'

'Okay, get your coat – there's a beach near here.'

She went out and took her trench coat and maroon woollen scarf from the stand in the hall.

Daniel didn't drive directly to the sea. He cut to the left, across a few boreens and down a couple of lanes. Eventually they came to the main coast road – a cove lay just beyond it. He drove over and parked the car on a pebbled stretch of foreshore.

Outside she tied the scarf around her head and neck. Their feet trod the pebbles, crunched the shells and squelched the seaweed.

'I've had to change the car twice before coming here today, Rosaleen,' he said. 'There's a lot of people looking for you. Your family. Relations. Priests. Newspaper men. Even television people over from London.' He turned to look at her face. It was serious, her eyes looking downward. 'This affects what you can do. They have your photograph. Now it's all up to you. Do you want to go back home?'

She shook her head.

'Then that means you have to keep out of sight. At least until you're sixteen. Then it's different – legally.'

'You mean stay in Mrs Moore's for two weeks?'

'No, they know most of our members. If you leave the country, go to Scotland for a couple of weeks, then maybe come back when you're sixteen.'

She looked out across the cold blue water, beyond the grey and green of Rathlin Island, to the luminous wet sky. Was she about to embark on an adventure?

'What part of Scotland?'

'We're looking into the possibility of building a church in Oban. It's in West Scotland.'

'Is it near the Isle of Mull?'

'I don't know. We've good friends there.'

'Would I just travel there by myself?'

'No, I'd take you. I'm the most expendable member of the church. Would you like me to take you?'

She looked up at his fresh, open face and said, 'Yes, I would.'

'Okay. I have to go back to Belfast to clear up a few things. But tomorrow morning we'll take the Larne-Stranraer ferry.'

They walked in silence for a short while. She was excited at the prospect of going to Scotland with Daniel. An escape, and a punishment for the man who hurt her – who refused to let her believe what she wanted.

'We'll get word to your family that you're all right. And that you don't want to go back. At this point in time. Is that all right?' he asked.

'Yes,' she said, 'tell them that.'

'Another point – I'm not sure how to tell you.'

'Be straight – please.'

'All the reports – especially the Catholic newspapers, say you're a fifteen-year-old schoolgirl.'

'I've left school.'

'Yeah.'

'And I'll be sixteen in two weeks.'

'I know. It's about tomorrow, when we're travelling. Maybe – I don't know – maybe if you could make yourself just a little bit older looking … there'll be people on the ferry, you know?'

Rosaleen went quiet. His blue eyes glanced sideways and scanned her face for any sign of emotion before he continued. 'You don't have to – I mean, like, you can dress whatever way you want …'

She stopped suddenly. He swivelled around.

'Do you know what I'll have to do, Daniel?'

'What?'

'Go back to Belfast for my grey granny wig.'

He stared at her face for an instant, then burst out laughing. 'You're an eejit,' she added.

He nodded his head slowly, saying, 'My folks would agree with you there.'

Back in the car, they drove along until they came to the road, and were just about to cross it, when she said, 'Can we go to the village?'

His eyes went up and down the road, as if he didn't hear, searching for non-existent traffic. 'What?' he asked.

'I need to buy some things. In the chemist.'

He gave out a dry cough for some seconds.

'You mean – drive down there?'

'Yeah.'

'– could you not wait until –?'

'No. I need to go to the chemist. Now.'

'– is there one in the village?'

'Yes.'

'Maybe I could go and buy –?'

'No, it's personal stuff.'

He chewed his lips for some seconds. 'Maybe Mrs Moore..?'

'No.'

His hands gripped the wheel, turning his knuckles white. 'We're supposed to be careful. Somebody might notice us.'

She turned towards him. Her big hazel eyes looked up through strands of light brown hair. The words were resolute. 'I have to go.'

'All right,' he said, swinging the driving wheel to the left.

They passed no cars on the way to Carnlough. Daniel crawled through the drowsy village and noted the handful of shops dotted amidst the terraced houses. 'I don't see any chemist,' he said.

'There's one back there.'

'Where?'

'The last one. Part of it is a chemist shop.'

He slowed down, backed into a lane and turned off the engine. 'Okay?' he enquired.

'Can you lend me some money?'

'Oh yeah, sure, I forgot – here,' he said, taking out his wallet and handing her two five-pound notes. 'I should have –'

'One's enough.'

'They gave me money for you. Go ahead.'

She took the notes and got out and crossed the road. A small girl came out of the shop carrying a lollipop. Daniel slumped down into the seat. The tips of his fingers started drumming his knees as he watched Rosaleen go in. Twenty minutes later she emerged carrying a bulging green plastic bag.

'Did you get what you wanted?' he asked, when she got into the car.

'No. They hadn't a great selection. But I got a few things. Can you hold this change? My pockets are too small.'

He put the palm of his hand forward. She piled it with coppers, threepenny bits and tanners. He slid these into his anorak pocket and started the engine.

The evening meal was a quiet affair. Mrs Moore expressed regrets, which seemed genuine, that Rosaleen was to leave in the morning. Daniel was muted and tense. When they saw him out to the porch, Rosaleen noticed his eyes were becoming slightly puffy, as if he hadn't slept lately. He drove off into the black night, promising to return early the next morning.

Rosaleen was beginning to find Mrs Moore's small talk annoying and boring. There was only so much to say about the weather and she didn't feel like making an issue about the radio or the general lack of news. She asked for a map of Scotland. The old lady disappeared into the library, came back with a school atlas and sat beside her.

'Do you know Scotland?' asked Rosaleen.

'Aye, I do. My folks come from there. Near Sterling.'

'Do you know where Oban is?'

'West Scotland.'

'Is it near the Isle of Mull?'

'Aye, why do you ask?'

'Oh, just a novel I'm reading.'

'Its a great part of the country. I wish I was going,' she said, finishing her tea and standing up.

Rosaleen offered to help in the kitchen. Again it was politely but firmly refused. She brought the atlas up to bed with her and perched the map of Scotland against a pillow while she read the novel. The story's journey across Scotland was a great, exciting adventure. Would hers be the same? Would it help get rid of the nasty memories of the past week?

A part of her was still there in that terraced house on the Falls Road – with her sister, mother, and even her father. But she had the strong, unnerving feeling that she had reached a major turning point in her life. The future was a blank page. Was she doing the right thing? Yes, she said quietly to herself, as tiredness closed her eyes and she put down her book. Yes, she didn't want to go back. She wanted to go forward. To Scotland.

Shortly after dawn, Mrs Moore gave the bedroom door two sharp knocks. The cocks crowed, the dog barked and the sheep bleated. It was a strange world. Rosaleen gathered a bundle of clothes and the green plastic bag and ran into the bathroom. The cold shot up her legs – her feet vibrated against the floor. She washed herself in hot water and put on the first layer of clothing, her best unworn underwear. Next, a pair of dark tights. A black skirt with a four-inch slit at the side, a brown leather belt with a brass buckle and a tight blood-red woollen jumper. Out from the green bag came foundation cream, a layer of Max Factor No. 4, bright pink lipstick, green eyeshadow, mascara and a black pencil for the eyebrows. She swept her hair back from her forehead and towards the right, a style she'd seen Barbara Stanwyck wear, and froze it into place with a lacquer spray. She dabbed Tweed perfume on the skin beneath each ear lobe. Rose-pink nail polish was carefully stroked onto each nail and dried with her hot breath. Then she slid into her stilettos and went downstairs for breakfast.

Though the fire burned brightly in the living room, the air was still cold. From the kitchen came the sound of a soft sizzle and the smell of frying bacon. Rosaleen blew on her nails, rubbed her hands and stepped across the carpet to the door of the kitchen. Mrs Moore poked a sausage with a fork – she suddenly turned, her hands shot up and the fork flew into the air.

'Rosaleen!' she cried. 'Merciful God! You're puttin' the heart crossways on me – don't be creepin' up on me like that again.' Pulling the perennial grey cardigan around her, she bent down and picked up the fork. As she did, her gaze fell across Rosaleen's black skirt, tights-clad knees and stilettos. 'You look so …so different, Rosaleen,' she stammered.

'I wanted to wear something warm.'

'– aye.'

'Is it all right?'

'For what?' asked Mrs Moore, her wide eyes taking in the whole exotic vision.

'The boat. We're travelling on the ferry.'

'That's a fine, heavy jumper you're wearing all right. But maybe I could lend you a good big coat that would cover you up better – the boats can be a bit cold and draughty, even at this time of year. I have a good big tweed one with a nice hood – you could pull it up over your head when the wind's blowing.'

Rosaleen considered the offer for a couple of seconds. 'No, I think I'll wear my trench coat. We'll be in the car most of the time anyway.'

Mrs Moore nodded and tried hard to conceal her disappointment. 'Whatever you think –' she said, leaning back against the handle of the pan. Her hand just stopped it from falling over the edge. 'My God! What am I doing?'

'Can I help?'

'No, everything's in order. Will you have some fried soda bread?'

'Please.'

Rosaleen felt uncomfortable during the breakfast. Sometimes Mrs Moore would lock her stare onto Rosaleen's painted nails, before suddenly looking up to her face – and then, sensing Rosaleen's discomfort, she would ignore her altogether and concentrate on her plate. A second offering of the tweed coat with the all-covering hood didn't help the atmosphere. Rosaleen finished her breakfast quickly, thanked Mrs Moore, and went up to the bedroom.

Kicking off her stilettos she tilted the mirror on the old dresser to take a head to toe look. Mrs Moore had shaken her confidence. She thought she looked nice. Glamorous even. Maybe too glamorous for an old farmer's widow. Marie would have been the perfect judge. She would have given her that little bolster before facing the hostile world. Daniel had asked her to dress older. She held her fingers flat and downwards so that she could see her nails sparkling in the mirror. Yes, she definitely did look older.

The sound of a car and crunching gravel sent her to the window. Daniel got out of the Morris Oxford. She slipped on her stilettos and proceeded to the top of the stairs. Below, Mrs Moore had opened the front door. Rosaleen straightened her jumper. She knew that from the waist up her figure was good, that the black skirt and dark tights diminished the slight fulsomeness of her lower half – that she could turn a head or two. She placed her right hand lightly on the banister and descended slowly.

Through the door she could see Daniel being subjected to animated urgings. And in his usual way, he cast his puzzled eyes downwards as he ascended the steps. Mrs Moore's lips were corrugated; her head shook from side to side. Rosaleen stopped four steps from the bottom of the stairs, and turned slightly sideways, her profile catching the light from the door. Daniel looked up and stopped dead, his mouth opened, his face flushed. No words came. Mrs Moore shot her a glance and then directed her gaze towards the coatstand.

'Rosaleen,' he began, 'I got the tickets.' His large hands plunged into the side pockets, then his left went up inside the anorak, pulling out two bright green tickets and proffering them towards her. 'We leave in about – eleven o'clock it leaves, are you … are you ready? I mean, we have time – not a lot … a few minutes won't make, is it? – are you all right, ready and everything – the water's not too bad though they're forecasting a light breeze, not too much I hope … well? How's everything, then?'

'Fine,' she said, coming down to the bottom. 'How do you think I look?'

  Mrs Moore's eyes were grave. She folded her arms.

'You look …' His head began jigging up and down '… fine. I mean, they're only forecasting a light breeze later on and –'

'Do I look older?' she asked.

'Yes! Definitely. You look older … doesn't she look … older, Mrs Moore?'

The old lady's eyes lingered on Rosaleen for some seconds, then went to Daniel's flushed face as she sucked in her cheeks, and finally came to rest on the coatstand. 'In my opinion,' she said, 'you will draw far too much attention to yourself.'

Daniel drew back, sensing Rosaleen flinch at the implied insult. 'In what way?' he asked.

Her eyes gave Rosaleen a triple head-to-toe up and downer. Then she said, 'In every way. She's dressed like one of them girls in the pictures. People will be looking at you, Rosaleen. I thought the whole idea was for people not to be looking at you. Not to notice –'

'Yes, but you see,' said Daniel, chopping the air with his hand, 'they'll be looking for a schoolgirl. She doesn't look like a schoolgirl, now does she?'

Rosaleen was thrilled. Like a girl in the pictures, the opposite of a schoolgirl.

'Yes,' said Mrs Moore, 'but there's no need to go from one extreme to the other. Perfume, lipstick, painted stuff ... like, how will she be able to get on the boat in them shoes?'

'I can manage fine in these shoes,' said Rosaleen.

Daniel stood back and gave her a clinical head-to-toe before nodding his head sagely and adding, 'I think she definitely looks older than fifteen.'

'Was all this your idea, then?' Mrs Moore asked Daniel. 'Did you supply her with all this ... stuff?'

'No, no, no,' he said, shaking his head. 'Rosaleen –'

'Everything's my own,' she confirmed.

'Well, if that's the way you want it.' The old lady cut the air with both hands. 'Though I can't see – does Dr Prichard approve of this get-up? I mean, did you get his approval for ... for this?'

'Oh, Dr Prichard approves,' said Daniel. 'He himself thought Rosaleen should try to look older.'

'In his sermons I haven't noticed any particular approval of painted women. In fact, I know of several women, including myself, who gave up these gaudy practices – and ours were extremely mild in comparison to this …', she said, her right hand flapping in the direction of the offender.

'What's wrong with make-up?' asked Rosaleen.

'The Reverend here is a minister of our church. The activities we are engaged in are irregular. Good ends, no doubt, but irregular. Everything has to be watched,' she said, pointing her finger in the air. 'Our enemies can and will use anything they can against us.'

'And I,' said Daniel, 'have taken great care so that nothing could be construed –'

'But have you?' she asked, her eyes wide, challenging.

He gulped, then gathered himself and replied: 'Yes. I have done everything that Dr Prichard said should be done. I have been very careful.'

'He has,' said Rosaleen.

A sideways glance from Mrs Moore was not altogether approving and she said, 'I'm only pointing out the pitfalls. We have to watch for what our enemies may see. Not what is in our hearts. For we have nothing to hide.'

'Yes. I agree. I agree with you there,' he said, glancing at his watch. 'We really do have to leave now. Where's your case, Rosaleen?'

'Up in the room. Everything's in it.'

Mrs Moore moved to the side as he climbed the stairs. She wasn't happy, refusing to look at Rosaleen, who took her trench coat from the coat stand.

'Thank you very much, Mrs Moore. For everything.'

She looked across at Rosaleen, warmth suddenly returned to her eyes, and she dashed forward and embraced her. 'Look after yourself, child. I'm only worryin' for you. You know that.'

'I know.' Rosaleen gave her a broad smile and returned the hug. 'Thanks.'

Daniel came lumbering down the stairs and dragged the case out through the doorway. Rosaleen followed and joined him on the driveway while he loaded the case into the boot. When she had settled into the soft leather seat, she turned around – Mrs Moore now looked frail, her head bowed towards the ground, her movement arthritic – she felt sorry for her. She waved. He started the engine.

'Good luck! Safe journey,' called Mrs Moore after them as the car moved towards the lane.

White flowered hawthorn hedges rolled by. Rosaleen was glad to be leaving. She had felt hemmed in, uncomfortable and cold. Mrs Moore was nice. But she didn't want to be around old people. She was young, about to embark on an adventure. People were looking for her. She would escape across the sea – to Scotland.

'Look at the mist,' she said, as they turned onto the coast road. 'Will it affect the ferry?'

Daniel's face was solemn. His hands gripped the driving wheel, he looked straight ahead and said, 'I think we should be okay. The weather forecast said the mist would clear.'

'Is something wrong?' she asked.

'No, why?'

'Oh –'

'What?'

'You seem worried.'

'Me? Naa. I'm not worried. Are you worried?'

She shrugged. Half-an-hour later they slid into the sleepy town of Larne and went up to the ferry. There were only six other cars and a handful of passengers who gave them no more than a passing interest. The mist was already clearing and small waves rippled the grey, glacial surface. Soon the car was parked, the ship drifted from the edge, the wide open sea beckoned. They stood on the deck near the prow of the ship and sipped tea.

Daniel stared down into the water, pensive. Rosaleen looked back at the great mass of land. This was her first boat trip. There had been so many firsts these past few months. She had to put it all behind her. Especially the nasty bits. The future was what mattered. The plaintive cry of the seagulls overhead did not match her mood – she wasn't sure about Daniel's.

'Have you ever been to Scotland?'

He took a while to reply. 'No.'

'Why are you coming?'

'– what?'

'You don't want to.'

'No, Rosaleen, I volunteered. I offered to come.'

'You make it sound like the army.'

'It's not you.'

'What is it then?'

'I like you. I'd like to be going off on a holiday with you. I'd love that. But this … this isn't a holiday.'

'That doesn't mean we can't enjoy it.'

His eyes screwed up, he turned to face her. 'Are you enjoying this, are you? Being hounded, hassled?'

'Maybe you should go back. I'll be all right on my own. They have buses over there, haven't they? Trains?'

'I'm taking you. I'm looking after you,' he said with a wave of his hand.

'You might be better off in Belfast.'

She could see that she was annoying him. She turned away.

'My place is here. With you.'

'Must you make it sound like a horrible despicable duty that Dr Prichard is forcing upon you?'

'Nobody is forcing anything upon me. I'm here because I want to be here.'

'That's not the message I'm getting.'

'Why? Do you not think I'm telling you the truth?'

She refused to look at his face and walked away along the deck. Aware that his eyes were following her, she quickened and turned a corner. The gathering breeze pressed her trench coat into her body. A middle-aged man, squinting at the open sea, turned and gave her an approving once-over. Amazing what stilettos could do to the unlikeliest of legs, she thought, hurrying along and dashing into the warmth of the lounge.

She looked around. A young family sat at one of the Formica tables in the corner. Through a window she could see Daniel plodding along the foredeck. Was he actually a bit too prairie for her? she asked herself as she slipped into the Ladies Room. The mirror told her what she wanted to see: eighteen, nineteen, maybe even twenty. She would redo her make-up and take her time about it. He could wait. Prairie men could do with a few hills and dales in their lives. And she had all the time in the world.

The sky was clear by the time they reached Stranraer. She was disappointed by the nondescript harbour and low-lying scenery. She had expected at least small mountains. When Daniel explained about the Scottish Lowlands and that they would, later, arrive in the Highlands, she postponed judgement.

The scenery was, nonetheless, pleasant. The sea and Arann lay to their left long the coast road, and the villages and towns were spruce. They stopped in a small hotel in Ayr and had a late lunch.

As they travelled along, Daniel became less tense and began talk about his home country and the things he missed. The warmth, the busy planting season, his folks. He was the younger of two sons, and they had wanted him to take over the farm. But one visit to the mission church in the State capital, where he had heard Dr Prichard speak, had made up his mind forever. The use of the word 'forever' frightened her a little, but mainly she felt warm, cosy and excited.

The Highlands beckoned. They by-passed Glasgow, cut up by the side of Loch Lomond – choppy water, pine forests and the occasional great house. This was the Scotland she had imagined. Then the stark, rugged climbs up into the sky – a bit like County Antrim, but more like Antrim's big brother. The road hugged steep inclines and plunged into sheep-dotted ravines. Soon they rolled down into Oban, a sandstone beauty at the edge of the sea, parading her wares before the Isle of Mull.

To her delight, the house they stayed in was right on the seafront. They were greeted by another old lady – she began to wonder if there were any landladies under seventy – and a similar contraction to that of Mrs Moore at the onslaught of her glamour. This one, a Mrs Weir, was a thin woman with flared nostrils. Her wrinkled right cheek had two small blood blotches, and her blue-grey eyes the gleam of a true believer. Bones rippled up and down her dark green woollen dress, and her left leg betrayed a slight limp as she stooped and led the way up the stairs. The weather was referred to twice, by each of them in turn, and Rosaleen particularly noticed her tact. No names were exchanged. Daniel introduced her as 'the new member of our church' – and promptly disappeared after depositing the case in the middle of the bedroom.

When Rosaleen was alone she sat on the satin-covered eiderdown. Pieces of highly-polished antique furniture were displayed around the room on thick rugs. Like all the fabric and the walls, the rugs were in different shades of dusky pink. Light streamed in from the west-facing window. Despite the warm colours and the light, the room was ice cold. The pokey grate hadn't been used in years. Her thoughts flashed back to the small, cosy hearth at home on the Falls Road.

She got up and went over to the window. Small fishing boats were stacked along the pier, and at its end a broader, fatter ferry-like boat pointed out towards the Isle of Mull. The sun was sinking into a wet western sky, a slate-grey sea lapped the stony beach. It had been a long day's journey. Was it the first leg of an even greater one?

Clip-clopping steps led up to her door, followed by a feeble knock. The brass handle turned. A head with grey hair, wide conspiratorial eyes peered in. 'Yer tea's ready, love, if ya want t' come down – would ya like some? A bit of fresh fish an' a few tatties?'

The meal was wholesome; the atmosphere strained. As if each was acknowledging that only the smallest of small talk was the best way to avoid discussing what was on their minds. Even the ubiquitous old radio was missing and Daniel managed the feat of not mentioning Ireland at all. Agricultural share-cropping in Northern Georgia did not rivet Rosaleen's attention.

As the meal ground to a halt, she announced her tiredness and the attractions of an early night. She followed Mrs Weir into a well-equipped kitchen – every surface gleamed – and waited on the pink rubber hot water bottle. Assuring the old lady that she had a copy of The Book, she took her leave, said goodnight to Daniel and went up the stairs clutching the hot water bottle to her tummy. Now, downstairs, she knew the real conversation was taking place.

She opened the case, extracted her pyjamas and another woollen jumper, and got ready for bed. With the Bible in one hand and *Kidnapped* in the other, she pushed the hot water bottle down with her feet to the end of the bed. First, the Bible: a random dip brought her St John's, Chapter Eighteen, and the trial of Jesus. She became absorbed, moved, read to the very end and put it down.

She now felt free to return to *Kidnapped*, David Balfour, Alan Breck Stewart and the Highlands. The room was freezing, the bed cosy, the tip of her nose cold. Outside, the sea and wind were restless. She travelled across Scotland with the characters, overcoming each obstacle. Would they eventually find their own warm, cosy hearth? Soon she was too tired to read, her eyes closed and she fell asleep.

A gust of wind shook the window; she awoke. A beam of sunlight moved across the room, and as her wrist turned over, she saw that it was just after ten o'clock. Her face felt sticky. She hadn't bothered to remove her make-up. A dash into the bathroom, a quick wash, then back. Yesterday was style, today she would go for a blend-into-the-background Scottish peasant look – flat school shoes, grey pleated skirt, woollen stockings, and a large loose brown polo neck. No hint of bosoms or legs – Mrs Weir should approve, she said to herself, going down the stairs to the dining room.

It was empty. So was the kitchen. On returning to the dining room, she saw the tell-tale signs of crumpled napkins. Breakfast was over. Anyway, she wasn't hungry. Putting on her trench coat, she tried the two other rooms downstairs – one a similar dining room, the other a spartan sitting room. She called upstairs. No answer.

Going out into the main hall, she opened the heavy front door and went out. A bracing breeze lashed in from the sea. All along the sandstone terraced houses there were gently swaying signs of B&Bs – their white-laced, bay-windowed dining rooms empty and forlorn. Further up the town, things looked a bit livelier: souvenir shops, postcards, teashops. She searched her pockets and found a half-a-crown.

Away from the harbour the town rose in steep terraces – offering good walking and great views: the stark, clean-lined architecture of the houses softened with a profusion of spring flowers. This was the prettiest town she'd ever seen.

After exploring the upper town, she went into the shops on the main street near the sea front. The clothes in the shop windows didn't seem quite up-to-date. She mentally compared prices; cheaper, if anything, she decided.

She felt peckish and went into one of the tea rooms just opposite the pier. She settled into a comfortable, cushioned seat near the window and ordered tea, scones, jam and fresh cream. Boats drew up alongside the pier, crates of fish were raised onto it and men loaded them onto lorries. The only customer in the tea room, she daydreamed – what might happen next? Where did her future lie? The Falls? Scotland? America? If she had to choose, she knew for certain which one it would be.

The sudden sight of Daniel shocked her. Not by his appearance in the town, which could have been reasonably expected, but in his agitated movement and the distracted look on his face. He craned his blonde head forward and peered into the windows of the shops opposite. She got up from the table, rushed to the door and waved.

He ran across the road, the black anorak flapping about him, and came straight up to her. He watched the young girl at the counter for a few seconds, then spoke in a low voice. 'Why did you leave the house?'

Her cheeks flushed pink. 'Why shouldn't I? I'm not a prisoner.'

'Hush!' he said, digging his hands into his pockets and glancing over her shoulder. 'There's people looking for you. Do you want to be found?'

'What am I doing that's wrong?'

'Nothing, nothing,' he said, shaking his head. 'Are you ready? To come back?'

'No,' she said.

She went back to her table. She cut a scone in two, buttered both halves, put two teaspoonfuls of blackcurrant jam on each piece, then used a desert spoon to heap fresh cream over the jam. Lifting one piece – the jam and cream dripping steadily onto the marble table, and then catching the tip of her chin – she bit into the scone.

Daniel looked away.

'Do you want some?' she asked.

'No thanks,' he replied, still without looking, 'I've had breakfast.'

'They're gorgeous,' she said, wiping the dribble with her napkin.

'Mrs Weir would have made you breakfast.'

'She wasn't there.'

'She's very annoyed.'

'About what? Missing one lousy breakfast? I'll have it when I get back. Though I prefer this,' she said, lifting the second piece of scone. 'You get sick of those greasy fries, you know? They're bad for the complexion.'

'I don't think she wanted you to go around the town.'

'I'm sick of these landladies and their oul freezin' houses. They spend a fortune on carpets and furniture and hardly a penny on heatin' the place – skinflints! Why don't you tell her t' light a few fires an' people wouldn't have t' go outside t' get warm,' she said, before popping the piece of scone into her mouth.

Daniel stared at the table and bit his lower lip. 'The house is cold – I admit that.'

'It's not cold – it's like the Antarctic. My nose is always red – I have t' keep powderin' it.'

'I think it's the Scottish climate.'

'It's not the climate – our house in the Falls is always warm – it's the landlady. She's too mean to heat the rooms. Tell her t' spend the breakfast money on a bit of coal.'

'She's just afraid people will notice you – that's all. And we're expecting a call from Dr Prichard.'

'Okay, let's go,' she said, standing up, scraping the wooden feet of her chair along the tiled floor. Behind the counter, from a kneeling position, the waitress raised her head and watched them leave.

Rosaleen marched out ahead of Daniel and strode along the pavement. He caught up and stayed to her left, protecting her from the traffic and the wind. In a few minutes they were back in the silent house, the heavy front door closed behind them, the only sound the ticking of a large grandfather clock from the landing on the stairs.

'Mrs Weir! Mrs Weir!' called Rosaleen.

There was no reply.

'My jailer's gone,' she said, giving a quick nod. 'What did she do – run off and pawn the radio? Tell me this, why is everybody so secret? We're in Scotland, for God's sake.'

Daniel licked his lower lip and said, 'She's just following instructions – that's all we're doing.'

'Whose instructions?'

'You know,' he said, turning away.

The front door swept open and Mrs Weir, bent over, slammed it behind her and directed her baleful gaze at Daniel. 'You have to ring him,' she said.

'Where's the phone?'

'You better use the one in the back study.'

He ran up the stairs.

Mrs Weir waited until he had disappeared before speaking. 'I have a big breakfast down in the kitchen for ye.'

'I've already eaten.'

'Eaten?' she gasped, clasping a hand to her bosom and reeling towards the banisters. 'But I have everything there. Cooked! It'll go t' ruin.' She waited for the implication of this to sink in before continuing. 'Good food! Bacon, sausages, two eggs, black, white puddin' and tatty bread – it'll all go t' waste if you don't eat it. Could ye not manage t' get some of it int' ye or else the bin'll have it.'

Rosaleen looked at her distressed face and said, 'Well, maybe I'll have … a bit.'

Mrs Weir's finger pointed like a dagger at the dining room. 'Go in there an' I'll have it out t' ye in a jif – ye have no need t' be goin' up the town t' eat rubbish when there's the best of stuff here. Besides, ye dinny know who's lukin' out the windy at ye – d'ye know what I mean, Rosaleen?' she said, taking her by the arm and leading her in.

The pristine dining room, decorated in the same dusky pink as the bedroom, had one place set at a large round table. As soon as Rosaleen was seated, Mrs Weir dashed back into the kitchen, her limp more pronounced when she hurried. Light sprayed in through lace-curtained bay windows. It was a cheery room, except for the emptiness.

The door pushed open and Mrs Weir came through at a slower gait, carrying a large metal tray. Rosaleen winced as she slid it onto the table. An enormous plate held two eggs, three sausages, four rashers, two halves of tomato, three pieces each of black and white pudding, two squares of potato bread and two slices of toast. Prolonged contact with the pan had shrivelled the fry, especially the rashers and tomatoes. The egg yolks had cellophane skin. And all the food was stuck to the cold plate with wedges of congealed grease. Mrs Weir smacked her lips, sucked them down onto the four natural teeth she had on the lower gum, and said, 'Yer lucky I dinny threw it out.'

Rosaleen gave her the ghost of a smile and gently poked one of the sausages with her fork.

Mrs Weir watched her. 'Don't be shy,' she said. 'Eat up. Ye need yer strength at your age. You're a growing girl.'

There was something in the wide-eyed expectancy of Mrs Weir that disarmed the rancour Rosaleen had felt earlier. After all, she was trying to be nice, doing her best. 'I'm not really that hungry, Mrs Weir – you see I had some –'

'Ye dinny pay good money t' them robbers up the town, did ye? They charge the moon – an' ye wudn't get good stuff like this.'

Rosaleen slowly cut off a piece of sausage and put it into her mouth under the watchful eyes of her host. She chewed slowly, looking off towards the window. 'That's a girl – don't be shy,' said Mrs Weir, lifting the large blue teapot and pouring tea into a mug. 'Just think of here as your home. I'd say ye have a good appetite at home, do ye?'

'Well –'

The sausage wasn't that bad, but it was with great relief that she heard Daniel's hurried footsteps on the stairs. The door flew open.

Another crisis. She could tell from the flushed cheeks, the nervous way his tongue moved on his lips.

'We have to go,' he stammered. 'At once.'

As Rosaleen rose, Mrs Weir gripped her by the shoulders and pushed her down. 'She's time for her breakfast. She can't be travellin' on an empty stomach.'

'I'll get my case,' he said, turning and leaving the room.

'What d'ye think?' asked Mrs Weir, tilting her head sideways. 'Isn't it good stuff?'

'It's nice. Very nice. It's just a pity I'm not … hungry enough to do it justice.'

'Rubbish!' she exclaimed, gripping her shoulder. 'At your age! Get it int' ye! Sure it's only a wee fry.'

Rosaleen pronged one of the large halves of tomato and cut a slice. As she was raising it to her mouth, Mrs Weir put an arm around her shoulders. 'Ye dinny have t' finish it all. But fill yerself up. I'll get ye a few books t' take with ye,' she said, turning and going out the door.

Rosaleen listened to the soft footsteps on the stairs. She went straight through into the kitchen and scraped the contents of her plate, with the exception of toast, into the bin. A pile of old newspapers lay beside the oven. She took one from the top, crumpled it up and stuck it down on top of the fry. Returning to the dining room, she buttered the toast and washed it down with lukewarm tea.

Upstairs, the phone rang. Mrs Weir's loud garbled voice, then a pause, followed by Daniel's softer tones. She left the dining room, crept up the stairs and quickly packed.

A few minutes later, outside the front door, as Daniel struggled down the steps with two suitcases, Mrs Weir thrust a small cardboard box of books into her arms. 'Good reading. Recommended by the man himself,' she said, ushering them down to their car.

A downward glance told Rosaleen that they were all religious. Interesting, no doubt, she told herself, and she assured Mrs Weir that they would be added to her reading list. *Kidnapped* she kept in her coat pocket.

Daniel started the car. It trundled along the shore, bereft of people, up through the narrow streets – not hurrying, but leaving.

Leaving, leaving, leaving – in the last few days she had been constantly leaving. They were nearly at the outskirts of the town before she asked. 'Why are we leaving?'

Daniel paused before answering. 'Dr Prichard said it was dangerous.'

'What?'

'Staying in Oban.'

'Why?'

Irritation was beginning to creep into his voice. '– he must have heard something.'

'What?'

'I don't –'

The car swerved up into a steep bend, just at the point where the view of Oban harbour is lost, and then the road straightened.

They both froze. About a hundred yards ahead, a black police car was parked, a temporary yellow stop sign was placed in the middle of the road, and two policemen were chatting. Daniel slowed down, stopped about ten feet in front of the sign and rolled down the window.

An older, stout, moustached policeman held back; a younger smooth-skinned man, short back and sides, tunic visible under a black raincoat, leaned forward and gazed at them. His voice was softer than his look. 'Can I see your driving licence, Sir?' he asked.

Daniel put his hand into his inside pocket and pulled out a bunch of papers. He slipped up a grey card.

'International driving licence?'

'Yes, Sir.'

'Can I see your insurance?'

He extracted a white certificate and handed it up. Rosaleen looked straight ahead. The policeman withdrew, read the certificate and went to his colleague at the side of the road. Some words were exchanged. He came back and leaned forward. 'What was the purpose of your visit to Oban, Reverend?'

Daniel coughed. Rosaleen was afraid to look at his face. 'We're … our church is thinking of building a new church in Oban. I had to see some people. About a site.'

'Are there not enough churches?' he asked, with a smile.

'There's never enough churches,' said Daniel, returning a larger, whiter smile.

'Have you any identification papers?' he asked of Rosaleen.

The smile vanished from both their lips.

'No – yes – they're in my case. In the boot.'

'She's a new member of the church,' said Daniel. 'We were in Oban on the same business.'

'Saving souls?'

They returned his smile.

'And where will you be travelling to?'

'Oh … the Highlands. Straight ahead.'

'Okay,' he said, standing back and waving them on.

After a couple of minutes Rosaleen was the first to speak. 'Do you think they were looking for me?'

'No.'

'You're sure?'

'Only two people know we're in Scotland. Anyway, you look older than fifteen.'

This pleased her. But she could see his knuckles, white on the driving wheel, his foot heavy on the pedal, the scenery whizzing by. 'Where are we going?' she asked.

'Inverness.'

'Why Inverness?'

He gave a helpless kind of shrug, his shoulders too big for the anorak. 'I was just given an address.'

'Dr Prichard?'

'Yeah.'

'– and are we in a big hurry?'

He gave her a tolerant glance, eased his foot on the pedal and said, 'No.'

'You're supposed to be my guide. Giving me the history of all these places.'

'Am I?'

'That's Loch Linnhe there.'

'Is it?'

'Very famous.'

'Okay. Give me the history lesson.'

She told him about *Kidnapped*. They skirted the foot of Appin, its head touching a white cloud, and hugged Loch Linnhe into Fort William. A bright wilderness of romance, where pine-treed mountains asserted their majesty over the land. Loch Lochy, Fort Augustus and the murky depths of Loch Ness. This was escape. Real escape from the grimy Falls. When they rolled into Inverness it was like visiting a maiden aunt after feasting with the Gods.

Their destination was a small, pebble-dashed, detached house close to the river that flowed through the town. Daniel picked up a key from under the rubber mat, opened the door and carried the cases into a bright living room. He set them down and went through to a small kitchen. Rosaleen followed him. There was a note on the table. He read it quickly and stuffed it into his pocket. 'Well, everything's here,' he said, pointing at the bags of groceries on the worktop. 'Mrs Hamilton works in an hotel. She'll come and see that you're all right.'

'Come?'

'When she can. Unfortunately, I have to go now.'

'Where?'

'Edinburgh, for a couple of days.'

'Can I not go with you?'

'No. It's – he thinks it best that you stay here for a couple of days.'

'On my own?'

'Mrs Hamilton will come – I'm sorry, Rosaleen. I'm just trying to do my best.'

She dropped her head.

'What do you want me to do? Ring Dr Prichard and tell him we're staying here together in the house?'

'You don't have to stay here at night. Edinburgh's miles away.'

'I have to do some business.'

'Business?'

'Yeah!'

'More important than me?'

'Well, no.'

'All I need is somewhere to stay.'

'Why are you angry? Is it Dr Prichard?'

'No, it's not Dr Prichard, it's you. You don't care what I want.'

Bafflement and hurt showed in his eyes in equal measure. 'How can you say that, Rosaleen? I'm doing this for you. I thought it was what you wanted.'

Her shoulders went up. 'Running around. Staying every-where for one night.'

'There'll be at least two nights here.'

'Oh, great!'

'… will I ask for three nights? Longer?'

'What are you? A message boy?'

His face turned crimson. His arms crossed each other and he stared down. She could feel his anger, from the toes to the fine short fair hair. His eyes came up and met her gaze. 'I don't think you're being fair, Rosaleen,' he said. 'What do you think I should be doing? Should I disobey Dr Prichard?'

She didn't answer.

'He's only thinking of you and your best interests.'

'I just think that somebody, sometime, should ask me what I want.'

'Okay, what do you want?'

She turned away, saying, 'You're so bloody predictable.'

His hands flapped the anorak. 'Rosaleen, I have to go. I have to meet a man in Edinburgh.'

'What is it? Another church, I suppose?'

'No, it's about you. He's a barrister.'

She turned around, her face slightly pale. 'A barrister?'

'It looks like there's going to be a judicial inquiry. In Belfast.'

'When?'

'An application's been made to make you a Ward of Court.'

'What does that mean?'

'You'd come under the power of the High Court. They decide.'

'What?'

'Your future.'

'No.'

'That's why I have to go to Edinburgh.'

'Two days?'

'There'll be a series of meetings. With legal people.'

A wave of fear came over Rosaleen. From the ordinary domestic irritation of landladies and breakfasts, there now rose a spectre of courts and judges. She had only been inside the Belfast Courthouse once in her life, a school visit, and that had been intimidating. 'Is there going to be a trial?' she asked.

'I hope not,' he said, glancing at his watch.

'And you definitely have to go?'

'Dr Prichard's lawyers say it's necessary. That's who the note was from.'

'Well, if they say it's necessary, you better go then,' she said listlessly.

'I don't want to.'

'They might replace you,' she said with a grimace.

His mouth fell open.

'In Edinburgh. Would you like that?'

'No. I'd like to stay. I'd like to see this thing through.'

He carried her suitcase up the stairs and she followed behind him. She picked the small front bedroom. He laid the case on the bed and stood for a moment looking out the window at the river.

'Do you know something, Daniel?'

He turned his head. The evening light streamed in and set his face aglow. 'What?'

'You've been in my bedroom for at last thirty seconds. Unsupervised. Not a landlady in sight.'

He smiled, then laughed, his shoulders moving under the anorak.

'Suppose word gets back to Dr Prichard? What would you do?'

'I guess I'd just have to leave the country.'

'They mightn't let you.'

'That's true.'

'You can rely on me. I won't blackmail you.'

'That's good to know.'

'Unless I'm crossed.'

Their eyes smiled at one another for some seconds.

'Well, I suppose I better go, then,' he said, brushing past her towards the door. 'It must be getting on to nearly a whole minute.'

They went downstairs. He handed her the key and carried out his case. She followed. At the end of the short driveway, as he put the case into the boot of the car, she pushed the gate back against the hedge. She watched his slow awkward movements at getting into the car that seemed too small for him.

He rolled down the window. 'See you soon,' he said, starting the engine.

With one hand on the gate she watched him move past her. 'Look after yourself,' she called.

He bumped the horn and drove into the narrow road along the riverbank, lined with poplar trees. Through these she could see rapids – brown water, white foam. A fly fisherman, waders up to his waist, flicked his line over the water. She turned back and went into the silent house and closed the door.

The evening sun spread its light through the rectangular window of the living room. She stood in its beam and looked out. The colours were hardening into silhouettes. She turned around. In front of her there was the small grate, the forlorn bag of coal and firelighters. She buttoned up her trench coat.

In the twilight gloom she thought of her mother, the new dress she had bought and how much younger it made her look. Why had she been so cruel to her? And Marie, whose love was never in doubt. She would never let her get this cold. This house was too cold for even a landlady.

Was Eddie still calling in his Italian suit? She smiled. Did her friends at school ever think of her? Sisters Gertrude.... and Veronica? She winced. Her Da? She bit her lower lip. The venom in his eyes, the fist coming at her face. The shock, the utter shock of his savage hate. Was he now paying for that in the way he deserved? Yes, he must be.

She was alone – no, she only seemed to be alone. There was Hilary and the girls from the meetings. Daniel and Dr Prichard. People who might prove themselves more than friends. Saviours. They were trying to help her. But first she must help herself.

The house was dark now. Breaking open a packet of firelighters, she threw some coal onto the grate and managed to kindle a small, trembling blaze.

There was a timid knock on the door.

Mrs Hamilton was a thin, highly-strung married woman in her early thirties. Shaking like a leaf, she showed Rosaleen over the house and lit two one-bar electric fires. She resolutely refused to look Rosaleen in the eye, and kept repeating that the good doctor would see that everything was all right. She left two more bags of groceries, and cold meat and salad from the hotel kitchen. When she departed, less than twenty minutes after her arrival, the house was slightly warmer. The table groaned under the mountain of food – were they expecting her to have to endure a long siege?

She sat down on the settee by the fire and read Chapter 18, St John, the account of the arrest of Jesus. When the Saviour answered that his kingdom was not of this world, it struck a chord. He was totally misunderstood. Didn't they simply hate what they could not understand? When she finished the chapter, she thought about it for some minutes. Would she soon be on trial? If she was, would she be up to it?

Her throat and tongue felt dry. She went into the kitchen, drank a glass of water and returned. The fire wasn't really catching, the heat was poor and she still hadn't felt warm enough to take off her coat. She went up to the bedroom, undressed, slid in between the cold sheets and perched *Kidnapped* on the slope of the pillow. Outside, beyond the poplar trees, Loch Ness was driving its captive water towards the sea. Soon she was warm and drifting towards the morning.

When she awoke a pale light was streaming through the window. The book lay on the floor. The gurgling of the river water sounded almost friendly. How less intimidating everything appeared in the morning.

She got up, dressed in her thick brown jumper, grey pleated skirt, woollen socks, and had some cornflakes. Afterwards, she sipped a cup of tea while gazing out the back door at the bright flowers that lined the small, square garden.

But the house was too silent. She longed for some noise, some bustle. She went out and headed for the main street.

What day was it? Wednesday? Thursday? A black Ford Prefect chugged past a post office and sweet shop. No big stores really, she thought, disappointingly, as she meandered through a gardening shop. The dresses in the clothes shops seemed a bit drab and old-fashioned. At the end of High Street she made a mental note of an Italian fish and chip shop with a juke box, and wandered into a record shop. At first they were playing old, corny Scottish tunes, but then came the excitement of Eddie Cochran's 'Com'on Everybody' – well worth the wait.

When she looked at her watch, most of the morning had passed. She didn't want to return to the house yet. She bought a newspaper and went into the Italian fish and chip shop.

The smell of chips and vinegar was too potent to resist. Sipping a coke, she spread the newspaper out flat on the yellow Formica top. The bold, black headline froze the chip heading towards her mouth:

BELFAST CATHOLIC SCHOOLGIRL ABDUCTED BY PROTESTANT MINISTER – SAID TO BE HIDING IN SCOTLAND.

Below the heading was a year-old photograph of Rosaleen – her hair shorter, the top of her uniform showing – but still recognisable. She dropped the fork onto the plate, held her hand across her brow, and through her fingers she read slowly down the column.

There were accusations of brainwashing, lurid and indecent suggestions, reports of a series of altercations in Stormont parliament between Unionist and Nationalist politicians, and demonstrations outside the Ravenmount church – all aimed at the Reverend Prichard, who was widely believed to have a major role in her abduction.

Rosaleen's cheeks were hot; her heart pounded. She quickly folded the paper, got up and moved towards the door. The middle-aged Italian waiter behind the counter looked over in surprise as Rosaleen dashed out.

The whole complexion of High Street had changed. From the pavements, the shops, the hairdressers, the bookies – strangers spied at her and were about to ring the police. Why had the police let them through the road block? Were they just giving them enough rope to hang themselves? Where was Daniel? Did he escape to America? Would she ever see him again? Were the police already back at the house? Should she return there? Where else could she go?

Head down, she marched on and away from the high street, cutting through lanes towards the river bank. A snarling terrier barked at her heels and then got bored with her lack of interest. Inside the house, she slammed the door and sat down on the settee by the grate.

The dead pieces of dusty coal absorbed the light. Her breathing and heartbeat were louder than the sound of the river. No wonder they hadn't let her listen to the news on the radio.

How? How? How had she – re-running all the events, from the first row with the nuns – let things come to this?

She got up, paced to the back door, returned, went up the stairs, into each small bedroom, then down to the living room and peered out the window.

Mrs Hamilton arrived at the gate with two more bags of groceries. Almost bumping into Rosaleen as she turned into the door, she jumped back and cried, 'God bless us and preserve us!'

Rosaleen waited for her to pick up two bulging black canvas bags and said: 'Why did nobody tell me?'

A strand of red hair dangled over Mrs Hamilton's two owlish green eyes. She came in, slammed the door with her foot, set down the bags and flicked the hair back over her head, all the time trembling and blinking, as if facing a deranged axe murderer. 'Tell you what?' she asked.

'The newspapers. I'm all over the newspapers.'

Mrs Hamilton shrank back and used her lips to form a perfect 'O'. 'Did you not know?' she said.

Rosaleen grabbed the newspaper from the settee and shook it in front of her. 'I just bought this on the high street,' she said.

The perfect 'O' expanded and brought forth a gasp. 'Bought it? Ya mean ya were out? God bless us and preserve us.' She closed her eyes and spread her hands. 'We're done for. We're goners. The game's up. We're finished.'

'I went out for a plate of chips.'

'A plate of chips? Sure I woulda made ya a plate of chips – there's tons of spuds in the bags. You're gettin' both of us thrown int' jail for a plate of chips? Where did ya have them?'

'The Italian fish and chip shop.'

Mrs Hamilton squeezed her eyes closed and bit her lower lip. 'Oh, you couldn't have picked a worst place. That's Martelli's. He hates Protestants and has connections all the way t' Rome – some say he's in the Vatican Mafia.'

Rosaleen swallowed hard. Everything she did or said seemed to make things worse.

'Did he folla ya?'

'– I don't think – I don't know.'

'It would be just like him to ring the police.' Her eyes became eggs. 'Maybe he's rung the police? Maybe they're on their way?'

'I'll go, will I? Will I catch the train?'

'Where to?'

'Edinburgh.'

'Ya canny go there. They'll see ya at the station.'

Rosaleen sat down and covered her face with her hands. 'What am I going to do?' she asked.

'Have you ever been in prison?'

She held back the tears that were forcing their way into her eyes. Where did they get these awful women from? 'No, I haven't,' she got out, without sobbing.

'Well, they have a new jail here in Inverness – I hear it's very comfortable.'

Rosaleen couldn't hold them back. The tears burst through her fingers. Her shoulders shook.

'Mind yerself, Rosaleen, we've done nothin' wrong. I'm just warnin' ya because they might hold both of us there – at least we'd be company for each other – the Reverend Pettigrew was held there last year for two weeks on his own. He'd nobody t' talk to.'

Using her fingers, Rosaleen spread the tears on her cheeks. This woman was no help, she decided. She would have to do something herself. 'Can you contact Daniel?'

Mrs Hamilton loosened a button on her tweed coat and said, 'I do have a number. But I'm only to phone in emergencies.'

Rosaleen looked her straight in the eye. 'Tell him I'm leaving this house today. With or without him.'

'Ya canny do that!' she said, shaking her head.

'I won't stay here another night.'

'What about the food? All that food?'

'I'm packing my things,' she said, rising and going up the stairs.

Once again she pulled the clothes from the drawers and flung them into the case. On the way to the bathroom she heard the front door opening. 'Rosaleen!' shouted Mrs Hamilton. 'I'm going to phone Daniel from the hotel. Stay where you are until I come back.'

She continued packing, not that she really had much to pack. Money? She emptied her handbag and pockets onto the bed. The fiver Daniel had given her. And some change. It wasn't a lot. She threw herself on the bed and closed her eyes.

* * *

Up towards Carrbridge, the icy peaks of Aviemore, along to Pitagowan and Pitlochry, then down to Perth, past the Firth of Forth and straight into the heart of Edinburgh. She was glad to be out of Inverness, away from the empty house and Mrs Hamilton.

Daniel hadn't come until noon the following day, but she forgave him that. And the great drive down through the Highlands was an escape of sorts. That was what she liked. Escape and movement.

And as they drove along Princes Street she felt happy – no matter that Daniel had been quiet on the journey. He looked dashing in his navy suit, and she was prim and fresh in her ruffled cream blouse and muted make-up. They could pass, she thought, for any young couple. 'Where are we going?' she asked.

'A house near here.'

'Do we have to?'

He gave her a nervous glance and said, 'It's all been arranged.'

She sighed.

'What's wrong? She's a nice lady. I think you'll like her.'

'Do you?'

'Well –'

'Can we go somewhere?'

'Where?'

'I don't know. Look, it's a lovely day – can we go somewhere first?'

He seemed relieved. 'There's a park near here. That okay?'

They continued along Princes Street and went up into Holyrood park. An early summer haze spread over the city – the castle perched high to the left, the streets down and around them, and the Firth of Forth just north.

'It's gorgeous, isn't it?' she said, getting out.

He smiled.

'Is there anything wrong?'

'No,' he said calmly, locking the car.

'There is – isn't there?'

'No,' he replied, shaking his head.

'You wouldn't tell me if there was, would you?'

'Yes, I would.'

'Honest? Honest to God?'

'Yes.'

'Why's your face all red then?'

He laughed. 'My face is red because it's always this colour – I'm a red-neck. My red neck goes with my red face.'

'Tell me what's wrong.'

'– it's nothing.'

'I know. You're worried about something,' she said, taking hold of his right hand. It was twice the size of hers.

'How can you know me?'

'Intuition.'

'Well, your intuition's wrong.'

She scratched the back of his hand lightly with her nails and squeezed it between her palms. 'Tell me or I'll squash it,' she said.

She squeezed.

'Rosaleen, I think you're going to have to try some other form of torture – it's not working.'

She pushed his hand away, saying, 'Daniel, wouldn't it be great if we could go wherever we wanted. Away from everybody – if you didn't have to go to see any solicitors – if I didn't have to be held captive by all these landladies.'

'Rosaleen, you're free to go anytime you want.'

'Then why is everybody hunting for me?'

'That's ... because of what you wanted to do yourself.'

'Yes,' she agreed.

'There is something,' he said.

'What?'

'Dr Prichard is coming under a lot of pressure in Belfast. Politicians, church people, your family. Would you ... could you record something on a tape that would express your own views? The solicitors think it's important that people know you're not being held against your will.'

'Is that what's worrying you?'

'I don't like any of this. Legalities. Tape recorders. What do I know about tape recorders? The solicitors have given me these,' he said, pulling out two sheets of paper from his inside pocket and handing them to her.

She started reading.

'To me, it's all legal talk – gobbledegook. If you're gonna speak into one of these tape machines, I think you should use your own words … to explain.'

Rosaleen read through the two pages of turgid legal prose. 'All the facts are there,' she said, handing them back.

'But it's not you, is it? It's not your voice. It's not Rosaleen Johnson.'

'No.'

'I think you should write and record your own words, your own reasons for what you're doing.'

'Yes...but –'

'What?'

'I'm not very good at writing.'

'I'll help you.'

Her eyes lit up. 'Will you?'

'Sure. I've to see the solicitors this afternoon. But after that I'll come round to the house and we'll write it together.'

'Great.'

'And then we'll record it.'

She liked the new house: solid old furniture, warm autumnal colours. From the bay window in the upstairs living room she could see the park in the distance and the shadowy castle. Princes Street was just around the corner.

It had been an enjoyable afternoon. A rebellion. Quashed his protests. She was not a prisoner. Inverness was small, Edinburgh was big. The nervous purchase of the newspaper. A seat in the garden under the castle. Not the first page, nor the second – she wasn't there. Anonymous. The relaxed visit to the castle, its horrible military history. Then the highlight – the museum of dolls' houses. A small girl had covered her eyes and turned away. 'Mammy! It's too beautiful!' she cried. Till closing time.

The return. Daniel, agitated and hunched over papers on the coffee table, afraid to open his mouth. She liked him being worried.

Now he was sitting on the same sofa, reading her handwritten pages, his pen poised. The sun had just set, a purple haze was spreading over the city, the streets were quiet. Behind her, the rustle of loose pages being brought together told her that he had finished reading. From the corner of her eye, she saw the red light of the tape recorder she had practised on fifteen minutes earlier. It sat on a chair. Narrow loose tape twisted down from the large spool and lay on top of the chrome microphone. She turned around.

His face was serious, his fingers touched the pages with a reverence. 'I thought you said you weren't good at writing.'

'That's the truth. Will it do?'

'Yes – Oh, yes. Are you ready to record it?'

She walked across the deep-piled carpet, took the pages from his hands and lifted the microphone.

* * *

The blinds had come down early on the windows of number fourteen Ivy Drive, as they had done every night for the past week. Outside, the street was dappled with shadow and light. Inside, a bulb in an orange lampshade threw its dim light on Frank Johnson. He leaned forward from the armchair and coiled his fingers around each other. The skin on his face was pale and taut; his eyes were hard, alert. Directly above his head he could hear Eileen putting on her high-heeled shoes.

The latch went up on the bathroom door and Marie came out. Black skirt, red jumper, and a sweet pungent perfume wafting before her. She sat down with a thump on the settee opposite Frank and crossed her legs. Her face was heavily made up, her eyes puffy. Frank looked down at the floor.

'Well?' she asked. 'Are you comin'?'

'Who said she'd be there?'

'Nobody. But do you not think we should be goin' along t' find out?'

'T' hear him?'

'Neither me nor m' mother are goin' there t' hear him.'

'He'll be there.'

'People are sayin' Rosaleen will turn up,' she said, folding her arms. Then a shrug. 'I don't know.'

'They're wrong.'

'How do you know?'

'She's not sixteen yet. Paddy Bolger says they won't let her appear in public till she's sixteen.'

'Well Paddy's goin'.'

'He doesn't expect her to be there either.'

'The Irish News said there were rumours –'

'Rumours!'

'Well, it's worth a try!'

'I don't want t' dignify that bloody man by goin' int' his oul bloody hall,' he said, standing up.

'All we want is t' see Rosaleen. And get her back home.'

'Hah!'

'We might get some information.'

'He's too clever for that. This'll be like everything else he does. A publicity stunt. A cheap publicity stunt and you're fallin' for it.'

Eileen's hurried footsteps scraped the stairs. She came into the living room and snapped her brown handbag shut. 'Fallin' for what?' she asked.

'Prichard.'

'Don't mention his name t' me.'

'I'm tellin' ya. All these rumours that Rosaleen'll be there. It's a gimmick. She won't.'

'I'm not sittin' here tonight,' said Eileen, drumming her handbag with her index finger. 'Wondering if she is or isn't. If I get the chance I'm gonna confront him. And so should you.'

'We've been to Ravenmount twice. Where did it get us? An announcement from the steps – publicity, more bloody publicity. Is that what you want to give him?'

'I wudn't give him the time of day, but I want to know where she is. I want to talk to her.'

'Tonight won't bring her back.'

'Stay. Stay home if ya want,' said Eileen, going over to the mirror above the fireplace. Her eyes were hot, glassy, and the powder only added to the puffiness beneath. She dabbed the slightly smudged lipstick with a tissue and put it into her bag. 'But I'm not gonna miss an opportunity t' give him a piece of my mind. He won't see us at his home or church – but he won't be able to avoid us tonight.'

'What makes you think you'll get in?'

'We're goin' now. That'll give us a full hour before starting time.'

Marie stood up and went for her camel hair coat at the foot of the stairs – Frank watched her. 'Maybe he's better stayin', Mammy,' she said. 'He might make a show of us.'

Eileen opened the door and went out and stood at the iron gate. Marie came after her. 'Wait!' called Frank from the house.

They lingered on the pavement. Two boys, playing football with a hard blue rubber ball, stopped to look. A lace curtain in the window behind them flicked back slightly. Frank came striding out in his tweed coat, his hands dug deep in his pockets. He raced ahead – Eileen and Marie exchanged looks and followed him to the bus stop.

Frank sat behind Eileen and Marie upstairs on the almost empty bus. No words were exchanged. He paid for the fares and stuck the tickets under the shiny metal seat-tops. As the bus approached Castle Street he rose, made his way downstairs in front of them and waited on the pavement.

There were few pedestrians on the short walk to the Memorial hall – a massive red-brick building with tall columns at the front and the two side doors. The latter were closed; the front door was manned by four burly middle-aged gentlemen in business suits. They had the over-friendly smiles of the elect.

The stony faces of the Johnsons did not diminish their smiles. One led them into the main hall, a vast theatre packed with portable chairs right up to the edge of a broad stage. A surrounding balcony stopped just short of this and on both sides men were adjusting spotlights. Behind the stage, lines of organ pipes rose up to a vaulted ceiling. The hall was already a quarter full.

Frank, a short distance down from the back of the hall, sat in a seat behind his wife and daughter. A constant stream of people filtered into the rows of seats and up and around the balcony. In twenty minutes the hall was apparently full. More people packed in along the sides and prepared to stand. A crush was felt from the back, excited talk rose up into the high vault, and the air breathed expectancy and tension. There was still twenty minutes to go before the meeting started.

The Johnsons did not speak. They just looked. They avoided the eyes of the congregation. They were different, they felt different, and they were perceived as different. Tonight they were spies on a mission. Amongst aliens who strutted a superiority. And they felt fear. And as the buzz increased, so did their fear. They had the sense of participating in a strange ritual where they were the enemy. The damned.

It was a relief when a balding middle-aged minister, the Reverend Campbell, carrying a red Bible, came out to the podium. Thunderous clapping. Calming their ardour, he held the Bible aloft. Muted words. Complaints from the back. The amplifier turned up. A short prayer. A summarised reading of the latest church financial statement – the discreet mention of the names of businessmen who had given generously to the church fund. New projects in the pipeline. The tone was calm. Polite interest from the congregation. More interest when a new church was mentioned. A special clap that one was to be built in the Republic. More details. Future fund-raising events.

Not so different, thought the Johnsons, from the homilies delivered at St Paul's. Except the coda. The sluggish beast in the hall pricked up its ears when The Man was mentioned. Its body grew tense at the hint of new evidence and important revelations.

The Johnsons flinched.

Two powerful beams of light strode the stage from side to side. Spine-tingling echoing brass music. A spotlight hit the door at the side of the stage. From the back trembling church organ music – a sudden silence, then darkness, except for the spotlight on the door.

The Johnsons felt sick.

The Reverend Lesley Prichard came striding through the door to thunderous applause – the spotlight followed him to the centre of the stage and he leapt the two steps up to the podium.

A quiet thank you to the Reverend Campbell, then he held the Bible aloft in his right hand. The applause increased. He wore a conventional dog collar and a charcoal suit; his wide square shoulders phalanxed the microphone. He bowed his glistening black head for a few moments, then he held up his free hand and fluttered it until the clapping abated.

'Please, please, ladies and gentlemen.' He smiled, then he laughed. 'Forgive me for laughing,' he said, 'I was just standin' in the changin' room in there – m' coat an' collar off – an' this wee girl dandered in. Lucky I hadn't gone any further – I know we promised revelations tonight but there are limits.'

A happy chuckle rose and faded.

'Do you know what she said? – do you play in a showband?'

Laughter engulfed the hall.

He stuck out his chin. 'I was gonna tell her she was in the wrong dressing room. But then I thought: she heard the music – she saw me changing. Why shouldn't I be in a showband? Wasn't there a showband playing in here last night? Maybe she thought my guitar was out here on the stage?'

More laughter. He waited until the congregation grew quiet. 'No, folks, I'm not in a showband. We leave that kind of worship to other, gaudier religions. We're not interested in shows – except where they spread the word of our redeemer, Lord and Saviour, Jesus Christ.'

There was some moderate clapping.

He spoke again when it stopped. 'The way of Our Lord, our redeemer, is not straight. Each generation has to find its own path, its own truth and guard against the corruptions and blasphemies that have been handed down by the Roman Catholic Church for two thousand years. That, my friends, is a showband – tinsel, glitter, vacuous noise – but we will not be fooled, will we?'

'No!!' the congregation thundered.

'The Vatican showband is the showband of all showbands – did you know that the early Popes gave their wholehearted support to the debaucheries that went on in the Roman Coliseum? Yes, the same Coliseum where they fed Christians to the lions. Of course, it was their kind of Christians – they fed the lions Protestants. Yes, an earlier version of Christian Protestants were fed to the lions by the Popes – and when they ran out of them they fed them wild animals from North Africa.'

An aghast rumble rippled around the congregation.

'Now, you may think that eventually they saw the light and stopped supporting this decadent barbarism. No! Do you know the only reason they stopped killing all the wild animals? They ran out of them. They used up all the wild animals running around North Africa and they hadn't it in their hearts to kill all the wild animals running around the Vatican.'

Raucous laughter rose and fell.

'A lot of these were, of course, the offspring of the Popes themselves. Maybe the lions couldn't stomach them – they hadn't got the Alka Seltzer in those days, you know?'

The congregation laughed.

The Johnsons felt a cold prickly fear.

'A certain case has been seized upon by the radio, the newspapers – and even the television from London has got in on the act. We had to keep them out of here tonight – though you can never be sure, the Pope's armies come in all disguises. There could be one sitting beside you now – here's a perfect test. Every woman in the hall take out a big hat pin – jab it in t' the man beside you – if he jumps up from the seat you can be sure he's from the BBC.'

The laughter rose, jokes were exchanged, the people on either side of the Johnsons gave them good-natured smiles.

'There's a lot of unsuspecting women out there tonight who didn't know where their husbands worked – this city is full of closet BBC people. Don't worry, don't worry,' he said, flapping his hands at the congregation, 'there's a medical unit set up outside for the extraction of hat pins.'

He waited a few moments. 'We don't really mind who comes to hear us. We're used to being misunderstood, our statements twisted into lies. The so-called communication industries broadcasting outrageous lies. We know they are the allies of our enemies – and let me tell you here tonight, we don't care! Publish your lies! Broadcast your infamies. Try to fool the people – you'll fool them once, twice even – but eventually the people will return to the glorious, imperishable truth!' He held the Bible aloft.

Waves of thunderous applause washed around the hall.

'We don't care,' he continued. 'We're used to it. But that's not to say we won't fight back. That we won't buckle our shields and face the enemy. With what? The truth!

'Why the truth? Because against the truth the devil has no defence. He breeds in the manure of lies and falsehoods, the half-truths that twist the dagger in the back. And, as each and every one of us here tonight knows, we have been calumnied in the newspapers, on the radio and on the television – by people who would jump up to the top of Mount Everest if you stuck a hat-pin into them.'

He stood back and gently rubbed his hands together, waiting for the applause to die down.

'You're all familiar with the lies and accusations that have been made against us, brethren. Me personally, other ministers, and members of our congregation. What do you do with a lie? Let's look at some of the great liars of history – let's take a recent one: Hitler. He said if you made the lie big enough the people will believe it. And indeed, the BBC and other gutter types have accused me of forcibly abducting a young Catholic girl, taking her away from her parents, her religion, kidnapping her and forcing her to be a Protestant – indeed, they use the word "Protestant" with the same sneer that generally accompanies the word "prostitute".'

A hush fell over the congregation.

'No matter. We're used to their sneers and insults. And let me be straight here tonight. We welcome people to join our church. We open our arms to receive new members – we do not, I repeat, do not coerce people into joining our church. Nor do we believe in coercion by any church. Religious belief, if it is not offered freely, is worthless. Did the Spanish inquisition really benefit the Church of Rome? Did it?'

He paused for a few moments, then moved his lips closer to the microphone.

'I know Rosaleen Johnson. I like her. She has visited our community hall and church on several occasions. She is a popular, normal teenage girl with, let it be said, exceptional personal qualities. Her parents should be proud of her. Her sister should be proud of her. To give you some insight into the nature of Rosaleen Johnson we are going to let Rosaleen talk to you here tonight. We are going to let her give you her version of what has happened. How she disappeared. Why she disappeared.'

Not a cough stirred in the hall. A tightness enclosed the Johnson family as if they were being welded into one unit.

'Rosaleen would have liked to have come here tonight in person. Unfortunately, she was afraid. Of what? Of coercion. Coercion by forces perhaps within, and without these walls. Instead she is giving us her words.'

He looked over at the door. The Reverend Campbell came through it pushing a trolley, draped in white linen and the eyes of the congregation focused on the grey tape recorder sitting on top of it. He stopped at the podium and retreated to the edge of the stage. The Reverend Prichard stepped down and lowered the microphone to the level of the tape recorder. He leaned over and spoke softly as he turned on the switch.

'Let Rosaleen Johnson, in her own words, tell you here tonight what happened to her barely two weeks ago.'

The Johnsons collectively felt as if someone was beginning to peel off their skin. Rumbling noises echoed around the hall, then the low hiss of a tape before Rosaleen's voice came on. For the first few seconds it was too low, then it was amplified until it reached every corner of the hall.

'My name is Rosaleen Johnson. Until a few months ago I attended St Monica's on the Falls Road. I left the school because of a disagreement with the nuns. Here's how it happened: one day I was brought into the head nun's office by the assistant head nun and ordered to admit to doing something which I hadn't done. Everyone in my class, including the assistant head nun, knew that I hadn't done it. When I refused to admit my guilt – in other words, tell lies – I was suspended from the school for two weeks. Because I was treated unfairly, I refused to go back to the school.

'This experience with the nuns set me thinking. They were more interested in justifying their authority and power than dealing with me in a fair manner or finding out the truth. I began to think about, read books on, and question the Catholic religion that I was brought up in. The history of the Popes made me doubt many of the things that I was taught by the Catholic Church. It seemed to me that the message of Christ had been twisted and used by bad men more concerned with the abuse of power than the word of Our Lord.

'Around the same time I got a job in Pattersons factory where I met a nice group of girls connected to the Ravenmount church. We discussed the Bible – we tried to find out the meaning of the Bible for ourselves. A priest or nun did not tell us what to believe – we believed what the Bible told us. In other words, the Bible spoke directly to our hearts and told us the truth. For me this was the greatest revelation of my life. Up to that time I had believed only what the priests or nuns told me.

'I started going to meetings at the Ravenmount church. The sermons by Dr Lesley Prichard brought the Bible alive in a way that made me feel I was in the presence of the spirit of Our Lord and Saviour, Jesus Christ. They made me feel the hidden depths and power of the Bible, in a way I had never experienced before.

'When I told this to my parents they didn't understand. They were angry at the interest I was showing in the Protestant religion. A priest was brought to the house. They forbade me to attend the Ravenmount community hall or church. This is something I didn't want to do. Religious belief is personal – it is between you and God and no one should try to make you believe something you don't want to. But I obeyed my parents – I left my job at Pattersons, cut off my relationship with my Protestant friends and stopped attending Ravenmount church.

'Two weeks later, a letter came to the house addressed to me. It was from a member of Ravenmount church – we had become friends. My father opened and read it. About ten days before, I had returned photocopies to the Church and said goodbye to my friends. On that occasion I had gone for a walk with one of my friends along the Lagan towpath. This was mentioned in the letter. My father got very angry and accused me of betrayal – he beat me and punched me in the face. I was afraid he might kill me. So I ran away from the house.'

A chair slapped back into the row behind and Frank Johnson shoved his way to the aisle amidst a welter of hushes. The Reverend Prichard glared down and stopped the tape – angry eyes willed the man in the tweed coat, head down, burrowing through the packed crowd, to be gone quickly. Their wish was answered – the bolt from the outside door rang out.

Immediately his seat was filled. No one noticed the distressed faces of Eileen and Marie Johnson – all eyes were riveted on the stage. The Reverend Prichard re-wound the tape and switched it on.

'– he beat me and punched me in the face. I was afraid he might kill me. So I ran away from the house. After wandering around the city for some time, I went to my friends at the Ravenmount church. They brought me to the hospital where I was treated for my injuries and they asked me what I wanted to do. I didn't want to go back home. I love my mammy and my sister – but I was afraid of what my father and the priests might do to me.

'Since that time I have been looked after by good people who have wished me no harm. I have also decided to become a member of the Ravenmount church. No one, at any time in the past couple of weeks, has prevented me from returning home. It is because of the great difficulties this would cause that I do not wish to return. It is possible, however, that I will return to Belfast in the near future to appear in Court. But at this point in time I do not want my whereabouts to be known by anybody but a few close friends. I'm signing off now … this is Rosaleen Johnson speaking …'

Eileen and Marie Johnson got up and edged along the row towards the packed aisle. The Reverend Prichard leaned over the tape recorder, switched it off, raised the microphone and climbed back onto the podium.

'Ladies and gentlemen,' he said, 'you have all heard the theories and lurid stories about the disappearance of Rosaleen Johnson. Abduction. Kidnapping. Brainwashing. Have all you BBC types out there got your notebooks out? "Svengali," they called me. Did any of these "News" hounds investigate the truth? Indeed, are they even interested in the truth? No, it was too easy. "Let's put the boot into Prichard and his congregation. They're easy targets." But everyone here tonight has heard the story from Rosaleen Johnson's own lips. It's not a nice story. It's not a pleasant story. But do any of you out there believe that it is not a true story? I doubt it. I can't say much more on this … for obvious legal reasons, but I think it's incumbent on all of us to stand and pray for that poor, wee girl's soul.'

The congregation rose in a unit, like an army called to battle. The Reverend Prichard bowed his head and said, 'Dear Lord, we ask you, in this hour of our need, to help Rosaleen Johnson overcome the …'

By the time they had reached Castle Street Marie and Eileen had talked themselves to a standstill. There were no buses around. It was the quiet time of the evening. They were surprised when they saw Frank coming out of the Hercules pub just up the street. He crossed to where they stood, his face pallid, whiskey vapours fanning from his open lips.

'We think it was a disgrace, Daddy,' said Marie.

Eileen blew her nose and dabbed her eyes with a paper handkerchief. 'I didn't think it sounded like her,' she said. 'It wasn't a bit like her. Not our Rosaleen.'

Frank ran his fingers through his hair and then pulled them down the side of his face. 'I didn't mean ...'

An awkward silence. Two men approached. One familiar – Paddy Bolger, the beefy, local Nationalist politician. A crumpled pinstripe suit, black receding hair and baggy shrewd brown eyes. He introduced a lean, distinguished looking man of about forty-five: square broad shoulders, high cheek bones, lightly freckled skin, cobalt-blue eyes, thick red hair with a side parting. His look was slightly boyish, intense, purposeful. He wore a black Crombie overcoat and carried his umbrella like a sword. Unlike Paddy, whose words seemed to come from his throat and die a short distance from his mouth unless he strained or shouted, when Richard Armstrong spoke his voice resonated with depth and authority. The Johnsons weren't surprised to learn that he was a well-respected barrister.

Both men had been at the Memorial Hall and wanted to speak to Eileen and Frank. A short meeting. They headed back down to Royal Avenue and went along it to the Grand Central Hotel. Ensconced in an alcove in the main lounge, Paddy ordered whiskeys for the men and lemonade for Eileen and Marie. The barman brought them quickly on a tray. Paddy paid, handed the the drinks around, then turned to Frank. 'Have you thought about the court hearing?' he asked.

Frank blinked back at him. His eyes looked dazed. ' – what court hearing?'

'Next Friday. The application to have her made a Ward of Court.' Frank's eyes drifted away. 'There's a good chance she'll appear.'

'Why?' asked Marie sharply.

Mr Armstrong put down his whiskey and spoke. 'The main reason is because it's the day after her sixteenth birthday. That will give her greater independence. In law.'

'But it all happened before she was sixteen,' said Eileen.

'– yes,' said Mr Armstrong, rubbing his small, smooth hands together. 'I don't believe a lot of that codology we heard in there tonight. Prichard is not short of legal cunning. Or advice. He has a few big guns in the background. But I think he's a menace. He preys on vulnerable, susceptible people.'

'That voice,' said Marie. 'It wasn't Rosaleen. Well, it was – but she wasn't herself.'

Mr Armstrong took a sip of whiskey, slipped the glass back onto the table and said, 'I've seen him at work. Rosaleen's not the first. Nor will she be the last. That's why this court hearing is important. A chance to show Prichard up for what he is.'

Eileen's head rocked from side to side. 'We've had enough publicity …'

'Before we go any further,' said Paddy Bolger, 'I think you should explain your own position, Richard. Where you're coming from –'

He shrugged his shoulders, joined his hands and spoke freely. 'I'm a Unionist. Protestant. Church of Ireland. I despise sectarianism in all its forms.' He paused. 'In my view the Protestant people haven't woke up to Prichard. I have three children – two boys, one girl. Northern Ireland is my home. I want them to grow up here. But I don't want them to grow up in Prichard's Northern Ireland. We've all heard him. We know what he stands for.' He leaned over. 'I feel personally for the terrible position this man has put you in. He's a master of propaganda. Exploitation. It shouldn't happen to any family. Catholic or Protestant. That's why I'm offering my services in the High Court.'

A few moments silence followed before Eileen spoke. 'The High Court? That'll cost an awful lot of money, Mr Armstrong.'

'Free of charge,' he said, making a neat wipe with the edge of his hand. 'I wouldn't dream of taking money. Prichard's clever and cute. He has good advisors. But he does make slips. If I can get him into the arena ...'

'You mean you think she'll come back?' asked Frank.

'Rosaleen doesn't know Prichard,' said Mr Armstrong. 'At least not the way I do. There's another side to the public persona and the jolly family man. This might be a great chance to sway people who've come under his spell ... like your Rosaleen.' He paused for a moment, and then added, 'I'm sure it must have been hell for you.'

Paddy Bolger asked if anyone wanted another drink. They all shook their heads. Then he said, 'When Richard first came to me at Stormont I ... well, let me say, I was surprised. But I know enough about him to value his honesty and sincerity.' He leaned back, folded his arms and continued. 'He's generally recognised as the best barrister in Northern Ireland – if Prichard sees him on our side, it'll certainly put the wind up him.'

'What about our solicitor, Jimmy O'Neil?' asked Frank.

'Jimmy thinks it's a great idea. He understands. If anybody can nail Prichard in the High Court, it's Richard Armstrong.'

'I'd like to have a go,' he said.

Frank and Eileen looked at each other. 'What do you think?' he asked of her.

'None of us have got anywhere. With him or Rosaleen. I think so –'

'We might as well,' said Frank. 'We'll give you all the help we can.'

'Thank you. If you don't mind I'll start tonight. I'd like all the details. Even the ones you don't think are significant – let me sort through them. Two of my staff are digging up all the information they can find on Prichard. I've set aside everything else so that I can give it my full attention before next Friday – and then in court we'll tackle the real problem.'

'What's that?' asked Paddy Bolger.

'Getting Prichard into the witness box.'

* * *

Rosaleen had finished *Kidnapped*. She found the last part of it a bit flat, like the Lowlands after the excitement of the Highlands. Indeed, a bit like Edinburgh after the novelty of the first couple of days. Daniel had disappeared for long periods and she felt she was waiting for something to happen somewhere else.

For half an hour each morning, she had been reading the Bible. Today, she had been trying to imagine what the Kingdom of Heaven was like. How wonderful, how brilliant it was. Like nothing we could experience on earth. A magical place where the souls of all the saved gathered together in an eternity of peace and happiness. Evil would be banished. No boring work. No nasty diseases …

The front door opened downstairs. She got up from the settee and went to the window of the living room. The mid-morning street was quiet. She heard eager, heavy footsteps all the way up the stairs. Daniel pushed open the door.

'Hi,' he said, panting. His respectable navy suit was newly pressed and the wind had ruffled his hair. He came over to where she stood and let the weighty brown leatherette hold-all that he was carrying drop to the floor. 'How's everything? I had to leave very early this morning.'

'Yes,' she said dryly.

'A meeting at eight o'clock. With the solicitors.'

'How interesting.'

'Well, it was, actually.'

'Oh I'm sure it was much more interesting than being here with me.'

'It was about you.'

'Really?'

She turned away and went over and threw herself on the settee.

'We're in Court. Friday. We're going back to Belfast,' he said, taking a white envelope from his inside pocket and handing it over.

'What is it?'

'Have a look.'

She slid open the envelope and pulled out five ten pound notes. 'What's this for?'

'You.'

'For what?'

'Buy things. Anything you need.'

Rosaleen stared at the notes. She had never seen this enormous amount before. They were crisp and new, sliding effortlessly over each other. 'What am I supposed to buy with all this money?'

'Well, I'll be buying the plane tickets.'

'Plane tickets? We're going by plane?'

'The day before the hearing. If that's okay.'

'My God. An aeroplane?'

Her stomach began to feel queasy. She was beginning to wish for a return to the boredom of the morning.

'We're better getting the Court hearing out of the way, aren't we?'

'Yes. This money –?' she said, forming a fan with the ten pound notes.

'Maybe buy some clothes?'

Her face blushed. Why was he looking at her grey pleated skirt and cream blouse like that?

'I ... I ... I don't think there's ... anything wrong with the clothes you have,' he stammered. 'Nice. Very nice. It's just ... maybe ... a court case, reporters, photographers.'

'Okay, let's go.'

'Where?'

'The shops.'

Princes Street was a delight for shoppers. The elegance of former times, and chic. With Daniel at her shoulder she walked the full length of it, peering into each window, examining the sleek models. He stood a couple of steps away from her, hands in his pockets, eyes watchful, and ready to nod with differing degrees of approval – interspersed with the odd, dissenting shake of the head when her lips twisted and she wrinkled her nose.

She returned to McKeevers, a large fashion store, where the clothes were slightly more modern and the assistants younger, and went in. An attractive young lady, discreetly made up, her brown hair swept around her head and dove-tailed into the neck, came over. 'Can I help?' she asked.

'I don't know,' said Rosaleen. The perfume and elegance of the girl took her aback. She noticed pale pink nail polish on her long slender fingers.

'Anything particular … or would you just prefer to look around?'

'I'll just look around, if you don't mind.'

The assistant retreated to behind a long wooden counter. Rosaleen, clutching the white envelope in her clammy hand, went over to the suit section. Her fingers stroked smooth wools and rough tweeds – a peek at the price of one woollen suit gave her a shock. She flicked the label up at Daniel – twenty nine pounds nineteen shillings and eleven pence. He sucked in his cheeks and followed her to the next rail – extravagant ball dresses, some low cut and others with speckled glittery material. She pulled out one with an ostrich feather diagonally across the line of the breasts and held the hanger upwards so that she could catch the full splendour of the rows of sparkling studs. Daniel's mouth fell open and his tongue formed a plum in his cheek. 'It is a … it is a court case,' he said, leaning over.

'Joan Crawford wore a dress like this in Madame X,' she said.

Daniel nodded and digested this piece of information. Then he asked, 'Was she in court when she was wearing it?'

Rosaleen nodded rapidly. 'Near the end. It was very sad,' she said, pulling the skirt out wide. 'What do I need, Daniel?'

He opened his mouth to reply but before he could get any words out she continued.

'I really need a nice suit, don't I? And a top. And shoes – medium heels. These are probably too high, aren't they?' She flicked up the heel of one of her stilettos. 'A bit –'

'... I like your shoes.'

'But everybody will be looking at me in the courtroom, won't they?'

'If you're on the stand.'

'My God,' she said, closing her eyes. 'Here, let's not think about that. Let's look at these suits over here.'

She picked out a navy suit. The jacket had padded shoulders – it tapered down to the waist and the lapels had a white trim. The skirt was tight fitting, just below the knees, with a two-inch slit. Daniel held her raincoat. When she came out of the changing room in her stocking feet he gave her a broad smile. 'It fits you very well,' said the assistant.

They watched her slip on the stilettos. She did up the jacket buttons covered in the same material, went across to the full-length mirror, and turned sideways and around. The assistant plucked tiny specks of fluff from the shoulders of the jacket. 'It's really a very good fit,' she said. 'It could have been tailor-made.'

Rosaleen retreated from the mirror, glancing behind her, then she went closer. Something wasn't right about the neck. She pulled on the lapels – they slipped under the ruffled front of her cream blouse.

'I think a blouse with a flat neck might be better,' said the assistant. 'You see, the jacket is such a good fit that the blouse puffs it up a bit.'

Rosaleen looked. The assistant was right. 'What do you think, Daniel?'

He partly closed his eyes and let his head go into a slow affirmative nod and said, 'The suit's beautiful.' Then he shrugged. 'The blouse …?'

'Will you be wearing it on a formal occasion?' asked the assistant.

Rosaleen and Daniel exchanged looks.

'– yes,' she said.

'Let me show you a new linen blouse that we just got in.'

She went over to a drawer, took out a cellophane package and placed it on the counter. Finely woven white linen, with two narrow layers of lace alongside mother-of-pearl buttons. In place of the top button there was a small emerald jewel in a gold setting.

'Does that come with the blouse?' asked Rosaleen, pointing at the jewel.

'Yes,' said the assistant, smiling and holding back a laugh.

Daniel leaned over the package and gave it a close examination. 'It's real pretty,' he said. 'Try it on.'

She took it into the changing cubicle and put it on. The material felt ultra fine and cool – not like the synthetic blouse she had taken off. It was the most luxurious garment she had ever worn. Her fingers stroked the lace at the front. It was too good, too delicate and too luxurious for her. When she stepped out she could tell what they thought by their eyes. 'How much is it?' she asked.

'Fifteen pounds, nineteen shillings and eleven pence.'

Rosaleen gasped. 'Nearly as much as the suit,' she said.

'The suit's twenty-nine pounds, nineteen shillings and eleven pence.'

The full-length mirror drew her like a magnet. She walked towards it, turned sideways and the mane of brown hair fell over the side of her face. 'What do you think?' she asked of Daniel.

'You look beautiful.'

She let the fingers of her right hand slide down the side of the blouse. 'What about the price?'

'It's your money,' he said.

The thought immediately struck her. No, it wasn't. And she hadn't even bothered to ask who had provided it.

'I have some more,' he continued, 'if we're short for other things. I don't think you'll find anything prettier.'

The assistant nodded slowly.

Rosaleen looked directly into the mirror and gave a faint smile. She looked older. And different. Hilary would like it. Marie would love it. Her parents? 'Yes, I'll take it,' she said.

Chapter 14

Rosaleen applied the final stroke of pale pink lipstick and dabbed a smudge with a tissue. She lowered her chin. Never had her eyelashes curled so black. Max Factor camouflaged the shadows under her eyes.

She didn't feel good. The morning's toast lay somewhere in the upper reaches of her stomach. Her eyes felt as if they wanted to close, and she had to strain to keep them open. On the single bed lay the navy jacket, the white-trimmed edges of the lapels forming a symmetrical zigzag pattern. The feel of the Police Custodial Centre bedroom, in shades of beige and brown, was warm and cold at the same time.

She drew back from the mirror. She loved the blouse, the emerald jewel at the neck, all bright and classy. A blast of air through the opened bottom-half of the window lifted the flowery pale brown curtains, but it didn't freshen the room. Outside a low, heavy, grey sky hung over Belfast, almost touching the green dome of the City Hall.

The clanking of the yard gate drew her to the window. A black limousine pulled into the cramped, busy yard. It looked the same as the one that had taken her from the airport to Dr Prichard's house, then to the police station, and to the Centre. Luxury on wheels.

Her stomach heaved. She knew Sidney Bradford, the barrister, and Nigel Campbell, the solicitor, would already be in the limo. The rehearsals in Edinburgh were over. Today was show day.

Her jacket was buttoned up when the policewoman knocked on the door. One minute!

A final check. The hair, swept high to the right, was neatly lacquered. The stilettos gleamed. Older, much older and wiser than the schoolgirl who had left Ivy Drive. A young woman. She beamed at the mirror; her smile collapsed instantly.

She swung the strap of her leather bag over her shoulder and went out. Down the stairs, the two men were waiting for her around a coffee table. Flashes of typed paper. Salient points. A jumble of words she couldn't follow.

She didn't like either of the men. Sidney Bradford was burly, with a square-set jaw, jowls, thick black eyebrows and prominent, often-pursed lips. His slightly hooded eyelids covered brooding eyes that surveyed the world with barristerial disdain. The voice was actorly with a splattering of Belfast grit. Nigel Campbell wore a dark grey suit to match his grey receding hair. He had smooth skin, an overly avuncular manner, and small shrewd brown eyes. His index finger always shot out, not at anyone in particular, whenever he was making a point.

The points swept over and around Rosaleen. Her head went into a perpetual glum nod. She knew she would forget every one of the salient points they made, the minute she stepped into the witness box. She was glad when they all got up to go to the limousine. The sooner she got there, the sooner it would be over. And there would at least be some familiar faces. Something would be resolved – today. That excited and frightened her.

It was the same chauffeur that had met her at the airport. He wore a peak cap with a brass badge. The legal team sat on either side of her, reiterating their endless points. She lost her bearing. Soon the bridge came up, black water underneath. The green dome of the City Hall. She knew the courthouse lay between them.

The blouse on her back was already moist. The traffic was noisy. She heard her name on the car radio – the chauffeur switched it off. The legal team were being terribly, terribly friendly now – saying how straightforward everything would be. She knew they were lying. She was wishing she wasn't here – better back in Edinburgh, even Inverness. Anywhere else.

The limousine slowed down. Off, an austere red-brick building, black railings, a gawking crowd, two lines of policemen. A snail's pace. Faces, the wax not washed out of their eyes. Heads, bodies straining. What kind of jungle was this? What had she let herself in for?

Suddenly they vanished. The car parked alongside others. She was led through high wooden doors and bright cream corridors – then came an enveloping arm from Dr Prichard and warm smiles from his wife. Daniel was there, tight-lipped and anxious, and Hilary too, standing well back against the wall. Other half-familiar faces from the Ravenmount meetings bobbed up and down in the swelling crowd. Sidney Bradford led the way and burst through a large oak door into the main courtroom.

Rosaleen surveyed the scene at glance: a buzzing amphitheatre then a sudden hush, three lines of packed tiered benches to the left, the high chair of the judge centre right, and below it to the left, the witness box. She was guided past two long tables in the centre towards three empty benches straight ahead.

The buzz returned. Nigel Campbell organised the seating arrangements: Rosaleen, first, at the front bench; Daniel at the back and centre; Dr Prichard and his wife towards the end of this bench. Hilary, three places down from Rosaleen, slipped her a peppermint sweet. Supporters filtered around and into the three benches. Soon they were packed. The legal team then sat down at the nearest long table.

Rosaleen took in the awesome trappings of the High Court. Straight across from her, on the front bench, sat Marie, her mother and father. A man with thick red hair, wearing a gown and holding a wig loosely in his hand, leaned over the shoulder of Paddy Bolger and said something to her family. They weren't listening; their eyes were transfixed on her. She looked back at them until she could take their angry, disappointed faces no more, and swept her gaze along the benches: Sisters Veronica and Gertrude, Father Wilson, neighbours, her Uncle Jim, and near the end, Eddie – reliable Eddie, in a red tie and his dark blue Italian suit, his Tony Curtis curls dangling down his forehead.

To her right, back from the broad centre, the tiered seating of the public gallery rose high up towards the back; Joan and two other girls from her class; a clutch of young people from the Ravenmount church and Pattersons factory; men in cloth caps, good cheap suits, others in expensive Crombie coats; women in furs or shawls or shabby coats.

A gavel silenced the courtroom. Everyone rose. A tall man wearing a wig and a gown entered and climbed slowly up to the high chair at the centre. His bright pink skin had been pulled tight around a long, thin face with high cheek-bones. His cobalt-blue eyes scanned the courtroom through small round-rimmed glasses. His nose was sharp.

Hilary leaned across to Rosaleen. 'That's Lord McDonnell,' she said.

He glanced at a sheet in front of him and cleared his throat. 'I am beginning this hearing today with the deepest regret. It involves a young person, her relationship with her family and other people. But an application has been made to have Rosaleen Johnson made a Ward of Court. And I, as the Lord Chief Justice, have to decide on the best course of action – taking into account her rights and the rights of her family.

'I understand both parties have legal representation here today – I trust that the well-being of the girl will be foremost in all our minds. Is she present in the Court?'

Sidney Bradford rose. 'She is, My Lord,' he said. 'And she would like to take the stand.'

'Very well.'

Rosaleen stood up. Her legs felt weak, her tongue and throat dry. She stepped down onto the wooden floor and began walking. The rattling steel tips of her stilettos was all she could hear – the clumsy noise was making a show of her. She turned at the first steps, which led up to the judge's chair, and started to climb. Immediately Sidney Bradford darted forward and Lord McDonnell leaned down. She retraced her steps, continued further to the witness box, went up to it and sat down. Now the only sound she could hear was her heart thumping in her chest.

The clerk came over with the Bible. On taking the oath, she looked above his head to the public gallery – a neighbour she didn't like, Mrs Rooney, was chewing her lips and staring down. Sidney Bradford came into focus. He pursed his lips and then said, 'Rosaleen Johnson, what happened in your home on Wednesday, April the twenty-eighth?'

Her voice was barely above a whisper and it quivered. 'I had a strong disagreement with my father.'

Lord McDonnell leaned over and spoke softly. 'Could you please raise your voice a little?'

'I had a strong disagreement with my father,' she said out loud.

Her eyes flashed to Frank Johnson. He bowed his head.

'What about?'

'Religion.'

'And then what happened?'

'I ran away from home.'

'Did anyone from outside the home try to persuade or induce you to run away?'

'No.'

'You had a strong disagreement. You were angry. You ran away. At any time after that would you have returned to your parents' house?'

'No.'

'You were on the streets?'

'Yes.'

'Did you seek out people to give you shelter and protection?'

'Yes.'

'So if these people hadn't come forward, you would have been a vagabond wandering the streets?'

'Yes.'

'Did any of these people at any time stop you from returning home?'

'No.'

'In short, your actions of the past few weeks have been entirely voluntary?'

'Yes.'

'Thank you. I have no further questions for Miss Johnson,' he said, going to the table and sitting down. Nigel Campbell immediately leaned over and whispered in his ear.

Lord McDonnell looked down sympathetically at Rosaleen and then turned his gaze upon her barrister, who was now flicking a pencil between his fingers.

'Of course,' said Lord McDonnell, 'Mr Bradford has chosen to leave out a crucial piece of information. Rosaleen Johnson was fifteen years of age when this crisis occurred. And it is a criminal offence to assist in the removal of a minor from her parents' home.' His eyes swept a short arc back to the witness. 'Could you explain in your own words, in more detail, why you ran away from home?'

'I thought they were going to try to make me believe something I didn't want to believe.'

'When you say "they", to whom are you referring?'

'My father … and the priests.'

'Were you afraid of them?'

'– yes.'

'Did they give you reason to be afraid?'

'– yes.'

'What reason?'

She hesitated. Frank Johnson pushed himself back against the bench, crushed his hands together and bent his head down.

'They made it clear that I wouldn't be given the freedom to believe what I wanted.'

'So you left home?'

'– yes.'

Lord McDonnell addressed the court. 'On the surface all of this appears to be a straightforward case of an internal family disagreement. Unfortunately, at least two of the people who seem to have played a significant role in her disappearance, have declined to assist the court in this inquiry. Is the Reverend Doctor Lesley Prichard present?'

Frank Johnson raised his head and stared across the courtroom. Dr Prichard stood up, straight, shoulders back. 'I am here, My Lord,' he said.

'Will you assist the court in this inquiry?'

'No, My Lord. My legal counsel had advised against it.'

'This is a great pity.'

'I don't want to act against the advice of my legal counsel.'

'Is the Reverend Daniel Upshaw present in the Court?'

Daniel stood up slowly, his face red, the large palms of his hands squeezing the sides of his black jacket. 'Here, My Lord,' he said.

'Will you assist the Court?'

'I'm afraid my answer must be the same, My Lord. My legal counsel –'

'Is this the same legal counsel as Rosaleen Johnson?'

Daniel opened his mouth, nothing came out.

'No,' said Dr Prichard. 'We have different solicitors.'

'Very well.'

They sat down.

'Mr Armstrong, you are acting on behalf of the parents. Would you like to question the witness?'

'Yes, My Lord,' he said, springing up from his seat. Hands behind his back, he paced the floor between the tables, the public gallery and the witness box like an animal marking out its territory. His eyes took in the courtroom as he spoke. 'How would you describe the relationship you had with your parents?'

Rosaleen fixed her gaze on the dark nylon stretched across her knees. 'It was okay,' she said. 'Most of the time.'

'Most of the time it was normal?'

'Yes.'

'Can you tell us when the trouble started?'

Her eyes came up and looked directly at her questioner's face. Freckles. Blue intelligent eyes. The voice … a real preacher's voice. Not really threatening, but the intelligence behind it was bound to make you wary.

' – it began when I started to question my religion. I read the history of the popes. I saw that bad popes had distorted the message of Christ and I came to believe that the Catholic Church was more interested in power than spreading the message of Our Lord.'

'This brought you into conflict with your parents?'

'Yes.'

'Was this before you left school?'

'It was around the time I left school.'

'Would I be right in saying that you had a dispute with the nuns at your school and left to work in a factory where you met girls who were members of the Ravenmount church?'

'Yes.'

'Was the relationship with your parents good at this stage?'

'… not great.'

'Bad?'

'Not good.'

'But not bad enough to make you want to leave home?'

'No.'

'You then started to attend evening meetings at the Ravenmount church?'

'Yes.'

'And who delivered the sermons at these meetings?'

'The Reverend Doctor Lesley Prichard.'

'Can you tell us in your own words what it was like to be present at one of those meetings?'

Sidney Bradford stood up and flicked his gown backwards. 'My Lord, is it really necessary to know every detail of an average run-of-the-mill religious sermon?'

Richard Armstrong gave the judge a wry smile. 'I doubt,' he said, 'if anyone in this court would describe the Reverend Prichard's sermons as run-of-the-mill. And surely whatever influences Rosaleen Johnson is relevant to this inquiry.'

'The question may have relevance,' said the judge.

'What were his sermons like?'

Rosaleen's eyes grew wide and she looked directly at Richard Armstrong. 'They ... they were wonderful. Exciting. They took the Christian religion right back to its basics. The Bible. And they brought to life the living Christ. He makes so much of what passes for religion today appear... shallow. Dead. Like it happened thousands of years ago. His religion is now. Today. I have never heard anyone like him.' She glanced across to her right and thought she saw Dr Prichard give her a smile.

'You liked his sermons?'

'Oh, yes.'

'And the man himself?'

'... I admired him greatly.'

'Were you attracted to him?'

'I think he's great. A great religious leader. He has great feeling when he speaks ... you know it's from deep inside him ... you know you're hearing the truth.'

'And you found this attractive?'

'Yes.'

'Did he talk about the religion you grew up in … the Roman Catholic religion?'

'Yes.'

'In what terms?'

'What do you mean?'

'Did he criticise it?'

'Yes.'

'Abuse it?'

'– well –'

'Did he vilify it? Did he describe it as one of the greatest abominations in the history of the world? Did he talk about the Catholic Church as if it was evil incarnate? And did he describe the present holy pope as – "Old Beelzebub"?'

Light laughter rippled around the public gallery. Rosaleen didn't laugh – or smile.

'He always made clear the distinction between Catholics and their church. Ordinary Catholics –'

'Like your parents?'

'– were misled by priests. They weren't evil.'

'But the Catholic Church was evil?'

'I don't know if he said the Catholic Church was evil.'

'He did. There are several recorded instances of it. So, Rosaleen, did the sermons have any effect on the relationship with your parents?'

'No.'

'But you have already stated that you came to admire the Reverend Doctor Prichard greatly. He regards the Catholic Church as evil. And your parents are Catholics, are they not?'

'Yes, but he always encouraged us to obey our parents.'

'Even if they were members of the Catholic religion?'

'Yes.'

'And these sermons, talks, ideas – from the Reverend Doctor Prichard – had absolutely no effect on your relationship with your parents?'

'No.'

Richard Armstrong circled around the centre of the floor, gently touching together the fingertips of both hands, his eyes down. 'At some stage there was a breakdown, was there not?' he asked.

'Yes.'

'What was it that led to this breakdown?'

'My changing religious beliefs.'

'Which had absolutely nothing to do with the Reverend Doctor Prichard?'

Rosaleen cleared her throat and spoke in an assertive voice. 'The Reverend Doctor Prichard is a minister. A man of God. It is his duty to teach the Bible in the light of his own understanding. My religious beliefs are my own personal beliefs. They are what I choose to believe.'

'And the Reverend Doctor Prichard did absolutely nothing to influence those beliefs?'

'He did nothing to turn me against my parents.'

'Directly?'

'Directly or indirectly. He always advised me to obey my parents.'

Richard Armstrong swivelled on his heels, his blue eyes shot her a laser of light. 'Even on the day you left home?' he asked. 'When you went over to see him at the Ravenmount church?'

Her mouth opened. Her eyes fled from his face to her parents, then Marie and finally came to rest on Eddie's red tie on the back bench. Her assertive tone wavered. 'I can't answer that question,' she said.

'Why?'

'I don't want to get anyone who helped me into trouble.'

'So there are limits on how far you should go in obeying your parents. And if not your parents – who should be obeyed?'

'I'm sorry.'

'Will you tell us what happened on the day you left home? Why and how you disappeared for these last eighteen days? And how you mysteriously turned up in court for this hearing today?'

Her eyes went down. She shook her head.

'I can't.'

'You can't or won't?'

'I'm here. I'm safe. I went away of my own free will. And I made my own decision to return here today.'

'Who advises you?'

Sidney Bradford stood up, the eyes owlish, the thick eyebrows like exclamation marks. 'My Lord, I am Rosaleen Johnson's legal representative. I advise her.'

Richard Armstrong turned as if a mongrel had snapped at his heels. 'And the Reverend Doctor Prichard?'

'She has one legal adviser.'

'So you refuse to tell us whom you went to see on the day you left home. Will you tell us where you stayed?'

'No.'

'Will you tell us who drove you to the house you stayed in?'

'No.'

'I presume your legal representative has advised you to provide all this non-information to the court.'

'No. It is my decision. I don't want to get anyone who helped me into trouble.'

Lord McDonnell rubbed his chin lightly with his fingers and said, 'It would be most helpful if you would give the court some details of your whereabouts over the past few weeks and the people you were in contact with?'

'I can't. I'm sorry,' she said, without looking up.

'I have no more questions of this witness, My Lord,' said Richard Armstrong, striding back to the table. 'For the moment.'

Lord McDonnell leaned over, trying to catch Rosaleen's eye. 'Would you not at least tell us where you have been?' he asked.

'I'm sorry.'

'Very well.'

'– can I go?'

'Yes, but please stay in the courtroom.'

Eyes down, Rosaleen began to make her unsteady way back to the bench. Sidney Bradford rewarded her with an affirmative nod as she passed. Hilary leaned over, smiled and squeezed her arm.

Lord McDonnell waited until she was seated before speaking. 'I must say it is deeply regrettable that the central witness in this inquiry has refused to reveal pertinent information. Taken with the knowledge that at least two of the other major participants are refusing to help the Court … it bodes ill for our endeavours to seek out the truth of the situation. Mr Armstrong, would you like to call any other witnesses?'

The barrister rose slowly. Just then the door to his right opened. A short stout man, tousled grey hair, neat deep-blue suit, came in , puffing and clutching a file. He projected a raised thumb, hurried over and sat down beside Richard Armstrong who opened the file and cocked an ear, saying, 'My Lord, could I have a few moments to consult my solicitor, Mr Robinson?'

A rumble of low-pitched talk spread around the court. Mr Robinson spoke without interruption, Richard Armstrong kept his eyes on the door. The Johnson family looked angry and tense. Sidney Bradford sucked his lips, drummed his fingers on the table and listened attentively to Nigel Campbell. Rosaleen and Daniel kept their eyes down. Dr Prichard surveyed the courtroom.

'Yes, My Lord,' said Richard Armstrong, standing fully erect. 'I would like to call a witness.' He moved away from the table, towards the centre, joining his fingers lightly together. 'When I started this investigation I found it almost impossible to elicit information from the major participants: there is a bad smell. A number of people from the Ravenmount church have striven to draw a sinister cloak of secrecy over the whole affair. Why? For a church whose members profess to be so obsessed with the idea of the truth, they seem to exhibit a remarkable reluctance to share the truth of this particular case with anyone outside their group. A bond of silence has smitten all the members who are in a position to help us. So the first thing we must ask ourselves is – why? What have they to hide? And, as we shall see, they do have a lot to hide.'

The door of the courtroom opened and a man stepped through it. Just under thirty, in a charcoal grey suit, he had a short back and sides haircut and a clear complexion. Rosaleen squeezed her lips tightly together. Daniel leaned over and gave her a gentle touch on the shoulder at the same time as he asked the man beside him to deliver a message to Dr Prichard.

'I would like to call Constable John Fenwick, of the West Scotland Constabulary, to the stand.'

The man hesitated. His eyes flicked everywhere as if he was taken aback by the size of the crowd. Then he moved forward, made his way up to the witness box and took the oath. Richard Armstrong observed the discomfort of his opposite number as he turned towards Constable Fenwick. 'Where were you on the second of May last?' he asked.

'I, together with Sergeant John Wilson, was manning a checkpoint out of the town of Oban, in West Scotland,' he said, in a soft Scottish accent.

'Was this an ordinary checkpoint?'

'No.'

'What was different about it?'

'Well, we were asked to look for a car containing two young people. A girl of fifteen years of age and a young minister of religion. If we spotted them we were told to note the details, car registration et cetera.'

'Did you stop a car containing young people fitting this description?'

'Yes.'

'What was its registration?'

He pulled a slip of paper from his inside jacket pocket and read: 'UZE 8426.'

'Did you check out its owner?'

'Yes. A Mr John Robertson from Portadown.'

Richard Armstrong turned to Lord McDonnell. 'Mr John Robertson is a member of the Ravenmount church,' then back to the witness. 'Do you see the girl who was in the car on that day in this courtroom?'

He looked across to his right and raised his hand. 'Yes. Rosaleen Johnson. That girl there.'

A collective exhalation of breath was followed by fidgety movement. Richard Armstrong waited a few moments. 'What general impression did you form of the young couple?'

'She seemed older than fifteen. He was okay. Maybe a little flustered. I suppose they appeared like any young couple.'

'Romantically involved?'

'– yes.'

'Eloping to get married?'

'If you like –'

'Did it surprise you that such a young girl was travelling freely … with this young minister of religion?'

'– yes. It did.'

'Why?'

'Well, we knew everybody in Northern Ireland was looking for them.'

'You knew she was underage?'

'Yes.'

'In possible moral danger?'

'– well –'

'Yet you did nothing?'

'We reported back to Glasgow immediately.'

'But you did nothing to stop them proceeding?'

'Yes.'

'Why?'

Beads of sweat began to sprout on the brow of Constable Fenwick. 'We were following orders,' he said. 'Instructions from Superintendent Lockhart in Glasgow.'

'Let's get this straight. You were ordered to set up a checkpoint to stop a young girl, a minor, who had been abducted from the family home. You discovered her travelling with a young minister of religion. You knew from newspaper reports, radio and television that the Northern Ireland Police Force, her family, various priests and politicians were all looking for her – they were distracted with worry about her disappearance. Did it not strike you for one minute that her moral welfare may have been at risk?'

'No, not really.'

'Why not?'

'He was a minister.'

'And ministers don't get involved in that sort of thing. Do you read the News of the World up in Scotland?'

Laughter rippled around the courtroom.

'I just followed my instructions.'

'When you reported it to your superiors – did they do anything to assist the return of this young girl to her parents?'

'Not that I know of.'

'No one took any action. Two policemen reported the presence of an abducted girl in the company of a young minister of religion to Superintendent Lockhart in Glasgow – and absolutely nothing is done about it? Is there not something incredible about that?'

'She didn't look as if she was being held against her will.'

'So, then, that makes it all right?'

'To me she didn't seem in any danger.'

'I suppose that depends on what you mean by danger. Her family thought she was in danger. Various priests and politicians thought she was in danger. I thought she was in danger. The law thought she was in danger – the law which it was your duty to uphold. Why did you not carry out your duty?'

'I followed the instructions of my superiors.'

'The plot thickens. We all know the power of certain people in the province. How it permeates every pore. So now we learn that this power has spread to Scotland. The heart of the Glasgow Constabulary. And it managed to ignore the law and allowed a young fifteen-year-old girl's moral welfare to be put at risk. Is the young minister of religion who accompanied Rosaleen Johnson that morning present in the court?'

'Yes.'

'Where is he?'

His index finger pointed across the courtroom. 'He's over there. The Reverend Daniel Upshaw.'

'Another one of our most reluctant witnesses!'

Daniel stood up, his face red and sweating, hands rubbing the side of his coat, Adam's apple throbbing against the white collar. 'I would like … I would like to take the stand, Your … My –' he stammered.

Sidney Bradford shot his chair backwards, saying, as he rose, 'My Lord, can I have a few words with the Reverend Daniel Upshaw?'

'My understanding is that you only represent Rosaleen Johnson,' replied the judge.

'There has been a change of circumstances.'

'Has there? Mr Bradford, this court is losing patience with certain quarters in this room. If there is to be a speedy resolution there will need to be more co-operation than has been hitherto forthcoming.'

'Indeed, My Lord.'

'Be quick.'

Sidney Bradford went over to Daniel who had come out from the bench. Richard Armstrong retreated towards the

Johnson family who sat squashed beside Paddy Bolger. From here he observed the opposing barrister's chopping hand movement in front of the red-faced minister.

'Mr Armstrong,' asked Lord McDonnell, 'do you have any other questions of Mr Fenwick?'

'Just one, My Lord.' He turned to the witness. 'Do you know why your superiors did not act on the information you supplied them?'

'No.'

'Thank you.'

Lord McDonnell looked over to his right. 'Mr Bradford, have you any questions of this witness?'

Turning around, his hand let go of Daniel's sleeve. 'No, My Lord,' he said.

Constable Fenwick stepped down from the stand and turned towards the door. His face was white and pinched. His eyes sought out Mr Robinson, who had buried his head in the file on the table. When he passed Richard Armstrong – smiling, his palm raised in friendship – he blew through his lips as if he was spitting out poison.

On the other side of the courtroom the argument continued. Daniel's head kept shaking from side to side. All eyes followed the action, except Richard Armstrong's. His were directed at Dr Prichard, who appeared to be unconcerned with the unfolding drama to his left, and was speaking casually to his wife. Daniel's head movement stopped, Sidney Bradford came striding back to the table and turned to face the judge. 'My Lord,' he said. 'My new client, the Reverend Daniel Upshaw, has decided to assist the court.'

Lord McDonnell's voice bristled with impatience and sarcasm. 'Your new client?'

'Yes, My Lord.'

Daniel marched across the courtroom to the witness box and stood rigid to recite the oath. Sidney Bradford didn't look at him. He read a page that came sliding along the table from Nigel Campbell. Richard Armstrong took off his wig, rubbed his hand across his moist forehead, and put it back on, without taking his eyes off Dr Prichard who folded his arms and smiled.

'How does it look?' asked Paddy Bolger in a low voice.

'They're throwing us the cub – I want the wolf.'

Paddy glanced up in surprise. The edges of Richard Armstrong's even front teeth slid slowly from side to side, a vein on the left of his neck pulsed. He watched him hurry back to his seat, sit down, close his eyes and knit his fingers together.

Sidney Bradford pulled himself upright and said, 'Reverend Daniel Upshaw, when you encountered Rosaleen Johnson on the day she left home, what kind of state was she in?'

'She was very distressed.'

'Why?'

'She'd had a row with her parents.'

'Was this just an ordinary row or a particularly bad row?'

'Particularly bad.'

'Did she want to go back home?'

'No.'

'Under any circumstances?'

'No.'

'Where did you take her?'

'To a house. In Belfast. Friends she knew from our church.'

'Had you full confidence that she would be looked after well in that house?'

'Yes.'

'Why did you find it necessary to go to Scotland?'

'Everyone was looking for her in Northern Ireland. She was afraid that certain people might try to force her to return home.'

'What kind of people?'

'Priests, politicians –'

'So you helped her to keep away from these people?'

'Yes.'

'Was Rosaleen Johnson ever in any danger or harm in all the time you spent with her?'

'No. Absolutely not.'

'My Lord,' he said, sinking into his seat, 'I have no further questions for Reverend Upshaw.'

Richard Armstrong still had his eyes closed and his fingers knitted together. He got up languorously, joined his hands behind his back and approached Daniel. The minister fidgeted in his seat, struck out his right leg against the front wooden panel of the box; the left leg came straggling out the open side, exposing a black, patent-leather, size–twelve shoe. His large hands gripped the rails as if he was about to spring out. His mouth opened to answer questions that weren't coming. His blue eyes were darting, puzzled.

The barrister gazed directly into his face, turned and went straight over to Rosaleen. Her eyes immediately went down. He stooped slightly and tried to catch her eye. She resolutely refused to engage. He ran his hand along the rail and moved down to just under the position where Dr Prichard sat, and while looking at him, he spoke. 'Reverend Upshaw, thank you for your belated offer to help this inquiry.' He then turned and took a few steps towards Daniel. 'You're a very young man. We must commend you for your bravery. Would that another party in this courtroom had your fortitude. When you were making the travel arrangements for Rosaleen Johnson and yourself, did anyone give you advice?'

'– yes.'

'Perhaps more than advice. Did you in fact receive instructions?'

'Sometimes.'

'From whom?'

'I'm afraid I cannot say.'

'– because your counsel has advised you –'

'I will answer for myself.'

'But not for people who have chosen not to make themselves available to this hearing.'

Sidney Bradford rose a few inches and said, 'My Lord, the Reverend Upshaw is acting strictly within his rights.'

'You will not name the person who was giving you instructions?'

'No.'

'You're a minister of religion, and training to be a preacher. Who's training you?'

'The Reverend Doctor Lesley Prichard.'

'A name that has been mentioned often, here in this court today, and throughout the land. The same person who has, unfortunately, chosen to skulk in the shadows and send out his apprentice into the arena.'

This time Sidney Bradford rose to his full height and emptied his lungs. 'I really must protest, My Lord, at the scurrilous insinuations of Mr Armstrong. You cannot impugn a person's character because he has accepted the advice of his legal counsel.'

'This hearing is not a trial,' said Lord McDonnell. 'I dislike the tone of Mr Armstrong's speech. But I do think the content is fair comment.'

Sidney Bradford returned slowly to his seat, his pursed lips and large egg eyes reflecting the unfair wounding of his feelings. If Dr Prichard was perturbed, his expression didn't show it. His face was serene.

Daniel's lips quivered. He brought a hand up and drew it across cheeks that seemed red enough to explode. 'I will only answer for myself,' he said.

'Do you know Rosaleen Johnson?'

'Yes.'

Richard Armstrong moved from side-to-side in front of Daniel, who had to keep turning his head to keep his eyes on him.

'Can you describe the nature of your relationship?'
'We're friends.'
'Just friends?'
'– yes.'
'How did you meet?'
'Through our involvement with the Ravenmount church.'
'Did you see her often?'
'Depends what you mean by often.'
'Once, twice a week?'
'Yes, up until –'
'Until what?'
'The time her parents stopped her.'
'Did you know she was disobeying her parents in going to the meetings?'
'– no.'
'You had no idea?'
'– well –'
'Lots of Catholics go to your meetings?'
'No. But it's not that uncommon.'
'How old are you?'
'Twenty.'
'And she's fifteen. Or was fifteen a few weeks ago. Did you regard her as a schoolgirl?'
'No, I thought she was mature. And very intelligent.'
'Are you aware of what precipitated the crisis in the Johnson family on the day she left home?'
'I think it was … a dispute.'
'You would be right in that assumption. And would it surprise you if I told you that you were central to that dispute?'
His head dropped, his words were muffled. '– I don't see how.'
'Pardon? Would you please speak up so that we can all hear.'
'I said, I don't see how.'
'Would a certain walk? A romantic walk along the Lagan towpath stir your memory? Indeed, your romantic walk – a

twenty-year-old Protestant minister of religion courting a fifteen-year-old Catholic girl from the Falls Road – does it not strike you as a calculated incendiary?'

'No. It was a walk. Nothing more. We were friends. She was leaving our church. I thought it would be our last walk.'

'So you had others?'

'No. Yes. Not along the Lagan, anyway.'

'So that was a special walk?'

'Only in the sense that I thought it was the last time I would see her.'

'And how did you feel about that?' asked Richard Armstrong, moving closer to the stand so that he could observe his face.

Daniel hesitated. His eyes were moist. 'I felt bad,' he said.

'Naturally. How would you describe Rosaleen Johnson?'

'She's nice. Warm. Lovely. Intelligent.'

'Yes, I'm sure everyone here today agrees with you. She's a nice, warm, lovely, intelligent young woman. What red-blooded young man wouldn't like to walk along the Lagan towpath with her? And you felt especially bad since you thought it was the last meeting with your new girlfriend?'

'We weren't –'

'Are you attracted to Rosaleen Johnson?'

Daniel swallowed hard. His Adam's apple pressed against his white collar. Richard Armstrong glanced over at Rosaleen – her face was creeping down towards the rail.

'Yes.'

'There's no shame in that. Natural. Perfectly natural. And you were attracted enough to write her a love letter?'

'No! I never wrote her a love letter. We were friends.'

'Would you like to tell us what was in that letter?'

'– I can't remember.'

'Let me jog your memory. Do the words – "There are so many things I like about you – your beauty, your charm – I will definitely be coming back for more!" Friendship? Was mere friendship ever described in words like that?'

'It wasn't like you're trying –'

'What was it like? Tell the court.'

'I … I … I admire her greatly. I wanted what was best for her. I was prepared to do all I could to help her. That was what I meant.'

'Does it surprise you that Frank Johnson understood from your letter that you and Rosaleen already had a relationship? An emotional as well as sexual relationship. And that you had already consummated it?'

'No! No! No! A thousand times, no.'

'Who suggested the honeymoon in Scotland?'

'It wasn't like that. Not like that at all. We were going to get away.'

'Who did you go to?'

'I can't say.'

'Under whose instructions were you acting?'

'I can't –'

'You were discovered together in Scotland, posing, in the words of Constable Fenwick "like any young couple", and finally you both turn up in Belfast the day after her sixteenth birthday – the very day her legal status changes – how convenient.'

'It wasn't like you're trying to make out.'

'I'm asking you one final question – Reverend Daniel Upshaw – do you love Rosaleen Johnson?'

He looked across at her. She had her head bent down so that only the thick brown hair was visible. Something moved inside his throat, his eyes dropped. 'Yes,' he said.

'I have no further questions of this witness. At this time.'

Daniel, eyes still down, stepped clumsily out of the witness box and went across the floor to his bench.

Richard Armstrong waited until Daniel was seated. 'My Lord,' he began, 'this inquiry is like the devil's onion. Each layer reveals a new depth of evil. Not only are we dealing with the sundering of a family unit, but it now emerges that we are witnessing a movement, a church that uses emotional and sexual infatuation to lure young girls into its clutches.'

Sidney Bradford's head had gone down into his jacket and gown, but he managed to pop it up and protest. 'My Lord, there is no evidence to support these ridiculous allegations.'

Lord McDonnell said nothing, Richard Armstrong ignored the protest and continued. 'A young twenty-year-old minister of religion is ordered to abduct a fifteen-year-old girl – to take her out of the country and travel with her for over two weeks – the same young minister whose love letter was crucial in the ignition of this fire – and who now professes that he loves her. I have no reason to doubt his sincerity. But whose sincerity do I doubt? And whose sincerity must everyone in this court doubt? And how much further must we cut into this devil's onion before the worm at its centre comes out to face the light of day? Your Lordship, I would like to call Marie Johnson, the sister of Rosaleen Johnson, to the stand.'

The sound of her name struck terror into Marie. She rose. The skin on her forehead felt hot, clammy and tight; the face powder on her cheeks had absorbed sweat, making them slightly blotchy; a jade-green cotton dress clung to her thin body; her hands and knees were jelly. When she reached the witness box and turned towards the great sea of faces, she clasped the wooden rail as if it was a lifebelt. Straight across the courtroom were the black broad shoulders of Dr Prichard, to his left the young minister, and at the front her sister, her face hidden beneath her hair.

Richard Armstrong coughed. She took the oath and looked to her left. Slouched against the bench, just down from her parents, he flicked his black gown to the side as if it was an annoying insect and came right up to the witness box. His face softened, his eyes were kind. When he touched the rail she noted the smallness of his hands, their fine texture, and how devoid of nerves he seemed compared to her.

When he spoke the tone was intimate. 'Marie, how was your relationship with your sister, Rosaleen?'

'We were very great. We shared a bedroom. Slept in the same bed. Talked about everything.'

'Is it a loving relationship?'

'Oh yeah.'

'You know her very well.'

'I think so.'

'Did you notice any change in her over the past few months?'

'Yes.'

'When did it start?'

'Around the time she left school and worked in Pattersons. But the really big change came when she started going to the Ravenmount church.'

'What kind of change?'

'She'd do things. Like tellin' me wee lies about where she was goin'. An' she'd stop talkin' about, you know, close things. And then she got a real set against the Catholic Church.'

'In what way?'

'Well, I don't agree with a lot of the things the Church says an' does. But she couldn't see any good in any … she thought they were all bad.'

'After attending the Ravenmount church?'

'Sometimes she seemed to be in a bit of a trance. Like as if I … or nobody could get through to her … she seemed caught up … in a spell.'

'Whose spell?'

'Doctor Prichard. He could do no wrong. Everybody was against him. Only he knew … about anything.'

'Did this affect your relationship?'

'Oh yeah,' she sighed.

'In what way?'

She joined her hands together. 'I … I felt I … I felt I was losin' her.'

'To Dr Prichard?'

'Yeah.'

'How do you feel about the events of the past few months?'

'I wish they had never happened. I wish we were back together. I wish she had never met Dr Prichard.'

'Why?'

'Because … because …' her voice trailed off.

'Marie, I know this is difficult for you. But could you describe the relationship between the different members of your family?'

She glanced to her left. Eileen, in a grey suit and dark green blouse, fiddled with her leather handbag and chewed her lower lip. Frank, a navy suit, white shirt and striped coloured tie, sat frail and rigid – his arms like two rods, his hands frozen around the rail. His face was white, pinched. His eyes had no look.

Richard Armstrong drifted towards Paddy Bolger, who sat at the end of the bench, beside Eileen and Frank.

Marie's eyes followed him as she spoke. 'We're just an ordinary family. Me an' Rosaleen are just like one. Like her an' m' mammy had the odd tiff … but m' mammy's more like a big sister really. Rosaleen was always the apple of m' daddy's eye. Especially when she was young.'

A jolting backward movement from Frank, the knock of his heel on wood – as he rammed his foot against the bottom of the bench. His hands drew back from the rail and squeezed into hard fists, the knuckles white. Richard Armstrong shot him a wary glance.

'… he used t' bounce her on his knee. Always had a soft spot for her. He took us both everywhere. Bellevue. Helen's Bay. Bangor. There was hardly a place aroun' Belfast he didn't take us. He loved her. M' daddy really loves her, that's why –'

Frank jumped up, his lips parted. At first no sound came – his jaw and face just quivered. His eyes burned, his right arm stretched to its limit, his finger pointing straight at the Reverend Doctor Lesley Prichard. 'That man seduced my daughter! He stole her! He tuk her away from us!' The words flew across the courtroom like an Old Testament thunderbolt, freezing the blood, holding time still.

Richard Armstrong gasped; Lord McDonnell flinched and drew his head backwards; Rosaleen and Marie both looked stunned; Eileen tried to pull Frank down but he remained frozen in his position. The eyes of the court observed the plaintive depth of feeling, the pain etched on his face.

Dr Prichard rose steadily to his full height and spoke. 'Your Lordship, I would like to assist the court. I would like to testify.'

Sidney Bradford's face went white. He dashed over towards the end of the bench as Dr Prichard, holding a large brown envelope in his right hand, edged out. 'My Lord,' he said, 'could I have a ten minute recess so that I can advise –'

'Advise who?'

'The Reverend Doctor Lesley Prichard.'

'Mr Bradford, earlier you informed this court that you only had one client – Rosaleen Johnson. You then acquired another client – the Reverend Daniel Upshaw. Are you now claiming a third client?'

'Yes, My Lord, but circumstances have changed.'

'This courtroom is not a marketplace for the advertising of your barristerial talents. Dr Prichard, do you wish to have Mr Bradford advise and represent you?'

'Yes. But I would also like to take the witness stand and answer for myself.'

'Very well.'

As Marie made her way back to the bench, Sidney Bradford pulled Dr Prichard by the sleeve and whispered: 'Armstrong wants you on the stand. Everything he says and does is designed to get you there. You're walking into a trap.'

'I have nothing to hide.'

Sidney Bradford scowled and swivelled away towards the wall where few could see him wincing and closing his eyes. Then he turned around and looked up at Lord McDonnell. 'Your Lordship, could I beg a ten minute recess?'

'It's not necessary,' said Dr Prichard, 'I will answer for myself. Now.'

A pained expression crossed the barrister's lips; his eyes were baleful, angry. He hurried back to the table, gave his gown a petulant flick and dropped into his seat.

Dr Prichard opened the top of the brown envelope, peeped into it and marched over to the witness box. Shifting around to get comfortable, he placed the envelope on the rail and put his hand on the Bible to take the oath.

Richard Armstrong leaned his head forward to Paddy Bolger, smiled and whispered: 'The wolf has left its lair.'

'What's in the envelope?'

'I don't know. But we'll soon find out,' he said, removing his wig. A wreathe of dark wet hair encircled the bright red crown of his head. He rubbed the sweat from his brow. Replacing his wig, he moved away, cutting a wide arc around the witness stand, gently knitting and unknitting his fingers.

'Dr Prichard, do you believe in the devil?'

'Yes, I do.'

'What form do you think he takes?'

'I think he can take any form, Mr Armstrong. He can even take the form of a red-haired barrister.'

Laughter swept the courtroom.

'Or a pope. Head of the Catholic Church. Old Beelzebub – is that what you call him?'

'One of the names.'

'And is this term of opprobrium confined to barristers and the pope?'

'No.'

'A selected few?'

'All popes – and a few barristers.'

Chuckles rippled around the benches.

'The heads of another Christian church. And people who have the temerity to question you in a public forum. Do the names: Mary Conway, Brigid McCarthy, Priscilla Andrews, Jane Rogers, Sinead McArdle, Rosemary Dunbar and John Hurson mean anything to you?'

'Yes, they are all members of our church.'

'And former members of other churches.'

'Yes.'

'Who have all gone to America and attended the Brinsley Hughes College in the state of Georgia?'

'Yes.'

'For preacher training?'

'Not simply preacher training. They study a diverse range of theology. The Bible. And other studies.'

'With a view to preaching in your particular church?'

'They are free to choose. If they choose to spread the gospel within our church, I will welcome them with open arms.'

'Their ages – three just over sixteen and two just over seventeen – do you accept that?'

'It's possibly true.'

Sidney Bradford, his face still sour, rose a few inches from his seat. 'My Lord,' he said, 'is the student history of a North American college really relevant to this inquiry?'

'I'm showing that Rosaleen Johnson is not an isolated case. Rather she is part of a institutionalised process whose managing director is sitting in that box.'

Lord McDonnell licked the edge of his pink lips, his eyes looked out over his spectacles, and he said, 'Proceed.'

'Six out of the seven are young girls?'

Dr Prichard shifted position – the eyes slightly puzzled, a thin smile spreading the lips – he folded his arms and said, 'Religious belief is not gender based.'

'Is there any particular reason why there is such a preponderance of young girls among these "converts"?'

He smacked his lips together and spoke with confidence. 'I would have thought the reason was obvious – it's my matinee idol good looks.' Laughter crackled around the court – he waited until it abated. 'These young people don't come to Christ – they come to gawk at my face. Hollywood have made numerous offers, all of which I have refused.'

The ripples continued. Richard Armstrong didn't smile. He bit on his lower lip and for the first time his confidence seemed to waver as he asked, 'So you don't think young girls are impressionable?'

'They may be impressionable to the lead singers of showbands and film stars – but to an oul married man with a wife and two young children? Would you have a titter of wit, Mr Armstrong?'

'So it's only a coincidence?'

'Clark Gable need have no worries.'

'Clark Gable is not luring young girls away from their families and the religion of their birth.'

His arms unfolded, his hands gripped the rail, and his eyes turned hard and protruding. 'I resent that remark! I preach the plain and simple words of Our Lord and Saviour, Jesus Christ. Do you dare construe the words of Our Lord as temptations designed to lead astray young men and young girls?'

'You refer to yourself as Reverend Doctor Lesley Prichard?'

The tone was still hot. 'Yes.'

'I studied for my doctorate at Queen's University for seven years. I know that the learned judge spent a similar length of time at Oxford, indeed your good counsel –'

Sidney Bradford stood up. 'My Lord,' he said, 'we're all very impressed with all our qualifications – but where exactly is it leading us?'

'The "Reverend Doctor" Lesley Prichard impresses young people with the self-styled title of "Doctor" – surely a brief examination of his academic credentials is relevant?'

Lord McDonnell nodded.

'Which academic institution conferred on you the title of "Doctor", Doctor?'

'The Brinsley Hughes College.'

'Seven years would be a normal period of study for the average doctor, but then I imagine that in this case we're not dealing with an "average" doctorate. How long did you spend on your particular course of graduate study?'

From the neck up, a light blush began to spread across Dr Prichard's face. '… I can't say exactly.'

'I can. I have your enrolment forms on file. You spent a grand total of six weeks earning your "doctorate". Six weeks was all it took for you to achieve the title of "Doctor" from the Brinsley Hughes College.'

'I have my diploma,' he intoned, thrusting his index finger into the air, 'from the Belfast Theological College.'

'I'm not asking you about your undergraduate diploma, "Doctor". I'm asking you about your doctorate?'

'I performed the set tasks. All the studies I was asked to complete. I know The Book backwards.'

Richard Armstrong turned and addressed the court. 'When I first started this investigation, I did suppose that it was possible "Doctor" Prichard was some species of genius. That he could accomplish in less than seven weeks what takes the rest of us mortals at least seven years at an establishment of higher education. But then I decided to check.' He addressed the witness: 'What kind of theological scholar would you say you were, "Doctor" Prichard?'

'I performed all the set studies.'

'Your secondary school was kind enough to supply me with reports on your final years there. You actually left school at sixteen. According to those reports, you were average, below-average, or slightly above-average –'

'My Lord,' exclaimed Sidney Bradford, standing again, 'what is the relevance?'

Richard Armstrong turned to face him. 'I want to know how an average or below average scholar manages to achieve a PhD in a six-week period of study?'

'I may have only been enrolled for six weeks,' said Dr Prichard, 'but my period of study was much longer.'

'Was it? Was it indeed! Well, I contacted the United States Department of Education and asked them for details,' he said, going over to the table. Mr Robinson handed him a letter and he started reading. '... The Brinsley Hughes College has been investigated by our department and found not to meet minimum acceptable standards for colleges and universities in this country. It is what we here in the United States call a degree mill – a bogus college.' Holding the letter aloft he handed it up to Lord McDonnell and said, 'How stands your doctorate now, "Doctor" Prichard?'

'I repeat what I said – I performed the set task of studies for my degree and I challenge anyone to question my knowledge of The Book.'

'We would have preferred to put that question directly to your mentor – Mr Brinsley Hughes – but unfortunately he was unable to join us here today. Primarily because he was involved in a little court case of his own last November, and was sentenced to two years in prison for embezzlement.'

'My Lord,' said Sidney Bradford, 'I fail to see what relevance all this has to the case under consideration.'

'Relevance!' cried Richard Armstrong, wincing in pained incredulity. 'There are hundreds of these degree mills throughout North America, specifically designed for people whose stock-in-trade is deception. Three-card-trick merchants of the religious world. People who use the title "Doctor" to impress young people, deceivers who want the title and respect without the hard slog and work of genuine achievement.'

Lord McDonnell gave a quick nod and said, 'I think it has a bearing on the case.'

'The Reverend Prichard specialises in packing young people off to bogus colleges for them to be brainwashed.'

Sidney Bradford shook his head, the wig swinging from side to side. 'You are making all kinds of allegations without one shred of proof,' he cried. 'My Lord, Mr Armstrong is taking advantage of the licence you are allowing him.'

'This is an inquiry,' said Lord McDonnell. 'No burden of proof is required.'

'Is there any proof,' challenged Sidney Bradford, 'that any of these young people were sent or held anywhere against their will?'

Richard Armstrong shook his head. 'My point is – that after the Reverend Prichard has finished with them, their will becomes his will.'

'Sheer unadulterated nonsense!' exclaimed Mr Bradford, little flecks of spit flying from his mouth. 'Does Rosaleen Johnson sound like a girl who has no will of her own?'

'We have already heard from her own sister about the change that came over her after attending Prichard's sermons. How critical, intolerant and disobedient she became.'

'Even if one or all of these claims were true – and it is all conjecture and opinion – are any of them a crime?'

'Perhaps not, Mr Bradford. But as we shall see, the step-by-step process that Prichard perpetuates does lead ultimately to crime.' He turned to Dr Prichard, who sat in the box gazing at him with sullen, watchful eyes. 'Do you claim to have the welfare of Rosaleen Johnson at heart?'

'– yes, I do.'

'Spiritual and physical?'

'Yes.'

'It doesn't take great imagination to know what it would be like in the average Catholic household on the Falls Road for a fifteen-year-old daughter to announce that she wanted to become a Protestant. Did you envisage it causing trouble in the family?'

'At the particular time you're talking about – I had no idea she wanted to become a Protestant.'

'No idea?'

'No.'

'You gave her no advice?'

'I advised her to obey her parents.'

'By doing what?'

'Obeying them.'

'And you had no idea that she was interested in joining your church?'

'No.'

'What is the purpose of your meetings?'

'To bring people to Christ through spreading the good news of Our Lord.'

'And get them to change their religion?'

'If they change their religion that is the work of Christ, through me. I am merely his instrument.'

'You're an empty vessel?'

'Not today, Mr Armstrong, I had a good Ulster fry this morning.'

'So the good Lord works through you to convert people?'

'I think you overrate my powers of conversion.'

'On immature minds?'

'I am not a psychologist.'

'Nor a doctor.'

'Do you not remember, Mr Armstrong, that in one of your newspaper articles you did confer on me the title of doctor.'

His eyes went wide. 'Did I?'

'Yes – a "witch doctor".'

Laughter swept around the benches.

'I was probably referring to your time in America when you consorted with American Indians – that they would have at least conferred a big degree on a heap important medicine man like yourself.'

'To my knowledge I consorted with no American Indians.'

'What? No bogus ones even? You've expressed concern for Rosaleen Johnson and her relationship with her family. Did you do anything to assist the sundering of that relationship?'

Dr Prichard lifted the brown envelope from the rail, held it between his fingers and said, 'No.'

'I think the good doctor should remember that he is in a court of law and under oath.'

'I'm fully aware of what I'm under.'

'You played no role in her disappearance?'

'Yes, I did.'

Movement stirred in the public gallery and the benches, a collective leaning forward.

'What precisely?'

'I assisted in her removal from physical danger.'

'Let's get this straight. You, wilfully and deliberately, assisted in the removal of a girl of fifteen years of age, a minor, from her family home?'

'You're twisting my words.'

'I'm merely trying to understand the barefaced audacity of a minister of religion who will stand up in this court and boast that he sundered the unity of a family and assisted in the removal of a minor from the family home.'

'You're using weasel words, Mr Armstrong.'

'I'm using "your" words.'

'Far be it from me – a mere minister of religion – to question your understanding and use of language. But I think we can all agree that I said: "I assisted in her removal from physical danger".'

'You helped to get her to leave home?'

'No.'

'On Wednesday the twenty-eighth of April?'

'When I met Rosaleen Johnson on that date she had already left home – she was wandering around the city.'

'You took advantage of a domestic dispute?'

'I was deeply worried.'

'About what?'

'What would happen to her.'

'At whose hands? The Johnson family? There they are,' he said, drawing his hand in their direction. 'You've heard her sister speak fondly of her. Mrs Johnson? Mr Johnson? – are they monsters?'

'No.'

'Yet you decided to render their family asunder. To worry them sick. To cause a sensation in parliament. To focus the attention of the world's press, radio and television on one unfortunate family whose daughter had the misfortune to attend one of your sermons.'

'I acted solely in the interest of Rosaleen Johnson. I believed her to be in great physical danger.'

'From a domestic disagreement? Come, come, "Doctor" Prichard. Look at the girl over there. It's just over two weeks since she left home. Does she look like someone who was in great physical danger?'

'No, not now, but she did when I saw her – this was how she looked,' he said, sliding a large coloured photograph of Rosaleen's face out of the brown envelope and holding it up. Her face was barely recognisable – badly swollen, with yellow and blue skin, and a brown slash above her closed, left eye.

The courtroom was silent. Frank Johnson's eyes went to the floor, his head sunk into his shoulders. Rosaleen covered her eyes with her hands. Eileen and Marie looked horrified. Richard Armstrong sucked in his lips and leaned back against the table.

Lord McDonnell broke the silence. 'Can I see the photograph, please?'

The clerk took it from Dr Prichard, went up the steps and handed it over. He gazed at the photograph for a short time. There was shock and sadness in his eyes. Eventually he looked up. 'Mr Armstrong?'

'Yes, My Lord,' he said, going over and stepping up to receive it. Coming back down he examined the blue stamp on the back of the photograph and turned to Dr Prichard. 'When was this photograph taken?' he asked.

'On the evening of April the twenty-eighth – the day Rosaleen Johnson left home.'

'Where was it taken?'

'The East Belfast hospital.'

'What camera was used?'

'The official hospital camera. It's dated and recorded in the hospital files.'

'What actually happened that evening?'

'Rosaleen arrived. Badly injured. She said her father had punched her. I advised her to go to hospital.'

'Did you go with her?'

'No.'

'Who brought her?'

'The Reverend Daniel Upshaw.'

'Who took the photograph?'

'A hospital doctor.'

'Is it normal for a hospital doctor to take photographs of people who come in to have injuries treated?'

'I don't know.'

'Well, let me make an addition to your education. It is not normal. It is extremely abnormal. Did you make a special request to have a photograph taken of her face?'

Dr Prichard hesitated. He shot a glance at Sidney Bradford. No help was forthcoming.

'– I asked for it,' he said.

'Why?'

'Because it was an abnormal situation.'

'And that's the only reason?'

'I thought it sufficient reason.'

'It didn't cross your mind that what you were about to embark on was a highly dangerous and illegal action – namely, the abduction of a minor, and like the proverbial and cunning magpie, you were gathering trinkets of evidence for your defence of this criminal act in the High Court of the land?'

'My concern was for the safety of Rosaleen Johnson. Any Christian in my position would do the same.'

'Take photographs of the poor girl's bruised face and flash it under the spotlight of the High Court to try and shame her family?'

'That is not my purpose.'

'Wouldn't any Christian do the same?'

Sidney Bradford shot up. 'My Lord,' he cried, his voice echoing up into the rafters, 'I object to the continuous harassment of my client. He is merely bringing evidence out into the light of day.'

'Facts are one thing,' retorted Richard Armstrong. 'Motivation is another. And surely the motivation of the star player in this criminal act is of the utmost relevance.'

'I object most strenuously, Your Lordship!'

Lord McDonnell looked down at Richard Armstrong and said, 'This is a hearing. An inquiry. No one is being prosecuted.'

'Not yet, My Lord.'

'He is inferring that my client is a criminal.'

'There is no one being prosecuted in this court here today. And the tenor of your questions should reflect that, Mr Armstrong. Do you understand?'

'Isn't the abduction of a minor from her parents a criminal act?'

'Mr Armstrong, I don't need you to tell me what is or isn't a criminal act,' said the Judge with some irritation. 'I will point out to you – again – that no one is on trial here today and that the tenor of your questions must reflect that.'

Richard Armstrong turned away from Dr Prichard, placed the photograph on the table and joined his hands behind his back. 'Let's move away from your sudden passion for photography. Let us examine the minutiae of the process by which the good "doctor" wins his converts.' He swivelled around. 'Don't you organise meetings for teenagers in your church hall?'

'Bible studies.'

'Dancing? Socialising?'

'That may or may not be part of it.'

'Boy meets girl. Girl meets boy. Sexual attraction. Girl falls in love with boy.'

'My Lord,' said Sidney Bradford, 'do we really need a lecture on the birds and bees from Mr Armstrong?'

'I'm exploring the mechanism of how the Reverend Prichard works his converts – how much of it is by design and how little is left to chance – indeed, the step-by-step process that has led us to this court today.'

'Proceed.'

'There's pop music. Socialising. Wasn't it at one of these functions that you introduced the Reverend Daniel Upshaw to Rosaleen Johnson?'

'No, it wasn't.'

'Where did you introduce them?'

'At my home. In the presence of my wife and family.'

'So you initiated the romance?'

'I did not initiate anything of the sort. I introduced two young people who had come to Christ.'

'Was their attraction for each other instantaneous?'

'How would I know?'

'You were there, I presume, observing the developing relationship.'

'What relationship? As far as I was concerned he was a young minister learning his craft as a preacher. She was a young girl interested in religion.'

'So you noticed no attraction whatsoever?'

'No. Not of the kind you are trying to insinuate.'

'Do you consider Rosaleen Johnson an attractive young girl?'

'Yes, she is.'

'And you heard your protégé here in the witness box today, the Reverend Daniel Upshaw, profess to a deep feeling for her?'

'Yes.'

'And you claim you had no inkling of that feeling?'

'No.'

'Nor the possible danger of throwing two young, attractive people together – alone – over a long period?'

'I trust the Reverend Daniel Upshaw. Rosaleen Johnson was in no moral danger whatsoever.'

'So you sent them off together. What was it? One, two, three nights in Belfast, on the Antrim coast? Then Scotland – the Highlands, Edinburgh – for over two weeks? A twenty-year-old man and a fifteen-year-old … girl.'

'My sole concern was for the welfare of Rosaleen Johnson. She voluntarily came to us – battered and bruised, as you have seen. She felt her life was in danger. What were we to do – send her back for more of the same?'

'Did you ever hear of the police? Legal protection? Protective custody?'

'What we were involved in was a crisis – there was no time for legal niceties.'

'"No time for legal niceties?" Let the court reflect on the Reverend Prichard's opinion of the law of this land. No time for the law. Yet you had plenty of time to drag her into a room in the hospital and take a photograph that you could use subsequently in court. And you had plenty of time to ignore the pleas of her family, of priests and of politicians?'

'The girl's welfare and safety was our only concern.'

'Was it? Was it indeed?' he said, turning to the side and looking down, distractedly, at a spot on the floor. 'Rosaleen Johnson was a normal Catholic schoolgirl. She has a boyfriend from her own community – I think he's in court here today.'

Rosaleen's eyes were drawn straight to Eddie's red tie on the opposite benches. His face was stone.

Suddenly Richard Armstrong swung around and directed his gaze at Dr Prichard. 'Yet you, concerned solely with her "welfare and safety", as you say, sent her off with a different twenty-year-old man, a protégé in your church bound by your instructions, knowing full-well in advance that there was a deep mutual attraction between them. In other words, you took full advantage of a vulnerable teenage girl and used whatever means at your disposal to exert your power.'

'I object, My Lord!' cried Sidney Bradford.

'Power has nothing to do with it,' said Dr Prichard.

'Rosaleen Johnson was absent from her home for seventeen days – who was her guardian?'

'She stayed in good Christian houses run by good Christian women.'

'Give us the details.'

'I don't know the details.'

'Let me enlighten you. Three nights in the house of a Mr and Mrs Henry Walker, Belfast; two nights with a Mrs Moore in Waterfoot; and one night with a Mrs Weir in the town of Oban, West Scotland. So far, do you agree?'

'I don't know the precise details.'

'Would it surprise you if I told you that the Reverend Daniel Upshaw and Rosaleen Johnson stayed in the same boarding house in Oban, on Wednesday, the third of May?'

'That may be true.'

'Which leads conveniently to another point. You all heard Constable Fenwick testify that the couple had been stopped on their way out of Oban. They were in the News. Mostly in Northern Ireland. But also in Scotland. Yet no information on her whereabouts reached her parents nor the police in Northern Ireland. Reverend Prichard – can you explain this?'

'No.'

'Do you know a Chief Superintendent Lockhart from the Glasgow Constabulary?'

'Yes, I do.'

'My Lord,' said Sidney Bradford, 'how much longer must we endure these redundant lines of inquiries?'

'What is the purpose of this line of questioning?' asked Lord McDonnell.

'The Reverend Prichard claims he is not interested in power,' replied Richard Armstrong. 'I would just like to highlight how successful he has been in his manipulation of power, and how high his influence can reach.'

'Proceed.'

'Is Superintendent Lockhart sympathetic to the aims of the Ravenmount Memorial Church?'

'I think you would need to ask him that question.'

'Is he a friend?'

'I know the man.'

'Well?'

'No, not well.'

'Do you know him well enough to have him as a house guest?' There was a pause. 'Have you had him to stay overnight at your house?' Another pause. 'Twice if I'm not mistaken?'

'It's common for … interested visitors … to stay overnight.'

'Of course. I'm sure you would have a lot to talk about. Topics of mutual interest and such like. Did you discuss the disappearance of Rosaleen Johnson with him?'

'No.'

'Did any member of the Ravenmount church discuss it with him?'

'I don't know.'

'Does it not strike you as peculiar that two policemen reported the whereabouts of Rosaleen Johnson to Chief Superintendent Lockhart and nothing was done about it?'

'That question is not within my area of competence.'

'I'm asking for an opinion.'

'I don't wish to express an opinion on it.'

Richard Armstrong shook his head and moved from side-to-side in front of the witness box.

Dr Prichard's eyes followed him.

Suddenly the barrister stopped in his tracks. 'The welfare of Rosaleen Johnson?' he asked himself, puzzlement spreading from the eyes into his screwed-up wrinkled face. 'When the Reverent Daniel Upshaw and Rosaleen Johnson left Oban, do you know where they went?'

'Not precisely.'

'Reverend Prichard, you are being less than honest with this court. For a man who orchestrated every single move in this saga you exhibit an abnormal lack of precision in your memory.'

'I knew they were in Scotland.'

'Would it surprise you if I said that they drove from Oban to 23 Riverview Cottages, Inverness? And we have all heard you claim how there were Christian landladies in attendance to chaperone this budding Ravenmount Memorial Church romance – was there a live-in chaperone Christian landlady at 23 Riverview Cottages?'

'I don't know.'

'Oh, really. Only a short time ago we heard you boast of the high quality control your resident Christian landladies were exerting on this budding romantic relationship. Was there a breakdown in communication in Inverness?'

'I was in Belfast.'

'Do you have a daughter of your own?'

'Yes.'

'What age is she?'

'One.'

'Let's suppose she was fifteen and turning into an attractive young lady. Confused. Troubled about the religion she was brought up in. Insecure. Vulnerable. And falling in love with a grown man, an adult, who happened to be a handsome young minister from a different religion. Would you gladly send her off on holiday to Scotland with this man? Would you let her be driven by that man, just the two of them alone, to 23 Riverview Cottages in Scotland, an empty house with no resident landlady at all? Would you be happy to permit that?'

Dr Prichard said nothing. His eyes were baleful, his lips were pinched and his tongue formed a plum in his right cheek.

From across the courtroom the voice of the Reverend Daniel Upshaw broke the silence. 'I can answer that question,' he said, standing erect. 'I didn't stay overnight at the Riverview Cottages. Nor did I touch Rosaleen in the whole time we were together … except …'

Richard Armstrong moved backwards so that the three formed the apexes of a triangle. 'Except what?'

'– our hands.'

Laughter rippled around the benches and the public gallery, then stopped abruptly.

'You held hands?'

The red skin on Daniel's face glowed, like bad sunburn, under the freckles. 'Yes,' he said.

'In the bedroom of number twenty-three Riverview Cottages at Inverness?'

'No!' he cried, then, the words caught in his throat, '– I don't think so.'

'You can't remember whether you held hands in the bedroom with a vulnerable fifteen-year-old girl? But you do remember that you and this girl were in the bedroom. Together. In a house in Inverness. Without a supervising resident Christian landlady?'

'I only carried her case up to the bedroom.'

'How gallant. How noble in the extreme. You carried her case up to the bedroom.'

'May I object, My Lord,' said Sidney Bradford, 'to these lascivious insinuations. The Reverend Daniel Upshaw is merely expressing his entirely innocent desire to help.'

'How do you know his desire was entirely innocent?' snapped Richard Armstrong.

'He is a young man of the highest reputation.'

'Does lingering in the bedroom of a fifteen-year-old girl whom he has just abducted from the family home and run away to Scotland add anything to her reputation?'

The words flew from Daniel's gaping mouth. 'I was only there a few minutes!'

'And what happened?' demanded Richard Armstrong.

'Nothing. Absolutely nothing. We just … talked.'

'Talked?'

'I really do object, Your Lordship,' said Sidney Bradford.

Lord McDonnell shook his head, saying, 'I think what happened during the girl's absence from Belfast is relevant. Continue.'

'You talked. Was it romantic talk?'

'No, not at all – we just talked. We joked.'

'About what?'

'She kidded me about what would happen if Dr Prichard knew I was in her bedroom. You see, I wasn't –'

' – supposed to be in her bedroom. Alone. In an empty house. Unsupervised. Who issued all these instructions?'

'I always obeyed Dr Prichard. I only stayed a few minutes. And afterwards I went straight to Edinburgh.'

'Thank you, Reverend Upshaw. The truth is sometimes slow in coming, but it always comes.'

Daniel sat down.

'I take full responsibility for the Reverend Daniel Upshaw's actions' said Dr Prichard solemnly. 'He is an honourable man.'

'Thank you, Reverend Prichard. I'm sure everyone here will appreciate your honesty. At least those of us who haven't grown old awaiting its arrival.' He stalked a wide arc in front of him, gently tipping the ends of his fingers against each other, letting the silence build its own momentum. 'So it has finally been revealed that you were the mastermind behind this great plan. The designer. The architect. You initiated her travel to the houses in Belfast and Waterfoot, the journey to Scotland – Oban, Inverness and Edinburgh. You successfully blocked any information reaching the Northern Ireland police on her whereabouts. And you arranged neatly for her to appear on your doorstep precisely one day after her sixteenth birthday – the very day her legal status changes.'

'I acted in good conscience,' said Dr Prichard.

Richard Armstrong turned and slowly moved towards the witness box, his blue eyes burning the air between them. ' So Reverend Prichard, your conscience is clear. You took in a distraught, immature, emotionally-disturbed girl. You encouraged a young minister who had romantic and I'm sure sexual feelings towards her. You instructed them to leave the country and travel to a series of houses where they sometimes stayed together. Alone. You thought nothing of its effect on her reputation. Her honour. Just as long as she was kept away from the influence of her family, her friends, and the priests of the religion she was brought up in. You were prepared to break any law in the land to bring this about – isn't that right?'

'I was determined that she would stay out of the clutches of the church of Rome.'

'And you deliberately broke the law?'

'When Rosaleen Johnson came to me she was beaten and bruised. I took her in, I took care of the girl. I saw that she underwent no harm. I brought her to Christ. And I'm proud of the part I played. There is no law in any land that is greater than the law of God.'

Barely two feet from each other, their eyes remained locked for some seconds.

Finally Richard Armstrong turned to the side and looked up. 'My Lord, I have no further questions for the Reverend Prichard.'

Dr Prichard rose, went down the steps and across to his bench. He smiled at Rosaleen and Daniel, moved in from the end, exchanged a few words with his wife, and sat down and folded his arms.

Richard Armstrong took the centre of the courtroom. 'We have managed to prise the facts of this case out into the open,' he said. 'It's not a pretty case. It's full of vulnerability, pain, regretful deeds, misunderstandings and plain criminality.

'At its centre there is the Johnson family. Rosaleen Johnson was a central member of that family. A normal young Catholic girl who came under the influence of the Reverend Lesley Prichard. And the unfortunate thing is – she is not alone. From the first night she visited that church, she became a changed girl. Everything her own religion stood for was – was bad; everything the Reverend Lesley Prichard said – was good. Try to put yourselves in the position of Frank Johnson – head of the household. Everything his daughter believed and was brought up in – is rejected. And she's spouting the same anti-Catholic venom as her mentor – the Reverend Lesley Prichard. He over-reacted. He struck her. And precipitated this crisis.

'Now put yourselves into the position of the Reverend Lesley Prichard – the injured, vulnerable, upset girl arrives on his doorstep, seeking help. Does he comfort her and talk about her duties, about loyalty, and understanding her own family? No, that is not his way. He abducts her secretly to various houses. He knows perfectly well the scandal this will cause, the publicity it will generate – no one has sought publicity more in this province, nor used propaganda more effectively.

'So what does this small-scale family tragedy become? A showcase, a showdown. Newspapers, radio, television. He despatches the vulnerable girl off with a young man as if they're going on a honeymoon – and then taunts the family with a tape of Rosaleen Johnson's voice in the Memorial Hall.

'Are these the actions of a man solely concerned with the welfare of a young girl who has come to him for help and advice? Or are they the actions of an opportunist, a master of propaganda who cunningly stage-manages the whole scenario – whose hatred for a rival religious institution will make him do anything, break any law – and in the process damage the vulnerable human beings who are unfortunate enough to come under his spell.

'The facts of the case speak for themselves. Calculated villainy was committed against a young girl and her family in the name of religion. My Lord, I ask you to redress that balance today and return the girl to the nurturing influence of her sister, her mother and her father, and let their love heal the wounds. Thank you.'

He walked over to the table, smiled grimly at Mr Robinson and sat down.

Lord McDonnell let the absolute silence continue for a short while before breaking it. 'Could Rosaleen Johnson please come to the witness box?'

Rosaleen dared not look up. She rose, edged to the end of the bench and began the walk across the floor. She looked up and saw her mother's stare, her father's closed eyes, Marie's open mouth – then diverted her eyes left, to the witness stand, her wet hands rubbing the sides of her skirt. So many eyes, faces, bodies. But she was dressed for the occasion. She was a new person. She must be determined. She sat down and crossed her hands on her lap.

Lord McDonnell turned towards her. 'Due to the very diligent investigative work of Mr Armstrong we now know a lot more about what actually happened. On that last day, the day you were injured and you went to see the Reverend Lesley Prichard – did he at any time try to persuade you to go back home?'

'I refused to go home.'

'Why?'

'I was afraid.'

'Of what?'

Her eyes went down to her hands. 'My father. I was afraid he might kill me. And I was afraid that the priests would try to force me to attend the Catholic Church.'

'Which up to that time you had attended for many years, isn't that right?'

'After my father hit me, I decided I was never going to a Catholic service again. I made a complete break. I joined the Ravenmount church – and I now consider myself a member of that church. A Protestant.'

Bodies stirred around the courtroom, among the benches at floor level and right up to the back of the public gallery, as if a beast had been pricked.

Lord McDonnell took off his glasses. His eyes were sad, resigned, and the bags under them seemed to have grown bigger. 'How would you feel about going back to live with your parents and sister?'

'I can't. It's not possible.'

'Even on a trial basis?'

'No.'

He put on his glasses and stroked his chin with the fingers of his left hand.

'How did the members of the Ravenmount Church treat you from the day you left home?'

'As a valued friend. And a member of their church.'

'Are you convinced that they acted solely in your interest?'

'Yes.'

'Do you intend to return to school?'

'No. I have been offered a position in the factory where I was working before. I intend to take it.'

'And where are you proposing to live?'

'At the home of my friend, Hilary Smith. Her parents have agreed to give me lodgings.'

'Are you one hundred per cent sure that you do not wish to return to your family?'

Her eyes flicked to the left. But they didn't catch the faces of her parents and sister: tired, drained of emotion. 'Yes,' she said.

'Very well.'

'My Lord,' said Sidney Bradford, rising, 'may I ask Rosaleen Johnson a question?'

'Yes.'

He rested the tips of his fingers gently on the table and began. 'In all the time you have known the Reverend Lesley Prichard – the advice he has given, and the actions taken in your regard – do you believe that he was acting solely in your best interest? Not even in any greater religious sense, but as an ordinary human being?'

'His sole concern was for my safety and welfare. I was never in any doubt – not for one hour, one minute or one second.'

'There are, nevertheless, aspects to this case which trouble me deeply,' said Lord McDonnell. 'Adults, under this jurisdiction, assisted in the disappearance of a young girl from her home. They did so knowing she was a minor. They deliberately broke the law.

'Whether there were mitigating circumstances is a debatable point. But what is not debatable is that the measures taken by the Reverend Lesley Prichard and his collaborators were extreme. They were not designed to facilitate the reconciliation of the girl to her family. The word "reckless" is not far from my mind when I consider the Reverend Prichard's position as head of a church and the burden he placed on the young Reverend Daniel Upshaw. These matters will have to be dealt with in another forum.

'But here, today, an application has been made to have Rosaleen Johnson made a Ward of Court. She is, in my opinion, an intelligent strong-willed girl who is now sixteen years of age. There is no way I can satisfy all parties. I have to make a difficult decision based on what is practical rather than desirable.

'I am going to allow Rosaleen Johnson to stay with her friend's parents over the coming weeks. In the meantime I would like all the parties involved to get together so that some amicable, humanitarian way forward can be found. I will leave the details to the representatives on both sides.'

Lord McDonnell got up and everyone followed. He came down the steps, turned past Rosaleen, the bench where the Johnson family stood, and went through the door.

Talk broke loose all around the courtroom. A stream of people headed by Hilary, Daniel and Dr Prichard met Rosaleen halfway across the floor. Smiling, anxious faces. She didn't return their smiles. Across Dr Prichard's shoulder she saw Eileen, Frank and Marie. It was as if they were at a funeral.

When the Johnsons came out from the bench, Richard Armstrong put his hand on Frank's shoulder. 'I'm sorry,' he said. 'I failed.'

Frank shook his head. 'No, no, no – you didn't. You were great, Mr Armstrong. We'll get her back, we will, we will,' he said.

Eileen looked directly into Richard Armstrong's eyes. 'What have they done to her?' she asked.

He shrugged his shoulders.

Frank spoke to himself and anyone else in earshot. 'Can't she see? Can't she see what they're like?'

The group drifted out the door. Paddy Bolger, hands deep in the pockets of his baggy trousers, his eyes soulful and sad, together with Richard Armstrong, listened intently to Frank. Eileen took her husband protectively by the arm. Marie said nothing; she held onto the sight of Rosaleen until the door closed and the talk started to ricochet off the shiny cream walls. At the end of the corridor she spied a familiar figure – Eddie, one sponge sole planted against the wall. She managed a wistful smile. His face was hard. He nodded and turned the corner.

Congratulations washed around Rosaleen; Sidney Bradford went on about how impressive she was. Daniel spoke of her courage, his admiration and relief. Dr Prichard gave her a warm handshake and avuncular hug. Hilary smiled. Other hardly recognisable faces beamed triumphantly. She didn't feel like a winner. She felt she had done something she had to do and was glad that it was over. Dr Prichard invited the group back to his house for tea.

Outside, the sky was still grey. Photographs were taken by members of the Press. Her family, standing in the middle of the car park talking to Richard Armstrong and Paddy Bolger, looked over. She followed Daniel and Dr Prichard, in the opposite direction, towards the black limousine.

High heels clattered behind her. Marie came running. Daniel, Sidney Bradford and Dr Prichard made to form a protective shield.

'No,' said Rosaleen to the men. They parted. Marie clasped her by the hand, then gave her a hug. 'I'll see you soon,' she said, turning and walking back.

The three men started towards the limousine, then stopped to wait for Rosaleen. She watched her sister walking away, noticing how the light cotton dress clung to her legs and body. She thought she was too thin.

Rosaleen turned, followed them and got into the wide back seat between Daniel and Sidney Bradford. She could feel goose bumps on her arms and a knot in her stomach. The engine hummed. The limousine passed the Johnsons, now huddled and peering. She waved her hand. No one waved back.

Their eyes followed the car out onto the main road until a granite wall blocked it from view.

A short distance on, the limousine stopped at traffic lights. Eddie passed in front of them. First he glanced at the car, then stared at Dr Prichard in the front seat. All the way across the road his head kept twisting around.

'Do you know him?' asked Daniel, turning to Rosaleen.

'Yes. He's from around our way. I used to go out with him.'

Daniel smiled. She waved her hand at Eddie. He stopped at the pavement on the other side and stared over, puzzled.

The car went on and slid into Oxford Street, alongside red and white buses belching out black smoke, and turned left onto the bridge. It seemed like a long time from when she first crossed it. A lot had happened. And she felt that her journey was only just beginning.

Chapter 15

Marie sipped the glass of chilled white wine. That was another Aussie habit she'd developed. The summer house was silent except for Gerry's quiet snoozing and the occasional muzzie flitting by her ear. She hoped the fumes from the candle would get them. Flies. That was Australia's curse. But it was clean. Cleaner than any freshly-scrubbed doorstep on the Falls Road. They knocked cleanliness into them early. No throwing your sweetie papers on the streets out here.

She got up from the table and winced. Her right hip yelped. How long more would she postpone the operation? Half-empty glasses annoyed her from every angle in the living room. She gathered some of them up and limped into the small kitchen, littered with even more glasses and the debris of the wedding cake. The air was fish-fried. Where would she start? No, she wouldn't start. She'd wait until some of them, big and ugly enough, came back. They were probably in an hotel, drinking. Should she wait on Rosaleen to ring? Or ring her? She'd wait a while.

She came back out and opened the door of the wooden cabinet beside the stone fireplace. Stiff, creaky. Like herself. Seven photograph albums slid down, scraping the wooden floor with the fine invisible sand that got into everything. The top five albums, glossy without and within, contained technicolour snaps of a cinematic country. The bottom two, covered with threadbare green cloth, contained the faded greys of fifties Belfast – they were what she really prized. The wine always made her want to rummage in the mongrel streets of the Falls Road.

The first picture was pure sunlight: two happy sisters together in front of the tennis courts in the Falls Park. Ten and twelve, Frank behind them. All three licking ice cream cones. Fast forward. Was she ever that thin? Like a greyhound. Beehive hair all luxurious and abundant. Now it was thin and dyed and when she washed it you could see her scalp.

Sudden stop. A newspaper cut out. The family leaving the High Court. Their faces said it all. Christmas around the table in Ivy Drive. The empty chair where Rosaleen usually sat. Ten pages on. Rosaleen's wedding in Georgia. The wooden church, the bell tower high up, white linen tables laid out in the open. None of them had gone.

Her visit to America. Flat yellow cornfields as far as you could see. The long, silent one had met her at the bus station and drove her out to the house without hardly a word.

Two photographs: Marie holding the baby, Ruth, and Rosaleen's bright eyes beaming up at their faces; the other around the dining table, with Daniel looking up, gravitas in his eyes, bodies stiff, no alcohol.

She said he was a laugh a lot of the time. A laugh? That depends, doesn't it? When did any of them get the time to laugh – running the house, the farm, the church? Set, rigid patterns – work, work, work – and no real personal time or chats in the whole two weeks she was there. Was that deliberate? She tried to bring up the court case one night. No discussion – only intense dislike, a hatred, of Richard Armstrong, the "devil barrister".

Two memories: Rosaleen, holding the baby on the porch, in a blue check cotton dress, as she drew up in the pickup – a big smile, the joyful look on her face. She knew that she wanted to put the baby down and run up to her and give her a great big hug. But something stopped her. And when she was leaving –

all right, they were in a group at the bus stop, and Daniel was there – but sisters don't shake hands, do they?

All those black-and-white photos were precious, irreplaceable treasures that her children could look back on in the twenty-first century. Or would they be interested? Would the photos crumble into the ground with her? Gerry twitched on the settee. Things were moving too fast to worry about a few old snaps. Out here the heat made everything crumble faster.

At least the wine was now licking her hip. She drained her glass. The bright phone lay insolent on the cane table. She picked it up and punched out the digits. The phone rang three times before Rosaleen answered. The voice a hybrid, American-Belfast.

'Marie here, Rosaleen, I rang earlier.'

'Sorry. I'm just in the door. I was gonna ring.'

'Thanks for the telegram. And the money.'

'You're welcome to it. One of Daniel's relations left us a bit. She's lucky. Usually we're broke.'

'It's far too much.'

'No. It's expensive. And you're on your own.'

'John's doing very well in accountancy. They're not short of a bob.'

'They'll find a use for it.'

'Oh, you can be sure of that. How's Ruth and Aaron?'

There was a pause. 'Well, Ruth is still teaching in Atlanta. We don't see a lot of her. Just Thanksgiving and Christmas. Aaron went off to the West Coast. He's working near San Francisco at some electronic thingamabob. And no sign of either of them getting married.'

'Plenty of time. See the world. Michael married them, you know?'

'– Michael?'

'My son. The priest.'

'Oh – Michael! The good-looking blonde one?'

'Being a priest is all different here, you know. Like he had on his collar for the ceremony in the church. But outside he just runs aroun' looking like a hippie.'

'I'd love to have been there.'

'It was a great wedding. A real riot.'

'Send me some photos, will you?'

'Sure. Why don't you come out some time?'

'To Australia?'

'Yeah.'

'Maybe the next time one of Daniel's relatives dies. If we don't go first.'

'There's great package deals available now. Spring or autumn's the best.'

'The problem is – we're involved in so many things. You know what Michael's life is like. It's the same for Daniel. And then there's the farm. We got away one week to Florida last year. And we stayed over with Ruth on the way down.'

'Perth's a lovely city.'

'So they say.'

'We had a barbie out here today at our summer house. All the children came …' She suddenly had a sense that maybe the wine was making her talk too much and maybe Rosaleen wasn't really all that interested. Finally she said, 'What about you, Rosaleen? Yourself?'

There was a pause. 'Well, my life doesn't sound nearly as exciting as yours.'

'Don't be talkin' nonsense. I've had wine,' she said, by way of apology.

'A lot of stuff connected with the church. Services. Christenings. Marriages. And we have some dairy cows –'

'Dairy cows! Are you havin' me on, Rosaleen?'

'They really clip your wings.'

'Dairy cows? Our Rosaleen? And do you … milk them?'

'Yeah. Well, I tie on the machines.'

'It was far from dairy cows that you were reared.'

'We get one annual trip to Atlanta. That's when I do my big shopping.'

'You'd like the shopping in Perth.'

'Would I?'

'Well, it's probably the same as Atlanta. Malls. Big shopping malls.'

'That's it.'

'They're all the same, aren't they?'

'All the same.'

'Remember Goorwiches, the Co-op, Robinson and Cleaver's?'

'I do.'

'Do you know what I think, Rosaleen?'

'What?'

'There's far too much shoppin' now. It used t' be special. Remember when you, me and m' Ma went uptown together.'

'We were always fighting.'

'Well, you two were always fighting.'

'Me fighting? Moi?'

They laughed.

'Do ya know somethin', Rosaleen? Ya've a terrible oul American drawl.'

'Have I?'

'It's desperate. Cud ya not get rid of it?'

'Are you thinking of giving me some elocution lessons?'

'Ya might be too far gone for them. But if you come out here t' Perth I promise ya'll go home with a Belfast accent.'

'Like yours?'

'Maybe even posher than mine. Malone Road – how wud that suit ya?'

There was a moment of silence.

'We must keep in touch more,' said Rosaleen.

'Yeah. Let's start writing.'

'You know what I'm like with letters.'

'If I write – do ya promise to reply? Remember – Daniel will probably go before you an' I'm all ya'll have left.'

'Lord preserve us!'

'Do you promise?'

'Yes, I do.'

'Girl Guide's word of honour?'

'Yes!'

'I'll start tomorrow. I'm gonna put it all down on paper,' Marie said.

'What?'

'Everything.'

'Everything? What do you mean "everything"?'

'Everything there is. Between us. Before we die.'

'You're getting morbid, Marie.'

'Am I?'

'And you used to be such a great laugh.'

'I'm still a great laugh. I'm a great, big, fat laugh.'

'How could you be fat? I'm the fat one. Sure you used t' make a greyhound look fat.'

'All the atin' an' drinkin'. How's your weight anyway?'

'Well, I have put on a couple of pounds. Just a couple.'

'You're probably bigger than a house.'

'Stop it!'

'Are you still in the same one?'

'The same what?'

'The same house.'

'Yeah. It's big enough. And convenient, too – there's a grave-yard down at the end of the garden.'

'And you're calling me morbid?'

'There's someone at the door. That's what I spend my life doing these days. Answering doors. Dealing with other people's wants and needs.'

'I hope yer not neglectin' yerself.'

'I never even think about it. Sorry, Marie, I have t' go. Thanks for ringing – we'll keep in touch. And tell everyone I was asking for them.'

'Ros –'

The phone clicked. She wanted to talk longer. They'd only started. There was so much to catch up on.

She went along the creaky floor into the small kitchen and opened the fridge. Still packed with drink. She filled her glass, came back out, sprayed herself lightly with insect repellent and went out to the back porch. The cane rocking chair lay close to the edge. She sat down.

The great vault of the sky lay before her. High up, to the right, a crescent moon cast a ghostly light – the dunes, the gum trees, the neighbouring houses sat mute. Stars hung thick to the rim of the Indian Ocean – it breathed and whispered along the shore. Even the Freemantle Doctor, the cooling wind from the sea, was taking a rest.

She felt better after the chat. Rosaleen was in good form. She was, wasn't she? And tomorrow she would write. What would she write?

She took two solid swigs from her glass. The space inside her head expanded nicely. She would write to her just like they were in bed together over forty years ago, having a great chat. And she wouldn't need to think about what to say because the words would come. Just as they used to.

Her eyes began to close. The dream came again. It always did in moments of great contentment. She's eighteen and wearing a jade green cotton dress and Rosaleen's nearly sixteen. She can see clearly the small violet flowers on the yellow dress she wore the day she left home. They're separated and lost in this maze – it's all zig-zags, boulders and obstacles of every description. Disasters come by the score – they fight their way through and then they finally find each other. Rosaleen gives her a great big hug and they hold hands as tight as they can and don't let go – and they feel all safe and warm for they know that they'll never get lost again as long as they stay together.

Printed in Great Britain
by Amazon